OFF THE MAP

In the Shadow: Book 1, a Christian Romantic Suspense

J L CROSSWHITE

To my brothers, Jeremy and Jason, and the times we pored over the map of America on the tent trailer tables on our camping adventures. Here's to future road trips!

Behold, I am doing a new thing: now it springs forth, do you not perceive it? I will make a way in the wilderness and rivers in the desert.

Isaiah 43:19

The lights in the spacious atrium dimmed, and a spotlight shone on the marble floor. Allie Ellis turned in her chair at the round banquet table to watch the bride, her friend Cait, get swept up in the arms of her new groom, Grayson, for their first dance. The band leader announced the bride and groom, and the band played "It Had to Be You."

Steve Collins—he'd always gone by his last name—was her date for the wedding. His gaze was steady on her but unreadable. She'd been half in love with him since their high school days, but was he just an idealized fantasy she'd created? Would getting to know him shatter the dream man she'd created in her mind? Could high school dreams even survive into adulthood?

The band leader invited everyone to the dance floor. Their table cleared. It had been full of their friends—all couples. Her sister Melissa with Scott, Kyle and Heather, and Joe and Sarah. She glanced at Collins. Would he expect her to dance to such an obviously couples' song when she wasn't sure if they were anything but friends?

He grinned at her and held out his hand. "Shall we? I have to warn you, I'm not a great dancer, but I can sway to the beat."

But Allie's heeled sandal caught in the floor-length table-cloth, and she whacked her knee on the table leg as she pivoted. Graceful.

"Are you okay?"

She nodded, hoping he hadn't seen her clumsiness and that her smile looked more confident than it felt as she placed her hand in his warm one. Was hers too cold or too sweaty? Why did being around him make her feel like she was back in high school?

His large, warm fingers enveloped hers, and tingles swirled along her arm. This was the first time he'd ever held her hand. But it was just out of courtesy. Wasn't it?

She rose, being careful not to tangle herself in the tablecloth, and let him lead her toward the rapidly filling dance floor. She turned sideways to avoid an older lady in a sequined jacket pushing out her chair in front of Allie. But that caused her heel to catch on the leg of another chair. She tugged on Collins's hand to slow his progress and steady herself.

He stopped and turned.

Just as Sequined Jacket spun into Allie with a full cocktail glass.

As the icy, sticky liquid splashed down the front of her organza bodice, she gasped and pulled out of Collins's grasp.

No, no, no, no, no! This could not be happening. She'd wanted this night to be perfect. And now her dress was definitely not.

Sequined Jacket looked up, just now recognizing what she had done. "Oh dear. I'm so sorry. Let me help you." She snatched up a cloth napkin from the table and handed it to Allie, but the polyester did little to sop up the wetness. "I'm so sorry. Oh your poor dress. And it was so pretty on you."

Was being the operative word. Allie sighed and looked at Collins. "Let me head to the ladies' room and see if I can't do something with this." She wove her way through the chairs and tables, scooting around the edge of the perfectly romantic atrium. She'd used her real estate connections as a corporate relocation specialist to secure it for Cait. Wedding venues were at a premium, but this was a luxury office space with a lush tropical-and-marble atrium that soared five stories. With fairy lights added to the existing lighting scheme, it was a beautiful place for a wedding. Their friend Sarah Brockman was the architect who designed it, and between the two of them, they convinced the building's owner to let them rent it. It had become a magical space for Cait's wedding.

As she left the atrium, footsteps followed her. She turned.

Collins was behind her.

"Oh, you don't have to wait for me. Go enjoy the wedding."

He shoved his hands in his pockets, a sheepish grin crossing his face. "I'd rather wait for you."

She got it. He didn't know the bride and groom. And everyone was on the dance floor.

He closed the gap between them, resting his hand lightly on her lower back as they continued down the hallway to the restrooms.

The sounds of the band faded, and the squeak of the restroom door seemed particularly loud as she pushed it open into the marble-lined ladies' room and made her way to the sink. The mirror reflected the wet red splotch that covered her pale-pink dress. She snatched a handful of paper towels and dampened them, dabbing at the front. It was so pretty. The pale pink organza swirled just above her knees, flattering her generous curves, and the hue brightened her nothing-special coloring.

Collins had certainly seemed appreciative when he'd picked her up, his eyes lighting up and his voice had deepened as he said, "You look beautiful" as he helped her into his large truck. But the ride had felt awkward. Had she made a mistake by inviting him? He seemed the perfect plus-one since he knew everyone at their table, even though he wasn't friends with Cait and Grayson. Neither was she, really, but she'd helped pull off the location, so she'd been invited.

She and Collins had reconnected last November, but then he'd left on an assignment to help as a detective for the police department in Holcomb Springs, a small resort town in the San Bernardino mountains about two hours from here. So they'd been texting and talking on the phone for the past four months. But friends did that too. She was hoping tonight would give her a better insight into the man he'd become from the boy she once knew.

But bringing him to a wedding… Didn't that imply something about their relationship? Did they have a relationship beyond old friends? That nervousness and uncertainty had made her clumsy. Well, she couldn't blame the ruined dress on her clumsiness. That landed squarely on the sequined shoulders of the older lady. But Allie was the one who would reek of alcohol all night.

She peered in the mirror. Despite her best efforts, the slightly less-red spot still dominated her dress. With nothing further to do, she tossed the paper towels in the trash. *Get a grip, Allie. Enjoy the evening. No one's even going to notice you, anyway.*

With a final fluff of her hair, she turned and pushed out the bathroom door.

Collins stood outside, gazing at his surroundings. His wavy hair was beginning to escape whatever product he had used to confine it. It made her want to play with his curls. She squeezed her hand shut.

He smiled at her. "This is some space, isn't it? Sarah's really good at what she does."

"Yes, she is. I'm glad we could use it for Cait and Grayson's wedding." She held her dress out. "I couldn't do too much with it. Maybe the cleaners will be able to fix it."

"I hope so. It's a pretty dress." Collins's gaze turned intense and he cocked his head. "Do you hear that?"

"The music?"

"Yes, but that song." He reached for her hand and pulled her a few steps down the hall. "Remember it?"

It sounded familiar, an alt-rock ballad from their high school years. "Oh, that's Lifehouse."

"Yep. It's 'You and Me.' We should go dance to it since I didn't get to take you to prom."

A thousand thoughts collided in Allie's head. "Oh, but my dress. It's still wet and… stained." *Brilliant, Allie.* State the obvious. And, he wanted to take her to prom?

He swung her around in front of him, sliding his hand along her waist. "We could dance here. The twinkle lights almost look like stars." He grinned.

She put her hand on his broad, football-player shoulder and began swaying to the music, laughing. "Wasn't that the theme of one of our proms, An Evening Under the Stars?"

"Something like that. All I know is that you went with Chris Mendoza before I could ask you."

She groaned. "He cornered me in the hall. I couldn't turn him down. I wish I'd known…you'd wanted to take me. I would have rather gone with you." Her voice softened, and she looked away. Had she said too much? She and Melissa had found a dress for her at a thrift shop and remade it a bit so she could go. Chris had paid for the tickets and bought her a wrist corsage that his mother had picked out.

Collins tugged her a little closer, apparently not concerned that her wet dress could touch his cobalt-blue dress shirt or navy tie. "We can make up for lost time."

She didn't know what to say to that, so she didn't say anything, just enjoyed the warmth of being in his arms as the music and memories swirled around them. She had been thinking of him as a wedding date, but now he'd taken her down memory lane to high school. And rewritten the history she thought she knew.

He'd wanted to take her to prom? She'd always thought that her crush on him was one sided, and she'd worked to hide it so as not to ruin their friendship or make things awkward. But perhaps their feelings were mutual. If she'd gone to prom with him… a different life spooled out in front of her. She shook the thoughts away. Her imagination was running away with her. *Enjoy the moment.*

The scent of him, clean like soap with a hint of something spicy, drew her closer. She forgot about her dress and let the music swirl around them.

Footsteps sounded on the marble floor, growing closer. Probably someone looking for the restrooms. She glanced up. Melissa.

She was frowning and biting her lip.

Uh oh. That look always meant trouble. Great.

Allie stepped out of Collins's arms and saw the confusion in his gaze. But Melissa wouldn't share her concern unless it was important.

Collins pressed his hand against the small of her back, maintaining their connection. She didn't pull away. But it was all she could do to concentrate on Melissa and not the feel of his hand.

Melissa glanced at Allie's dress. "Oh, no! What happened?"

She shrugged. "An older lady bumped into me with her cocktail. The cleaners can probably get it out. I'll be fine. What's up?"

Melissa shoved her cell phone into Allie's hand. "Both Daniel and Brittney are bailing on us."

She studied the screen. "The Great American Road Trip? You can't be serious." No wonder Melissa looked upset. They'd planned this trip for years and finally were able to agree on dates and get it on the calendar last Thanksgiving. Planning future trips around an old map kept them occupied as kids during some difficult times. This trip was supposed to make those dreams a reality finally.

"Why did he text you right now? Didn't he know we were at the wedding and that Scott was down from Washington?" Allie handed the phone back to Melissa.

Melissa shrugged. "He never pays attention to our social lives."

Allie touched Melissa's arm. "Let's not think about it now. Go back in and enjoy the reception. We can figure something out tomorrow."

Melissa opened her mouth, but Scott stepped up and slipped his arm around her waist. "I know you, Melissa. Just let it go for now. Allie's right."

As Scott led Melissa back toward the wedding, Allie turned to Collins, shaking her head. "We had been planning a sibling road trip, something we'd dreamed about for years. But it looks like Daniel and Brittney can't make it. So that just leaves Melissa, Matthew, and me. Well, and Scott. He was going to go with us." She let out a sigh. "I know Melissa will turn it over in her brain, trying to think of solutions instead of enjoying the evening. Speaking of which, we should get back in there." She brushed her hand down the front of her dress. "Nobody's going to be looking at me anyway."

Collins frowned. "Why do you have to cancel the trip? Why can't the rest of you go? Maybe you can all try to go another time, but it doesn't mean the rest of you should miss out."

"Daniel has the trailer. None of the rest of us has one or anything to pull it with. And I don't want to sleep in a tent. The amount of gear we'd have to buy..." She shook her head. "Let's go back inside. I think they're going to cut the cake."

Collins reached for her hand, intertwining their fingers.

She tried to act casual, like it didn't mean anything, like she didn't feel as if her feet would float off the ground as he navigated them back to their table. But in that moment, she was suspended between two realities, two dreams that had been a part of her life for far too long: Collins and the Great American Road Trip. Maybe childhood dreams were never meant to see the light of day.

She focused on the feel of her hand in his. Because if they couldn't pull off the sibling road trip, would it mean her dreams of a future with Collins would disappear like a misty dream as well?

Chapter Two

W illard drove his Porsche past the typical Laguna Vista, California, suburban two-story with the OPEN HOUSE sign, his pulse ratcheting up. This was the sweetest moment, when his plans clicked into action. He parked down the street then entered the house and looked around. Another couple moved through the rooms. He'd seen their car out front.

The Realtor came toward him, smiling. "I'm Elaina Gonzales." She handed him a flyer. "Sign our guest book, please, then feel free to look around. We've got some fresh-baked cookies." Her glossy, dark curls and soft brown eyes invited him to something more. "Don't hesitate to ask me any questions."

He smiled back. "Thanks, Elaina. Did you bake these yourself?" He grabbed a cookie off the tray on the counter and took a bite.

"Yes, I did."

"That must be the special touch I taste, then." He signed the book Richard Ramirez and put down the address of a vacant lot in Garden Grove.

Elaina glanced over the form. "So Richard, are you looking for a family house or is it just you?"

"It's just me." He winked. "For now."

"You'll find this house has plenty of space for whatever your needs are."

Yes, that's what he was counting on. He wandered through the rooms, killing time until the other couple left. He slipped to the front door and locked it.

His heart beat in his ears, and he could hardly contain his excitement. He'd found exactly what he was looking for. It was the perfect spot. "Elaina, could you explain this to me?"

"What's that?" She left her seat at the dining room table, leaving her phone, and following him into the hallway.

He pointed to the air conditioning return vent in the ceiling.

She frowned and stepped closer. "I don't see what you mean."

He slipped his arm around her biceps and tugged her close.

She snapped her head around with a scowl. Until she saw the knife he held. Then trembles shook her body.

He repressed a laugh. Reaching up, he fingered one of her beautiful, dark curls. He grasped it in his hand, the texture just as he imagined. With a quick slice, he freed the lock from her scalp.

She yelped. "Please, don't hurt me." Her voice shook.

"How about you give me the personal tour?"

* * *

COLLINS STEPPED OUT ONTO THE PATIO AT HIS LVPD partner Kyle's house the next day where Kyle was manning the grill. The Southern California March sun was warming up the perfect spring day. Collins and Allie had just arrived after attending church together.

The wedding last night hadn't provided many more opportunities for him to be alone with her until he took her home. She'd been nervous all night, and he couldn't seem to do anything to reassure her. They were just beginning to find their rhythm, to relax, when Melissa had dropped the bombshell about their road trip.

By the time they got home, it was late and both were tired. He walked her to the door and gave her a hug goodnight with a kiss on the cheek. He picked her up again this morning for church. While they were getting to spend time together, it was always with other people. Which wasn't a bad thing. Seeing a person with their friends was a good way to judge their character. And right now, he could see that Allie was as sweet and giving as she'd always been. The fact that she had curves in all the right places didn't hurt things at all.

The whole gang was here today to spend time with Scott while he was down visiting from Naval Air Station Whidbey Island in Washington where he trained F/A-18 pilots. The last time Collins was at a party at Kyle's, the women congregated in the kitchen and the men out here. Today probably wouldn't be any different.

"I don't need any help, thanks." Kyle grinned at him. "I've learned to do things just fine without a partner these past few months."

Collins lifted his chin. "Nice to be appreciated. I'm sure I'll get stuck with a pile of paperwork when I get back."

"I've been saving it just for you." Kyle's gaze strayed through the French doors into the kitchen. "Did you and Allie have a good time at the wedding last night?"

"We did. Though she's pretty bummed about the road trip she and Melissa were supposed to go on with their siblings. I guess they'd planned it a long time and their brother and other sister backed out. It kind of put a damper on things."

"She'll figure it out. She's a woman of amazing resources. I couldn't believe she found a condo for Kim last year and then helped Cait and Grayson with the wedding venue. She's creative."

The patio door opened, and Joe stepped out with an empty platter. "You done ruining those burgers?" He was a fire captain and had been friends with Kyle and Scott since they were kids.

"Burned them just for you." Kyle scooped the patties off the grill, the smell of sizzling meat and spices wafting up. He slid them onto the platter Joe held. "You and Scott are entertaining the ladies, I presume."

"It's what we do best." He winked at Collins. "But I think they're ready for your company." Joe returned inside with the burgers.

Kyle turned off the grill. "Grab me a Dr Pepper from that cooler, would you?"

"Sure." Collins grabbed two, one for each of them, and handed it to Kyle before following him inside.

After Kyle gave the blessing, the group filled their plates and seated themselves around the dining room table that had been made large enough by the addition of leaves. While Collins had been Kyle's partner for five years, he'd only recently become acquainted with Kyle's friends. He enjoyed their company, and they had enriched his life. Especially since he found out that Allie was connected to the group.

Sarah put down her hamburger. "So, Heather, did you get any ideas for your and Kyle's wedding last night?"

Heather shrugged. "We've got a permit to get married on the beach and have the reception where we had our first date. It's amazing how much planning is involved. I think Cait lucked out. Sarah, you did such a beautiful job designing that space."

Sarah's face pinked, and Joe, her fire captain boyfriend, slipped his arm across her shoulders and gave her a squeeze. "Thanks. I'm just glad it was repairable after all that happened to it last year." Sarah had been a witness and possessed evidence for a crime last year that made her projects a target for an arsonist.

"More importantly, Kyle," Joe put in. "Have you figured out what your getaway vehicle is going to be? Grayson set the standard pretty high with that sweet restored '69 Charger of his."

"Like I told Collins, I just hand over my credit card and show up." He chuckled as Heather smacked him on the arm.

"Never mind. I'll join forces with Allie, and we'll find something suitable." Heather shifted her gaze to Melissa. "What's happening with your road trip?"

Melissa let out a long sigh and looked at Scott, her naval aviator boyfriend. "I don't know. Scott had already gotten his leave cleared, and we're not going to waste it. But with the trip less than a week away, it's going to be hard to find someplace that's not already booked. Plus, I had this detailed itinerary of what we could go do and see. It's just disappointing to have it not happen. Frankly, I don't know how the five of us kids will ever find the time. Look how long it took us this time." She played with her napkin. "Maybe it was just a childhood dream." She forced a smile.

Allie's brow furrowed. "We can make something work out. Just because Daniel and Brittany can't make it doesn't mean we have to give up the trip. Really all we need is a trailer, or a truck that can tow Daniel's trailer."

Collins's pulse notched up. He had a truck that could pull a trailer. It was part of why he'd bought it. He planned on getting a trailer for camping to make weekend trips to the mountains or beach campgrounds easier. In a moment, the idea of spending a road trip vacation with Allie sounded like the best deal, and it blocked out any other thought. "I can do it. My truck will pull a trailer. And it sounds like a lot of fun."

And then he remembered this was a siblings' trip, though Scott was going. "I mean, if you don't mind me coming along." He had a lot of comp time coming and had planned to take it before getting involved in too many cases at work. Plus Kyle would be taking time off for his wedding and honeymoon, so if Collins didn't go now, who knew when he would be able to? And what better place to use it?

Allie touched his arm, shooting warmth up it. "Collins, would you? That would be wonderful! We could keep the same plans." Her face glowed like it was lit from within, and a smile stretched across it.

"What plans?" Kyle's younger sister, Kim, walked into the kitchen.

"I knew I should have made you give back your key," Kyle pretend grumbled. "You're here more than you're at your place."

"You have better food." She popped a dip-covered veggie in her mouth. "So what are you planning?"

Heather scooted closer to Kyle. "There's room here, Kim. Come join us."

Kim filled a plate and joined the table while Melissa explained. "When we were kids, we had this tattered old map of the US. We'd spend evenings studying it, tracing routes we'd take, places we'd like to go. It was a fun way to dream. Last Thanksgiving, Brittany brought the map out. I didn't even know she'd saved it. We talked about actually planning one of these trips instead of just talking about it. We picked a date where it wouldn't be too hot and that everyone could get off. So we're touring the Southwest. The Grand Canyon, Monument Valley, Arches, Bryce, and Zion. Ten days to do a big loop."

Allie continued. "Originally it was supposed to be the five of us kids plus Scott." She nodded at him. "But our brother Daniel had a scheduling conflict, and Brittany got a new job and can't take time off. They needed someone who could start right away."

"I don't think Daniel ever wanted to leave his girlfriend behind, and she refused to come." Melissa scowled. "She doesn't camp."

"That doesn't bode well for that relationship," Scott said, and Melissa elbowed him. He grabbed his side like he was hurt then grinned.

"So anyhow," Allie continued with a glare at Scott. "It's going to be Melissa and Scott, our brother Matthew, and me. And Collins." She shot a glance toward him, her face slightly pink. "So two girls, three guys. Collins is going to pull Daniel's

trailer. Kim, you should come. It'll even out the numbers."
Allie's gaze darted to Melissa.

Collins studied Allie's face, almost certain she hadn't meant
to blurt out the invite to Kim without asking Melissa first.

But she plowed on. "Collins is replacing Daniel; you can
replace Brittany. It's perfect."

Except that Collins absolutely didn't want her thinking of
him as her brother. But, yeah, other than that, it was a perfect
solution. Now he just had to make sure he could fulfill the
promise he'd just made. And figure out how to spend ten days in
close quarters with people he only casually knew.

ALLIE RESTED HER HEAD AGAINST THE WINDOW ON THE
passenger side of Collins's truck. Where had the invite to Kim
come from? Melissa always was the one who made the plans. Yes,
she consulted with Allie, but Melissa was the planner, and Allie
was the executioner. Melissa didn't seem too upset that Allie had
invited Kim. Probably because Scott was around. She was
focused on him since she didn't see him much.

Allie didn't know Kim that well. She'd helped her find a
condo last year, and they'd become friends with all the folks they
had in common. But to do a road trip with someone? Well
they'd either be better friends by the end or not speaking.

And then there was Collins. She wasn't sure how she felt
about him being on the road trip with them. She loved that he
was able to save the day, but to spend a week and a half with
him could be wonderful or terrible. She thought there were
always options to problems, but this was a solution she'd never
imagined.

She leaned back against the headrest.

Collins glanced over at her. "Kim seemed excited to be
invited along. I know I'm amped to be going." He smiled at her.

"Thanks so much for saving the day. I know you weren't planning on that."

"I've got some comp time coming. I love camping, and I've always wanted to tour the Southwest. I haven't been to the Grand Canyon since I was a kid." They came to a stoplight. He turned to her, his gaze soft. "But the best part will be getting to spend some time with you."

Warmth like heat lightning shot through her body and back. After the wedding yesterday, the way they had danced together, she was pretty sure he wanted to be more than friends. But Melissa's news had taken the energy out of the night.

She smiled at him. "I'm looking forward to that too. It's going to be a fun trip. Kim wants to get inspired for a new clothing line. Melissa and Scott want to spend time together. My brother Matthew is funny. He'll make sure we all have a good time. It'll be a trip to remember." And she was beginning to believe it. This really could work.

The light turned green, and Collins returned his attention to the road. "There's just one condition."

Her heart stopped. What could he mean? Of course they'd pay for his gas. Her brain started whirling. *Stop, Allie. Wait until you hear what he wants.* Good grief, she was her own worst enemy. "What's that?"

"I want you to help me find a house."

Chapter Three

Willard slammed his fist on the counter as he read the text message from Olivia. She didn't want to see him anymore? Well, he'd see about that. Someone was feeding her lies. There's no way any sane woman would resist being with him. He had the charm, he had the looks, he had the car, and women loved him.

He'd tried it the therapist's way. A real relationship, the man had told him, was based on shared control and decision making, where the other person's wants and desires had equal weight. Give and take, put her needs first.

It hadn't worked. It never worked. He promised his brother he'd give the therapist and the meds a chance to work. It was useless; Willard had known it would be. But he tried anyway. He always tried. That's what nobody seemed to understand.

It didn't matter. His way was better.

Even Elaina had done what he wanted. With a little persuasion. He thought about the plastic bags hooked to the inside of a cupboard door in his bedroom. Beautiful curls, each with the name of their owners carefully labeled across them. Right where he could look at them from his bed. Elaina's made a wonderful addition.

As he paced away from the counter across his living room, a thought dawned on him. Olivia was playing games. That's right. She enjoyed having him chase her, show his interest in her. She thought she was the one in control, making him beg for her attention. Maybe she needed to see the therapist and listen to his advice about give and take.

He'd show her who was in control. And when he was done, she'd be begging for more. It would just prove that he didn't need the medication that head shrinker had given him. He was just fine without it. Better, even.

Olivia thought she was so smart. She wanted games? Well game on. She had met her match. He pulled up the tracking app on his phone that showed him where she was.

For a moment, he stood in his living room thinking, then grabbed the keys to his Porsche.

He knew just what he was going to do. A smile crossed his face as he locked the door behind him.

Monday morning, Allie opened her laptop in her office, reviewing what she'd come up with last night after Collins had dropped yet another bombshell about her helping him find a house. Yes, Kyle had teased Collins last winter that Collins needed to stop paying rent and allow Allie to find him a place. But then he'd been sent to help another police department, and she never knew if he had taken Kyle's suggestion seriously.

It appeared he had.

She'd asked him a few questions last night about what he was looking for. But he didn't seem to really know. He hadn't given the idea a whole lot of thought. Because she specialized in relocations, this was fairly common. Often her clients were moving to this area without knowing much about it beyond what they'd seen on TV. So she had a form she used that helped her understand her clients' wants and needs a bit better.

She'd go through it with Collins today. It worked well, and she was sure it would work with him. But last night, she'd done something a bit unusual. She'd picked out a house for him and set up a viewing appointment without getting his input first. It seemed perfect. At least for the Collins she had known in high school and was getting to know again now. There was another house they'd look at first, but she didn't think it would be a good fit. Still, she wanted to give him options. But mostly she wanted him to see that she could find the perfect house for him. If there was any part of him that still viewed her as a high school girl, she wanted to replace that image with one of the professional, successful woman she had become. At least that was how she felt most days.

She glanced at her Apple Watch. He'd be here in fifteen minutes. Today she picked a cotton, A-line skirt with a great print and a tailored wrap blouse. It was one of her favorite outfits, comfortable but confidence boosting by skimming her curves, which she often felt were a bit too generous, and making them look proportional. It was a warm spring day, so it felt just right. Chunky jewelry completed the ensemble.

Her desk phone buzzed. She punched a button, and Rachel's voice came over the line. "Steve Collins is here for you."

"Thanks, I'll be right out." Nerves had suddenly erupted. She didn't have time for them. She shoved down the insecure high school girl that had awakened inside, one she hadn't even realized still existed. Forcing herself into professional mode, she eased open her office door and stepped out.

He wasn't looking at her, instead he leaned casually against the counter, chatting up Rachel. He could charm a smile out of Oscar the Grouch. Which wasn't too far off in Rachel's case.

Allie put her hand against her office door, slowing its closure, willing it to click shut quietly. The moment she took a step, her heeled sandals would tap loudly on the travertine tiles. She studied him a moment. He'd looked fantastic at Cait and

Grayson's wedding Saturday, and today his dress shirt didn't conceal his broad chest and shoulders.

She took a few steps, and his head swiveled her way, a smile brighter than the polite one he'd given Rachel. "Hey, nice office you have here."

"Thanks." It wasn't large, just a small reception area with two leather love seats, a deep wooden receptionist's desk, and the hallway that led to her office and the conference room. But the big windows and tropical plants made it seem like a bit of a hideaway. She wanted it to feel professional but warm and comfortable at the same time. How she wanted her clients to feel about her. It set the stage. It was good to see it through his eyes.

She tilted her head. "Come on back to my office." She turned. "Rachel, hold all my calls, please."

Rachel raised her eyebrows and smirked. "Sure thing."

Allie resisted rolling her eyes. She'd tried everything she knew to help Rachel understand what was expected of her, like how to behave appropriately around clients. She wanted to mentor Rachel and help her become a great, professional admin. But without confrontation. Allie hated confrontation and saved it as a last resort. There were almost always better ways.

She'd hired Rachel because the director of the Christian business professionals mentoring group, Leroy Simmons, had said Rachel desperately needed a job. She was also his niece. It was the first time Allie had been assigned to be a mentor by the very group that had helped her get her business off the ground. And everyone knew they could count on Allie to help out. She liked helping. She'd built a business on it. Which Rachel might be putting in danger. Allie just had to figure out how to unlock the right motivation for Rachel like Leroy had done for her.

Pushing out a smile, Allie led the way to her office, feeling Collins's gaze on her back. In her office, she picked up her laptop and gestured to the sofa and chair grouping in the corner. She preferred to talk to her clients here instead of behind her desk. Relocating to a new city was hard enough without the impersonal barriers of a desk and a computer. Her clients were trusting her to help them get started in their new life, after all. And in Collins's case, it would be odd to sit across a desk from him.

He slid onto the couch, and while she usually took the chair, this time she eased down next to him, deciding quickly on a more friend-than-client distance.

With his nicely-muscled arm stretched along the back of the sofa, he looked like he was in his living room, not her office. He glanced at the map that papered the wall behind her desk. "That might be the most colorful map I've ever seen. And we've created a few interesting ones."

"What? Oh, that?" Her face warmed. It probably looked amateurish to a police detective. "It's my own little coded system. I have different places marked in different colors. Makes it easy for me to look for something at a glance. Clients with elementary-aged kids want to be close to schools. Others might want to be near hiking trails or have easy access to the beach. I have a digital version on my laptop too." She was babbling, something she did when she was nervous. And usually didn't do with clients. She clicked over to the client form she had started for him.

"I'm not surprised. I remember you used to highlight your notes with different colors." His deep-brown eyes sparkled with a familiar humor.

"It got both of us to pass a lot of tests, so it worked."

"That it did. So what do you have to show me?"

"Well." She didn't want to blurt out what she'd planned. "Let's go through a few of my standard client on-boarding forms and see what we come up with."

"Sounds good." He leaned toward her, his woodsy aftershave wafting toward her and reminding her of their dance at the wedding.

Focus. She turned her computer toward him and led him through a series of questions and even some Pinterest boards she had set up to get a sense of her clients' tastes. As she did, her heart sank until it hovered somewhere above her heeled sandals. The house she'd picked for him—the one she was sure was perfect for him—went against everything he said he wanted. She didn't want to look like she hadn't listened to him. And maybe he'd changed. Maybe he didn't want the same things he had when they were younger.

She licked her lips. "I did set up two viewings for us today, just based on what I thought might interest you. They may not work at all, but if you have time, we could go look at them." And maybe she'd learn something more about him and what he was looking for.

He lifted his hands. "I'm all yours."

I wish. Alli tamped that thought down before it became evident on her face. She'd been down that road fifteen years ago. Would this time be different?

"I'd love to see what you picked out. Honestly—" he waved his hand at her computer—"I'm not sure if anything I told you is actually what I prefer. I think I'll know it when I see it. I trust you."

Her temperature must have ticked up a few degrees. Was it her imagination, or had his voice dropped a bit on that last sentence? *I trust you.* She hoped he wouldn't be disappointed. The good news was there were a lot of houses for sale in an area as big as Orange County.

"Okay, then, let's go." She snapped her laptop shut and stood just as he did, bringing her face close to his shoulder. Reminding her again of the dance they had shared. She stepped back. *Be a professional.* She grabbed her leather tote and cell phone. "Oh, I'm driving."

He grinned. It had been a constant argument between them in high school. She didn't have a car, so he'd let her practice driving his. Sometimes. "I take it you don't have a stick shift?" He motioned her forward.

"As if." She smacked him on the arm, pretending to be

offended. In reality, he wasn't wrong. She never did get the hang of driving a stick shift. "If it makes you feel better, you can drive."

"It does."

As they passed through the lobby, Allie paused. "Rachel, we're heading out. If it's urgent, you can call my cell."

Rachel propped her chin on her hand, revealing a mouth of overly white teeth to Collins. "Have fun." Her voice lilted, making *fun* sound like something naughty.

Allie wanted to respond but couldn't think of anything to say that wouldn't sound like a slam against Collins. She finally settled on, "We're old high school friends."

"Those are the best kind." Again with the lilt.

Allie wanted to roll her eyes again. Just when she thought Rachel understood the concept of professional, she did something like that. But for now all Allie could do was ignore it. She'd have to deal with it soon, though.

Collins held the door of his F-150 for Allie, catching a faint hint of something lightly vanilla. He went around to the driver's side and climbed in. "Just tell me where to go."

Allie gave a small laugh as they pulled out onto the main road. "I usually feel like a tour guide as I take clients around, giving them the information on the area as we drive. But you're a local. I don't need to do that for you."

"I'll listen if you want."

She laughed. "Are you back in town for good, or do you have to go back to Holcomb Springs? I keep forgetting to ask you."

"That assignment ended early. I'm back, in between assignments, helping Kyle get caught up on paperwork." Until he got sent somewhere else. Or if he decided to take the job that

Holcomb Springs had offered him. In which case, what was he doing looking at houses? Finding an excuse to spend time with Allie. Or seeing if finding the perfect house, or not, was God's way of opening or closing doors. He didn't really know what he was doing. He just knew this sense of restlessness had been following him for about six months. And he wanted God to show him how to resolve it.

She directed him to an area in the foothills not too far from Kyle's house. It looked like it had been built in the same era as Kyle's. He remembered how much work Kyle—and he—had done on that house. He wasn't looking forward to buying a fixer upper.

He pulled to the curb in front. There was a car in the driveway.

"The agent said she had a showing before ours but that it should be over by the time we arrived. She thought she might still be around because she was going to meet a repair service here. I didn't think you'd mind."

"No, I'd prefer it, actually. It's always good to know what you're getting into." His phone buzzed. It was Kyle.

"Go ahead and take it. I'll just go on in and see if her showing is finished." She slipped out of the truck.

Collins swiped across the screen, but his attention was on Allie as she walked to the front door.

Allie approached the front door. The lockbox was off to the side, open, so Amanda Park, the listing agent, must still be inside. She knocked on the door as she opened it, calling out. "Hi, it's Allie. My client will be just a minute, so I thought I'd pop in."

Amanda didn't appear, but Allie thought she heard a noise down the hall, toward the bedrooms. She headed that way. "Amanda?"

Now she definitely heard something, like someone bumping into furniture. But why didn't Amanda answer? Maybe she was on a call.

A blood-curdling scream came from the last bedroom, followed by the sound of a door banging open.

The hair rose on the back of Allie's neck, and she broke out in a cold sweat, but she pushed on. What was she walking in on? But Amanda might need her help. Maybe she fell.

Allie shoved open the ajar master bedroom door. Amanda was pushing herself upright on the bed, her hair and clothes in disarray, her nose and lip bleeding.

Allie rushed to her. "Are you okay? What happened?"

Amanda's face crumpled, and she pointed to the open French door that led to the backyard. "That man attacked me."

Glancing where Amanda was pointing, Allie didn't see anything. Hoping the man wouldn't come back, her first thought was for Amanda. "You're hurt. Do I need to call an ambulance?"

She shook her head and sobbed.

Collins appeared in the doorway. "What happened? I thought I heard a scream."

"She was attacked. He went that way." Allie pointed to the open French door.

Collins sprinted outside.

"Let me get a washcloth for your face." Allie took a step toward the master bathroom.

Amanda's hand snaked out and clutched Allie's wrist. "Don't leave me. Please?"

Allie sat on the bed and put her arm around her. "You're safe now."

Some of Amanda's glossy black hair had been hacked off. Allie shuddered at the thought of how close the knife or scissors must have been to Amanda's neck to do that.

Collins reappeared a moment later, on the phone. "The

police are on their way. I didn't see him. Can you give a description?"

Amanda relayed a jumbled description of a man with a goatee dressed in a business suit on the thin side, average height, dark hair, dark eyes.

Collins passed it on and hung up. "I'm sorry. I'm sure the uniforms will ask you the same questions. And then the detectives. Anything you can think of from your contact with him will help." He turned to Allie. "Are you okay?"

She nodded. "He was darting out the door as I came in. He must have heard me announce myself. These houses are so soundproof with their triple-paned windows and extra insulation that I'm amazed you heard anything at all."

"I probably wouldn't have in the truck. I had just stepped out." He went to show the police in, and after he and Allie had given their statements, they were allowed to leave.

"Why don't I take you home before going back to the office?" He escorted her back to his truck.

Allie looked up at him. Her mind was spinning. She'd gone from being a Realtor to someone who had interrupted a crime. Her brain couldn't keep up. "Why?"

He pointed to her blouse.

Amanda's blood stained it.

WILLARD SAT BEHIND THE WHEEL OF HIS PORSCHE PARKED down the street, enjoying the rush of adrenaline mixed with the leathery smell of his car. He chuckled and fingered the dark hair in his suit pocket. He'd never come close to being discovered before. The rush was amazing.

Before he entered the house with Amanda, he had parked his Porsche a few houses down. Now safely inside his car, he watched between bushes and trees as the police pulled up. That was his cue to leave. But he had a minute. A businessman in a

Porsche wouldn't raise any eyebrows in this neighborhood, and he wanted to gather as much information as possible, savoring the rush. The truck, the man driving it, and most of all the woman who had interrupted his plans with lovely Amanda.

Allie, a fellow Realtor, it sounded like. And when he'd peeked in the bedroom window after making his escape, he'd gotten a good look at her.

Well, he'd like to meet the woman responsible for ruining his plans. Yes, he would. And soon. Up close and personal. He'd have some plans for her.

Chapter Four

Collins pulled into the parking lot for Allie's office. They were going to try again today to see the house they hadn't gotten to yesterday. After the attack on Amanda Park, giving their statements, and then taking Allie home to change her blouse, they had missed the window for the showing. And neither of them had been in the frame of mind to reschedule it for later that day.

He pulled open the door, and she was immediately on the other side, practically pushing him back out before he stepped in.

"Hi, I'm all ready to go. Do you want me to drive?" She smiled at him and gave a quick glance back inside before letting the door shut behind her and heading to the parking lot.

He raised his eyebrows. Okay. "How about I do?"

She laughed.

He helped her into his truck, and they drove back in the same general direction as before. This time they turned into a different neighborhood. He glanced over at her. "How are you doing after yesterday?"

She shrugged. "I'm more aware of my surroundings. I was careful when I opened up the office this morning." But she didn't meet his gaze. "I'm glad you agreed to meet me at the office. I didn't like the idea of walking into an empty house. And I'm glad I don't hold open houses or work with clients I don't know. But it does scare me for my female colleagues who do."

She darted a look at him and let out a breath. "I didn't get much work done yesterday afternoon. I searched for something else to show you today, but nothing really fit. So we have just the one to see."

He took the change in subject in stride. "If it doesn't work, we'll just keep looking until we find something. There's no rush."

They pulled into a driveway. Collins immediately felt better about this house than yesterday's. Nothing about this house looked like a fixer. The landscape was basic, the paint fairly new. A two-story in the typical Mediterranean-influenced California style. He looked around. Seemed quiet enough. Not a high crime area.

Allie hopped out, and he was right beside her, not wanting any surprises. She headed for the front door shaded by a porch then used an app on her phone to unlock the lockbox, pulled out a key, and opened the door.

But he put a hand out and walked in first, scanning the area before taking another step inside and ushering her in.

The entryway was travertine tile with dark wood floors in the living areas. There was a great room that combined the kitchen and den. The den area had built-ins for the TV with bookshelves and drawers. "This has definitely been updated. I was expecting a fixer like Kyle had."

She smiled at him, following a few steps behind, letting him experience it first. "I know you said you liked lighter colors, and this has dark wood floors and cabinetry."

"But it doesn't feel dark. There's a lot of light from the windows, and the light travertine is a really nice contrast to the dark wood."

Allie moved toward the French doors off the great room.

"This was actually what made me think of you." She unlocked the door and stepped out into the backyard.

He followed. "Oh, wow." He turned and looked all around him. "This looks a lot like my backyard growing up." The yard wrapped around the side of the house and was terraced at the edges leading up the slope that surrounded them. "Of course we didn't have this cool outdoor kitchen or pergola."

"See what's over here." Allie led him to the side yard out of view. The terrace dropped lower here, creating a sweet, small flower garden. Very much like the one he and Allie had spent hours sitting in and talking.

He shook his head, stunned. "How did you find this? It's amazing."

Her pretty blue-green eyes sparkled above her smile. "It's been on the market awhile. I'm not sure why. But from the first time I saw it, I thought of you."

A rustle in the bushes made Collins instinctively step closer to Allie. A calico cat appeared and hopped onto the terrace wall.

Allie moved toward it, hand out. "Hello, kitty."

The cat stared at her and let her pet him. Or her.

"Do you still have cats?" Collins moved closer but didn't want to scare the cat away.

"Yep, just not the same ones." She laughed.

They had spent a whole session of study hall whisper arguing over the merits of dogs versus cats. It was a running joke between them. Standing in this backyard with her made him feel a bit like they'd gone back in time.

She gave the cat one final pat. "Do you want to see the rest of the house? I know it's more bedrooms than you need, but the office and garage both have some pretty sweet built-ins."

"Lead on. I like the built-ins in the den."

They headed back inside, and Allie made sure the door was locked behind them. "I have great respect for someone who loves built-ins."

Was she talking about him or the owner? Either way, he was

sold on this house. And it was vacant. That had to mean they wanted to deal, right?

The rest of the house was just as if someone had designed it for him, even though he could see it wasn't anything like what he'd told Allie he wanted. But she knew him better than he knew himself. Better yet, he could see Allie here too.

He was getting way ahead of himself. He kept his expression neutral. He didn't want her to read his thoughts on his face. They had only begun to reconnect. He'd blame it on the memories that had transported him back to another time, a time when he couldn't help but picture her in his future. Only then he hadn't had the guts enough to do anything about it. He never quite knew if she felt anything beyond friendship for him. And he didn't want to risk that friendship to find out. He was still walking that tightrope with her.

"What do you think of it?" He turned to face her at the front door.

She blinked and paused before answering. "It's a great house. I think you could get a good deal on it. It's bigger than you need, but you could grow into it." She glanced away at her phone. "It's more important what you think."

He also wasn't going to rule out a future with her. If she couldn't see herself living here, he didn't want to buy it. But how to say that to her? *Dig deep.* "Would you live here?" he blurted.

She started to open her mouth then looked around, nodding. "Yes, I would. I love the built-ins, the light, the backyard." She met his gaze. "It would be a great house to live in."

He didn't think they were talking about the house anymore. He propped his hand on the wall behind her shoulder, leaning into her space. The smell of vanilla—shampoo, perfume?—drifted over him. "Have dinner with me tonight." Then he remembered her frequent glances at her phone. "Do you have other plans?" He eased back.

"No, I don't. But I have a better idea. Do you still like steak?"

"Who doesn't?"

"Vegetarians, but since you're apparently not one, how about I throw a couple on my backyard grill? We can talk about the house and the road trip."

Her idea was even better than his.

They exited the house, and while she was locking up and putting the key back in the lockbox, he strode around the front yard, viewing it with fresh eyes. This could be his. He could be happy here, becoming a homeowner instead of a renter. And every image that flashed through his mind included Allie. It'd been a lot of years since high school. She'd always been cute and smart, but now she was a confident, stylish woman running her own company. She had a whole life he didn't know about, as weird as that seemed. He'd had a life without her too. They'd have to get to know each other all over again. Something he was definitely looking forward to. Starting tonight.

AFTER TAKING ALLIE BACK TO HER OFFICE, COLLINS headed into the Laguna Vista Police Department, his mind still on Allie. He was fascinated by how she made everyone feel at home, from helping Cait find the right place for her wedding to finding the perfect house for him when he didn't even know what he wanted. She even stepped up to comfort Amanda yesterday after her attack.

He'd taken the whole day off yesterday to get caught up on everything he'd neglected while at Holcomb Springs. But if he was going to make good on his promise to keep the road trip going, he'd have to get cleared for the time off. It shouldn't be a problem. He hadn't been assigned any active cases yet. He had comp time coming. And between now and the road trip, he could help Kyle with his backlog. Seemed like a win all the way around to him.

But that wasn't how the lieutenant saw it when Collins

made his way into his office. "Collins, you just got back, so I know you don't know what's going on. But we're short staffed, and Patino's already asked for that week off. If you can get him to swap with you, fine. I don't care. I just need bodies here."

What were the odds Patino would swap with him? He needed to gather some intel. He headed back to the cubicle he shared with Kyle, who happened to be there.

"Look what the dog dragged in." Kyle stood and shook Collins's hand. "Tired of resort life up in the mountains? I didn't think you were coming in until tomorrow."

"I wasn't. But I wanted to talk to the lieutenant about using my comp time for the road trip Allie and Melissa are planning."

"And he said no."

"Yeah. You could have warned me."

"Always better to learn the info first hand. How do you think Allie's going to take the news that the trip is off? Or are you going to let her use your new truck?"

Collins jerked back at the idea. He remembered too clearly trying to teach her to drive a stick. She'd just about burned out the transmission in his Ford Ranger. "I can swap with Patino."

Kyle raised his eyebrows. "He agreed to that? He's been talking about his house renovation nonstop, even roping me into doing some work."

"Then I can sweeten the offer by offering my services." He was glad Kyle had dropped that bit. It gave him more ammo to make his case. "Speaking of houses, we went back to look at a house today. In your neighborhood, as a matter of fact. Just a few blocks over."

"I'm glad you decided to stop throwing away money on rent. But the house-buying process can be stressful. Even if you're not stumbling upon Realtors who have been attacked."

Collins nodded. "About that. How's she doing? Anything on the perp?"

"It's like the other recent Realtor assaults. Similar description. At the previous attack, which took place at an open house, the guy signed in as Richard Ramirez, but he's not Hispanic."

Collins raised his eyebrows. "The Night Stalker?"

"The guy has a sick sense of humor. We talked to the neighbors yesterday and got surveillance footage from anyone who had security or doorbell cameras. We're going through all of that now." Kyle leaned back in his chair. "But you'll be on a road trip, so this won't be your problem. What did you think of the house you saw?"

"I think it's the one. It's perfect for me. Yesterday I reached out to a lender I know so I can make an offer tonight." It was the first time he'd said the words out loud. Should he pull the trigger on the house? Why not? He loved it, and it was in his budget. Though asking Allie to show him more places would give them more time together. But he was having dinner with her tonight. And if they could talk about the future a bit, he wouldn't need the house-hunting excuse.

Kyle nodded. "It's hard to make a bad investment buying real estate in California if you can hang on to it long enough to ride out any ups and downs."

Collins nodded, but the Holcomb Springs job offer flitted through his mind. He hadn't seriously considered it, but maybe he should pray about it before dismissing it out of hand. Especially before he bought the house. He'd been so eager to spend time with Allie, he'd gotten ahead of himself. No matter how hard he had worked or how many dues he had paid or how many opportunities he had passed up to hitch his wagon to this particular star, when it came down to it, he wasn't guaranteed tomorrow. And this job was getting riskier every day.

Collins tapped his knuckles on the desk. "I'll be back in the morning. I'm sure you'll have plenty waiting for me."

Kyle gestured to a stack on Collins's desk. "Just a few things. Good luck with Patino. You know if he's not at his desk, he's probably at Taco Bell."

Collins laughed as he exited the cubicle and headed toward

Patino's. His fondness for the quasi-Mexican fast food was well known. If Collins had known he'd have to trade with Patino, he could have brought a bag of chalupas to sweeten his offer.

He was in luck. Patino was at his desk. Now to convince him that it was in his best interest to swap with Collins.

Chapter Five

Why do I always do this to myself?" Allie asked Melissa, who was on the other end of the cell phone coming through her car speakers and too far away to be any help other than moral support. "I have way too much to do in the time I have to do it. I could kick myself." Instead she smacked the steering wheel lightly. "What on earth made me think I could get to the store, get home, tidy up the place, and change into something comfortable in an hour? By midnight maybe."

"Oh, Allie—"

"Good grief. One of these days I'm going to actually think before I open my mouth and stick in my foot—even if I do like my pedicure." She glanced down at the little flowers dotting her big toes. "But no, I want Collins to think my life runs so smoothly I just need to pick up a few things, return to my immaculate townhome, and change. What fantasy world am I living in?"

"Well, I think—"

"Reality alert. My house needs more than tidying, I need more than a few things at the grocery store, and—" feeling the dampness under her arms and down her back—"I need a shower."

"Allie! Take a breath!" Melissa's shout caused Allie to blink.

She directed the air vents toward her chest, hoping to cool down. "I know, you're right. Collins will just have to deal. He'll understand. I think he's pretty happy with the house we looked at today. Actually, that's not even why I called you."

"Uh oh. What'd she do now? I don't know why you don't just fire her."

"Why do you assume this has to do with Rachel?"

"Well does it?"

"Yes, but you don't have to assume that."

"Honey, Rachel is the bane of your existence. If you don't fire her soon, she's going to ruin your business. She makes you look bad."

"You're right. I just don't know how I can. Today, Mr. Winchell—the older man with the little dog that looks like Toto—he called looking for a recommendation for a vet, and Rachel told him to Google it. He's not our biggest client since he moved here to retire and isn't a corporate account, but he has a lot of corporate connections still."

"That's exactly what I'm saying. Look, I know you hate confrontation with a passion. You're a softie, but you're not doing yourself or Rachel any favors by letting her act that way."

Melissa was right; Allie knew that. Melissa had run a multi-million-dollar defense contracting firm as vice-president of operations before she opened her own boutique consulting firm at the end of last year. Allie just hoped Melissa wasn't right about Rachel ruining her business.

"Have you ever had to fire anyone?" Allie couldn't picture herself firing Rachel, just couldn't. She broke out in a cold sweat even thinking about it.

"Yes. It's never fun. But sometimes you're doing them a favor, letting them find a job that they really enjoy."

Maybe. "Is there some sort of education technique that I'm just missing? That's the whole purpose of the mentorship group we are a part of, learning how business works. This is the first time I've been asked to be a mentor, and I don't want to blow it. And I don't want to let Leroy down. He specifically asked me to take on Rachel. He's done so much for me, I couldn't say no. Plus, she's his niece. I know he's expecting me to make this work."

"Haven't you tried teaching her?"

"Well, yes. But maybe I wasn't clear enough. Maybe I'm the problem."

"Hmpf."

Apparently Melissa didn't agree. "Well, anyway, pray for me that I don't make a fool out of myself in front of Collins, and that I'll have wisdom to deal with Rachel."

"Courage is more like it. But you and Collins seemed pretty cozy dancing at the wedding."

"Yeah." Her voice softened. "I'm just afraid he still thinks of me as the girl with the embarrassing crush on him from high school."

"I highly doubt that."

Encouraged by her big sister's words, Allie hung up and focused on her next challenge: tonight. Collins seemed pleased with the house she had picked out. But when he'd asked her if she could picture herself living there, she'd answered honestly. All afternoon she'd turned that over in her mind. Was he asking her as a Realtor or as his possible-girlfriend-maybe-something-more-someday?

From a practical standpoint, if he was going to be serious with any woman soon, he should have her input on a house she might live in. But she and Collins hadn't even been on a date. Tonight didn't count. Did it? Oh, sometimes her thoughts could get her head whirling like the washing machine on the spin cycle. Maybe tonight would bring more clarity.

As she pulled into Ralph's parking lot, she didn't enjoy that her stomach felt like she'd eaten a whole plate of jalapeños for lunch.

Reusable grocery bags cutting grooves into her arms, Allie kicked the door shut connecting the garage to the kitchen. The clock on the stove read 5:45. Great. Her shirt sticking to her back told her just how un-ready she was for company. It wasn't that hot out, so it must be nerves. Which was ridiculous. She had people over all the time.

She dropped the load on the floor. Rajah, her orange-and-brown calico cat, sniffed the bags. Food could wait. Prep work would give them something to talk about. Grabbing papers, magazines, an empty Diet Coke can, and a pair of sandals, she hurried to her bedroom upstairs. "I'll feed you in a minute, Rajah." The cat followed, racing up the stairs ahead of her.

She dumped everything on her bed and flung open her closet doors. What to wear? That decision process alone could take an hour. Grr. She grabbed a maxi dress. Cute, casual, and comfy. And a quick dunk under the shower should refresh her.

Ten minutes later she was feeling better. She fed Rajah in the laundry room then scanned the living room. Everything in order? Pretty much. She fluffed a pillow. The whole place needed a good dusting. What was that advice? Light candles and no one will see the dust? She turned on her favorite relaxing station on Pandora, connecting to the Bluetooth speaker. Grabbing the candlelighter, she flicked it on and lit a couple of candles out of Rajah's reach. The smell of hot wax and sulfur tickled her nose and prompted a sneeze.

Anything else?

The doorbell rang. Collins was still punctual. She shoved the lighter back in the drawer and hurried to answer the door.

"Hey, you found it." She stepped back, slightly self-conscious, like she should make some sort of sweeping Vanna

White gesture to welcome him inside. Rajah trotted over to inspect the newcomer.

"Siri gives good directions." He stepped into the Saltillo-tiled foyer. "This is nice."

Rajah sniffed his shoe.

As he looked around, Allie realized what was playing on the station. A romantic song, a little too loud. *Ooh baby, baby. I love you, baby.* The candles, the romantic music… She wanted to die. Imagine how it must appear to Collins. An invitation back to her place. He must think she was trying to succeed where she couldn't fifteen years ago. She was such an idiot.

She hurried past him. "Wow, I had no idea the music was that loud. I didn't even see what was in it. You know, usually being home alone, I just put it on random." She clicked the volume down to barely audible. "Okay, then. Sorry, I was rushing around a bit and haven't started dinner. But it shouldn't take too long." Babble, babble. *Just shut up, Allie.*

Collins followed her into the living room, a slight smile across his face. "No hurry. I don't have anywhere to be but here." He gave her that winning grin, and her stomach time-traveled her back to high school.

"Great." She clasped her hands. "Well, you can keep me company while I get some things together." She moved into the kitchen and opened the refrigerator. "Iced tea or a Coke? Or just water?" Babbling again.

"Iced tea's great."

Collins seemed pretty relaxed, settling himself on a barstool at her counter. She caught a whiff of soap and a note of something woodsy, what she was beginning to think of as his signature scent. He'd changed into jeans and a shirt with the sleeves rolled up and clearly had taken a shower and shaved. Her stomach did that funny thing again.

What of it? Some guys liked to shave at night or after a shower. Big deal. She stopped examining his freshly-shaved cheeks before it became too obvious. Still, she remembered how that skin felt at the wedding. Get a grip. She ducked into the fridge and pulled out the iced tea pitcher. She poured a glass and slid it across to Collins.

Collins picked up his glass and sipped. "I really liked the house you showed me today. I spoke to a lender this afternoon, and I have a pre-approval letter all ready to go. I think we should put in an offer."

We? Her gaze moved to his face almost of its own accord. Something cold ran across her hand, and she jerked. Iced tea overflowed her glass. Her jerking knocked the pitcher against his glass, and it tipped over, onto the counter. Iced tea hit the floor, tinkling against the tile like BBs.

Rajah darted out of the kitchen. Smart cat.

"Ah, I'm sorry! Did I get you?" She grabbed for the towel hanging on the oven door handle. And hit the pitcher with her elbow, knocking the rest of it down the front of her. Ice-cold liquid plastered her dress to her front.

Collins laughed. "You got me a little, but you got yourself way worse."

She plucked the bodice away from her, making a sucking sound. She tossed him the towel. "Here, clean yourself up. I'm going to go change."

"Good idea." He chuckled.

She escaped the kitchen and flew upstairs. Rajah joined her, hopping on the bed and studying her. Even the cat thought she was nuts. At least Collins was laughing. Good grief, could she be more of a klutz? Or had her swirling thoughts unnerved her that much?

No, she'd always been clumsy. That part of her hadn't changed. It reminded her of the time they had stopped at In-N-Out after a football game. He played varsity, she cheered—thanks to a generous scholarship. Most of their lives, in just about every aspect—church, school, friends, work—intertwined. So after an away game they had all stopped for something to eat. She was gesturing while she was talking—something else that hadn't changed—when her arm hit the tray holding what was left of her fries. They flipped up in the air and sprinkled the floor.

In a typical teenage moment that embarrassed her now, she'd laughed that she'd leave it for the fast-food workers to pick up. They got up to leave. Allie grabbed her purse off the back of her chair to see Collins on the ground picking up her fries. Chagrined by his thoughtfulness compared to her flip attitude, she bent down to help him.

God, I know I'm impulsive when it comes to doing things for others, and maybe inviting Collins over wasn't the smartest move without more preparation. But please don't let me sabotage myself tonight. Did she just ask God to protect her from herself? Well, it wasn't the worst idea. A verse niggled at her, but she couldn't recall it. Served her right. She'd been putting too many hours in at the office trying to save her business and had let her attendance at Bible study group slide. And now with this road trip…

Flinging open her closet for the second time this evening, she knew she didn't have time to deliberate. Since she was wearing her now-drenched maxi dress, she was going to have to go for whatever was decent. Yanking her dress off and tossing it in the laundry hamper, she then toweled off the damp residue on her skin before shimmying into a floral peasant top and skinny jeans. Checking in the mirror to make sure she didn't have something sticking to her face—because that would just top this whole evening of embarrassing moments—she hurried back downstairs. Joanna Gaines she was not.

Collins was mopping up the counter.

"Oh thanks, you didn't have to do that." His kindness hadn't changed. "How badly did I get you?"

He stepped back from the counter to reveal an iced-tea-dotted shirt. "Not too bad. You got the worst of it."

"Well, I deserved it. Let's hope I can light the barbecue without blowing up the place." She moved toward the patio sliding door, but he caught her hand.

"Allie, don't stress about it. It's fine. Really."

For a moment, as the warmth of his hand enveloped hers, she just looked at those deep-brown eyes. She hadn't done that in a long time. And the desire for those eyes to gaze at her and only her hadn't needed much coaxing to come back to life.

Trying to gain control over the burst of longing, and certainly not wanting him to see it, she flashed some sort of smile and snuck her hand out of his grasp.

A few minutes later the grill was lit, and while they waited for it to get hot enough, Collins helped her prep the salads and mashed potatoes. They carried everything to the small table she had out back. It was a good evening to eat outside.

Collins studied her patio. "This is nice."

She tried to see it with his eyes. An over-sized clay jar filled with river rock became a burbling fountain. Solar-powered lights accented the landscaping of potted palms, bougainvillea, mandevilla, gardenias, and other semi-tropical plants. Their heavy, floral scent mixed with the smell of grilled meat and a whiff of propane to make something that smelled like almost summer even in the spring. Contentment finally settled over her.

She set the steaks on the now-hot grill and poured more iced tea while they waited. When the steaks were ready and they were seated at the table, Collins reached for her hand while he asked the blessing. As the seconds passed, this felt exactly right.

She hated to break the moment, but she had to ask. "Did you find anything out about Amanda Park's attacker?"

"It could be the same guy from the other Realtor assaults. They pulled footage from any neighbors who had cameras, and they're going through that now. He thinks he's smart, but we'll get him."

"I'm just glad we were able to be there to interrupt him before Amanda was hurt worse."

"I'm glad you don't routinely meet clients you don't know in empty houses." His gaze held hers for a long second. The tenderness she saw there was almost her undoing.

She turned her attention to her plate. "Me too."

Collins must have sensed the shift. "So tell me about this Great American Road Trip. Where are we going?" Collins put a bite of steak in his mouth. "Mmm. Perfectly medium rare."

"You were able to get time off?" She hadn't been sure since it seemed kind of short notice. While she hadn't told anyone, she'd still been thinking of backup plans.

He nodded. "It'll cost me some Saturdays working at the house my buddy Patino's renovating. I had to swap with him. But I'm free to go. Wherever it is that we're going."

A weight rolled off her shoulders. "The plan is to head to Phoenix and meet Matthew and Daniel there. Matthew has a small pickup truck, so we won't have to all be squished in your truck. Five people aren't too bad with the crew cab but six wouldn't be good. We can get the trailer from Daniel and head to Flagstaff for the first night. From there we head to the Grand Canyon for a couple of days and then drive through Monument Valley to Arches, then Bryce Canyon and Zion, with a couple of days at each. Ten days total. It's really just a quick trip that hits the highlights, but it's the best we can do."

"It always ends up being that way. But it's a great way to know the places you want to revisit and stay longer in the future."

She nodded. "There's really so much to see even for a weekend trip to either the mountains, desert, or beach."

"That's why I got the truck. I want to get a trailer, too, but I haven't had the time to pick out what I want. Daniel's trailer will be a good test to help me figure that out."

"It sleeps six, if two people want to sleep on the dinette-slash-bed and couch. So we were figuring that the girls would sleep inside and the guys would sleep in the tent." She studied his reaction. "I hope you're okay with that."

He waved a hand. "It's fine. We won't spend any time in there other than to sleep. I've got a good sleeping bag and pad.

It's cooking that's the hassle with tent camping. No good place to keep the food and prep it."

"The trailer will be a big help with that. Melissa has it down to a science. She's got a menu planned, a shopping list, a prep list. She'll get you a copy of what you need to bring."

Collins chuckled. "I saw her in action last year with everything that happened at Broadstone Technology. She's a force to be reckoned with. It's going to be a great trip."

"My brother Matthew likes to needle her. He's always up for any kind of adventure, and he teases Melissa with his wild ideas just to get a rise out of her. You'll get a wonderful look at what it's like to be part of a family." Collins was an only child, which was why they had usually hung out at his house in high school. That and her house was barely controlled chaos that she didn't want anyone to see. She shivered.

"Cold?"

"It's getting cool. We can bring the dishes and food in. I have some strawberry shortcake from Samashima Farms courtesy of Cait that we can eat inside."

"Sounds great. We can talk about the house buying process over dessert."

They worked companionably to bring in the food and dishes. Collins doubled checked the grill was off and wiped down the outside table as she put things away inside. It was like they'd done this before. She'd redeemed herself, proven that she was a grownup who could serve a meal and carry on a conversation without endangering herself or anyone else. *Thank you, God.*

Collins helped her with the coffee and dessert, carrying it all into the living room, setting their coffee cups on the low table.

"Let me get my computer." She hurried upstairs and back down again empty handed. "I left it in the car when I brought in the groceries." But she wasn't going to castigate herself this time. She'd had a nice, comfortable evening with Collins, and she wanted it to continue.

Returning with her laptop, she had a decision to make.

Collins was sitting on the sofa, close to the middle, petting Rajah, who had deigned to join them. How close did she sit to him? Friend close? Or more-than-friend close? If only she'd sat down first. Refusing to analyze it, she sat close enough to show him her screen.

He scooted closer and put his arm across the back of the couch.

Rajah tried to climb on Allie's lap, where the computer was. Allie nudged her away. She went back to Collins. Allie laughed. "I guess Rajah likes you."

"I think she wants attention and resents your laptop." He scratched Rajah's ear, and she purred, settling deeper into his lap.

"Well, now she's got you doing just what she wanted." She focused on her screen. "Do you want to see any other houses?"

He shook his head. "Nope. That's the one."

They walked through the offer process between bites of dessert, discussed what price to offer, and she emailed him all the forms to e-sign at home. "And that's it. I talked to the listing agent earlier today and let her know you were interested. It doesn't sound like anyone else is, and the sellers have already bought another house, so I think they'll be reasonable. We should have an answer fairly quickly tomorrow after we send everything over." She closed her laptop and set it on the coffee table next to their empty dessert dishes.

He reached out and touched her hand. "Thank you for everything, Allie. Dinner, the house, all of it. You're really an amazing woman."

She shifted, a little uncomfortable with his praise. He'd always been a big encourager in her life. Until now, she hadn't realized how much she missed it.

"Hey, I wanted to talk to you about something." Now it was his turn to look uncomfortable. "Remember at the wedding how I said I wished I'd asked you to prom first?" His gaze was intent on hers.

She nodded, not trusting her voice.

"I never wanted to do anything to ruin our friendship. And I don't now either. But I also want to see if we have something more." He gave a low chuckle that did funny things to her stomach. "Seems like ten days together on a road trip would be a good way to test that out. What do you say?"

She gave him a soft smile. "I wish you'd asked me to prom. And I value our friendship too. I would never want to lose it. But, yeah, I don't want to live with any more what ifs."

He tucked a strand of hair behind her ear, and his knuckles trailed along her cheek. "I'm looking forward to spending ten days with you."

"Me too." Was her voice really as breathy as it sounded to her? Something she'd dreamed about, words she'd dreamed she'd hear him say, a status she'd longed for came crashing true. On her couch, in her living room, things that showed she'd gained a measure of success quite different from the life she'd led in high school. No football team or cheer squad surrounding them, no rumors in the hallways or being seen together in public. No, this was nothing like what she'd dreamed about in high school. No, it was better.

He held her gaze for a long moment. "I should be going." But it was another long moment before he actually stood.

She walked him to the door. He opened it and turned to her. "Dinner was great. The company was wonderful. Thanks for everything. I'll talk to you tomorrow." He pulled her into a firm hug that was both longer and shorter than she wanted.

"Um, good night. Drive safely."

He gave her a grin topped off with a wink and shut the door behind him. She locked it. Smelling Collins's aftershave on her, she ignored the dessert dishes and climbed the stairs to bed, Rajah racing her to the top. Maybe if she fell asleep quickly, she'd see him in her dreams.

COLLINS TOSSED HIS KEYS ON THE COUNTER OF HIS apartment and glanced around. If all went well, he wouldn't be here much longer. In fact, it hardly looked like he lived here, even though he'd been here almost five years. There were no homey touches like at Allie's townhome. He'd never thought he was missing them, but after feeling comfortable at her place, maybe he'd been wrong.

He headed to his bedroom, thinking about what Melissa's list might contain and what he would need to bring. His eyes fell on his guitar case sitting in the corner of the bedroom. On a whim, he brushed off the dust and opened it, pulling out his Martin guitar, one of his most prized possessions. Yet he never played it. A quick strum across the strings told him how out of tune it was. He fiddled with the tuning pegs and strummed until it was in tune. He tried to pick out the chords of Lifehouse's "You and Me." While he tried to recall the melody, he kept getting distracted by the memory of her in his arms, of them having dinner as comfortably as if they had been doing it for years.

At the wedding, he had studied the band. It was something he enjoyed doing whenever he listened to live music. He was glad Cait and Grayson had opted for a band instead of just a DJ.

What had made those band members choose that career path instead of something else? Yes, they probably all had day jobs, but what kept them going when other people gave up on music? People like him. What would it be like to follow your heart and not someone else's expectations?

He enjoyed his job. He did. But at times he wondered what might have been. He thought of Allie. If he'd had the courage in high school to be more than just her friend, to act on his feelings for her, where would they be now? Everything happened for a reason, he believed that and that God was in control with a good plan for him. But still… he couldn't help but think about a lot of what ifs.

One thing he was certain of: He wasn't going to let what ifs stand in the way this time. He was going to see if he and Allie had a future together. No matter what it took.

The road trip had cost him, putting him at Patino's mercy. Buying a house would certainly cost him, even though it was an investment.

Allie was worth it. Right? If he pulled out, the whole trip would fall apart. And while he had no obligation to her or her family, he loved seeing her smile. He wanted to make her happy and spend time with her. The road trip seemed like a great opportunity to do both. Plus, he needed to know if they had something as adults, not just his leftover feelings from a high-school crush.

The house. Well, the house represented his dreams of the future that seemed almost within reach. He'd spent some time in prayer this afternoon sitting on the small balcony of his apartment after talking to the lender, making sure that this was part of God's plan for him. And that the job offer in Holcomb Springs that he'd brushed off wasn't something that he needed to consider more thoroughly. But he had a sense of peace after his time in prayer. What were the odds that the perfect house was just waiting for him? It had to be a God thing.

He strummed another chord and then put the guitar back in its case, latching it shut. No, he'd probably never play for her again. Who was he kidding? His guitar playing days were long ago. He should probably just sell the guitar. His heart clenched a bit at the thought.

Instead, he flipped open his laptop. His mind was spinning; he wouldn't sleep soon. It'd be better to get those documents e-signed so Allie wouldn't be waiting on him tomorrow.

He chuckled. It was refreshing to see her spill tea on herself tonight. She could almost be intimidating if she weren't so kind, as successful as she was. And given where he knew she'd come from, it truly was an accomplishment. They'd had AP classes together. In math, she dominated him. Probably still did. On more than one occasion, he'd felt stupid as they worked through a problem that she breezed through and he struggled with.

Tonight had been so much better than he imagined. He'd wanted to take her out to dinner, so she would know that it was a date. But it still felt like one at her house, without the pressure to give up their table. And with her comfortable patio, they were able to relax and talk far longer. Once again, her idea had been great. And had she actually been nervous around him? At the beginning of the evening, it seemed like she might have been. Why? Was she uncertain about dating him?

Well they were going to have ten days together to figure it out. One way or another. He scanned his email. There was the paperwork from Allie. And the checklist from Melissa. He chuckled. He moved through the paperwork, clicking in the appropriate spots for his signature. When that was complete, he emailed her a copy of his pre-approval letter.

Should he text her to let her know it was on its way? And tell her again how much he enjoyed tonight? But then he looked at the time. No, too late. She was an early-to-bed girl. As far as he knew, she'd never pulled an all-nighter, saying sleep was better than cramming. She was probably right. He'd text her in the morning.

He opened Melissa's camping checklist and laughed out loud. Allie was right. Melissa was incredibly detailed. She didn't want to assume that you'd remember everything, including deodorant, soap, shampoo, toothbrush/paste, etc. He printed it out then closed his laptop. He'd add to the list.

His eyes flicked to his guitar again. He had memories of playing it around the campfire when he'd gone camping with the guys. He'd even played for Allie during high school when he was still in the ensemble.

But that was a long time ago. He couldn't imagine playing in front of people without a lot more practice. And he didn't see that happening in the next three days. No, forget it.

He tossed the printed camping checklist on his dresser and got ready for bed, knowing that sleep wouldn't come quickly.

One thing he did know. When it came to the future with Allie, he was in. He was all in. He just had to convince her of that.

WILLARD CLICKED THROUGH THE WEBSITE ON THE LAPTOP in his apartment. His patience had paid off. He'd followed the man's truck yesterday morning from the neighborhood back to what must be their townhome, since both of them went inside. Given the amount of traffic, it was easy to blend in and not be spotted. But that cut both ways. He was surprised he'd pulled it off, having nearly lost the truck twice. He didn't know if the man was Allie's husband or boyfriend, but he seemed glued to her side, and his body language screamed that he was protective of her.

Good. The revenge would be on both of them then when he got ahold of Miss Allie. He knew where they lived. And today he'd narrowed down where she worked. Good thing Realtors had their faces plastered everywhere, just asking to be contacted. There were only three Allisons in Laguna Vista licensed as Realtors. He had the addresses of their offices.

As disappointing as Amanda had been, this new chase would be very sweet. He opened his cupboard where Amanda's hair was safely stashed.

Revenge was definitely a dish best served cold. He couldn't wait.

Chapter Six
____

First thing Allie did at the office the next morning was to text the listing agent that they were putting in an offer. Then she opened her laptop and got to work. She saw the emails from Collins. He must have worked on this last night after he got home, based on the time stamp. She sent the packet of paperwork over to the listing agent.

Rachel still hadn't arrived. Allie pushed down irritation and went to get coffee in their small station set up in the conference room. As she popped a pod in the Keurig, she considered Melissa's words. Yes, she needed to do something about Rachel. The question was, what? With leaving on the trip, she had the option of letting Rachel man things here, and possibly mess them up or firing her and having no one here. Frankly, she wasn't sure which was worse. No, she'd have intermittent Wi-Fi and cell phone access; she couldn't leave the office unmanned.

She dosed her coffee with Almond Joy creamer and leaned against the credenza that served as their coffee station, looking through the glass partition into the reception area. They didn't have any on-going projects right now. A few small, repeat clients on the books, but she needed a big anchor client, and soon, or retaining Rachel would be a moot point. She'd have to close the office and work from home. She had feelers out at several companies that could come to fruition any day. She just hoped that happened sooner rather than later.

She headed back to her office and sat behind her desk, putting her coffee a safe distance from her laptop. Her phone showed a text from the listing agent. The buyers had countered their offer. It wasn't an unreasonable counter, so it looked like this deal was going to go through. She texted Collins.

Just heard back from the listing agent. The buyers countered your offer but it's not a big deal. Have time to talk about it on the phone?

Two seconds later, her phone buzzed. Collins's face popped up below his name, a photo she'd taken of him at the wedding. Her heart almost stopped each time she saw it. "Hey, that was fast."

"You summoned; I responded." His deep chuckle turned her bones liquid. "So, what do you think about their counter?"

They chatted through a few of the details. "Ultimately, it's up to you, but I think they just want the pretense of dealing."

"I think you're right. I love the house. Let's go for it. I accept their counter."

"Great. I'll text the agent, amend the contract, and send it to you to e-sign. But I suspect we'll know tonight whether or not you have a house."

"Thanks, Allie. You're the best."

She smiled. "How's your first day back going?"

"Kyle's trying to drown me with paperwork. But I'll survive." Kyle's faint reply in the background came through the phone, but his words were unintelligible. Maybe that was for the best. "We should go out to dinner tonight to celebrate. And you're not cooking this time."

She'd spent the past four days in his presence. And then they were going to spend ten days together soon. Perhaps she should decline. But he wanted to celebrate, and she wanted to celebrate with him. Spending yet another night home with Rajah didn't sound terribly appealing. "Sounds great. I'd love to. I'll text you when I hear back from the listing agent."

They ended the call, and Allie finished up the paperwork and her coffee. When she had sent everything off, she still hadn't heard Rachel come in. Should she be concerned or annoyed? She thought about Amanda. Could something have happened to Rachel? She often pushed the boundaries of her starting time, but this was late even for her. Allie grabbed her coffee mug and headed out to the reception area. Nope, no Rachel. She shot her a quick text.

Everything okay? Did you tell me you were coming in late and I forgot?

She stared at her phone a minute, but there was no answering reply. She washed out her mug, thinking of what to do next.

She moved to the reception desk and plopped in Rachel's desk chair. Maybe there was a clue here about why she was late. Allie really hoped nothing bad had happened to Rachel. She thought of news stories where someone hadn't reported for work and then after several days was found dead in their apartment after meeting up with someone they met online.

But Rachel still lived with her parents. Surely they would miss her. Should she call them? Their information had to be in Rachel's file, but it seemed a bit extreme.

A magazine lay open to an article on summer trends. A floral-and-vanilla scent floated by as she turned the page. A perfume sample. Other than the magazine, an empty Starbucks cup, a pad with random doodles, and some gum wrappers dotted the desk. Not much in the way of clues.

The door swung open. Rachel. Unconcerned about her lateness, by her nonchalant saunter into the office.

Relief quickly gave way to anger. Allie stood and proffered the chair to Rachel with a flourish that would do a maître d' proud. Maybe it would lighten the mood and get Rachel to be more cooperative.

Rachel plunked in the chair and propelled it across the tile, tossing her bag out of sight.

Allie leaned against the other L of the desk, bracing her hands behind her so she wouldn't cross her arms. She didn't want to come off as the Inquisition, just…inquiring.

"Did you get my text?"

Rachel pulled her phone out and set it down. "Oh, yeah." She looked up at Allie and smiled. "As you can see, I'm fine. There was this great sale at Nordstrom Rack that I had to hit before coming in. Guess I forgot to tell you."

Allie drew her mouth in a tight line. "I'm happy to give you time off. Just let me know in advance next time, please."

"Sure." But Rachel didn't look at her, just booted up her computer while scrolling through her phone.

Allie's phone buzzed. Another text had come in from the listing agent. She headed back to her office, footsteps tapping down the tile, out of ideas for dealing with Rachel. Plus, she needed to switch gears and focus on work. It looked like everything was a go for Collins's house. Allie scanned over the documents. It was nearly time for lunch. She needed to get out of here.

Gathering her purse and phone, she told Rachel she was leaving and headed for a small salad-and-sandwich shop nearby. It was early, so she shouldn't have much of a wait. And she didn't. She took her salad and sat on the patio, letting the sun melt the tension out of her shoulders.

What was she going to do about Rachel? If Allie wasn't in the office, would Rachel even come in? Perhaps she should just send the office phones to her cell phone, add a voicemail explaining her delay in returning calls. She should be able to get service at least once a day somewhere. She didn't have any big projects coming up or clients that needed handling. Rachel would probably be grateful for the time off.

That problem solved, for now. But she did need to talk to Leroy about his niece. Maybe he could tell Allie what she was missing. She picked up her phone, found his number in her contacts, and tapped his name.

He answered on the second ring. "Allie, how great to hear from you. How is business?"

They exchanged pleasantries and caught up for a few moments. Leroy was semi-retired, but he maintained a wide network of contacts.

"Actually, I need your advice about something. It's Rachel." She gave him a quick rundown of the facts about Rachel's job performance and what Allie had done to correct her. "I'm at my wit's end as to what to try next. Do you have any suggestions?"

Leroy chuckled. "Personnel management is one of the trickier things about running a business. You've counseled her; you've given her training. What haven't you done?"

"I can't think of anything. That's why I'm calling you. I was honored that you chose me to be her mentor. I learned so much from you, I wanted to repay that to your niece."

He was quiet for a moment. "Rachel has been given everything she could ever need or want. I don't know that my brother and his wife have done her any favors. When I assigned Rachel to you, it was because I thought you could give her what she needed. I trust you, Allie. You'll know the right thing to do when it's time."

That was a less-than-satisfactory answer, but Leroy had always been the kind of mentor that made you work through your own problems, with his nudges in the right direction. Right now, she wasn't sure if he was disappointed in her or felt she had done all the right things. But it didn't look like she was going to get any further direction. She promised to keep in touch and ended the call.

She took a few more bites of salad as she pondered Leroy's words. *Lord, I could use some advice here.* What was Leroy trying to tell her?

She shook her head. Time to move on to something where she could make progress. She texted with the listing agent and made closing arrangements. Next item of business, the inspection.

No. Allie dropped her fork into her salad. She'd had Collins's house and the road trip in two different segments in her mind. But now they would overlap, in an unfortunate way. They only had a small window of time to get the home inspection done, and most of that window was taken up by the road trip. Collins didn't need to be there for the inspection; he could just get the report. But traditionally the buyer's agent was there. She'd have to do some work on this, make some calls to her favorite inspectors to see if they could inspect the house and write the report up in the time frame she needed. She'd work on that this afternoon when she got back to the office.

She texted Collins that the offer had been accepted. He texted back quickly.

So now it's official we have something to celebrate. :) Pick you up at 6?

See you then. :)

Smiling, she finished the remains of her salad. She had plans to execute on several fronts. And a date tonight. Which was a rare enough occasion.

She downed the last of her iced tea when Melissa texted her.

Grocery shop for the trip tonight? Sorry I forgot to ask earlier.

Ugh. Melissa wasn't going to like her answer. She should have thought things through a bit more. This road trip had taken a back seat to finding Collins a house and all the details that went along with that.

I can't. Collins and I are celebrating his buying a house.

That was fast.

Yep, and it's perfect for him.

The house too :)

Allie sent back an emoji with its tongue sticking out.

Can you go Thursday instead? I can go then.

Need to prep the food Thurs. Too much for one night.

Yeah, that was true. She felt bad.

I'll help with the prep for sure.

No worries. Have fun tonight. You can tell me all about it as we cook.

She smiled. Yes, Melissa would drag out all the details about Collins. Better get it out of the way before the trip.

An email notification slid across her screen, this one from her good friend Glenn Hunter. He ran Hunter and Beyond, LLC, a marketing firm that served the same clientele she did. He was a good source of connections, not to mention he was her go-to marketing colleague.

And this time, he'd hit the jackpot. DataCorp had decided to open a branch in Orange County, and they were looking for resources for locations, staff, the works. She'd heard rumblings about this for the past year and had her feelers out. She didn't have any connections with DataCorp other than through Glenn. And apparently, he'd just given her name to their chief operations officer, Edward Jacobsen, and passed on the tidbit that they were requesting proposals—RFPs—due next Monday.

This would be the anchor client that she needed to stay afloat. If she could swing it. She read Glenn's email again. "I know it's less than a week away, but you can pull it off," it had said.

No. No, she didn't have less than a week. She had less than two days.

She picked up her phone to text Collins that their date was off.

WILLARD SWUNG OPEN THE DOOR TO THE LAST OFFICE ON his list. The first two hadn't panned out, something that was immediately obvious as soon as he saw the agents' pictures. That meant this had to be the jackpot.

The door opened to a waiting area and a receptionist's desk.

The girl at the desk belatedly looked away from her phone, eyebrows raised. "Yes?"

"I'm looking for Allison Ellis. Is she in by any chance?" He gave his charming smile to the girl, who smiled back.

"Nope. She's out at lunch. But she should be back soon. Want me to have her call you?"

"Actually." He leaned casually against the desk. "I was really hoping to meet with her. I've heard great things about her, and she seems just like the person to handle my house purchase."

"You know she's not a regular Realtor, right? She only works with corporations. Well, sometimes she works with friends." She tapped something out on her phone.

"Oh, yes, I knew that. It's for my company. I'm the owner. Do you have her calendar? Can you make me an appointment?" He smiled again and extended his hand. "I'm Richard. What's your name?"

"Rachel." She shook his hand then slid her gaze to the computer.

"I'm sure she must rely on you to keep things running."

Rachel nodded. "You don't even know." She looked back at him. "She's going out of town Friday, and she's going to be gone for like ten days."

"Oh, wow. That sounds like some trip. Where's she going?"

"She's doing some family reunion thing. They're going to the Grand Canyon and then that place where they shoot all those cowboy movies."

He thought for a moment. "Monument Valley?"

"Yeah. That place. Then a couple of places that sound like they're out of the Bible. It's a big trip. Sounds boring to me."

Moab and Zion maybe? "That is a big trip. I've always wanted to tour the Southwest. I hope she has a fun time. She's leaving Friday, you said?"

"Yeah."

"I'll try to catch up with her when she gets back. Thanks, Rachel. You did a great job." He gave her a grin with a little salute and headed out the door. Now what to do with this new information?

COLLINS READ ALLIE'S TEXT TWICE. A WEIRD MIX OF disappointment and elation churned through his gut. He was happy about the house, sad Allie couldn't help him celebrate. Happy that she had a potential new client, sad that she had to work to get everything done before the trip. That was life, he supposed.

Anything I can do to help?

Pray. I'm not sure I can get it all done in time.

You got it.

But he was also going to be practical. She'd need to eat. And if they couldn't go out, he could bring food to her.

He and Kyle had gotten further on the stack than they'd hoped. After working together for so long, they had a rhythm he'd missed when he'd been in Holcomb Springs. He stretched. They were done for the day. He just needed to know if Allie wanted dinner delivered to her home or office.

He sent her a quick text and discovered that she was headed home to spend the evening on the couch with Rajah and her laptop.

Don't stop for dinner. I'll bring something over for you. I won't stay long. Chicken wraps sound good?

You're so sweet. Totally not necessary, but I appreciate it. If you could spare a few minutes to eat with me, I could use the company.

You got it. See you in a few.

He placed the order on the app on his phone. Within an hour, he'd picked up the food and was at Allie's door. She answered the door barefoot and with her hair piled up on top of her head, wearing a soft pink T-shirt and yoga pants. It'd been a long time since he'd seen her dressed so casually. She'd let her guard down, and it twisted something in his chest.

"Thanks for bringing dinner by. That's so sweet." She padded across the floor to the small dinette table in the kitchen.

He followed her, setting the bags of food on the table. "I'm sorry we can't celebrate the house together tonight, but we will find time." He touched her arm. Her soft skin and the worried look in her eyes made him want to pull her into his arms until everything was better. But that wouldn't solve her problem tonight.

She nodded, but her thoughts were clearly elsewhere.

They sat at the table, and he said a blessing on the food, asking for strength and clarity for Allie, and thanking God for the smooth house process. When he said, "Amen" and looked up, some of the tension had eased from her eyes.

"So tell me how I can help." He picked up his wrap and began eating.

She explained about DataCorp, what they were looking for, and what it would mean to her to get the account. "Or, maybe I should just stay home. But that would break Melissa's heart. And after everything she went through last year with losing the company she'd spent her life building and finding out her mentor and father figure was a fraud, I want her to have something good, even if Daniel and Brittany don't come."

He didn't want to go on a road trip with people he didn't really know without her. But he'd already committed to it. All he could see were ten long days without her. He reached for her hand. "I feel a bit biased saying this, because I don't want to go without you. But you guys have planned this a long time. I'm sure we'll have some connectivity every day from somewhere. Do you think you'll be able to get everything done in time? You could even work from the road if you needed to."

"I think so. I'd really hate to disappoint Melissa by not going. I already had to bail on shopping for the food with her tonight because I thought we would be celebrating. I told her I'd make it up to her by helping prep the food Thursday, but I don't think I'll be able to do that either."

"I'll help her. Don't worry about that. Then I can get the scoop on you from her." He grinned.

She laughed. "Wait, maybe I should rethink this. No, that's very sweet of you." Her voice softened. "You've really done a lot to help us make this road trip happen. I appreciate it." She squeezed his hand before pulling back.

"It's going to be a great trip. We just have a few hurdles to get over first." He gathered up their trash and tossed it.

She moved to the couch and opened her laptop. "Okay, here's what has to happen. Maybe talking it out with you will help me."

He sat next to her, closer than he had last night, and put his arm across the back of the couch, studying what she'd pulled up on the computer. Rajah jumped into his lap, and he petted her soft fur. She settled in and started purring.

"She must like you."

"She likes the attention." He kinda knew how the cat felt. He surely liked Allie's attention on him.

Allie ran through what DataCorp was looking for and what she was planning to offer them. She covered some of the financial details for one of the properties. Some sort of lease/purchase land deal she seemed to grasp with her calculator-like mind.

He was a bottom-line guy when it came to numbers. He learned over the years that his strengths lay with people, not numbers, and he was good with that. Still there was a tinge of—something—about her ability to deal with numbers better than he could.

His stomach churned. She'd asked for his help, and other than bringing her food, he wasn't sure he could help her at all. He was just beginning to understand the complexities of the services she offered to companies relocating or opening new branches.

Worst of all, he had no idea if she should go on this trip or not. He wanted her to, but he didn't want her to lose a big client either. He felt helpless, and that wasn't a feeling he did well.

"I had no idea that what you did was so involved. That's really amazing. How long did it take you to pull a proposal together the last time you did something like this?"

"I'd prefer to have a week. I have done it in three long days before. So I hope I can pull it off. But, Collins"—she turned those blue-green eyes on his—"I really need this client. I don't have a big anchor client right now, just a lot of smaller ones. This could provide cash flow for several years."

He picked up her hand and wove his fingers through hers. He'd love to sit here all night and watch her work, but somehow he thought that wouldn't be productive for her. "You are a smart woman. You know what you're doing." He kissed her fingers. "I'm going to go so you can concentrate on work. But you can always text me if you need moral support. And I'll be praying."

She squeezed his hand. "Thank you. That means more to me than you know. I really appreciate you helping out with Melissa."

He stood. "You hate to let anyone down."

"True." She rose, too, and wrapped her arms around his waist, her head against his chest. "Thank you for everything."

The feel of her body pressed against his was so good, so right he didn't want to let go. But he had to. He pulled back. "I'll talk to you in the morning if I don't hear from you tonight." He kissed her forehead and let himself out, hearing the lock snick home behind him.

He drove home in silence, thinking about the side of Allie he'd just seen. The side that reminded him of why he'd never asked her out in high school, why they'd never been more than friends reared its head again. She was so much smarter than he was. She'd never intended to do it, but his teenaged ego had been bruised more than a few times by her careless words.

But wasn't he past that now? Wasn't he the kind of man who could be proud of how smart his girlfriend was? Yes, he was totally proud of her and impressed by her. But would she feel let down being with a detective instead of some high-powered mover and shaker in the corporate world? Yesterday that thought wouldn't have occurred to him, but today after seeing her in action… He just didn't know.

Maybe helping Melissa tomorrow would shed some light on things. He just hoped that he didn't end up with a wrecked heart at the end of this road trip.

Chapter Seven

Allie stood from her desk the next morning and stretched her back. She'd stayed up too late hunched over her laptop. By the end of the evening, she was second guessing her approach to the DataCorp RFP. She'd called it a night and headed for bed. But her dreams were about firing Rachel and being chased across the desert by a spreadsheet. It wasn't restful sleep.

She texted Glenn Hunter and asked if he had time for lunch. He was her best contact on DataCorp and what they might be looking for. He agreed, and she gathered her things.

"Rachel, I'm headed out for lunch," she said as she passed the reception desk.

Rachel's barely perceptible nod was the only indication that she'd heard what Allie said.

Allie repressed a sigh as she pushed out the doors. She hated being cooped up inside, especially when it was such a perfect day.

When she arrived at Cafe Rio, Glenn had already grabbed a table on the patio, the sun glinting off his shaved Black head. Often he wore a Cal ball cap, his alma mater, but today he was dressed in a deep-purple button-down.

"Mr. Hunter, I see you're still associating with me." She laughed as she gave him a hug.

He kissed her cheek. "I'm just flattered that I got time on your schedule."

"I know you didn't get dressed up for our lunch."

"As much as I'd like to say yes, I do have a client meeting this afternoon." They got in line and placed their orders, bantering back and forth a bit. Their conversation was easy, and she always felt better after talking with him. And she often came away with another good idea to implement.

When they sat with their food, she began. "As much as I love talking to you, I do have a real reason for lunch."

"I'm all ears."

"I'm working on the DataCorp RFP." She launched into her plan but asked for his opinion on it.

He'd confirmed her thoughts and had given her a few ideas as well. It was good to know that her instincts about this project were right, even if her ideas were a bit unusual. She was on the right track. Lunch sat easier on her stomach.

Feeling like she might actually get the proposal done, feel good about it, and enjoy the road trip, they finished lunch with a promise to reconnect when she got back.

When Allie walked in, Rachel was scrolling through her phone and barely glanced up.

"Since I'm going out of town starting Friday, I've decided to close the office. I'll forward the phones to my cell. You can have Friday and the following week off, but I may need you to come in and do a few things for me. How does that sound?"

Rachel smiled. "Sounds great. Thanks!"

"Just please answer any calls or texts from me as soon as possible. I won't have a lot of Wi-Fi or cell service, so when I call, I need you to respond right away. I have a big proposal going out, and I may need your help with it while I'm gone."

"Sure. No problem." She nodded and went back to her phone.

"Rachel." Allie waited until she had the girl's attention. She only had enough nerve to get through this once. "This is important. I need to rely on you. If I can't, we'll have to make other arrangements."

"What does that mean?" Rachel frowned.

"It means you'll have to find another job."

Rachel stared at her a moment, then smiled. "Sure. But I can always talk to Uncle Leroy."

"I already have."

That seemed to take the wind out of Rachel's sails.

Allie gave her a tight smile then headed back to her office. She hoped the threat as well as the time off would ensure Rachel's help while Allie was gone.

She slid into her chair. An email from one of her contract clients caught her eye and she opened it. They were due to renew next month.

No. She reread the email. They weren't renewing. Allie had done such a fantastic job getting them established with everything they needed, they were ahead of schedule and wouldn't need her services.

She didn't have to go to her budget to see what would happen without this account. DataCorp was the only thing on the horizon that could keep her afloat.

She shoved down the panic. The best thing she could do right now was work on the RFP.

But her thoughts drifted to last night and how sweet Collins had been. If she'd told him how desperately she needed this account, would he still have advised her to go on the trip? Even Melissa didn't know how tight things had become. Allie didn't want to worry her; she had enough going on with getting her own company started and being away from Scott.

Collins had been sweet in high school, too, but he'd grown into his muscles, and his caring had a serious side to it now. Spending time with him was one more vote for the road trip.

But her company hung in the balance. This contract with

DataCorp could be the saving grace. She reined in the panic that threatened to rise. God was in control. If DataCorp was the way he was going to provide for her, great. If not, there'd be another way. He'd always taken care of her, no matter how close things had come.

She needed to remember that. Letting her fear go and putting the whole DataCorp thing in God's hands, she made a final decision. She was going to finish the RFP. She knew she could do it, and Glenn had given her some good ideas. Pacing the office waiting to hear back from DataCorp while her friends and siblings were on a road trip without her looked like a prescription for misery.

She was going. And she prayed it wouldn't cost her her company.

Olivia's hand whipped up, a can of pepper spray in her grip. Her lovely dark curls swung around her face.

Willard backpedaled. She'd outplayed him. He almost laughed. He hadn't seen that coming. "Hang on. Just calm down. No need to get upset." He gave her his charming smile, the one that women loved. "I misread your signs. No crime in that." His gazed flicked up and down her. "With that outfit, is it any wonder a man would think you were putting out signals?"

Her eyes narrowed. "Get away from me. I don't ever want to see you again. I don't know how you knew where I was, but I'm calling the police and filing a restraining order against you."

Keeping his smile frozen in place, he raised his hands placatingly, pushing down the boiling rage inside. "Your wish is my command. I can't help it if we ran into each other coincidentally. But I won't bother you anymore." He took a few steps back from her.

Her guard weakened, and her hand lowered slightly, but her other hand was in her purse, likely searching for her cell phone.

This wasn't a good place to make a move. He gave her a mock salute, pivoted on his heel, and headed for his car. Once inside, he safely let the rage out, pounding the steering wheel in frustration. Today, he thought he had the perfect opening. He called her a filthy name before starting his car. If she was calling the police, he needed to get out of here, lay low for a while. It wouldn't be too long before they figured out who he was.

If Robert found out, he'd disown Willard. He was on the last straw with his family.

He wasn't going back to prison.

He wasn't going back to the shrink.

He wasn't going back on those mind-numbing meds.

A plan began to form in his mind.

He headed for his storage unit, parked the Porsche inside, and snapped the lock shut. It was a sweet ride, and the chicks dug it, but it attracted too much attention, something he didn't want right now. He needed something more low profile for what he had in mind.

He pulled out his cell phone and called Robert. "Hey, can I borrow your truck for a while? Thought I'd go camping, get away from it all before everything gets too crowded during spring break."

"Sure. It's just sitting here. You might need to check the oil before you go."

"Happy to. Can you swing by my storage unit and pick me up?"

"See you in a few."

His brother—half brother, different fathers—would do anything to keep him on the straight and narrow. And Willard had to keep him thinking that he was. He chuckled to himself as he walked down the aisle between the units and stopped in front of another one, unlocking it, and stepping inside. He pulled out a tent, a sleeping bag, and other camping gear.

While he was waiting for his brother, he pulled up the tracking app. Olivia wasn't showing up. She'd figured it out. He smacked his hand against the side of the storage unit. This could get very bad. At least with Elaina, there was nothing linking him to her. With Amanda, he might have played it too close to the edge. Or maybe not. Cops weren't that smart. And the rush was fantastic.

His brother appeared around the corner in the older model truck. Willard waved and stowed his stuff in the shell in the back. Joshua Tree National Park seemed like a great place to head to right now. Not too hot and just far enough away.

He climbed in the passenger seat. "Thanks for doing this."

"Not a problem. Where you headed to?"

"Not sure yet. Thought I'd just go where the road takes me." He flashed his brother a smile as they pulled out of the storage unit lot and onto the street.

If it weren't for *Allie*, he could still be driving his Porsche and he wouldn't have to go camping, something he hated. Maybe she'd even gotten to Olivia. Yep, the road would give him a lot of time to fantasize about how to make Allie pay for ruining his life.

COLLINS RANG THE BELL TO MELISSA'S TOWNHOME, HAPPY to be away from work. He and Kyle had taken a report from a woman who had a man stalking her and wanted to get a restraining order. Kyle would look into it while Collins was on the road trip. Kyle and Patino were still working the Realtor assault case, as well as a previous case about another Realtor who had been assaulted during an open house, looking for connections. He was glad Allie wasn't that kind of Realtor. Those cases were always hard. He didn't have sisters, but he thought of the women in his life. He hated that they could be in danger because some wacko decided to take an interest in them. And frankly, a restraining order was only good after the fact.

Melissa opened the door. "Come on in. Kim's already here,

and we're just getting started. Did you eat dinner? I ordered a pizza."

He followed her inside to the kitchen. "Sounds great. I'm starving. I was afraid I might eat the camping provisions."

"Thus the pizza."

"Hey, Collins." Kim was already at work in the kitchen at the cutting board.

"Your brother said to tell you hi and that you should stay out of trouble. I told him you were going to be with me and Melissa, and he said, 'I repeat the warning.' What trouble does he think we're going to get into?"

"He's just my over-protective big brother. I ignore him." Kim brandished the chef's knife she was using to cut vegetables.

Collins raised his eyebrows. "I hope you know what you're doing with that thing." He stayed out of arm's reach.

"Well, I did have a bit of trouble not too long ago." Melissa popped a baby carrot into her mouth.

That was an understatement, considering she had been the vice president of a defense contractor and had nearly lost her life after stumbling across evidence that implicated her boss, his son, and brought down the whole company. "I don't think there will be any corporate espionage over our camping menu." Collins snuck a carrot too.

Kim swatted at him with her non-knife hand.

"Let's hope not." Melissa picked up a piece of paper. "Okay, before the pizza gets here, here's the plan. I have the menu for each night and what needs to be prepped in advance for each meal."

Collins grinned. Melissa always had a plan. In some ways, it was great because he didn't have to worry about planning any event she was involved with. She'd cover all the bases. And then some. He just hoped she wouldn't be a drill sergeant on the trip and loosened up a bit.

Just as Melissa had finished running down what they needed

to do tonight, the doorbell rang. She glanced at her phone app to check the doorbell camera. "Pizza's here."

After what he'd seen today, he was glad she was cautious. But it was nice for once to put work aside and hang out with other people, working on a project together. It reminded him a bit of music ensemble in high school. He hadn't thought about that in a long time.

They ate and chatted a bit about the trip. Melissa and Collins talked about what they were looking forward to.

Kim made a face. "Okay, you both know I've never gone camping, right? I'm open to the experience and hoping to get some ideas for a new clothing line inspired by the Southwest. But I don't know about the rest of it."

Collins tossed his plate and washed his hands at the kitchen sink. "You never went camping with Kyle?"

Kim grimaced. "Ew, no. Not with those stinky boys in a tent." She hip checked Collins out of the way at the sink. She was the closest thing he had to a little sister. He enjoyed it, having been an only child. The sibling dynamic fascinated him.

Melissa laughed. "Well the stinky boys have the tent again this trip. The trailer should be pretty comfortable for us girls. You'll be in a bunk bed with sheets, not on the ground."

They began cutting, dicing, and packaging at Melissa's direction, finding a good assembly-line rhythm. "Kim, you'll love it." Collins sliced into a bell pepper. "There's nothing like being outside under the stars, talking around a campfire. It's one of the best ways to get away and relax. And we won't be competing with the summer crowd."

"Don't you ever worry about someone robbing or attacking you in your tent? It's not like those things have locks on them." Kim gestured with the wooden spoon she was using to stir the ground beef she was cooking.

"I've never had anything stolen all the years I've gone camping. Campers are a friendly, neighborly bunch, and you're probably safer there than a resort or hotel that caters to tourists and the opportunists they attract. Plus, there are park rangers that patrol. And you'll have me and Scott to keep you safe." He grinned. "Kim, we won't let anything happen to you. I promise."

Melissa zipped up the plastic bag she was storing the food in. "Don't forget Matthew, though he'd probably try to distract any burglars with a joke. When we went camping as kids, it was because it was the cheapest vacation. We borrowed most everything and never had anything worth stealing."

Kim didn't look convinced. "What about that dad and his daughters that went camping? He was killed, and they went missing."

"A rare occurrence, if you look at crime statistics."

Kim rolled her eyes. "Now you sound like my brother."

"I am your brother in absentia." He popped her on the shoulder. "But seriously, you're in more danger at Fashion Island or South Coast Plaza than camping." He needed to change the subject. He didn't want Kim to worry, and he wanted to find out more about Allie, what made her tick. "It's too bad Allie couldn't join us tonight. Did she tell you about the big proposal she's working on?"

Melissa nodded. "Yeah, I talked to her about it again today, telling her what I would be looking at from the operations standpoint. She's got solid and fresh ideas. Her proposal will stand out."

"It's not a world I know much about. I just hope she's able to relax and enjoy this trip. Sounds like you guys have planned it for a long time." Collins looked up from his slicing to gauge Melissa's reaction.

"Me too." Melissa nodded. "The timing's not the best, but once she gets on the road, she'll be all in on the trip."

"That's what I'm hoping."

Melissa stacked the now-full plastic bags on top of each other and popped them in the freezer. "I can't believe you guys hadn't reconnected until last winter. In high school, it seemed like you two were inseparable."

He nodded and met Melissa's gaze, feeling comfortable enough with her to share his thoughts. "I sometimes wonder what life would be like now if I'd had the courage to rock the boat a bit."

Melissa held his gaze. "I believe God's timing is perfect, no matter how it appears to us." She patted him on the shoulder as she moved past. "You can take the risk now. It's hard for Allie to let her guard down, to let someone take care of her. She's always had to take care of everyone else. You know what our life was like growing up."

He hadn't quite realized the extent of it at the time, only knowing as a kid that Allie had a lot of responsibility for taking care of the house and her siblings, things he never had to do. But looking back now, he realized how hard it must have been on all of them to have an absent parent and one who was there physically but not for much else.

"I imagine security is important to her. Which is why the DataCorp account means so much."

Melissa nodded. "It is. But so are relationships. She's incredibly loyal to anyone who is her friend."

He wanted to ask her if Allie would be more interested in a corporate type than a detective. He wasn't a street cop working a beat anymore, but his job still could be dangerous and unpredictable. That had been a big issue for Heather when she started dating Kyle. Would it be for Allie? A corporate type would have more stability and safety.

"Did she tell you about the house she picked out for me? I know it's not what she normally does, and she did it as a favor to you, Kim, and for me. But this house is just perfect. She's really good at it. I knew she was smart in high school, and she still is. It must run in the family."

Melissa had gone to a different high school—commuted to her old school when their mom had moved the family to the other side of the Inland Empire—but you didn't get to be where she was without being smart. In high school, everyone knew that you went to Allie for tutoring. His old insecurity raised its ugly head. Was he even ready to run with this crowd? They had high school in common, but even then, their differences in background and intelligence was obvious. He wanted to know what it would be like to be part of this group, but maybe he didn't really belong.

Melissa laughed. "Wait until you meet Matthew." She picked up her list. "Okay, we've only got three more meals to pack."

Collins wasn't going to get his questions answered tonight. He picked up his knife and started chopping the next round of vegetables Melissa pushed his way. But he had the whole road trip to figure it out. He'd know at the end if these people would be lifelong friends or people he wouldn't want to see again for a long time.

* * *

ALLIE READ THROUGH THE LIST OF SUPPORTING documents she wanted to include with the RFP. By thinking through everything they might request ahead of time, it would minimize the amount of contact they might need from her while she was on the road.

She clicked through folders on her computer. Where was the after-action report? It covered things they ended up changing from the original proposal, obstacles they ran into and overcame. Davis Marketing had come back and extended the original project, asking for additional services, things DataCorp would likely want as well and which Allie had included in her proposal for them. It would be the icing on the cake to include it. But she didn't have it.

Then she remembered. Yes, it was on the external hard drive. It hadn't gotten uploaded with the archived file because it had come in later, after the project was done. She ran her hand through her hair. She'd have to go back to the office. Not that she had the time. She still hadn't packed. But it was necessary.

She didn't want to ask Rachel to pull it for her while she was on the road. She hoped she didn't have to ask Rachel to do anything while she was on the road.

She hopped in her car and headed back to the office, thinking through what else she might want to grab off the hard drive while she was there. It was dark, and she was tired. She didn't love the idea of heading to her office at night alone. Maybe she should have let someone know. It was just going to be a quick trip. She did it all the time. But she couldn't get the image of Amanda Park out of her mind.

At the stoplight before her office, the light turned yellow, and she hit the brakes. A violent shove pushed her car forward. She snapped toward the steering wheel, her momentum arrested by the seatbelt strapped across her chest. Her gaze flicked to the rearview mirror. The car behind had crashed into her. Shaken, she put on her flashers. They needed to get out of the road. With a loud creak, her car moved forward, and she eased over to the side. Hands shaking, she reached into her wallet for her driver's license, pulled the insurance card out of the glovebox, and got out. Her rear bumper and hatch were crumpled inward. This was not what she needed the day before a big road trip.

The other driver was out of his car too. "Are you okay? I'm so sorry. I guess I thought you were going to go through the light."

"I'm fine. Just a little shaken. You're not hurt?" Allie rubbed her arms. It was cool out and the adrenaline was still coursing through her system. "No. My car is even drivable. So let's just exchange information and let the insurance companies sort it out."

"Agreed."

They took pictures of each other's insurance cards and driver's licenses and then left.

Allie continued to the office. Something seemed to be rubbing on the car, but she was close enough to the office to head there. One more thing on her overflowing to-do list. They were leaving in the morning. She'd have to file a notice with the

DMV about the accident and notify her insurance agent. She didn't have time for this.

She'd stepped out of her car before she remembered to be more wary of her surroundings. The accident had shaken her up, but she still needed to be on her guard. There were no other cars in the parking lot, so she hurried into her office, unlocked the door and locked it behind her. Making her way to her office, she plugged the external hard drive into her computer. While it spun up, she pulled down the SR-1 form from the DMV and filled it out. Then she sent an email to her agent with the other driver's info attached.

Okay, what did she need to get? Her neck and shoulders were starting to hurt a bit. She'd need to pop some ibuprofen when she got home. She had a headache. She flipped through the archive folder on the hard drive. There were a couple of companies she'd done similar projects for, so she grabbed those files as well as the Davis Marketing ones and looked around her office. Everything seemed okay.

She disconnected and closed her laptop. A moment later she locked the office behind her, checking her environment, then climbed in her car. It made it all the way home, though it didn't sound great by the time she pulled it into her garage. She'd deal with it when she got back.

Inside, she set her laptop on the table and plugged it in so it would be fully charged when they left in the morning. She took a couple of ibuprofen and brewed a cup of tea. She needed to review the RFP and get it sent off and pack before she could get that much-craved hot shower and bed.

Chapter Eight

Allie rushed around, hoping to pull everything together before Collins arrived. She was a little sore this morning. A few more ibuprofen with toast and coffee while she double checked the RFP and sent it took the edge off. She wished there had been time for Melissa and Glenn to review it before it had to go. But two days was barely enough time as it was. She prayed as she hit *send* on the proposal. *God, it's in your hands now. Help me to relax on this trip and accept whatever the outcome is as your will.*

Another cup of coffee or no? Collins would be here at nine, then they were picking up Kim, and Scott and Melissa. Then a long road trip. One more cup. She needed the caffeine, and she'd have a few opportunities for a bathroom break.

She went over her packing list, making sure she'd brought everything. Melissa's list was thorough, but Allie couldn't shake the feeling that she was forgetting something. Well, they'd be around some town every day. If she forgot something, either Melissa would have it or she could buy it. It wasn't like they were leaving civilization.

Hauling her bags to the door, she dropped them then picked up Rajah, who knew something was up. Allie's neighbor had an eight-year-old daughter, Lucy, who loved Rajah. They'd come over every day to feed her, check on her, and play with her. Still, Rajah wasn't thrilled with Allie's leaving. She never was. "You be good, kitty cat. No clawing the furniture." With a quick hug, she set her down.

One final scan and a quick check that all the doors and windows were locked. Thermostat switched off. Water hoses to the washer and dryer turned off. Rajah had food and water. There was nothing left to be done.

Her doorbell rang. Collins was here.

She opened the door. He was in a gray Henley, sleeves pushed up, worn jeans, and hiking boots. Her heart skipped. He was made for the outdoors.

He pulled her into a hug, one that felt solid and reassuring. "Did you get the proposal off?"

"I did. About an hour ago."

He studied her face. "It'll be fine. You've done the best you can, and they'll reach out if they need anything else."

She nodded. "I know. I just can't help but feel like I'm forgetting something."

"If you are, we can pick it up. Or I'm sure Melissa will have it." He grinned and glanced at the bags at their feet. "Is this everything?"

"Yep. Oh, we need to get the ice chest out of the garage."

"I'll start loading the truck." He grabbed her bags and headed down the walkway.

She went to the garage and opened it. The ice chest was on a shelf, and she tugged it down.

Collins met her from the outside. "What happened to your car?"

Oh. She'd forgotten about that. "Um, I was in a fender-bender last night. No big deal. I'll get it fixed when I get back. I emailed the insurance agent last night and filed the forms with the DMV. Everything's taken care of."

"Where were you?" Collins circled the car, examining it.

"Just a block from the office. I had to get something off the hard drive there. I stopped short for a yellow light and got rear ended. The guy was nice. We exchanged info and everything."

Collins frowned. "A man hit you? What'd he look like?"

What was he getting at? "I don't know. Average. Want to see his driver's license? It's on my phone." She tugged her phone out of her pocket, swiped to photos, and handed it to him.

He studied it for a moment. "Will you send this to me?" He handed her phone back.

"Sure. Why?"

"I don't believe in coincidences. You stop an attack in progress and then three days later you're rear ended. I want to check it out."

"The guy seemed nice and didn't try anything at all. We just exchanged info and left."

"And now he knows where you live." His gaze was steady on her.

Oh.

"I'll pass the info on to Kyle and see if he comes up with anything. Luckily you'll be gone for the next ten days, but we'll have extra patrols swing by. Tell your neighbors to report anything that seems odd, like the same car driving by or someone parked in front of your townhome."

She nodded.

Collins grabbed the ice chest and headed back to the truck. She closed the garage, a sick feeling in her stomach. This was not how she wanted the trip to start.

She grabbed Rajah and gave her one last hug. "I'd take you with us, but you'd hate it." She plopped her on the stairs and sent her neighbor a quick text with Collins's instructions. She locked the door behind her, tugging on it.

Collins came up the walk. "That it?"

"Yep, unless you wanted to say goodbye to Rajah." She grinned as she swung her backpack over her shoulder.

"I don't think she'll miss me."

"She might not even miss me. Lucy next door plays with her more than I do. I think she also sneaks her kitty treats." She climbed into the truck and looked around as he pulled out. "It's a good thing your truck is big enough for all of us and the stuff we have to haul until we get the trailer."

"The crew cab was a good call. I figured it would make road trips more comfortable. What's the point in having a truck if you can't haul all your friends and their gear too?"

"I like how you think."

He gave her another heart-stopping grin, a nice change from the scowl earlier.

She mentally reviewed her list. She'd contacted her transaction coordinator to begin the paperwork on Collins's house. She knew they would be out of town, so a delay wouldn't surprise her. Rachel was taking today and the next week off. The proposal was sent. Rajah was taken care of. It probably was just that she hadn't gotten enough sleep. She'd been pedal to the metal the last few days that now it seemed weird to sit back with nothing to do. That was probably it.

They pulled up in front of Kim's condo. She answered the door, still throwing things in a bag. "Sorry! I was up late last night and overslept. Here." She handed Allie her pillow. "I'm going to sleep in the car."

"Wish I'd thought of that." Though she didn't think she could actually sleep in front of Collins. What if she did something weird like snored or drooled?

At Melissa's, they had Scott's help. He'd flown in last night and stayed with Joe, who'd dropped him off on his way into work at the fire station. Which was good because there were three big ice chests to get loaded. Allie glanced at Melissa. "Bringing guys along on a trip is a great idea. For once, we don't have to do any heavy lifting."

Scott flexed from the bed of Collins's truck. "Happy to be your labor. We work for food." He hopped down and pulled Melissa in for a quick kiss.

The guys got everything loaded in the bed of the truck and strapped down. Melissa examined everything. "I think we're ready to hit the road. Any final bathroom breaks before we go?"

Collins laughed. "You sound like my mom."

She popped her hands on her hips, a mock scowl crossing her face. "Someone has to be."

Kim scrambled out, phone at the ready. "Wait, we've got to get a picture before we take off." She assembled them in a quick group in front of the truck and squatted down in front to include herself in the group selfie. "Great! Now we can go."

Collins rolled his eyes. "Is every stop going to be like this?"

"Yep." Kim scrambled back in, reclaiming her spot with her pillow. "I'm documenting our trip for my followers. I'll tag all of you."

Collins shared a glance with Allie and raised his eyebrows. She shrugged. "It'll make for good memories."

He stepped next to Kim. "You won't be able to tag me because I'm not on social media. Take all the pictures you want, but please don't post any on social media of me."

"Or me," Scott added.

Kim shook her head. "Not a problem. I never put any up with my brother either."

Allie grabbed the crew door. "Scott, your legs are longer than mine. Why don't you sit up front with Collins? All of us girls can sit in the back." She swung herself in and grabbed the middle seat, and Melissa followed her.

Soon they were on the freeway headed toward Phoenix, Arizona, where they'd meet Daniel and Matthew.

"Anyone create a playlist for the road trip?" Allie asked from the back seat. She glanced at Melissa.

"I assigned that to Scott."

"And I always complete my missions." He waved his phone. "I just need to pair it to Collins's sound system here and we'll be good to go." He chatted with Collins and fiddled with a few things before the strains of classic rock poured through the F-

150's speakers. The Eagles' "Hotel California" was first up. "The Great American Road Trip requires great American music."

Kim rolled her eyes.

Allie leaned back and let out a breath. For good or for ill, they were headed out.

Melissa eyed her. "How late did you stay up last night? Did you get the proposal out?"

"Yeah, first thing this morning. I was up until eleven and then back up at six. I felt so rushed packing that I can't help but feel like I've forgotten something."

"You'll be fine. If you did, I probably have it."

"True. I think I just wished there had been time for you and Glenn to review it before I sent it off. I was so sleep deprived I'm afraid I did something stupid like misspelled their name."

"You talked it over with both of us. You did a good job. Try to relax."

Allie nodded. "So Matthew's meeting us at Daniel's place, right?"

"Yeah, I confirmed it again with both of them last night. Plus I had some questions about how Daniel has outfitted the trailer. Or rather, not outfitted it. I felt like I had to haul along practically my whole kitchen. That's supposed to be the advantage of having a trailer. You can leave it stocked and just bring groceries."

Allie gave her a look. "Daniel always worked off a list you had given him. You should have given him a list this time."

"Wish I'd thought of that earlier. Oh well. He said that Mom is really serious about that guy Larry she's been dating."

Allie raised her eyebrows. "Really? Well she's been with him six months, which is a record for her."

Melissa nodded. "And you won't be surprised to know that Daniel's planning on proposing to Nikki."

"I'm not. He said they were serious last time I talked to him. Glad you spent some time on the phone with him."

"My new life is a little less hectic than my old one." Melissa's gaze strayed to Scott's profile. "Something I'm grateful for." She'd started her own boutique consulting firm after the collapse of the defense contractor she'd worked for.

"Me too. Guess that means the idea of a sibling road trip won't ever really happen then. Since Nikki hates to camp." Allie's shoulders slumped a little at the thought, a sadness swirled in her stomach. So many things had gone wrong with this trip. She hoped the rest would be smooth sailing, even if it wasn't what they'd originally envisioned.

"Not necessarily. Camping in a trailer isn't really camping. It's more like glamping. She just doesn't know what she's missing."

It was turning out to be another warm day. Collins flicked the AC on as they left Orange County and headed into the Inland Empire of the San Bernardino valley, through the Banning Pass, and headed toward Palm Springs. Wind machines sprouted on both sides of the freeway like some odd form of desert trees.

Collins pointed to a road sign for an upcoming turn off. "Ever camp at Joshua Tree National Park? Crazy hot in the summer, but it's great in the winter and not too far from us."

Scott nodded. "We've gone a few times. You can't believe the stars at night. You can see the Milky Way. I know some guys that come out here just to photograph the night sky."

"One of the best parts about camping. I'm looking forward to having my own trailer so we can make weekend trips. There are a ton of places to go within driving distance."

Mount San Jacinto loomed over them on the right as they crossed the desert. Scott glanced back at Melissa. "Remember our trip up the Palm Springs Tram to Mount San Jacinto last winter?" He snaked an arm back and squeezed her knee.

"That was a fun trip, something we should all do again." She smiled, sharing memories in that telepathic way that couples had.

Would she and Collins end up like that? Allie studied Collins's profile, and he met her gaze in the rearview mirror.

Conversation lulled as they crossed the Coachella Valley and started up the grade toward Chiriaco Summit. The road narrowed to two lanes each way, and Collins passed a number of semitrucks struggling up the hill. Between the warmth of the cab, the stress of the past week, and the late night, Allie found herself drifting off. She could use a dose of caffeine, but they were far from anything until they reached Blythe. The least-aptly named place ever.

Scott pointed out the window at the open desert. "We used to dry camp out here near Corn Springs. No facilities or anything, just open desert. One year, Kyle's dad got a bunch of ATVs for us to ride. There are sand dunes on the other side of the highway. For a bunch of boys, it was a weekend of dirty, messy fun. We had a blast."

Allie thought back to their camping trips as kids. They would go to the mountains near Holcomb Springs usually for a three-day weekend. It was one of the few times Mom was actually present with them. They'd play games, cook together, go on hikes, listen to ranger talks. For once they felt like a real family.

She knew this trip was a chance to recreate that feeling again, to pull together her adult siblings who had scattered in separate directions. Without Daniel and Brittany, it didn't look like that now. But it could still be good. She could get to know Collins better, and Melissa could spend some much-needed time with Scott and get a break from everything that had happened to her last winter.

Allie wanted everyone to have a good time and bring back good memories. Which meant not telling Melissa about the car accident. She'd have to swear Collins to secrecy as soon as she could get him alone. Melissa would worry and hover. And neither of them needed that. She pushed her unease away and closed her eyes.

Collins checked his fuel gauge as he took the off-ramp at Blythe. He'd fill the tank in town since there wasn't much between here and Phoenix except endless desert. He'd taken the truck in to have the oil changed and everything checked out before they left. He felt responsible for these folks, even though they were all perfectly capable adults in their own right. He glanced at Scott. Maybe even more than he was.

He pulled into the Mobile station. "Baja Fresh was on the itinerary, right, Melissa?"

"Right. It's across the street, so we can walk over there while you're getting gas if you want. It'll be good to stretch our legs." She opened the crew cab door and got out.

Scott joined her at the front of the truck and took her hand as they headed for the Mexican grill.

Kim scrambled out, snapped a few pictures, and followed them. Collins shook his head. Whatever made the trip enjoyable for her.

Allie moved to the back of the truck where he was pumping gas. Seeing her in casual clothes and a little flustered this morning was refreshing. He was less than thrilled about the car accident.

"Aren't you going to join them?"

"No, I thought I'd check my email and wait with you."

He grinned at her. "Thanks for keeping me company. How are you feeling after the accident? Any pain?"

"Just stiff and sore. I took some ibuprofen at breakfast. I'll take more if I need it. Just don't say anything to Melissa. I don't want her to worry." She pulled out her phone and scrolled through it.

"Any word from DataCorp?"

"No, but it's early yet. My insurance agent got back to me. He just said to let him know when I was back in town, and he'd send an adjuster out to look at my car."

Collins replaced the nozzle and screwed the gas cap back on. "That's one thing you don't have to worry about." He held up his hands. "I'll wash them first thing at Baja Fresh."

"Just don't mention it to Melissa. I don't want her to know."

"Your secret's safe with me." He didn't understand why, but it was her decision.

But as they headed across the street, the rest of the gang was walking back toward them.

"What's wrong?"

Melissa blew a strand of hair out of her eyes. "They had a water leak, so all their water is turned off. They aren't serving food."

Scott pointed down the main road. "There's McDonald's, Taco Bell, Subway. Del Taco, and a couple other places."

Melissa nodded. "Okay. Change of plans. Scott, you know the area best. Lead the way."

They piled back in, and Collins squirted on hand sanitizer before heading down the main strip. The group had decided on Albertacos. It was hard to go wrong with tacos.

They spilled back out, ordered, and ate their fill of tacos outside the small stand. Collins checked for a response from Kyle about the guy who'd hit Allie. Kyle said the guy was clean and there wasn't anything that would tie him to the Realtor assaults other than the general description of tall, thin, and average. Considering they didn't have many leads on the assault cases, he didn't find any of it reassuring. He was glad Allie would be with him for the next nine days. Maybe Kyle would catch this guy while they were gone.

They were getting ready to leave when Allie stood just as Melissa did and bumped Melissa's tray, knocking her drink off and into her lap.

"Ahh!" Melissa's narrowed gaze shot to Allie. "You always talk with your hands. Be more careful where you swing those things."

"Oh, I'm so sorry! Here." Allie thrust napkins at Melissa. "I'll get more." She ran and got a handful from the dispenser.

But Melissa's jeans were soaked across the thighs. It would make for an uncomfortable trip. In more ways than one.

"Oh, that's what I forgot. I usually throw a pair of yoga pants in my backpack to change into." Allie studied the back of the truck. "Can we get into any of your bags so you can change?"

Melissa followed Allie's gaze and let out a long sigh. "Not easily. We put all the food and supplies toward the back so we could load them in the trailer." She glanced at Allie. "I can't believe I didn't think to bring yoga pants in my backpack. I'm adding that to my packing list."

Scott hopped in the back of the truck, and Collins followed him. "Which one of these is yours, Melissa?"

She pointed.

Between Scott and him, they dug through bags and moved things around until her duffle was free.

She quickly pulled out a change of pants and headed toward the bathroom. But he didn't miss her glance at her Apple Watch. They were behind schedule. Did it matter? As long as he didn't have to hook up the trailer in the dark, they'd be fine. Was this spark of tension a sign of how the trip was going to be?

He and Scott organized the truck bed and got everything tied down again. He gave Allie a quick squeeze around the shoulders.

But the worried look on her face eased only slightly.

They climbed back into the truck and soon were crossing the Colorado River into Arizona. His eyes flicked to the rearview mirror as Kim snapped a photo of the Welcome to Arizona sign.

They'd gone about an hour with a bit of quiet conversation when the traffic slowed and then came to a stop. Both lanes. The right one was filled with big rigs. There was a truck stop about twenty miles up the road in Tonopah, but right now they were stuck in the middle of nowhere at a dead stop. The traffic alert on his navigation panel mentioned an accident up ahead a few miles.

"With nowhere to exit, any accident could back up the traffic for quite some time, especially if there are injuries and they need to life flight someone out." Collins shifted into park and turned off the truck. People around them were out of their cars, stretching their legs.

Kim held up her phone. "Yep. An accident with an overturned big rig and several cars."

"Gonna be awhile." He glanced back at Melissa.

She was texting on her phone, probably alerting Daniel that they would be late.

He glanced at the clock on the dash and rolled down the windows. It was eighty-seven degrees out with a slight breeze. The Arizona Department of Public Safety State Troopers patrolled this area. But it was only March. It would be hot out here in July. A simple car breakdown could become life threatening with the heat. The idea made him thirsty. "Anyone want a water? I thought I'd get a few from the ice chest in the back."

Everyone did. He climbed out and walked a few paces to the front, seeing if there was anything for him to see. Just cars stretching out in front of him. He grabbed the water bottles out of the ice chest dedicated to drinks and carried them back to the cab. Of course, they couldn't drink too much since even though the rest stop was only a few miles up the road, it might as well have been in Phoenix for the good it did them. Unless they wanted to walk. He didn't think they'd be that desperate.

He'd be glad to reach Phoenix and get the trailer loaded and hooked up.

They had four hours until sunset. That shouldn't be a problem.

WILLARD OPENED THE ICE CHEST HE HAD SITTING NEXT TO him on the picnic table and grabbed a beer. He popped it open while he contemplated his next move. The White Tank campground at Joshua Tree was the smallest and the most remote. Stars littered the sky last night, and he even spotted the Milky Way spilling overhead. But during the day, the landscape was filled with giant boulders and dirt. And it was warm. Not as warm as it'd be in a few months, but there was no sea breeze or even any humidity from the marine layer to dampen the unrelenting sun bouncing off the rocks and dirt.

A parade of cars, trailers, and RVs had driven by his campground today. If it wasn't full yet, it'd likely be so by the end of the day. A park ranger cruised by and nodded at him, looking at his campsite tag. It expired today. The ranger stopped. "You staying another night?"

"Just thinking that over right now."

"All right. You've got another half hour to decide and pay the fee."

"Yep." He gave a half wave, half salute. Nothing to see here. Just a guy getting away from it all.

The ranger waved back and moved on.

And getting away from it all wasn't an exaggeration. There was no cell service out here. Not even any water. Pit toilets. He wasn't made for this kind of life. Someplace with more amenities was more his style.

He'd found Allie's Instagram account last night when he went into town for dinner. Surely she'd chronicle her family reunion trip. Without cell service, he didn't know if she'd posted anything today. At some point, he'd have to get to town and find out. He knew her first stop was the Grand Canyon.

He'd always wanted to see the Grand Canyon. He finished off his beer and hopped in the truck. He opened the glove box. His treasures were still there, like he knew they'd be. Always good to have company on a trip. He fingered the bags before pulling out.

Chapter Nine

Allie wished Melissa could just relax and enjoy the trip. Not that the fun part had really started yet, but still. Melissa's shoulders tightened as they neared Daniel's house. Between the wreck on the highway and traffic coming into Phoenix, they were definitely behind schedule. But they hadn't missed anything.

Allie's phone dinged. A message from Lauren Chao. Wow. She hadn't heard from her in a long time. She lived in Scottsdale, and they had connected for lunch when Mom had first moved out here and Allie was visiting. She tried to get together with Lauren when she came out, but often Allie's trips were so short there wasn't time. How did Lauren know she was in town?

Oh, Instagram. Kim had tagged her, and Lauren must have seen it. She wasn't sure what to respond. Maybe they could meet Lauren for dinner.

"It's this house." She directed Collins to a white house with blue trim on the corner. He pulled to the curb.

The trailer was backed into the driveway. Daniel came out the front door, letting the metal screen door slam shut behind him. "Hey, you made it."

Melissa jumped out and gave him a hug. "We did." She glanced around. "Where's Matthew? I don't see his truck."

Daniel shrugged. "He went to play basketball with some friends when he heard you were delayed. I texted him a few minutes ago that you were almost here."

Allie followed Melissa out of the truck. She didn't know if anyone else could tell, but she knew Melissa well enough to see the steam coming out her ears. Matthew knew just how to push her buttons. And he enjoyed doing it under the guise of getting her to laugh or lighten up.

Melissa lifted one shoulder. "I guess we can leave him behind if he doesn't get here in time."

Allie glanced at Scott, who raised his eyebrows. Maybe he hadn't seen this side of her yet. Should make for an interesting trip.

Collins moved next to Allie. She felt his presence immediately. "Daniel, do you remember Collins from when we were in high school?" Daniel had been two years behind them.

"I do. It's been a long time." Daniel stuck out his hand.

The men shook. "You're taller than I remember." Collins laughed. "Thanks for letting us take your trailer. Want to show me what I need to know?" The two moved off with Scott joining them.

Melissa tossed her hair over her shoulder as she texted, probably Matthew. Allie could only imagine what she was telling him.

She suppressed a sigh of envy. Even after a six-turned-eight-and-a-half-hour road trip, Melissa's auburn curls looked like she'd stepped out of a magazine photo shoot. Allie felt limp and frumpy, her nothing-special brown hair thrown up in a messy bun to get it off her neck.

Kim joined them, doing something on her phone.

A minute later, Matthew pulled up in his truck, music blaring.

Melissa's eyes narrowed, and she stalked over to his truck. While her exact words didn't carry, her tone did.

Allie hung back. She'd let the dust settle a bit.

Matthew left his truck and strode across the lawn, unfazed by the chewing out Melissa had given him. "Hiya, Allie! I'm gonna hop in the shower, and then we can start this road trip." His gaze caught on Kim, and he stopped. "Hey, I'm Matthew. We haven't met."

"Kim Taylor." She stuck out her hand.

He took it and grinned. "It's gonna be a fun trip. I'll be right back." He half jogged inside.

Allie laughed. Oh, Matthew would indeed make this a fun trip.

Melissa came over and nodded to Kim. "So that's Matthew. Not quite the baby of the family. That honor belongs to Brittany. But close."

"Lauren Chao texted me. She saw Kim's Instagram post about our trip and wants us to meet her for dinner tonight if we can. What do you think?"

Melissa blew out a breath. "Why not? We're already off schedule. It doesn't really matter at this point." She glanced around. "I'm surprised Mom isn't here to see us off."

Allie shrugged but texted Lauren.

Sounds great. How about Macayo's in Glendale? It's on our way to Flagstaff.

It was across the Valley for Lauren. Maybe she wouldn't make it.

"Good thing we're staying at a motel in Flagstaff. I'd hate to have to try to set up the trailer and tent in the dark." Allie shoved her phone in her back pocket.

"We've done it before."

"I know. That's why I don't want to do it again."

The guys seemed done with their inspection. "Why don't we start loading up the trailer? That way everything will be secure in the motel parking lot overnight instead of being in the truck bed." Melissa headed toward the truck.

Allie and Kim followed her. But they had only lowered the tailgate when the guys came over.

"Melissa, why don't you hop in the trailer and organize stuff as we bring it to you?" Scott suggested.

Lauren replied back.

Ok. See you there.

"Hey, guess who we're meeting for dinner," Allie said to Collins.

He shrugged. "No idea. Your family?"

"Nope. Lauren Chao."

His eyes widened. "No kidding. She lives out here?"

"In Scottsdale. We've kept in touch. She saw Kim's post on Instagram where she tagged me and asked if we could meet up. She'll be shocked to see you here."

He hefted bags out of the truck. "Yeah, I don't know that I've seen her since college."

"That's right. You didn't come to our ten-year reunion."

"It was just before I moved to Orange County."

Collins had dated Lauren in high school and in college. In fact, Lauren had been his date to the senior prom when Chris Mendoza had asked Allie. Until the other night when Collins had mentioned wanting to take Allie, she'd assumed he'd always planned on taking Lauren. It was a long time ago, but her gaze moved to his face almost of its own accord, like a moth searching for the proverbial flame he might still be carrying for Lauren. She'd told Allie it had been an amicable parting. They'd been in the business track together at college when Collins switched to criminal justice. After that, they'd drifted apart.

So dinner should be interesting. With Lauren and Collins and Melissa and Matthew, the potential for fireworks seemed higher than Allie was comfortable with. This road trip was getting off to a potentially explosive start, to say the least.

She carried one of the last bags to the trailer and climbed in.

It was older, but in good shape. To the right of the door was the big bed separated from the main areas with a wall and a curtain. Against that wall was a couch that must flatten out to a bed. Along the back wall was the sink, stove, and fridge. The dining table was across from that. And in the back were two bunk beds and the bathroom.

"You, Kim, and I can flip for the beds." Melissa shoved bags around. "There's plenty of room here for us. I think it'll work out great."

"Good." A bit of tension slipped from Allie's shoulders. Melissa was back in her groove. She was fabulous at plans and executing them. She wasn't so great at being flexible when things changed. But she usually got there once she was past her initial disappointment. "A good dinner and a good night's sleep should get us ready for our adventure to the Grand Canyon tomorrow."

Melissa glanced around before leaning close to Allie. "Isn't Lauren the girl Collins took to the prom and dated?"

Allie nodded.

"Huh."

She started to say more, but Scott stuck his head in. "Everything set in here? I'm hungry. We need to get this trailer hitched up and on the road."

"Yep. Is Matthew ready to go?"

Matthew's face appeared in the door. He gave her a salute. "Yes, ma'am. Reporting as ordered."

Melissa shook her head. "Let's go eat." She hopped out of the trailer.

Collins locked it behind her. He and the guys managed to get the trailer hooked up to his truck in no time at all. They double checked the connections and were ready to go.

Melissa watched from the side. "Hey, Kim, why don't you ride with Matthew? Allie, you can sit in front and show Collins where to go. Scott and I can manage the back seat for the trip to the restaurant. It's not that far."

Allie studied Melissa's face. What was she up to now? "Okay."

Kim shrugged. "Sure. Don't want to feel like a fifth wheel among the couples."

Allie's face heated, but she didn't think Collins had heard. Soon they climbed into the trucks, waved goodbye to Daniel, and hit the road. Allie helped Collins watch the mirrors and make sure the trailer was pulling correctly, and after a few miles he relaxed. By the time they got to Macayo's Restaurant, he comfortably maneuvered them into an empty part of the parking lot and pulled through several spaces.

He double checked everything again when they got out and headed toward the restaurant.

Lauren was waiting out front.

"Hey, guys! Collins? Oh my gosh! I had no idea you were here!" She stepped over and wrapped Collins in a hug. "So good to see you again."

Allie felt her smile turn from genuine to brittle as their hug went on. Then she was being grabbed in a monster hug by Lauren. "We've got to get together more often. I don't know why we don't."

They hadn't been close friends growing up. Nothing bad between them, just different interests and most often they were thrown together because their moms had become friends when they had moved in high school.

Allie introduced Lauren to the rest of the group. They entered the restaurant, and the hostess showed them to their table.

As a pharmaceutical sales rep, Lauren was clearly doing quite well based on what Allie could see. Designer bag, shoes, and jeans that fit like they had been made for her. Simple but quality jewelry that clearly cost far more than the boutique and artisan-made pieces Allie usually wore.

"I was in the mood for Mexican food," Lauren confessed. "Glad you guys obliged."

"You don't have to twist my arm." Allie dipped a warm, salty chip in salsa. "Thanks for making the trek over here."

Lauren gestured between Allie and Collins who sat next to her, her brow wrinkled. "So, Collins, are you on this road trip? I didn't see you tagged in the post."

Kim rolled her eyes. "He's not on social media. Neither is my brother, who happens to be his partner. It's a cop thing."

"It's a waste of time," Collins said under his breath for Allie's ears only. She giggled. "Yeah, their brother couldn't go. So I volunteered my truck to pull his trailer. It seemed like a great trip, and a good opportunity to get away and spend time with Allie." He smiled at her, one only for her with a touch of heat that made her toes curl, and he slipped his arm across the back of her chair.

Was he serious or just putting on a show for Lauren? Had their breakup not been as amicable as Lauren had made it out to be?

Lauren nodded with a satisfied smile, like she had figured out a secret. "Well, since you're not on social media, put in your contact info." She handed him her phone, and he typed in it before handing it back to her. "What are you up to these days?"

"I'm a detective at the Laguna Vista Police Department. Been there five years now."

She told him about her job as a pharmaceutical rep.

Allie reached for another chip. She always ate too many and then didn't have as much room for dinner. But they were too good to resist. Though they went straight to her thighs, a part of her body that definitely didn't need any padding. She wasn't going to worry about what Lauren thought she knew. After dinner tonight, it'd probably be another six months to a year before she saw her again.

But now that she'd reconnected Lauren and Collins, did she need to be worried? Would she spend the trip worrying about those two, or would she be able to relax and enjoy herself? Sometimes it really felt like high school never ended and they were all just playing at being grownups. Where was the manual for this kind of thing anyway?

Dinner went better than Allie expected. They were all hungry after the day's adventures. Conversation flowed naturally, and surprisingly, Lauren and Collins didn't talk too much about old times.

Allie piled salsa on a homemade flour tortilla. She was stuffed, but this was so good she couldn't resist. Her mouth filled with a combo of fresh and spicy and yeasty as she took a bite.

Melissa caught her eye and pointed to her Apple Watch.

Allie looked at hers. Wow, it was much later than she thought. They needed to get going. She took a last swallow of her iced tea. "Thanks for reaching out, Lauren. We've got to go. We still need to get to Flagstaff tonight, and it's been a long day."

After they'd settled the bill, they walked out. Allie gave Lauren a hug. "Thanks for meeting us for dinner. It was wonderful. We definitely need to get together next time I'm in town."

"My pleasure. Thanks for bringing the company. I think it's a total God thing that we're all back together again." She gave Collins a hug, and Allie couldn't help but wonder if Lauren held on a bit long.

COLLINS DISENGAGED HIMSELF FROM LAUREN'S HUG AND was happy to walk away. It was fully dark now. The trailer had pulled just fine coming up the freeway here, but there was a significant grade going to Flagstaff. He'd see what his truck could do.

He turned on the flashlight app on his phone and scanned the trailer hitch again, shaking it, making sure nothing had vibrated loose. It looked solid.

Scott joined him. "Looks good." He turned to Melissa. "Sure

you don't want to find a place to stay here tonight? We could start early in the morning."

"It's not that late. Collins, you okay with driving to Flagstaff tonight?"

"Yeah. I don't think it'll be a problem. Let's stick with the plan." He grinned at Melissa. He'd make brownie points with her for that remark.

"I'll ride with Matthew again." Kim slung her backpack over her shoulder and followed Matthew to his truck. "He has better music."

"Scott, you can sit up front. I don't think you'll want to sit three hours with your knees bent in the back seat." Allie tugged open the crew door and slid in the back with Melissa.

Soon they were on the road, Matthew following them in case there were any issues. After they were safely on the I-17 heading north, Collins glanced back at Allie in the rearview mirror, but it was hard to see her face in the dark.

He wasn't sure how he felt about seeing Lauren again. He couldn't remember the last time they'd talked or emailed. Their two-year relationship had ended on okay terms, but Lauren had been disappointed in him. When they were in the business program at college, she had wanted him to join her father's new venture that she was sure would make them all rich.

Collins had wanted to be a cop, transferred to the criminal justice program, and their relationship had ultimately ended over it. Lauren didn't want to be with a cop, something he hadn't spent much time thinking about in regards to Allie. He'd gone on to a successful career, and he couldn't help feeling a bit like he had proved to Lauren his decision had been a good one.

It didn't matter now. He'd made the right decision. God had confirmed it to him over and over. And Lauren's opinion didn't matter. The only opinion that mattered was Allie's. She hadn't indicated any hesitancy about his job in any of their conversations, but there was a difference between being friends with a cop and being seriously involved with one. So what did that mean about his relationship with Allie?

He intended to find out on this trip.

The road to Flagstaff was dark, and the lights coming at him were mesmerizing. The cab had gotten quiet except for the strains of *The Best of Kansas* pouring out the speakers. Dinner made him sleepy too. Especially since his vigilance over the trailer had settled down. It pulled just fine up the incline, maintaining a steady speed, and the truck didn't heat at all. He should have grabbed a Dr Pepper for the jolt of caffeine.

Scott glanced over at him. "So what's it like to have Kyle for a partner?"

Collins appreciated the overture for what it was: an attempt to keep him awake and alert from a naval pilot who had probably had to be both many times. They talked the rest of the way about their experiences with Kyle and Joe. Until recently, Collins hadn't been much a part of Kyle's friendships, but since last winter, he'd been included in their circle and was grateful for it.

When Kyle started dating Heather and began to have a life outside of work, Collins began to do some serious looking at his own life as well. Spending time in Holcomb Springs where life moved a bit slower had been a good break and given him some time for introspection. He suspected God had some life changes in store for him.

"Let's game plan tomorrow." Melissa's voice came from the back seat. "We can't check into the campground until noon. It's about an hour and a half from the motel, but by the time we get set up and everything, it could be well after two before we get into the Grand Canyon. There is RV parking at one of the shuttle stops. We could just park there, take the shuttle into the Grand Canyon, and check into the campground at the end of the day. Thoughts?"

"As long as we get back in time to set up camp while there's still daylight." Allie's voice floated up to him.

"I agree. Especially setting up the trailer the first time, I'd prefer to have daylight."

"If we leave the park by five, we should still have daylight and more time in the park than if we tried to set up camp first," Scott put in.

"Okay, good. So that means we need to leave the motel fairly early in the morning, say be on the road by nine?" Melissa asked.

Collins nodded. "Sounds good."

"There's a restaurant next to the motel. We can meet there for breakfast by eight." This time Melissa made a statement, not a question.

He chuckled to himself. Probably none of it was actually a question. More like her getting buy-in on her pre-existing plan. He was fine with that. She'd spent the time figuring out the best way to maximize their trip. She knew what she was doing.

They arrived in Flagstaff late. Melissa had called the motel to reassure them that they were still coming. She hopped out to check them in, then he pulled around back to the RV parking. The rest of them spilled out of the truck, blinking and stretching their legs. Collins unlocked the trailer and handed out the bags they would need for tonight before locking it back up. They met Melissa coming out the back door of the motel. She handed out key cards.

"We have a problem. The rooms they gave us don't have space for a rollaway, even though I specifically asked for that. There are two queens. For us girls, it's not a big deal. Allie and I have shared a bed before, and Kim can have the other one. With you guys, I don't know. Do you want to grab sleeping bags?"

Matthew glanced back. "I can sleep in the trailer. It has a nice bed. Besides, it'll probably be my only chance." He grinned.

Melissa nodded. "Okay, thanks."

Collins unhooked the trailer key from his keyring and handed it to Matthew. "Sweet dreams."

"In about five minutes." He jogged back to the trailer.

The rest of them filed inside the motel. The patterned carpet contrasted with the plain walls, and it smelled like carpet shampoo and disinfectant. Based on the relaxed set of Melissa's shoulders, Matthew must be back in her good graces. The family dynamic should be interesting to watch on this trip. As an only child, Collins hadn't experienced that.

Their room was across from the girls', which made him feel better. He pulled Allie into a quick hug. "Sweet dreams."

"You too." She smiled and followed Kim into their room.

Melissa kept her voice low. "See you guys in the morning."

Slipping into their room, he left Scott and Melissa some privacy, something he was hoping he'd get more of with Allie.

He checked his phone for messages. He had one from Lauren.

So good seeing you again tonight. A wonderful surprise. Let's stay in touch. Let me know when you guys come back through Phoenix and we'll meet up again.

He didn't know what to think about that. He didn't want to be rude, and he had good memories with Lauren, but his focus was on Allie. He didn't want a relationship with his ex-girlfriend. He sent back a quick, basic text and got ready for bed. Slipping under the sheets, he was certain he'd be asleep as soon as Scott turned the light out. But his mind buzzed with unanswered questions, and sleep eluded him longer than he liked.

Chapter Ten

Allie wasn't surprised to find Melissa already up when the alarm went off the next morning. Melissa always had this extra energy at the beginning of the trip until everything found its groove. Allie slept hard last night, which surprised her. It'd been a long time since she'd shared a bed with her sister. As usual, they put a pillow between them. Melissa hogged the sheets, and she claimed Allie kicked in her sleep.

She was particularly careful as she sat up, holding back a groan. Once Melissa went into the bathroom, she eased into some stretches, blowing out her breath. The second day was always the worst, so after today, the pain and stiffness would get better, right? She checked the weather app on her phone. Thirty-five degrees. It'd warm up to the sixties today, but the dry air really allowed it to get cold at night. That and being at nearly seven thousand feet. Good thing she'd brought layers because the cold would make the stiffness worse.

Kim sat up in bed, rubbing her eyes.

"How'd you sleep?"

"Not too bad."

"Mind if I open the curtains?"

"Go for it."

Allie slid open the blackout drapes, letting in the sunlight. Instantly she felt more awake. Coffee would help, but the in-room stuff was likely not as good as what she could get in the restaurant. And there was always Starbucks.

Allie grabbed her clothes and hopped in a hot shower so she could move without groaning.

The girls were ready and had their bags packed at quarter to eight.

Melissa grinned as she peeked out. "I bet we beat the guys. Let's see." She crossed the hallway and knocked.

Male voices floated out, but the words were undecipherable. The door opened, and the smell of soap drifted out on the wisps of steam. Scott's face appeared in the opening.

Melissa laughed. "I knew it! We beat you. We're ready to go."

Scott pushed the door open wider. "So are we." Collins stood behind him, and their bags were packed and at their feet.

"Hmm." She tossed her hair. "Well, let's get moving."

Scott reached for her bag. "We'll take the bags to the trailer and wake up Matthew. You guys go get us a seat at the restaurant and get the coffee ordered."

"Good plan." She reached up and kissed him on the cheek.

Allie winked at Collins and giggled at the interplay of Scott and Melissa. It was good to see her sister happy. And it looked like she'd met her match with Scott. Now if she could just keep Melissa from worrying about her, their trip would be off to a great start. The last thing she wanted was for Collins to see Melissa mothering her like she was a child. Old habits were hard to break, but Allie would be happy if Melissa would see her as the capable professional she was.

Matthew looked half asleep when he followed Scott and Collins into the restaurant. They ate a full breakfast, drank lots of coffee, all of it documented by Kim. Allie popped a few ibuprofen when Melissa wasn't looking. Between that, the shower, and the food, she was starting to feel human.

Scott saluted Kim with his coffee mug. "So you're going to make a movie of all this when we get back, right? We can show those other poor schmucks what they missed out on."

Her eyes lit up. "Yes! I hadn't thought of a movie, but I'd better remember to shoot some video. Good thing I brought two power banks. A movie will be fun. We can have movie night at someone's house when we get back."

"That's your assignment then." Scott pointed at Matthew. "You can help her. You young people know about all that technology stuff."

Allie almost spit out her coffee. "Like you're so much older. You're what, only five years older than Kim and Matthew?"

"Ah, but I've lived more experiences."

She was still laughing when they reached the trailer. Melissa distributed plastic bags of trail mix and bottles of water. "We might be late getting lunch, so this should keep you hydrated and not starving."

After filling up their backpacks, they climbed in the truck. The "young" people had opted to ride together. It seemed like that was the default arrangement now, and Allie was glad Kim and Matthew had connected and seemed to be enjoying each other's company. Matthew could have a good time anywhere, but Kim only knew Collins and Scott as friends of her big brother and Allie a little from helping her find her condo.

Allie had been concerned that everyone had strong-armed Kim into the trip because she happened to walk into Kyle's house in the middle of the conversation. But now that Kim had a project, a purpose, and a partner in crime, it seemed like she'd have a great time.

Collins input the campground's address into the truck's navigation system. "Will that get us close enough to the shuttle parking lot?"

"Yes, we'll reach it before the campground. It's behind the IMAX theater, so we can't miss it," Melissa answered.

"The I-40 to the 62? Or the 180?"

"The 180 is a scenic highway, and it's not much different time wise."

"Then let's take it." Collins checked the mirrors, pulled out of the parking lot, and headed north. "We're even fifteen minutes ahead of schedule."

Melissa laughed. "Good. Then I don't have to get out my drill sergeant whistle."

Allie relaxed and watched the scenery as they drove through the woods and the mountains. Last night was too dark to see much, but her whole body relaxed at the sight of trees and mountain ridges. Even her soreness was manageable. Breakfast and ibuprofen had helped. This was vacation. It always had been for her. They were going to leave all the troubles behind and enjoy themselves.

Today they would see the Grand Canyon, have a campfire, and it would be a good day. Melissa didn't suspect a thing about Allie's injury, and that was just the way she wanted it.

***

They pulled into Tusayan, and Collins found the IMAX theater and parking lot with no problem. Easy trip so far. They headed toward the shuttle stop just as the shuttle was coming up the road. "Perfect timing."

"Yep, that's what I strive for." Melissa grinned.

Scott wrapped his arm around her. "That's my girl."

Melissa showed the pre-purchased passes, and they got on, two to a row. "We're getting off at the visitor center."

Allie slid in next to a window, Collins beside her. The high seat backs gave them the feeling of being in their own little cocoon. He slid his hand over hers and interlaced their fingers.

She turned and smiled at him, squeezing his hand.

The view out the window was similar to what they had coming up from Flagstaff, so he turned his attention to Allie for the short drive into the park. When they bypassed the line of vehicles at the entrance, he was glad Melissa had the foresight to take the bus.

At the visitor center, they got off. The low-slung buildings with trellises across the front looked like they'd been designed not to compete with the beauty around them.

They gathered in a group, and Melissa showed them the map she'd printed off. "Here's what I was thinking. We can head to Mather Point to get a great view of the canyon. Then we can come back and pick up our bike rentals and continue onto Hermit Road. It's about ten and a half miles, and there is a steep section, but you can stop and pick up the shuttle if you get tired. We can also take it back if we want. It will hold three bikes, so we can't all do that at the same time, but the shuttles run every fifteen minutes. I doubt that Scott and Collins will need a break, anyway." She grinned at them.

"Sounds great. Thanks, Melissa, for planning all of that out," Allie said.

"I really do enjoy it, all the logistics and stuff."

"I know you do." Scott kissed her forehead.

Collins grabbed Allie's hand again, and they headed down the wide sidewalk with other visitors toward Mather Point and their first peek of the Grand Canyon. At first the scenery looked no different than what they'd been among, with the pinyon pines and sagebrush. But then the trees parted, and the far rim eased into view. They continued down the stone steps to the fenced-in edge.

Breathtaking—as trite as that was—seemed to be the only word for it. How had the first Europeans to see this land felt when they saw it? They would have had no frame of reference. The multi-hued layers of earth looked like a giant had taken a trowel right through and carved out a canyon. After a family trip here when he was a kid, he tried to recreate it in the backyard, using a hose to create a river for his boats. Mom didn't appreciate it.

The morning light cast deep shadows among the carved

layers of dark red, tan, and green. Kim probably knew more exact terms for the shades. And at the edge you could look down thousands of feet.

The view was amazing, almost hard to take in, it was so vast and indescribable. And it was even better with Allie's hand in his. Hers was so much smaller that his engulfed hers. The acute awareness of her and the electricity that shot up his arm and through his body distracted him from the stunning view in front of him. In very rare moments had he ever allowed himself to imagine something like this, an adventure with Allie.

And the restlessness that he'd been feeling on and off for the past six months had stilled. What was God trying to tell him?

He slid his arm around her. "I need to do this more often. Get away from work and everything. Just enjoy nature."

She looked up at him. "Me too. I think that every time I'm out in nature. And then I don't do it enough. After this past week, it's restorative."

He pulled her closer to him. "Then let's agree to do this more often. We can hold each other accountable."

A smile lit her face, the one he felt might just be for him. "Yes, let's."

Matthew ran by and leaped up onto some rocks before quickly hopping back down, acting like he was about twelve.

"Matthew!" Allie shook her head at him.

Melissa stepped over. "This is no place for spontaneity. You could get hurt or hurt someone else."

He grinned. "I just wanted Kim to have a great action shot." He looked over at her. "Did you get it?"

Kim laughed.

"Hey, sibling photo in front of the canyon." Matthew pulled Allie's arm and disengaged her from Collins.

He immediately felt the lack. It almost took his breath away. He didn't have siblings. Sometimes he felt like he barely had parents.

The three siblings posed while Kim snapped their pictures.

He watched while something a lot like envy snaked through his stomach.

He pulled up the photo app on his phone and handed it to Kim. "Get one of me and Allie, would you please?"

"Sure."

He slipped up next to Allie and put his arm around her shoulder, gently pulling her close again, careful of her soreness but not wanting to make it obvious. "Kim's going to get a picture of us." He leaned even closer as Kim counted to three. That photo was going to be his new screensaver.

"Now, group photo!" Kim snagged a park ranger. "Could you get a picture of us?" She handed the ranger her phone.

Kim arranged everyone to her liking before slotting herself in and giving the ranger a thumbs up.

Collins didn't care how many pictures Kim took as long as he got to hold Allie close during them.

The ranger took a few photos, and she and Kim directed the group into different positions. A thin guy with medium-brown wavy hair wearing tailored shorts and a polo stood behind the ranger, watching, smiling.

Kinda creepy. Collins studied the guy. He seemed friendly enough, but something in Collins's gut didn't feel right about him. Still, it was a public place, and he supposed national parks drew all kinds. The rangers had their work cut out for them. He held Allie's hand a bit tighter.

The ranger handed Kim's phone back to her. Melissa glanced at her smart watch. "We'd better head back. Our bike rental starts soon."

Kim stopped them as they passed by the Grand Canyon National Park sign. "We need a shot here." They draped themselves around the stone monument while Kim flagged down another park visitor with her camera. Photo op over, they finished the walk to the bike rentals. The warm sun felt good in the chilly air. They'd be shedding layers soon.

On the way to the bike rental shop, Collins thought this

might be the oddest group date he'd ever been on. Not that he'd been on many, but spending time with the woman he was interested in and her family and friends, well, it was interesting to say the least.

The bike rental shop got them situated on their bikes and gave them each a map with the return time written across the top. He kept an eye on Allie as she eased on to the bike with a slight wince. This could be a rough day for her.

Once they were all ready, they headed down the paved Greenway trail that was just for bikes. They headed through more trees and the Village before they turned and broke out into a trail along the rim. This time there was just a small curb of stone and a few feet, if that, before the canyon gaped open.

They stopped at the first overlook. Allie grinned at him. "Almost makes my stomach drop riding so close to the edge. It's unbelievable." She looked at her sister. "Melissa, you did good."

Melissa opened her map. "This was originally a wagon road. Can you imagine cutting this road and taking a wagon over it?"

"I'm just glad we're separated from the road and the pedestrians until I get my bike legs back." Allie grimaced. "I haven't ridden a bike in forever." She and Collins stayed at the rear of the group.

As they rode along the rim, taking in the majesty from different angles, each view seemed more impossible than the next. Though he couldn't help but also enjoy the view of Allie, wind blowing through her hair that peeked out beneath her bike helmet. They definitely needed to do more of this. Even if it was with a group of people.

Once they reached Hermit Road, Matthew glanced over his shoulder with a wicked grin. "Race you to the next stop!" He stood on his pedals and took off.

"You're on!" Scott was fast on his heels.

Kim got it on her phone.

Melissa shook her head. "Boys. I'm not sure which one of them is worse."

As the rest of them rode up to the shuttle stop, Scott and Matthew leaned against their bikes swigging water.

"Who won?" Kim asked.

They shrugged then laughed.

It probably wasn't so much the winning as it was the racing they enjoyed. The rest of them parked their bikes at the shuttle stop and walked the trail to the Maricopa Point overlook. Collins had to admit getting off the bike to walk was a welcome change. And watching Allie take a few stiff steps, he imagined it was for her too. Plus, it gave him another opportunity to hold her hand.

The Point was out on a finger of rock like a peninsula into the canyon, giving them a wide-angle view. The sun was higher, and they'd gotten warm riding. They all were shedding their jackets and tying them around their waists.

After a few moments of soaking in the view and Kim snapping pictures, they headed back to the shuttle stop. The problem with having to get the bikes back on time meant they couldn't dally as much as they'd like. However, the view from the bike was unmatched. You could cover the ground a lot faster than walking the paths.

"Uh oh." Allie frowned at her bike. "Does my back tire look flat?" She squeezed it, and it pancaked down. "I thought it felt a little soft."

Collins followed her. He squeezed Allie's back tire. Yep, it was soft. He leaned in to whisper for her ears only. "How are you feeling?"

"I'm not that upset the tire is flat. I've hit my limit on this bike anyway," she whispered back. "But I don't want to mess up Melissa's plans."

Melissa walked over. "What's going on?"

"My tire's flat. I know there's a number we can call, but I don't want to hold everyone up while they bring me a new bike. Why don't you guys go on without us? Either we'll have them bring us a new bike or we can ride the shuttle back and return the bike. But you all keep on going. No need for all of us to stay here." Allie put her hands on her lower back and stretched.

Melissa met Allie's gaze for a moment. Some sibling communication took place between them. "Are you okay? You've been moving gingerly all day. Did you hurt yourself?"

"Um, no. Not today. Just stiff from the car ride."

Melissa peered at her then put her hands on her hips. "What aren't you telling me?"

Allie's gaze cut to the side before darting to Collins. "I was in a minor fender-bender the night before we left."

"What? Why didn't you say something?" She looked at Collins. "Did you know?"

He nodded. "Yeah, she told me." He slid his arm over her shoulder.

"Allie, why didn't you tell me? Are you sure you feel okay? Do you want to go back to the trailer and lay down—"

"This. This is exactly why I didn't tell you. You're not my mother. I'm an adult and can decide what I need to do or not do. Now, why don't you all go on without us? We'll take care of the bike and figure something out."

Melissa held her gaze a second more.

Collins was fascinated by their interplay. And a little concerned. He wasn't used to seeing that kind of tension. Should he defend Allie or let her handle Melissa on her own? Considering they had far more experience with sibling relationships, he figured his best move was to sit back and see how it played out. He could always pick up the pieces later if needed.

"Okay. Let's meet at the Maswik Food Court in the Village at three if we don't meet up before then." Melissa hopped on her bike and took off with Scott, Matthew, and Kim. She gave a final glance over her shoulder at Allie before disappearing around the bend.

Collins and Allie dragged their bikes over to the side. She perched on a low wall, and he joined her, and they both removed their helmets.

He rubbed her back. "You okay?"

"Fine."

He wasn't sure if he should say anything about her interplay with Melissa or not, so he didn't. But sitting in the sun, next to her, it was actually kind of nice. Even though her bike wasn't working, it was just the two of them. Not so much of a group date now. He glanced up.

The preppy guy from earlier walked over.

Great.

"Looks like you have some bike trouble."

Brilliant observation. "Yep. But it's under control."

"Need a hand?"

"Nope. We've got it."

Allie gave the man a polite smile, but her eyes were troubled. She had her phone in her hand.

The man took a step toward Allie. The guy was just taking a closer look down the road, though Collins wished he'd do it farther away from Allie. He hoped the guy wasn't waiting for the shuttle bus too. Maybe he'd take the walking trail down to the next few lookout points that were grouped together.

This guy didn't seem interested in either moving back or heading on down the trail to the next overlook.

Allie looked at Collins. "I don't have much of a signal. Do you?"

He slid out his phone. "Yeah. Let me call the shop." He frowned. Lauren had sent another text. He swiped it away without reading it then punched in the number on the phone. He explained their situation. He lowered the phone and turned to Allie. "It'll be a bit before they can get here with a replacement bike. Do you want to just take the shuttle back?"

"Yeah, let's do that."

Collins updated the bike shop and hung up. Preppy guy was still around. He really didn't want to discuss their plans in front of him. He reached for Allie's hand. "Are you disappointed?"

She shrugged. "A little. But we've already seen such amazing sites. Plus, it's been a long time since I've ridden a bike. I'm sure I'll feel it tomorrow on top of the soreness I already had. And this is only the first real day of our trip."

Preppy Guy laughed.

Collins frowned. Didn't anyone ever tell him it was rude to eavesdrop on someone else's conversation?

Allie held up her phone. "I got a text from an unknown number supposedly from Edward—he's the COO at DataCorp —asking about an email. But it's a Saturday. So it's probably best if we head back where I might have some cell service to figure out what's going on."

The shuttle bus pulled up, and people got off. Collins and Allie pushed their bikes to the rack on the front of the bus and secured them then hopped on. Preppy Guy was already in a seat, and Collins nudged Allie to the back away from him.

They listened to the guided tour as they rode the rest of the way. They passed their group on the road as they neared Hermit's Rest. He and Allie waved, but he wasn't sure they saw them. "Do you want to get off at Hermit's Rest? We can hang with the rest of the group until the next shuttle?" Then Preppy Guy could be on his way and away from them.

Allie chewed her lip. The text. She'd want to get to it.

Just then, Preppy Guy stood as they pulled into the Hermit's Rest shuttle stop.

"Never mind. We'll get back to the bike shop, and you can check on your text."

And he could breathe a sigh of relief.

At the Village, they changed buses to the Village line back to the visitor center and bike shop. Allie watched the bars on her phone. Had she forgotten something on the RFP for DataCorp and Edward was asking for it? But what email? She hadn't gotten anything from him.

Then she remembered. The company email went to Rachel's account. She had forgotten to redirect it to her own account. And Rachel clearly wasn't monitoring it. Still, she'd given Data-Corp her personal email for this very reason. She opened her email and waited for enough bars for it to load. She checked the spam folder and searched for DataCorp and Edward's name. Nothing new showed up.

They arrived at the visitor center, and she and Collins got off the shuttle and retrieved their bikes. "No luck, huh?"

Allie shook her head. "What I really need is my laptop. Then I could check the company general email account and see what email he's talking about. If it even is Edward and not some coincidental spam. But I can't do that from my phone. And the laptop is in the trailer."

She saw the thoughts flitting through Collins's head.

"No. We're not leaving and going back there. Plus, it's a Saturday. No one will expect me to respond before Monday."

This was a vacation. And she was alone with Collins. Something she'd dreamed about. The spectacular scenery had helped to take her mind off the pain. So she was going to push thoughts of Edward and DataCorp out of her head and focus on enjoying herself.

At the bike shop, she and Collins considered what to do.

Allie looked at the map. "We're too far to catch up with the others. We could walk along the Rim Trail to the Village and poke around there until it's time to meet up with them."

"So you're good if we just turn in the bikes?"

"Are you?" This was his vacation too. If he wanted to keep going, she'd do it for him.

"I'm fine with it." His smile warmed her through.

After they turned in their bikes, they headed down the Rim Trail. It was hard to put into words just how vast and stunning the vistas were. And her contentment with walking along the trail with Collins, her hand in his. It was something her high school self could have only dreamed about. This peace she had with him, this contentment was something she hadn't realized had been missing. The stress over keeping her business afloat—not to mention dealing with Rachel and living up to Leroy's expectations—had worn on her more than she had known.

They passed Verkamp's visitor center, the Hopi house, the El Tovar hotel, the lodges, and arrived at Lookout Studio. The views from this stone building that perched on the edge of the rim were astonishing. They took the stone stairs down to the terraced levels that peered out over the rim. Allie tightened her hand in Collins's grip. Her stomach felt a little swirly at the drop. They settled on a low stone wall.

Allie was grateful for the rest. She stretched her back and neck a bit and glanced around. "Can you believe people used to come out here by stagecoach? Then once the railroad arrived, things boomed."

"And now we come here by cars. It's hard to imagine what things were like over a hundred years ago. No air conditioning." He nudged her shoulder.

"Yeah, it had to be brutal in the summer. Right now is nice, though. I'm amazed at how many of these buildings were designed by a woman, Mary Colter. Unusual for the time." It was a challenge being a woman business owner now. How hard it must have been for Mary Colter working in a male-dominated career one hundred years ago. While there were some things she wished she could go back in time for—being more honest about her feelings for Collins in high school—she was glad she lived in an era of modern conveniences.

"The West must have seemed to provide more opportunity to people who wouldn't have had it elsewhere."

Allie nodded. Thoughts of Rachel crept in. Would Mary Colter have given her the boot? Or would she have been inspiring to someone like Rachel? The purpose of the mentoring group was to give opportunities to people who might not other-wise have them. Allie's heart was always bent toward helping others, so it was a great fit, not to mention she had benefited from the group herself. But were there people who couldn't be helped? If so, how would she know? And what should she do?

Collins frowned. "You look deep in thought."

She gave him a smile. "Wondering what a strong woman like Mary Colter would have done with someone like Rachel. Though I know what Melissa thinks."

Collins got to his feet and held out his hand to help Allie up. "It's your company. You'll know when it's the right time."

His gentle confidence in her buoyed her spirit. As much as she valued Melissa's advice and looked up to her, she wanted to be seen as her own person and step out of Melissa's shadow.

They crossed the Village toward Maswik Lodge. "We should come up here by railroad sometime and stay in one of these lodges." Collins gestured around him. "I bet it's beautiful in the winter."

"I've always wanted to do that. Maybe we can make something like that work for a sibling trip."

Collins winked at her. "I have a feeling we'll get a lot of ideas for other trips from this one."

Her heart tripped at his assumption that they would be making more trips together in the future. Yep, she was going to push work out of her mind and concentrate on enjoying what she'd wanted for so long.

Willard plopped down at the picnic table at his campsite in Mather campground, considering his options. While Allie hadn't posted anything, her friend Kim had, tagging her. And since Kim seemed the type to post everything, he wouldn't have to worry about losing them.

And as usual, his plans had paid off. Hanging around the visitor center had been a good plan. There were enough people around that he was able to follow them without attracting notice. He'd picked up a bit of information about them and their plans. They'd been having a good time and not paying attention to him.

He couldn't shake the image of the woman with the chestnut hair who was with Allie's group. Her long, beautiful curls were just his type. When the sun hit it and she wasn't wearing her bike helmet, streaks of red appeared. He thought he'd heard the young guy call her Melissa. So maybe this trip would really pay off. Two for one.

Except that Allie's boyfriend—he didn't see any rings, so he didn't think they were married—was a cop. He was way too suspicious. Willard smiled. There were ways around that.

The other guy who was with Melissa—his gut churned at the thought—he wasn't a cop, but he carried himself with an awareness. Probably military. Those two guys could be a problem. In fact, right now Willard couldn't see a way to get any of the girls alone.

Maybe he should find someone else. Realtors were easy targets, but any woman would fall for his charm with the right circumstances.

No. Allie needed to pay for messing up his life. And Melissa? She was his. She just didn't know it yet. But she would. And the obstacles would just make the chase all the more sweeter. He let his mind drift back to the rush he felt with Amanda, the cops closing in and his escaping them easily. He laughed. This would be even better.

Tomorrow they were driving the Desert View. He'd hang out at the Watchtower. Eventually they'd end up there.

He'd bide his time and wait for a plan to form and an opportunity to present itself. It always did.

Chapter Eleven

Collins hung out the window as Scott guided him and the trailer into the campsite. They'd been lucky to snag one of the few with trees.

"That's good." Scott held his fist upraised.

Collins threw the truck into park and climbed out. He and Scott worked to get the truck unhooked, the trailer jacks down, and everything level. He was glad that everyone had agreed to his suggestion to head back after they'd eaten at the Maswik food court. It had been a long day, they still had to set up camp, and he knew Allie was hurting and wanted to get back to her laptop. He was doubly glad when he saw Allie's grateful smile.

Matthew's truck didn't fit on the campsite, so he and Kim unloaded their things and moved it to an overflow parking area.

Melissa looked at them. "You ready for us to start setting up inside?"

"Yep." Scott opened the compartments under the trailer, and they began getting the tent and camp chairs out.

Melissa, Allie, and Kim headed into the trailer. He was sure Melissa had a plan to organize it. Plus the girls had real beds that needed to be made up with sheets and blankets.

He and Scott got the ten-person tent up in no time. With

three guys and their stuff, it should be just about right. Whoever determined tent sizes must have been fine sleeping stacked together like cord wood.

Sleeping bags laid out inside, chairs set up around the fire ring outside, and still no sign of the girls. He poked his head inside. "How's it going in here?"

Melissa turned around. "Good. We're just about ready to start dinner. Hungry?"

"Starving." Considering they'd eaten a late lunch, he was surprised, but they'd burned a lot of calories today.

"Okay, let's develop a plan here since we really can only have two people in the trailer if someone is cooking." She stepped out of the trailer. "Allie and I can cook tonight, if Kim and Matthew can do the cleanup. There won't be much. Then Kim and Matthew can cook tomorrow with Scott and Collins doing the cleanup. And we can just keep rotating. I have a menu posted on the fridge inside. How does that sound?"

Everyone nodded. "Sounds great."

"All right. We're having walking tacos tonight. I'm going to heat up the taco meat and then we can put all the toppings in paper bowls. That ice chest is for drinks, so you guys can get in there and help yourself whenever you want. If we get low, we'll have to stop and get more. We'll probably need ice in there more often too. The other ice chest contains all the frozen stuff for meals. It has dry ice in it, so it should be fine, but let's not open it any more than we have to. And I unloaded the other ice chest with the breakfast stuff and condiments that belong in the fridge in the trailer."

"Great job, Melissa. Thanks for being so organized." Collins smiled at her and winked at Allie.

"Great job, honey." Scott kissed her cheek. "Want us to get some firewood for tonight?"

"That would be great! I forgot to mention we have s'mores for each night. Special s'mores." She raised her eyebrows.

Allie and Matthew laughed.

"See? They agree. But you'll have to wait until after dinner. I'll get to it." Melissa disappeared back in the trailer.

Collins turned to Scott. "Let's head to the camp store. We can check out the campground."

They headed toward the camp store and picked up a couple of bundles of firewood. "You guys have a good time on the bike ride?"

"Yeah, we did. It's been good to get away and spend time with Melissa in person instead of over FaceTime."

Collins nodded. "I was hoping it'd be a bit more picturesque here to walk around the campground after dinner. But it's mostly dirt."

"The Arizona Trail is behind the campground. I was thinking about running it in the morning. You up for that?"

"Sure. We might get fat and lazy on this trip." He grinned. Okay, that probably wasn't in the cards. But then neither was getting more alone time with Allie tonight.

He'd hoped she would be able to deal with her work email and then be able to forget about it for the rest of the trip. But instead, she was helping Melissa get everything set up. But between her soreness and worry about work, it wasn't turning out to be a great first day for Allie. But maybe he could make it better.

***

MATTHEW WAS LOOKING FORWARD TO S'MORES TONIGHT. IT was one of the best things about camping. And this trip had gone pretty well so far. Better than he thought it might with his sisters and two guys he didn't know. And Kim was pretty cool too. That was something completely unexpected.

She was sitting at the picnic table with a sketchbook, pencils, and her phone in the waning light of the day, her blonde hair falling over her shoulder.

He peered over her. She was sampling colors from her

pencils along the edge of the paper, trying to match the image in her phone.

She turned. "Hey."

"Trying to draw what you saw today?"

"More like trying to develop a color palette. Then I can sketch out some images to inform my designs. I've been so inspired by the colors and shapes I saw today. The way the indigenous people used nature to feed, clothe, and house themselves. There's a lot to take in."

He straddled the bench next to her. "It is. Biking along the rim was awesome. You must have a ton of pictures."

"I do. Want to see them?" She pushed her phone toward him.

"Sure." He scrolled through the photos, watching her with his peripheral vision as she continued sketching. She did have a good eye for things. The group pictures and more than a few of him doing something silly told a story. Unlike his sisters, Kim seemed to find him entertaining, laughing with him instead of scolding. It was refreshing.

He hadn't made many trips to Orange County to visit, other than to go to the beach in the middle of summer. But since Kim lived there, visits could be a lot more fun. Plus, there was the job he was considering. He enjoyed working as a salesman for his technology company, but as usual, he got restless once he'd mastered the job and its opportunities. There was a position in Orange County that likely could be his if he wanted it. He hadn't mentioned it to Allie and Melissa, but it was with DataCorp and their new branch. The question was, did he want it? It was something he'd hoped to think about on this trip, maybe talk it over with his sisters, get their opinions.

Scott and Collins strode back into camp carrying firewood. They dumped it next to the fire ring as Allie exited the trailer carrying paper bowls of lettuce, tomatoes, olives, and a jar of salsa, which she put on the picnic table.

Kim gathered up her sketchbook. "Time to eat. Let me put my stuff away."

Matthew watched her leave, intrigued in a way he hadn't been in a long time.

ALLIE HAD STUFFED HERSELF WITH TWO BAGS OF WALKING tacos. It was one of their favorite camping meals, and easy to make since it involved an individual bag (or two) of tortilla chips slathered with taco meat and whatever toppings you wanted, such as cheese, sour cream, salsa, tomatoes, onion, avocado, and lettuce. Something about camping made everything taste better.

She ducked into the trailer as Melissa was showing Kim and Matthew where everything went. They had drawn straws for the beds. Melissa got the big one and Allie got the lower bunk. She climbed on there and opened her cubby looking for her laptop. She must have put it there. It wasn't in her backpack. She couldn't remember where she'd put it, but they had unpacked so many things, it all ran together. Not in her cubby. Where would she have put it?

She wanted to take care of this before it was time for s'mores. Another favorite when camping. She dug through her backpack again. No, it just had the things she needed today at the Grand Canyon. She wouldn't have lugged the laptop around all day. Then she grabbed her bags and went through those. No laptop.

Frustrated, she started at one end of the trailer and opened every cupboard and drawer, no matter how ridiculous of a place it seemed to be for a laptop.

The trailer rocked as someone entered. Collins appeared. "Did you get it figured out?"

"I can't find my laptop. I've looked everywhere."

"Did you check the truck?"

"Nope. I can't imagine how it would be in there, but I'd better look." She followed him out the trailer and to the truck.

He opened the driver's side and she went through the passenger door. They scanned every part, looking under seats, in crevices. No laptop.

Tears sprung to her eyes. What was she going to do?

"Are you sure you brought it with you?" Collins came around to her side.

She tried to think about the morning they left. She was running around trying to get everything packed up. That feeling that she was forgetting something kept nagging at her. No. "It's sitting on the dining room table, still plugged in."

He pulled her into a hug. "It's going to be okay. You're on vacation. You got everything off to DataCorp. You probably don't need it."

She wanted to believe him. She really did. Pulling back from him, she attempted a smile. "Let me check my phone, see what I can do." She climbed back into the trailer, grabbed her phone of her bunk, and plopped into the dinette.

Collins slid in across from her.

She opened her email app, double checking that a message from DataCorp hadn't ended up in the junk folder. Then she opened the browser and signed in directly to the company's email server. She scanned the inbox. Nothing but the usual junk. She looked in the trash. And then all the folders. Nothing. Was she missing something?

She scrubbed her hands over her face. She couldn't believe she'd forgotten her laptop. She could only hope that she hadn't forgotten something important on the DataCorp RFP too. "I can't find anything. I don't know what to think. And I still need to figure out how to route the company email to my account." She pulled up the hosting website and called the tech number. But no one answered. It was a Saturday. Maybe she could do it herself. Could she remember the password? Hopefully it'd be stored on her phone.

On the hosting site, which was not designed to be viewed on a phone, she was able to get into her account. She had to keep enlarging the screen and moving things around to see what was on the page. But eventually she was able to get to the email section and forward it to herself. Success, at least in one area.

"Well, I can't find the email Edward is talking about. If it's Edward. Let me see if I have his number anywhere." She went through the emails until she found it. "Yep, it matches the one that sent the text. So it was him. I can't find his email, but I've fixed future emails. Some mixed results for sure."

Melissa climbed in the trailer and rooted through the cupboards for the s'mores supplies. She came out with an armful of Hershey bars, Twix, Reese's, and a few other things that Allie couldn't see. "Why don't you call Glenn and see if he knows anything?"

"Who's Glenn?" Collins looked between the two of them.

"My marketing colleague. He's got a contact at DataCorp. He's the one that alerted me to the RFP. That's a good idea. I'll try him tomorrow."

"It's the weekend. No one is expecting anything before Monday even if they did send you an email."

She gave a half laugh. "That gives me another day to worry about it."

He held out his hand. "Let's go eat these special s'mores of yours." He smiled, but worry shadowed his eyes.

It was nice to be worried about instead of always being the one that did all the worrying. She put her hand in his and followed him out of the trailer. "Those s'mores will change your life." She laughed.

He squeezed her hand and winked.

They'd at least take her mind off things for the evening.

Collins stepped out of the trailer and froze. Matthew was sitting around the campfire, tuning a guitar. But Collins's guitar case sat on the picnic table.

Matthew looked up. "I grabbed your guitar for you. I didn't know you had one too. Let's play something together."

Allie moved around him, but he couldn't move. It had been a last-minute, late-night impulse that had him adding his guitar to his bags. He'd forgotten about it, but Matthew had found it. He had zero desire to play it in front of Allie and make a fool out of himself. If he'd had some time to practice, maybe. But what excuse could he give?

Maybe if he put it off, they'd all forget about it.

"I have to have one of these special s'mores first. Allie, show me how it's done."

She led him to the picnic table where an assortment of goodies were visible in the glowing campfire light. The typical marshmallows and graham crackers, plus an assortment of candy bars, chocolate syrup, and peanut butter. It looked like a stomachache waiting to happen.

"What's your favorite?"

Allie picked up a marshmallow and threaded it on a skewer. "Roasted marshmallow between two peanut butter cups. Matthew likes Twix with peanut butter and graham crackers. Melissa usually goes with boring old Hershey bars but drizzles her marshmallow with chocolate syrup. Basically, whatever your sweet tooth demands."

He'd never heard of such a thing—messing with the classic s'mores recipe—but if it got him out of playing the guitar, he was all for it. "Scott, what are you trying?"

Scott squatted in front of the fire roasting a marshmallow. "Haven't decided yet. I know I'm more adventurous than Melissa is."

She nudged him with her knee, and he laughed.

He picked up a skewer and impaled a marshmallow and followed Allie to the glowing coals. "Important question for you. Lightly toasted or flaming torch?"

She grinned. "I don't eat charcoal. Matthew does."

"It's good for the digestion." Matthew strummed a chord.

Allie turned to Collins. "Well?"

He dunked his marshmallow into the flames and watched it catch fire before blowing it out. "I'm with Matthew."

She made a face. "I think you boys just like lighting things on fire." She stood with her lightly toasted marshmallow and squeezed it between two Reese's cups. As she bit into it, a look of rapture crossed her face.

He carried his carbon over to a Twix bar and sandwiched it between two bars. It was surprisingly good. A step up from plain graham crackers and chocolate.

Allie settled into a chair, and he took one next to her. "Remember that trip where you and Daniel were trying out those experiments from your Boy Scout experience?"

"My favorite is still the one where you put a paper cup of water in the fire and it doesn't burn." Matthew adjusted the tuning pegs and strummed again.

"If you don't mind ashes in your water." Melissa licked her fingers.

"Desperate times…"

"Really desperate." Allie carried her skewer over to the table then returned to her chair.

"No more?"

She shook her head. "One is enough. Even if we did burn a lot of calories today."

Collins didn't think he needed another one either, but Matthew cast a look in his direction. "I think I'll try the peanut butter cups this time."

"Remember the time we went hiking and got lost?" Matthew gave Melissa a pointed stare. "Never let her tell you there's a short cut. You'll end up climbing the side of a mountain."

"Hey, we got back okay," Melissa protested.

Scott raised his eyebrow. "I have to hear this story."

Collins was curious too.

Melissa leaned her head back. "We learned a lot that day. We were camping near Holcomb Springs and went on a short hike, what we thought was a nature trail. We did everything you shouldn't do on a hike. We didn't tell anyone where we were going. We tried to take a short cut. We didn't have any water or anything with us. How dumb were we?"

Allie's voice lowered. "When the trail we were on petered out into nothing and we were on the side of a mountain with quickly lengthening shadows… I was pretty scared."

"Yeah, but you and I got our punishment having to carry Brittany and Matthew piggyback because they got so tired. We're just lucky we got back before Mom called the park rangers. Some quick nature walk." Melissa pointed at Matthew. "I think you should carry me on the next hike."

Allie settled back into her camp chair. "At least it didn't kill my love for hiking. Just made me more cautious and better prepared."

"How'd you find your way back?" Collins asked.

"That was Allie." Melissa nodded in her direction. "She knew that our camp was on the other side of that mountain. The mountain was just a lot bigger than we thought. She has an uncanny sense of direction."

Allie shifted. "I knew my way around."

The silence lingered but wasn't uncomfortable. For a moment, Collins had a peek into what life had been like for them, especially Allie and Melissa, having to be responsible and in charge. It was a different perspective than what he knew of her in high school. It was why she was the way she was. And he was determined to help make her load a little lighter.

"All right, Collins. Get over here with your guitar. Let's see what we can play to entertain these folks."

All the eyes, but especially Allie's, shifted to him. There was no way out of this. He just hoped he didn't embarrass himself too much. He really should have practiced some if he was going to bring his guitar. What had he been thinking? He was going to make a fool out of himself.

He opened the case and removed the Martin, taking care as

he picked his way back to his seat in the shifting light of the campfire. He settled the guitar in his lap and tuned it, muscle memory coming back at something he'd done a thousand times.

He strummed, his fingers finding the chords clumsily. His face grew hot, and he was glad for the dark shadows. His fingers found the strings, found the fret, as if coming home. The weight of the wood across his thighs, the flickering firelight, the dark shadows created a concert venue unlike any he'd ever played in. This audience was more carefree with fewer expectations, less critical and exacting in their demands. Perhaps this was what he had needed to begin playing again.

Matthew began, "Get Your Kicks on Route 66," and Kim sang along with him. He sang and played the way he seemed to do everything, with full heart and not much finesse. But he clearly didn't care. He enjoyed himself.

Collins thought about how his guitar teacher would have cringed at Matthew's technique. But at least he was playing.

Matthew segued into "Kumbaya" and a few other campfire songs.

Collins surprised himself by keeping up, mostly. His fingers felt thick and clumsy, and he fumbled the chords, but he wasn't making a total fool of himself. The dark helped. That and the fact that no one seemed to be expecting concert-level performances. It was a new experience to play just for fun, with no expectations. And Matthew's enthusiasm covered Collins's mistakes.

When Collins took his aching fingers off his guitar, he noticed Allie's gaze on him, her soft smile in the warm glow of the fire.

"That was great. I had forgotten about your playing. I'm glad you remembered to bring your guitar."

If it got her to look at him that way, he'd play until his fingers bled. Maybe having Matthew around to push him into uncomfortable places wasn't the worst thing.

He glanced up, and Matthew grinned at him, giving him a salute with his pick.

ALLIE FINISHED GETTING READY FOR BED AND STEPPED OUT of the tiny trailer bathroom.

"Want some Sleepytime tea?" Melissa held up the tea kettle.

"Yes, please." She slid into the dinette across from Kim. "Kim?"

"Sure." Kim looked up from her iPad.

Melissa lit the burner then brought down the tea. "What did you think of the Grand Canyon?"

"Amazing. I'm just going through the pictures now. They don't do it justice, though."

"Allie, you and Collins did okay even without riding with us." It was a statement not a question, followed up by a grin.

Allie shrugged. "We had a good time exploring the Village, picking up some postcards for his mom." Eager to get the attention off herself, she turned to Kim. "You didn't mind that we stuck you with Matthew on the road trip?"

"Nah." Was that a faint stain of pink on her cheeks? Hard to tell in the trailer's dim light. "He's fun."

Melissa brought over the kettle and poured into their mugs. "That he is." She studied Kim's face. "Cute too."

Kim's face was definitely pink now. "I hadn't noticed." But her casual remark wasn't fooling anyone.

"Uh huh." Melissa sipped her tea.

Allie grinned. "I saw you and Scott looking awfully cozy today. Must be nice having him around again."

Melissa's smile turned wistful. "It is. After seeing him nearly every day this past winter, it's been hard being apart."

"How long is that going to last?" Kim glanced up from her iPad and sipped from her mug. "Ooh, minty."

"Hopefully not too much longer." Melissa leaned back. "I

created my new company so I can work anywhere." She waggled her ringless finger. "Once he proposes, we'll start looking for a place near his base. I'm not pushing to rush anything. This trip will be good for us. We need some time together that's not filled with a crisis to see how things are."

"It's going to be an interesting trip, for sure." Allie blew across her tea. "Collins and I hadn't seen each other in forever, and then suddenly he's back in my life last November. Then he left to go to Holcomb Springs PD, and now he's back. Guess we get to see if we have anything more than great high school memories."

Kim scoffed. "I've seen how he looks at you. I don't think you have anything to worry about."

Allie wasn't so sure. She turned to Melissa.

"The girl's right."

They could have all the opinions they wanted, but they didn't have to live with the consequences. "So, Kim, anything you want to know about Matthew? We've got all the dirt on him." She giggled.

Melissa started laughing. "Yeah, he wouldn't appreciate it, but we've got photographic evidence too."

Allie and Kim joined her and soon they couldn't stop laughing.

A knock sounded on the trailer door. "You girls okay in there?" Scott's voice sounded more amused than concerned.

Melissa giggled again. "Oh yeah. We're fine."

Allie clamped her hand over her mouth, and Kim just laughed.

"Okay then. Well, keep it down. Some of us need our beauty rest."

Which only made them laugh harder.

Chapter Twelve

Sun edging through the curtains woke Allie. Her legs ached a bit from yesterday, and she maneuvered around to stretch them without banging her head on Kim's bunk above her. Her back and neck were still sore but better than they had been. The trailer wobbled. Melissa must be up and moving around.

It wasn't long before they were both dressed. Allie started the coffee, grateful for the coffeemaker that allowed them to make multiple cups of coffee at once. She was also grateful for the electrical hookups that allowed them to recharge all of their devices. Cell phones and their cords covered the dinette, like a weird electric spider. Which reminded her that she needed to call Glenn today. He'd be at church this morning, so it'd have to wait until they got back this afternoon.

The guys had mentioned going for a run before breakfast, at least Scott and Collins had. When they returned, Melissa had Scott setting up the Coleman stove outside to cook bacon. She worked the griddle for pancakes, and soon they were eating breakfast.

"Bacon is a must have for camping." Matthew dipped a piece in syrup.

"It does seem to taste better," Scott agreed. "Must be the campfire."

A quiet fell over the group as they ate and nature woke up around them. The cool morning would soon be offset by the warming sun.

"I know it doesn't feel like a Sunday, but I was thinking we'd do a small worship service before we hit the road today." Melissa looked around the group. They'd always done this when they were camping.

"Can I pick a passage to read?" Scott looked up.

"Please do."

He grabbed his phone and scrolled through. "I like the Psalms when I'm out among God's creation, especially the ones that talk about the majesty of the Lord." He began reading. "This is from Psalm 27. 'The Lord is my light and my salvation—whom shall I fear? The Lord is the stronghold of my life—of whom shall I be afraid?...One thing I ask from the Lord, this only do I seek: that I may dwell in the house of the Lord all the days of my life, to gaze on the beauty of the Lord and to seek him in his temple...I remain confident of this: I will see the goodness of the Lord in the land of the living. Wait for the Lord; be strong and take heart and wait for the Lord.'"

Scott lowered his phone. "Most of you know about what happened last year when my F/A-18 malfunctioned and crashed. It killed my electronic warfare officer and left me with a traumatic brain injury. I wasn't sure what God's plans were for me after that. I didn't particularly like his timing either. But there are a lot of verses about waiting for the Lord. And I think that must mean as humans we aren't really inclined to be patient, that we are often on a different schedule than God is. At least I know I am. And I have found I learn more in the waiting about God than I do when things go the way I want them to."

A murmur of agreement rippled around the group. Matthew strummed his guitar and played the praise chorus, "I love you,

Lord." Everyone joined in, and a silence fell on the group as the last note faded away.

Collins lifted his voice. "Lord, thank you for bringing us here today, this particular group of people to get to know each other better as we explore the beauty of this creation you've given us. I pray this will be a good time of fellowship, of safety, and of learning to love you more each day. Thank you for the gift of your Son, and in his name we pray, amen."

Amens echoed around the group. The peacefulness seemed like a living thing that Allie, and apparently everyone else, was reluctant to shatter.

Matthew raised his hands. "This is the day the Lord has made. Let us rejoice and be glad in it. So let's hit the road and explore what he's made."

Everyone laughed. Leave it to Matthew to lighten the mood, even if it didn't need lightening.

Melissa packed up plastic bags of deli meat, cheese slices, cut-up veggies, fruit, crackers, and a container of dip into the empty cooler along with bottles of water. She turned to Scott. "Can you get another bag of ice from the camp store for this one?"

"Sure."

Allie caught Collins studying her. She gave him what she hoped was a reassuring smile. He reached for her hand. "How did you sleep?"

"Not too bad. A little sore still but better. How was your run with Scott?"

"Good. It's a nice trail back there. It's part of the Arizona Trail that runs the whole length of the state, so it was good for running. There were a couple of mountain bikers back there too. Scott's a good guy. I knew that from Kyle, but it's been fun to spend time with him."

"I'm glad. I wasn't sure how you felt about going on this trip with people who were almost strangers to you."

He held her gaze, his deep-brown eyes boring into hers.

"Allie, you're not a stranger to me. And I'm enjoying getting to know your family better." His thumb grazed the back of her hand.

Her heart pounded, and warmth shot through her. The world around them shrunk to just the two of them and a magnetic pull seemed to draw her to him.

Matthew bounded up and smacked Collins on the shoulder. "Thanks for playing last night, man. We should talk today and create a playlist."

Collins nodded distractedly and squeezed Allie's hand.

She frowned at Matthew.

Kim walked up, backpack slung over her shoulder and a tripod in her hand, looking at Matthew. "Are you going to bring your truck around or should we just head out there and wait for them to catch up?"

Melissa hopped out of the trailer waving a piece of paper. "Matthew, you need your entrance pass."

Allie grinned at Collins and shrugged. She took a step closer and spoke into his ear. "Still enjoying getting to know my family?"

Scott came back with the ice, and they had Collins's truck loaded up in short order. Today they had to wait in line to get into the park, but it wasn't as bad with the pre-paid passes. As they headed toward the visitor center, they turned right onto Desert View Drive. They enjoyed the expanse of the canyon peeking in and out of the sagebrush, junipers, ponderosa and pinyon pines as they headed toward Grandview Point.

Drives in nature reminded her of growing up. There were times Mom decided to be present, and then they'd all pile in the minivan and go wherever she felt like. They'd explored all sorts of places they wouldn't have found otherwise. And they also got stuck a few times too. Still, the call of an unexplored road seemed to speak to her soul in a way not much else did.

Even as they were driving to Grandview Point and knew it was there, the trees blocked the view of their destination. It didn't seem at all like they were getting closer, and yet she knew they were. But if you didn't know the canyon was there, like perhaps early explorers, you could be fairly close and miss it. There were probably many things like that in life. Things you passed by and didn't know how close you were because you weren't looking for them.

They got out and walked out to the point, the morning sun burning off the lingering haze that hung over the canyon. Collins wrapped his arm around her waist and pulled her close as they studied the view, enjoying the peacefulness.

A family came up behind them, the grade-school-aged kids running and laughing. They scrambled over the rocks wearing flip-flops. The girl had a unicorn backpack that matched her flip-flops. One boy's backpack had Marvel comic book characters.

Allie bit her lip. That was a good way to twist your ankle or get scraped up. The kids balanced on the rocks within falling distance of the edge, the parents laughing and taking pictures. She glanced at Collins then at Scott. Both of them had their eyes glued to the kids.

Didn't people understand this was wilderness, not an amusement park? There was no guarantee of safety if you did something stupid.

She edged closer to the kids. If the parents weren't going to keep an eye on them, then she could at least get closer. Collins seemed to read her mind. The decomposed rock on the slope made for slippery footing even in hiking boots.

The boy pretended to be a comic book hero and chased his sister around. She tripped and slid face first down the slope.

Collins sprung forward and snagged her arm, halting her forward progress that would have ended with her over the cliff and onto the rocks below. He held her arm until she got her feet under her, then he pointed her in the direction of her folks. "You okay? You took a bit of a spill."

The girl stared at him with wide eyes.

The parents came over and dusted her off. "Thanks," the mom said.

Collins nodded and glanced behind him, wincing. The drop-off was nearly vertical.

The mom's gaze followed his, and she gasped. "Why don't they have a guardrail here? Someone could get hurt." She pulled the girl close to her and called for her other kids. "We're leaving. This place isn't safe."

Collins nodded and walked away, slowly rotating his shoulder, lips thinning. When he reached Allie, he leaned in. "No, it's not. That's why you don't let your kids run around in flip-flops near the edge of a cliff."

She took a deep breath and released it. For a moment, she thought for sure that little girl was going to end up over the edge and this day would end very differently for that family.

But Collins didn't look right. "Are you okay?"

He nodded. "Yeah, just tweaked my shoulder a bit. I had a weird angle on her."

"We should get some ice on it."

"I'll be fine."

"Hmm." Allie rolled her eyes. Stupid macho attitude. Why couldn't he just do the smart thing and put ice on it? She'd grown up with Matthew and Daniel and their various injuries, but they were younger than her, so she could just tell them what to do—well, usually it was Melissa giving the orders—and they generally did it. She didn't think that would go over too well with Collins.

He held out his uninjured hand to her. "Ready?"

"Yeah."

Back in the truck they headed toward Moran Point. She noticed Collins drove with his right hand and slung his backpack over his right shoulder. They walked out to a flat expanse on the edge of the canyon. Allie was glad not to see the family here. It was even more dangerous. Her stomach flipped as she slowly eased closer to the edge.

Parents were supposed to protect their children and teach them how to navigate the world safely. She glanced around at her siblings. They'd had to figure it out themselves without much guidance. She knew that had left her with some scars and coping mechanisms that probably weren't healthy.

"We can get some ice out of the ice chest." Allie eyed his shoulder, which was no hardship, filling out his dark T-shirt.

He touched her chin with his index finger. "I'm fine. You don't need to worry."

At Lipan Point, they had a view of the Colorado River cutting its way through the layers of rock. The clouds cast shadows, painted the rocks with patchwork colors. It was as if a sunset had been trapped in the stone, lending their hues to the rock.

Kim was taking pictures and seemed to be in a zone of deep thought. Allie was glad she was enjoying the trip and getting inspired by it.

Matthew pointed to the Colorado River. "Next time we need to take a rafting trip down that. Can you believe that the explorer John Wesley Powell did that in a canoe? With one arm?"

"No wonder three of his team deserted him, thinking he was on a suicide mission." Melissa pulled out her map of the area. "Here's something he recorded in his diary. I can't believe it—or they—survived. 'We are three-quarters of a mile in the depths of the earth, and the great river shrinks into insignificance, as it dashes its angry waves against the walls and cliffs, that rise to the world above; they are but puny ripples, and we but pigmies, running up and down the sands, or lost among the boulders.' I think he describes exactly how the canyon makes me feel."

Matthew was undaunted. "Allie, you went whitewater rafting. What do you think?"

"Collins was on that trip, too, with our high school youth group. It was fun, but not as dangerous as down there."

Collins chuckled. "We did have our share of adventures on

that trip. I think Matthew would enjoy the bailing bucket fights we had. We'd wait around a bend and ambush another raft floating down the river. I'd want Scott on my team for logistics."

Matthew laughed. "You don't want Allie and Melissa ganging up against you. They have a secret code. When we'd have water balloon fights, they'd yell 'pickle!' and double-team the other person. Usually me."

Scott raised his eyebrow. "Pickle? Have to say I've never heard that code word."

Allie laughed. "We thought we were really clever. Use a common word that no one would suspect."

Scott shook his head and chuckled.

"Didn't Donna lose a contact on our river trip?" Collins dropped his backpack at his feet and reached into it for a bottle of water and opened it, handing it to Allie.

She took it, her eyes traveling up until they met his. "Thanks. Yeah, it got shoved up behind her eyelid."

"Yikes." Melissa said that. "Sounded like fun up until that point."

Allie's focus remained on Collins.

"That trip wasn't without its problems." Collins took a swig of his water. "Pastor Ted had that diabetic episode when we were on the river and that other group had to help us. Then Marty fell on the hike and broke his tailbone and still had to hike out two miles."

Melissa shook her head. "We've had some sort of disaster or injury on our trips."

Allie gave a half laugh as she studied Collins. "Hey, maybe it's us. Maybe we're cursed." Looking at Collins's shoulder, she was only half joking.

BY THE TIME THEY REACHED THE DESERT VIEW Watchtower, Collins was ready for lunch. Some protein and carbs would help the ache in his shoulder. He was careful not to grimace since Allie was watching him so closely. He liked her attention, just not the reason for it.

He slotted the truck into a parking spot and was grateful when Scott grabbed the ice chest and Matthew the insulated tote with the other picnic supplies. They walked along the path, the seventy-foot stone tower looming in the distance.

"Here's a picnic table." Melissa pointed to one under the nearby trees. She and Allie began setting the food out, and everyone filled their plates.

As they ate, Melissa pulled out her guide map. "This is another building Mary Colter designed. She wanted to model it after native structures she had seen in the area. She insisted that the rocks not be cut so they would maintain their weathered appearance and would blend in with the canyon walls. I would have liked her; she was a stickler for details. I guess she had left for the day at one point, and the men continued laying stone. When she came back, she made them take it all down and start over. My kind of woman."

Scott slid his arm around her shoulders and hugged her close. "You're my kind of woman."

Melissa pretended to be annoyed and swatted at him before kissing his cheek. "Just for that, I'll show you what I brought for dessert." She reached in the bag and pulled out a plastic container. "Cowboy cookies."

"What's that?" Collins asked.

"Just the best thing ever." Matthew reached across the picnic table and stole one as she removed the lid.

"Like an oatmeal-chocolate chip cookie but with pecans and coconut flakes too."

"Sounds fantastic." He started to reach with his left hand, but pain shot through his arm as he moved it. He must have reinjured that old rotator cuff tear. He used his right hand instead, but Allie had noticed and frowned.

She reached into her backpack and a minute later dropped two ibuprofen into his hand. "These will help."

"Thanks." He took them with a swallow of water. Her attentiveness resulted in her kindness. She saw a need and did whatever was needed to meet it. Her clients must love her.

They packed the lunch back up. Matthew grabbed the ice chest. "I'll take this back to the truck. I want to head into the deli over there and grab a Coke. Anybody want anything?"

"I'll go with you." Kim stood. "I want to stop by the trading post as well. We'll meet you all over at the tower."

Collins took Allie's hand, and they began the walk to the tower looming in front of them. "I can't imagine hauling those stones without modern equipment."

"It's truly amazing."

He thought she was amazing, but he just winked at her. They entered and climbed the eighty-five steps that circled around the inside of the tower, each window teasing them with a more spectacular view until they reached the top. Long, horizontal windows circled the tower, and they wandered from view to view. The Colorado River made a big bend and continued to the west.

Allie pointed out the window. "That's the North Rim, over ten miles away, and on a clear day you can see over one hundred miles. Imagine seeing that far and yet not seeing any signs of civilization like roads or buildings. So different from back home."

They settled on one of the benches under the window and enjoyed the view. Maybe his shoulder would get him out of playing guitar tonight. Nah, then Allie would worry. Besides, last night hadn't been that bad. Of course, the group was just being nice, and Matthew's enthusiasm covered a lot of errors. They were playing simple campfire songs, after all.

Still, he'd forgotten how good it felt to play with other people. The feeling of having a part and working with others to create something bigger than all the individuals. Maybe he should make the guitar part of his routine again.

He hadn't gotten the alone time with Allie last night that he'd wanted. In fact, he'd spent more time alone with Scott than with anyone. This morning's run had been a good one. Not too strenuous, and they were well-matched running partners. Reminded him a lot of Kyle but not as serious.

After a while, Matthew bounded up the steps.

Kim was behind him, her DSLR camera out, shooting photos of the murals and paintings that adorned the walls. She circled the room almost in slow motion, taking in all the details. She snapped a few of him and Allie on the bench as well before joining them. "I love how much Mary Colter respected the local culture and their design and that the murals are representative of the Hopi people."

Matthew pointed out the window. "Is that a California condor?"

A great black-winged bird soared out over the canyon, ugly and beautiful at the same time.

"Do you know why they have no feathers on their heads? It's because they are like vultures, they eat carrion. And not having feathers on their heads means they can stick their heads into the body cavities and not have rotting flesh up there to worry about."

Allie smacked his arm. "Nice, Matthew."

"I know a few things." He grinned.

Collins turned to Allie. "Want to go down to the lookout outside?" Maybe they could get a few minutes alone. He stood and held his hand out to her.

"Sure."

They descended the stairs, spiraling down this time, and continued outside and down the terraces that clung to the side of the canyon. He didn't think the view would ever get old. They followed the paved area out to the farthest point, a peninsular strip of concrete surrounded by a fence that reached out into the canyon. He studied the Colorado River, thinking about the previous rafting trip he'd taken with Allie.

They'd had a few moments alone one evening, walking by the river's edge, skipping rocks. He'd so wanted to say something to her, but he was terrified the rest of the trip would be awkward if she didn't return his feelings. Fear of playing the guitar, fear of disappointing his parents, fear of speaking his heart to Allie. He'd made a lot of life decisions based on fear. It was past time for that to change.

Scott and Melissa came down the walkway, and he and Allie moved back to make room for them at the end, then they wandered back toward the terraced area. They had just taken a seat on the low wall when Preppy Guy sauntered by. He headed toward the railing where Scott and Melissa were.

Collins's fist clenched. He hoped that guy didn't spot them. He didn't need that today.

Preppy Guy made a comment to Melissa and Scott and laughed. Scott nodded but soon guided Melissa back where Collins and Allie sat.

Matthew and Kim had just joined them when Preppy Guy sauntered over. "Hey, did you ever get your bike fixed yesterday?" His gaze fixed on Allie.

"We just returned them and enjoyed the rest of the day on foot."

"Aw, that's too bad." He glanced around. "Are you guys all together? Related?"

Allie gave a small laugh. "Mostly."

"Well, we must be on the same tour path since we keep running into each other. How long are you staying here?"

Matthew chimed in. "Today's our last day. We're headed to Monument Valley and then Arches. What about you?"

"Funny coincidence. Me too. Lots to see here in the Southwest."

Collins shot Matthew a look he didn't see. He really didn't want Preppy Guy knowing where they were going. The guy was probably harmless, but Collins's job made him look at everything with a suspicious bent.

But Preppy Guy stuck out his hand. "I'm Willie. Since we keep bumping into each other, we might as well introduce ourselves."

"Matthew." He shook Willie's hand. "And my sisters Melissa and Allie."

Willie shook their hands. "Ah, yes. I can see the sisterly resemblance."

"Steve." He made his grip a bit firmer than usual and held Willie's gaze, hoping the man saw enough of the warning there to not mess with them. He didn't like his given name and didn't go by it much, but he'd prefer this guy not know his last name.

"Scott."

"I'm Kim."

Collins breathed a bit of a relief that no one else had volunteered last names. Some bit of wisdom had gotten to them. Still, what else could they have done? It would have been rude not to respond to the man, and he could be completely innocent, and Collins could just be overly sensitive due to his job.

It was possible.

It was also possible that his aching shoulder was giving him a negative view of this Willie guy who seemed to appreciate the view Allie, Melissa, and Kim provided more than the Grand Canyon.

He didn't want to put a damper on anyone's trip, and Scott had been through way worse after his accident.

Scott got to his feet. "Ready to head out?" He glanced at Willie. "We've got a schedule to keep."

He'd remind himself to thank Scott later.

Chapter Thirteen

Allie knew Collins's shoulder hurt more than he let on as they retraced their route back to the visitor center, parked the truck, filled their backpacks with snacks and water, and hopped on the orange route bus to the south Kaibab trailhead. Of course, he didn't want to let on how much it hurt, which just made him seem like more of a hero, keeping the cost to himself.

After seeing the beautiful vistas from the rim, she was excited to descend a bit into the canyon itself. The dirt trail carved into the rocks and clung to the side of the canyon. The switchbacks were narrow enough that she couldn't imagine doing this when there were a lot of hikers going both ways. How did you pass someone when it required walking so close to the edge? She couldn't imagine.

Collins positioned himself toward the edge of the canyon and let her cling to the side of the mountain.

No one spoke much. The vistas were awe inspiring, and there were enough rocks and loose gravel that she needed to watch her footing. The trees that clung to the rocky outcrops were a testimony to nature's tenacity in the most challenging of environments. There was probably a lesson to be learned there too.

She was grateful for the concentration the hike provided and the distraction. Her mind had drifted to the call she needed to make to Glenn when they got back to camp and what information DataCorp might need. There was nothing she could do about it from here, so she needed to enjoy the time they had in nature.

Collins wasn't letting his sore shoulder slow him down, though he did only carry the backpack by one strap.

As the trail moved onto one of the fingers of rock projecting into the canyon, they broke out into full sunlight, and the canyon spread out before them. They continued down the trail as the sheer rock walls gave way to the flat expanse of Ooh Aah Point. It was aptly named. The sun hung over the rim to their left while endless carved plateaus of the canyon stretched out in front of them as the trail fell steeply away.

They arranged themselves on a cluster of rocks with the canyon behind them, taking selfies and group shots. She got one of her and Collins on her phone. That was going to be her new screensaver.

"I hate to leave, and I wish we could keep exploring this canyon from down here." Allie cast her gaze back up from where'd they'd come. "But what goes down must go back up."

Collins snugged her close and kissed her forehead. "We'll come back again and explore more. And we still have so many places to go and see."

"It might be sensory overload by the time we get back."

"That would be a nice problem to have."

They sipped on water and ate a few snacks before heading back up the trail. The views were different going this way, but just as spectacular.

At the top, they plopped on the benches waiting for the shuttle bus to take them down one more stop to Yaki Point.

Melissa looked at her smart watch. They had about an hour

until sunset, and Melissa was counting on watching it from Yaki Point. Kim was, too, and had brought her camera for this purpose.

When they swung onto the shuttle bus, Allie was grateful for the break. Her legs were worn out. This was more of a workout than she usually did. They got off with most of the rest of the shuttle passengers and made their way down to Yaki Point.

Kim studied the various angles and set up a spot, then Allie joined her. The sun hovered over the rim and was casting every layer of the canyon in a molten red glow.

The warmth of the day disappeared with the sun. She reached into her backpack to pull on her zip-up fleece and tucked her arms around her knees.

Collins slid his arm around her. "Warmer now?"

"Yes. Thanks. How's the shoulder?"

"It's fine." Though the tight lines around his mouth told another story, she didn't think he'd ever give her a different answer.

"I can't believe this is our last day here. It feels like we just got here."

"I know. There's so much to see. And I bet we'll feel that way about every stop."

She nodded. And she was glad Kim and Matthew were doing the cooking tonight. She was worn out and hoped her eyes stayed open long enough to enjoy the campfire.

As the sun slipped behind the rim, she almost felt like they should cheer, like for the end of a show. *Good job today, God. One of your better ones.*

And she realized it was true. No matter what happened with DataCorp or what Glenn did or didn't tell her, God was still in control creating amazing sunsets every day for her to enjoy.

WILLARD SMILED IN SATISFACTION AS HE LEANED AGAINST the picnic table at his campsite. His plan had worked. They always did. With an added bonus. He knew where they were headed next, which helped since Kim posted on Instagram after they'd been at a location.

And he had all their names.

He was mulling over his options with the noise of rambunctious kids in the background. This campsite was surrounded by families. Kids ran in and out of the trees and rode their bikes on the campground roads and through the sites. A pack of kids tore through the edge of his site on their bikes. Trailing them was a girl on a pink and white bike with a unicorn backpack. "Wait for me!" she wailed. She slid to a stop at the edge of the road, wobbling and putting her flip-flopped feet down for balance. "Guys! I'm telling Mom!"

The other kids were out of sight. Were they being mean and trying to ditch this girl? He remembered that feeling all too well. The collection of kids that belonged to his mother from her liaisons with men was vast and varied. But what they all had in common was a hatred of him. He'd been ditched, wedgied, swirly-ed, and stuffed in trash cans. Only Robert had been somewhat kind to him.

The girl looked all around, tears streaking her dirty face. Then she broke into sobs.

Willard set his beer on the picnic table and strode over to her. "Hey, are you lost?"

She nodded so vigorously her bike helmet slid down over her eyes. She shoved it back.

"I can help you find your campsite. Do you know which way it is?"

She pointed back the way she'd come through the trees.

Not overly helpful. "What kind of car do your parents have?"

"It's a minivan. A blue one."

Okay. Well they could walk around the campground until

they found a blue minivan that belonged to her parents or he found a ranger. Whichever came first.

He walked alongside her bike as they headed down the road in the general direction she came from. He scanned for a blue minivan. She couldn't have gone too far.

Sure enough, they'd only gone about a dozen campsites when her face lit up. "There it is!" She pedaled faster and turned into the campground.

He followed her enough to make sure it was the right place.

She ran up to a woman and gave a lengthy explanation about how the others had left her behind then she pointed back at him.

He lifted a hand. "Just wanted to make sure she got back okay."

The mom took a few strides in his direction. "Thanks so much. I told them to stay together."

"Good advice. You never can be too careful. There are some dangerous people in this world." He waved again and headed back to his own campsite, to continue thinking through his plan.

It was dark by the time they got back to the campground. Kim and Matthew pulled out the items needed to make the spaghetti on tonight's menu, along with a pre-packaged salad and garlic bread. Kim's stomach growled just thinking about it.

Her head still whirled from all she had seen today. She was torn between working as furiously as she could to capture all the inspiration and the frustration of knowing it was as futile as trying to catch the wind.

Luckily, Melissa's instructions were easy to follow. She was appreciating Melissa's attention to detail and schedule. While normally she might find it constricting, she instead found it freeing, not having to worry about what was coming next, just enjoying the moment.

The meat was cooked, so they just had to warm it up with the sauce and cook the pasta. The trailer had a small oven to toast the garlic bread. A cookie sheet wouldn't fit, but some foil worked just fine.

Matthew had turned out to be a fun companion. She wasn't sure what this trip would be like with people she hardly knew. Scott and Collins were like brothers to her. Allie had helped find her condo, and she was sweet. But Matthew had been a pleasant surprise. He was always up for something fun and more than willing to include her. He thought her ideas were cool and even made a decent assistant, helping her with camera angles and lighting.

The trailer rocked as Matthew came back in lugging a big pot of water. Kim lit the burner so he could set it to boil.

"This may take awhile. These trailer burners aren't very powerful."

Kim nodded. "I'll start reheating the meat and add the sauce. We won't put the garlic bread in until the pasta goes in." She dumped the ingredients from their plastic bags into another pot.

Matthew plopped onto the dinette cushion. "So today was pretty cool. Have you looked at your pictures yet?"

"Not yet." She reached up on her bunk and pulled her DSLR camera and phone down. She put the phone between them on the table and opened her photo app. They scrolled through the pictures. "Wow. These turned out better than I thought."

Matthew looked up at her. "You're a good photographer. You have an eye for composition, the light. Have you gotten more ideas for your clothing line?"

She nodded as they continued to swipe. "Yeah, just a lot of rough ideas. But I'm thinking about more natural lines, flowing, with muted colors inspired by the reds, golds, and greens of the canyon and the trees. Maybe some chunky jewelry with native designs. Just a lot of possibilities. My head is spinning right now, but tomorrow during the drive I'll get out my sketchbook and work."

Matthew grinned. "I've never chauffeured an artist before."

She smacked him on the arm. "Have you chauffeured anyone before?"

"Well, no, but…"

She jumped up and stirred the meat. The water hadn't boiled yet. She enjoyed Matthew's attention. He had a way of looking at her like she was the only person in the world, like he was truly interested in what she had to say. It wasn't something she was used to. She loved her brother, but he treated her like she was still his teenaged little sister.

It didn't hurt that Matthew was a hottie. Lanky, with a swath of hair that he was constantly brushing out of his eyes. She was sure it helped him in his job in sales. What woman could resist his attention?

But, she had to remind herself, he probably turned that charm on every woman he met. She'd have to be careful not to take his attention too seriously.

She checked on the not-yet-boiling water and slid back into the dinette bench. Matthew's gaze was on her, something more serious replacing the usual mischief in his eyes. "What?"

He lifted a shoulder, not taking his gaze off her. "I don't think I've ever met anyone like you. Creative yet determined. You know what you want. You don't let others discourage you. You see the world through some sort of magical lens." He smiled and leaned forward. "You've made this an unexpected trip, Kim Taylor."

Warmth rushed through her body, probably setting her face aglow. She wasn't sure what to say. Picking up her camera, she flicked it on to review today's images. But then she raised her gaze to his. It hadn't moved. "You, too, Matthew."

Before either could say anything, the trailer door opened, and Allie stepped in. "Smells great!"

———

ALLIE PULLED THE CURTAINS TO HER BUNK SHUT AND pulled on a pair of fleece-lined leggings. The cool night air was too much for her capris. Then she grabbed her phone and headed outside, calling Glenn as she paced the far edge of their campsite. Scott and Collins had a fire going. That would feel good.

Glenn picked up. "How's your trip going? And why are you calling me?" He laughed.

She joined him. "It's been great, just fantastic. But I got a weird text from Edward asking if I'd gotten his email. But I don't have anything in my inbox or on my phone. It just struck me odd that he'd text me on a weekend to ask about an email, so I thought I'd see if you had any thoughts on the matter."

"His message didn't say anything other than asking if you got his email?"

"Right. My direct contact information was on the proposal, so I don't know why he would have emailed the corporate account, if that's what he did."

"Ah. That sounds like Jacobsen. He likes to push the edges, check out the information that you didn't give him. So he might have seen how he could contact you in ways you didn't provide, just to see what happens. He fancies himself a black hatter."

Allie laughed. "This isn't corporate security or trade secrets."

"He's got quite an active imagination, from what I hear."

"So what do you make of it? Is there anything I should do?"

Glenn was quiet for a moment. "I'm just guessing here, but if he was trying to poke holes in your responsiveness, to see how available you would be to him, he might have tried the office number or email. The request itself was probably inconsequential. He was likely just seeing if he could reach you on the weekend and how fast you would get back to him."

"So regardless, I need to get back to him. Even though I don't know what was in his email and I'd have to admit that." She rubbed her forehead.

"It's a risk. It would be better if you knew what happened. I don't think anyone else at DataCorp would reach out over the weekend unless there was something specific they needed."

"That's the thing that worries me. What if I forgot something in the RFP or they needed additional information?" Being rear ended had really shaken her up in more ways than she had imagined.

"Even if Jacobsen called, it's not an unreasonable boundary to return his call first thing Monday morning. You could check in to see if they needed any additional information."

"Unless being hyper responsive is what he's looking for."

"Then you have to decide if that's the person you want to be or if that's the kind of client you want."

She wasn't sure she had a choice. Without the DataCorp contract, things would get tight soon if something else didn't come along quickly.

"You're right. I'll just check in tomorrow morning mentioning the text and asking if there is anything they need."

"Sounds like a reasonable plan. Just remember two things."

"What's that?"

"With Jacobsen it's always Edward, never Ed. Certainly not Eddie."

"I'll remember that." She wasn't one to give people nicknames unless they were her close friends, so she didn't think she'd mess that one up. But it was a good reminder.

"And two, try to enjoy your vacation."

"I will." She grinned as she hung up. She always felt better after she talked with Glenn.

Collins walked up and slid an arm across her shoulder. "What did Glenn have to say?"

She gave him a quick recap.

Collins nodded and took a step away.

"Oh, Collins? Get a plastic bag with some ice for that shoulder." She gave him what she hoped was a winning smile that would make him do her bidding.

"Allie…"

She raised her eyebrows.

"Fine." He gave her a sardonic grin before wandering off.

Melissa walked up. "Did you get ahold of Glenn?"

"I did." Allie gave her a quick recap.

"You are on vacation," Melissa said.

"I know. But Edward doesn't know that, and I don't want him to." She paused. "Things are not good financially. A solid client didn't renew their contract because I'd done too good of a job, and they didn't need me. I need the DataCorp account."

Melissa studied her. "You can always come to me for help."

"I know." But she didn't want to have to. She wanted to make it on her own. She stared up at the vast sky beginning to be dotted with stars. Maybe she should find a way to head back home. This job was too important.

But so was this trip. And there would always be some job to chase after. Where was she going to draw the line? Wasn't that what Glenn was saying? Didn't she want a life outside of work, maybe even one with Collins?

Melissa studied the sky with her. "Remember that glow-in-the-dark book we had on the constellations?"

"Yeah. I still can't remember them, though."

"But God can. And he remembers you too." Melissa pulled her in for a quick hug.

"I need to remember that." God was in control. This wasn't too big for him to handle. "Thanks, sis."

Melissa smiled and walked over to Scott.

Collins came up, holding ice on his shoulder. He pointed to it and smiled. "Following doctor's orders. Everything work out okay?"

"Yeah. I'll call Edward Jacobsen in the morning before we leave and see what he wanted."

"Dinner's ready!" Matthew called from the picnic table where he'd set a lantern, a big pot, and a big bowl.

The smell of tomato and garlic wafted toward her, making her stomach growl. She was starving. Tonight would be a good opportunity to trust in God, not worry about what Edward might say to her tomorrow, and get some sleep.

Collins saw his chance to talk to Scott when they were on clean-up duty after dinner. They were in the trailer putting the leftover food away and cleaning the few dishes that weren't disposable. "What do you make of that Willie guy?"

"I don't like him. Seemed a little too friendly." Scott wiped out the spaghetti pot.

"That was my read too." He'd set his ice pack aside to clean up. Allie had been right. It did help. He'd put it back on when they were done. "I'm not thrilled that Matthew let him know our plans."

Scott nodded. "Yeah, but they were general enough. It's not like the guy knows where we're staying. And plenty of people will be at Monument Valley and Arches, even this time of year." He turned and looked at Collins. "It's possible we're both just feeling overprotective. The guy could just be harmless enough, lacking social skills, and entranced by the beautiful women in our company." He grinned.

Collins shrugged, the movement reminding him he needed more ice. He put away the freshly washed dishes. "He could be lonely. He seemed to be traveling alone. Most people who camp are friendly and helpful."

Scott nudged Collins's good shoulder. "Besides, even with that bad shoulder of yours, we can take him if he tries anything."

"True." Collins chuckled.

"How is that shoulder, anyway? And don't lie." Scott pointed a dishtowel at him.

Collins reached for the icepack and plopped it on. "I reinjured an old rotator cuff injury. It hurts, but the ice and ibuprofen are helping. There's not much else to be done. I just have to remember not to use it. It's a good thing it's my left shoulder."

"Don't try to be macho for the women. If you need anything, let Matthew know." Scott grinned. "That kid has more energy than both of us put together."

Collins laughed and followed Scott out of the trailer and to the campfire. Those special s'mores were calling his name.

Kim was assembling her s'mores ingredients on a plate as he walked up. He hadn't done a good job of checking in with her like he promised Kyle he would. "How's the trip going for you?"

"Good. I'm getting a lot of ideas."

"Having fun? Are you okay riding with Matthew all the time?" He lowered his voice.

It was hard to tell in the light of the lantern sitting on the picnic table, but it looked like her cheeks reddened. "Um, yeah. Us young people have more fun than you old folks." She nudged him.

"Hey! Be grateful your brother isn't here."

"Oh, I am. I may not have gone on trips with these folks, but I've been around them enough to see what trouble they can get into. My brother's usually right in the middle of it. Remember last year with Melissa? And then last summer with Sarah? And Heather last year? They attract trouble like a magnet. I'm just glad the rest of them aren't here. Should make for a much more peaceful trip."

From her mouth to God's ears, as his mother used to say.

But it reminded him that he should text Kyle and get an update on the assault cases and the guy who'd rear ended Allie.

Chapter Fourteen

The next morning after breakfast, Allie took her phone to the edge of the campground. Collins had showed her where the Arizona Trail was, and she still had cell service, but it was quiet over here. She felt bad leaving breakfast clean up and the packing up to the others, but they all assured her that it was fine, that she needed to go take care of business.

She pulled up her contact information for DataCorp and asked for Edward Jacobsen, deciding not to call or text him on the number he had texted her from.

"Edward, it's Allison Ellis. Just checking in with you to see if you needed more information on the proposal."

"Ah, so you did get my message. I was wondering since I didn't hear back."

Allie didn't take the bait. She refused to apologize for not responding to a business call on the weekend. If it were an existing client with an emergency, that was one thing. But she'd spent a lot of time thinking about what Glenn said last night. She didn't want to be at the beck and call of a client who wanted something that could easily wait until Monday. She was going to have to trust that if God wanted this business to succeed, he'd supply the clients. And if that wasn't DataCorp, then it would be someone else. But making the decision and carrying it out were two different things.

"What did you have a question about?" She kept her voice calm and even.

"I was looking through your proposal. It's impressive. I'm particularly interested in the work you did for Davis Marketing's relocation. You hit the highlights here, but do you have more details on the work you did for them? They were the closest comparison on your proposal to what we're trying to accomplish."

"Absolutely. I can send over the proposal package I wrote for them, outlining the details, and add an explanation of how the final project turned out. I believe their contact information is there as well if you'd like to contact them to ask them directly about their experience with my firm."

"Yes, I plan on doing that. I would like more details of the project first."

"I'll get those right over to you."

After she ended the call, a large weight fell off her shoulders. Her step was lighter. Edward seemed satisfied with her response and was even excited about the fact that she had done similar work for another firm. It seemed like she had a real shot at this. And she knew Jim Davis would give her a glowing review.

Now she just had to figure out how to access that information without her laptop.

As she entered their campsite, Collins looked up from checking the trailer hitch. "How'd it go?"

She tilted her head. "Potentially good." She gave him the recap. "I just need to figure out how to give him the info he needs without my laptop. How's the packing up going?"

"Good. By the time we do this a few more times, we'll be a well-oiled machine."

"Just how Melissa likes it." She stepped inside the trailer where Melissa was securing things. "Thanks for doing all the work."

Melissa turned. "How'd the call go?"

"He likes what I sent him, and he wants more. And I have it. I just don't know if I can get it to him from my phone. Let me check really quick then I can pitch in."

"No need. We're nearly done."

Allie plunked on her bunk and opened a browser on her phone, connecting to the cloud server. She went through her file hierarchy. They weren't a current client, so it wouldn't be in that folder. She looked in the Archived folder. Only one client folder was there.

She wanted to smack herself in the forehead. Of course. It was one of the files she'd pulled off the external hard drive at the office. It was on her laptop. At home. That's what happened when she got rear ended and discombobulated.

Now what was she going to do? She had just promised Edward that she'd get them to him ASAP.

How else could she reach those files? She could conceivably get them from the backup server, but that was slow, and her connection here wasn't good. Could she even download them via her phone and forward them? She wasn't sure. Regardless, the time-consuming attempts would put them behind schedule.

If they got too far behind, they'd be setting up camp in the dark. No, she didn't want to make her problem everyone else's problem. And she wanted Collins to continue to see her as a strong, capable business woman. She also didn't want to run to Melissa for help. She was going to figure this out on her own.

Once they left Tusayan, she'd have very little cell phone connection until they got to Moab tonight.

She picked up the phone and called Rachel.

COLLINS SLID THE LAST TENTPOLE INTO THE BAG. ALLIE hadn't reappeared from the trailer yet. Hopefully she'd be able to get what she needed sent off and then be able to relax. They were going to see some spectacular scenery today, and he wanted her to be able to enjoy it and not worry about work.

Scott and Matthew had hitched the trailer to the truck. He let those two do the manipulating of the hitch and locking it in so he could keep from straining his shoulder. And Matthew and Scott didn't seem to resent Collins's lack of help at all. They jumped in to protect his shoulder without being asked. They were good guys, and this had been an enjoyable trip so far.

He could use another cup of coffee, though. He'd send Matthew and Kim over to the Starbucks across the road before they left. He'd had trouble sleeping. He'd fallen asleep okay, but he really needed something under his shoulder to support it. He ended up wadding up a couple of sweatshirts to shove under it. But the pain made for a restless night.

Kyle had texted him back. The assault victims were working with Heather as a sketch artist to create a composite of their attacker, assuming he was the same one. And Kyle promised to compare it to the driver's license photo of the guy who rear ended Allie. But not until they had finished with Heather. But mostly he told Collins to relax, enjoy his vacation, and leave the detective work to him.

Collins conceded Kyle had a point. They were in another state, away from all that was happening back home. He should enjoy it while he could.

He'd let Scott drive some of the way today. It was over four hours to Monument Valley. His shoulder would probably need ice some of that time. Then it was another two and a half hours to Moab. Melissa had planned it that they could spend about two hours in Monument Valley and still get to Moab with about half an hour of daylight to spare to set up camp. Of course once they crossed into Utah, they'd be in Daylight Saving Time, which Arizona didn't participate in. So they'd lose an hour.

At least Allie was happy after her conversation with the DataCorp guy. He hoped to take her on a date when they were in Moab. It was a big enough town that they should be able to have a real date with just the two of them. The group atmosphere was fun, but he wanted some time with just her.

Allie was chewing on her lip as she stepped out of the trailer, a contrast to the springy steps that had marked her going in. Her backpack slung over her shoulder seemed to hold the weight of the world.

"What happened?"

She told him about the requested files on the external hard drive and her options, her tone artificially upbeat. "I left Rachel a voicemail and a text with specific instructions on what to do. I know I won't have cell service until Moab. And considering I told Edward the information would be coming soon, I hope she does what I've asked." But her worried body language told the true story. She didn't expect Rachel to do it.

"If I had an extra key to my townhome, I could send someone over there to get the files off my laptop. But Melissa has the extra key. Or maybe I'll be able to get them using my phone once we get some strong Wi-Fi." She scrubbed her hand over her face. "It'll be fine, one way or the other."

Collins didn't think she believed that and wished he could help her. He didn't like feeling helpless, but there was literally nothing he could do. He handed her his cell phone. "Watch the bars on my phone. We have different carriers. If I have more service, we can pull over and you can try Rachel from my phone."

Her smile to him was heartfelt and warm. "Thank you."

It was the least he could do. He just wished it could be more. He'd keep thinking.

They loaded up into the various vehicles and, with Starbucks in hand courtesy of Matthew and Kim, they were out of the park by nine a.m. and on the road, retracing their path through the park to Desert View Drive, the Watchtower, and headed out the east entrance.

Once they left the park, the scenery looked like much of the high desert anywhere in the Southwest. Creosote bushes, scrub oak, chaparral, rocks, and gravel stretched on either side of the pavement along the flat horizon.

"Time for the Ungame." Melissa rustled around in her backpack.

He glanced at Scott who shrugged.

"What's that?"

"Just the best road trip-slash-campfire-slash-sleepover game ever."

He caught Allie's grin in the rearview mirror. "It's kind of a get-to-know-you game. There are two levels of questions on the cards. Level Ones are more lighthearted. Level Twos are more introspective and personal. We used to play it on every trip."

"Who wants to go first?" Melissa asked.

"Since you and Allie know how to play it, why don't one of you go first and show us?" Scott suggested.

"All right. I'll take a Level One." Allie took a card from Melissa. "'Describe an ideal vacation.' Wow. Does this road trip count?"

"Good answer." Collins chuckled. "But isn't being honest one of the rules of this game?"

"It doesn't have any real rules," Melissa said. "You can pass if you don't want to answer. And you can't make a comment unless you get a Comment or Question card."

"I can answer. It's only a Level One. Let's see. Someplace warm, near a beach with *warm* water."

Everyone laughed. The Pacific wasn't known for its warmth and even in August could barely get to seventy degrees.

"Maybe a hammock where I could read and nap. Oh, and get a massage." She handed the card back to Melissa. "See? It's that easy."

"I'll go next," said Melissa. "And I'll even take a Level Two. 'Share a childhood experience with death.'"

Wow. These did get deep. He could see why it was good to have the option to pass if you didn't want to answer. Was there any topic he wouldn't want to discuss with them? He wasn't sure.

"We had a dog that died when we were kids. I think that was the first real death that I had experienced. He was old, but completely lovable. But he got so sick we had to put him down. The house felt empty without him."

Allie gave a slow nod. "I remember him." She glanced around. "I think supportive comments are okay."

"Scott, you're next," Melissa said. "One or two?"

"Uh, One."

Melissa handed him a card.

"'Talk about a childhood experience that changed you forever.'" He turned the card over. "This is a Level One? Um, well, my brother was killed by a drunk driver when I was ten." He paused a moment. "It changed the dynamics of our family forever. I occasionally wonder what we would be like if Christopher had lived."

Collins never would have guessed that the almost-cocky naval aviator would have had such a tragedy in his past. He didn't have anything so tragic. In fact, he didn't have much to complain about at all growing up.

Melissa took the card Scott handed her. "Collins, Level One or Two?"

"One." He was almost afraid to look. "Scott, want to read it to me so I can keep my eyes on the road?"

"'How do you think your mother would describe you?'"

"Hmm. My mom likes me." Everyone laughed. "I'm an only child, so it's hard to have any perspective on this, but while I don't think either of my parents wanted me to be a cop, they're proud of me." He glanced back at Allie. "And she's really going to like the house I just bought."

Chuckles went through the cab, lightening the mood.

The road occasionally cut through the rocky folds of the earth, and off to the north they could see a smaller gash in the horizon that was the Little Colorado River. He pointed out the window.

"This area seems so barren and endless, and then you come

across something spectacular like this out of nowhere. Want to stop?"

Down the road was a sign for the Little Colorado River Gorge Overlook. Collins pulled into the parking lot. It was a good chance to stretch their legs. He took Allie's hand as they made their way along the wide rock steps along the blue railing. They studied the landscape in silence. The gorge was much smaller than the Grand Canyon, with a smaller, muddy river at the bottom. But it was still impressive.

She handed him his phone. "You have some texts." Her voice sounded calm, but she wrapped her arm around her waist.

What was that about? He took his phone. A text from Lauren. Ugh. "I guess Lauren's following our progress on Instagram. She's been taking this getting back in touch thing a little too seriously." He swiped the message away.

"Aren't you going to respond?" A cloud of worry floated through Allie's gaze.

"Nah. She can find out what we're up to by following Kim." He squeezed Allie's hand and handed the phone back to her. "Unless you want to respond to her?"

Allie lifted a shoulder. "She didn't text me."

He didn't know what to say to that, so he didn't say anything.

Back at the truck, everyone helped themselves to waters and snacks.

Collins tossed the keys to Scott. "Mind driving a bit?"

"Not at all."

They switched positions and were back on the road, this time in a starker, more desert landscape.

"Another round?" Melissa asked, leaning forward and looking between the guys.

"Sure," Scott said. "But this time, I dare you all to go to Level Two."

Melissa scoffed. "There's no daring in the Ungame."

He shrugged. "Makes the whole 'getting to know you' thing go faster."

She shook her head. "It's not always about speed, Flyboy."

He lowered his aviator sunglasses to look at her in the rearview mirror. "But it's fun."

Laughing, she handed him a card. "Just for that, you can go first. I'll read it since you're driving. 'Share your feelings about financial security.'"

He laughed. "Well, I work for the US government, so I think that answers that question."

At the intersection with Highway 89, a large, desert-inspired roundabout greeted them, the red-and-black center circle bricks laid in a native design. They followed the highway north.

"I'll go next." Allie took a card. "'Share something you enjoy doing with your family.' Road trips?" She laughed. "Actually, that's kind of true. We always enjoyed looking at maps and planning trips. And Mom's idea of fun was piling us all in the minivan and heading off to parts unknown for the day. Sometimes it was great. Sometimes it was not so great. But we often played the Ungame to make the time go faster."

Melissa cleared her throat. "Except Mom never really played. It was just us kids."

"What do you mean? She played with us."

"She pretended to, but if the question was at all personal, she made a joke or passed or changed the subject."

"I don't remember that."

"It's because you're younger." Melissa's voice had grown taut. She handed a card to Collins. "You're next."

Okay. He never would have guessed about the dynamic between Allie and Melissa that he was seeing hints of on this trip. Maybe it took this kind of intense time together to really know people. That and the Ungame.

"'Talk about a recent news story that has captured your interest.' Well, given my job, we're often the ones investigating the stories behind the news. I guess the most recent string of

Realtor attacks has caught my attention. Up in Holcomb Springs, I didn't deal with anything that serious, and it was a nice break." He caught Allie's gaze. "I'm just glad Allie doesn't show homes to people she doesn't know. Sometimes it all hits a little too close to home."

In Cameron, they stopped to use the facilities. The historic Tanner's Crossing Bridge crossed the Little Colorado there.

Matthew ran up to the chain-link fence that cordoned off the bridge. "Too bad we can't walk across it. I bet the view of the river from the middle is awesome."

He pulled out his phone. "Ooh, I have a signal. Let's see what Wikipedia says. Huh. This was the longest suspension span west of the Mississippi when it was built in 1911. It provided a northern access route to the Grand Canyon and was damaged by an overload of sheep in 1937." He looked up. "I didn't expect to learn that on this trip. Who knew sheep could overload a bridge?"

"I'm just surprised that Melissa has rubbed off on you. Usually she's the one reading us facts about historical sites and points of interest." Allie checked her phone then shoved it back in her pocket.

But Collins's phone had service. He unlocked it and handed it to her. "Use mine."

"Thanks." She tried Rachel again. Her face said it all as she left another voicemail and a text saying she was calling from Collins's phone and to reach her at this number instead.

He pulled her aside and took her in his arms. "Lord, we bring this situation before you. We know none of it is hidden from you or out of your control. We'd love for Allie to be able to relax on this trip. Please let Rachel do her job and return Allie's call and send off the appropriate documents. That's what we want. But, Lord, we leave it in your hands and your plans. You know what is best. Please cover Allie with your peace. Amen."

She pulled back and looked at him, her eyes brimming with tears. "Thank you. That is the sweetest thing. I appreciate you praying with me and for me." Her shoulders didn't seem as bowed down as they had before. "I've done all I can do. Whatever happens is in God's hands."

He'd done something for her. Maybe it was the most important thing he could have done.

ALLIE FELT LIGHTER AS THEY GOT BACK IN THE TRUCK. She'd seen Melissa's worried eyes on her and was determined not to let her problems show. She had to remind herself God was in control. And to remind Melissa that she was a grown adult who could handle her own situations.

They headed up Highway 89 to Highway 160 where they turned northeast.

"Melissa, it's your turn to take a card," Allie reminded her.

"'What kind of emergency scares you the most?'" Melissa paused a moment. "Last year I might have said getting trapped by fire. But since we've lived through that—" Scott reached back and squeezed her knee— "I don't know. I think something where someone I care about is in danger and I can't do anything to help."

Nods went around the truck. And they sat in the quiet. It wasn't uncomfortable. Allie thought about what everyone had said, particularly Melissa's words about Mom. Melissa had a more strained relationship with Mom than any of the siblings. It was probably because she'd borne the brunt of caring for all of them longer than Allie had. But it shaded her view of anything Mom did.

Allie's view of her mother shifted, like those old View-Master slides when, if you didn't press the lever enough, the picture didn't advance all the way, leaving a white paper border through your vision. In the cab of this truck, speeding down the desolate highway in northeastern Arizona with some of the most dear people in her life, one image had been replaced with another. Melissa's tension, her longer relationship with Mom, gave credence to her words, and Allie could see the truth of them from her adult perspective looking back. No, Mom had never answered the hard questions, the deep questions of life. Ever.

Melissa handed Collins a card. "Read this for Scott."

"Level Two, huh?" he asked. "Guess we're not messing around."

"Go big or go home," she sassed.

"'Say something about illness and how it has affected your life,'" Collins read.

"Did you peek at these?" Scott glanced at Melissa in the rearview mirror.

"I swear I didn't." She raised her hands. "It's the weird thing about this game. It's like it reads your mind."

"Hmm." Scott didn't seem to believe her. "Well, my traumatic brain injury last year turned my life upside down. Or maybe it was right side up. Anyhow, it was life changing. Ultimately, though I couldn't see it at the time, God has used it for good." He reached back and patted Melissa's knee.

"Allie." Melissa handed her a card.

"'Talk about a joyful time in your life.' Hmm."

Collins swiveled his gaze toward her.

Did her happiest moment involve him? So many of her high school memories did. But hadn't she had fun since then? The pressures of being an adult, going to college, learning her business and going out on her own hadn't left a lot of time for the kind of fun she'd had in high school, where the combination of freedom and independence had created unique opportunities. "We had a lot of fun in high school with the youth group. The white water rafting at summer camp that we talked about earlier." Her memory slid to a moment where it was just her and Collins walking along the river's edge. Where she hoped… Her face heated. "Uh, I think they all involved being in nature and doing things with a group of my friends. So maybe this trip will be my new happiest memory." She met Collins's gaze as he smiled.

Lauren had also been on that trip, though she and Collins hadn't been dating. Did Allie have anything to worry about now? Lauren had held on to Collins for an awfully long time when she hugged him at Macayo's. And now she was texting him. Maybe it was just friendship. Because if it were something more, Allie wasn't sure her heart could take it.

When they reached Tuba City, Scott asked if they needed to stop for anything. Everyone said no. Collins asked if he wanted to switch driving.

Scott shook his head. "I usually drive a classic 'Vette. It's fun driving a truck. A lot more legroom and a higher view of the road. And this digital-display dashboard looks a lot more like my F/A-18 than my analog 'Vette's."

Allie tuned out the guys' discussion of cars and stared out the window. It seemed like it took a lot of courage to be one of the people that settled out here, especially in the days before air conditioning. Why did people decide to live all the way out in the middle of nowhere? It was something she always wondered. Why did people live where they did? Did they choose it? Follow a job or family? If her family had moved less growing up, would she have settled somewhere else? What if she had never gone to school with Collins? That thought turned her stomach.

She liked a lot of things about where she lived: the weather, the easy access to the beach, and being not too far away from the mountains or desert. But there were also a lot of people in Orange County, and it wasn't cheap. What would it be like to live in a small town? Or in the middle of nowhere? It would be a lot harder to do her job, that's for sure.

"Collins, it's your turn." Melissa handed him a card.

"'Complete the sentence: "I hope…"' I hope Scott doesn't wreck my truck."

Everyone laughed.

"Nah, in the spirit of being vulnerable like everyone else, I hope we have a great time on this trip and that we all get to know each other better. I'm honored to come along with you all."

They passed two rock formations called the Elephant's Feet. And she could see why. They looked like two stone feet mid stride. With few other rocks in the mainly flat area, they stood out for miles around. What had happened with the earth that caused these guys to be here? The endless wonders of nature were part of what she enjoyed about road trips. God sure was creative. Her life tended to be predictable and routine, even when she took on new clients. They were all looking for the same thing. But on a road trip, the unexpected was part of the allure.

They passed a lone gas station in the middle of nowhere. Why was it there? Who used it? People would probably look at her like a crazy person if she actually asked those questions. But for a moment, it was nice to let her mind wander wherever she wanted and not think about work.

"Melissa, you're the only one who hasn't gone three times," Allie prompted.

Melissa pulled her gaze from the window and drew a card. "'Talk about the importance of a religious faith in your life.' Well, like Scott, last year was a challenging year. I lost the company I had spent my whole professional career working in. I lost my mentor. I almost lost my life." She swallowed. "But I gained so much more. I realized that God had a bigger plan for me than I could even dream of. He was watching over me with his tender lovingkindness, his *hesed* in Hebrew. I never could have survived without him."

That seemed a good note to end the game on, and a companionable silence filled the truck as the desert slid by the windows. It gradually began showing more plant life and greenery as more scrubby bushes appeared and the highway swung north and northeast toward Utah. Mesas dotted the horizon more often.

At Kayenta, Arizona, they stopped and stretched their legs while Collins filled the truck's tank.

"We've got to stop by the Burger King," Kim said as she climbed out of Matthew's truck.

"Craving a burger?" Scott asked.

"Not really. They have an amazing display on the Navajo Code Talkers."

"At Burger King?" Melissa asked. "How'd I miss that?"

Matthew smirked. "You don't know everything."

She rolled her eyes at him. "Let's go. I want to see this."

They headed over to the Burger King and got drinks while they browsed the near-museum quality display. The Navajo code was the only unbreakable code in modern military history. It allowed the US to take Iwo Jima in World War II. The Burger King was owned and operated by the son of one of the Code Talkers.

As they left, Allie turned to Collins. "This is the kind of magic that only happens on road trips. You discover things you didn't even know you were looking for. You find heroes even in the middle of nowhere."

Collins switched places with Scott. "Last leg of the journey." He glanced at the navigation display.

As they left the town turning onto Highway 163 north, the rocks and dirt took on a ruddy hue, and the formations were more numerous and closer to the road. A rocky spire in the distance seemed out of reach, and they never seemed to get closer for the longest time. Kinda like some of her goals. Always just out of reach.

When they passed it, more buttes and mesas dotted the horizon in front of them. Such a contrast to the flat desert that had been their view for the early part of the day. The variety of nature never ceased to amaze her.

"I'm beginning to feel like I'm in an old western and cowboys on horses are going to ride up beside us any minute." Collins chuckled.

They crossed the border into Utah and promptly moved an hour ahead. They turned onto Monument Valley Road and headed to the visitor center. It was on Navajo Nation land, so the tribe ran the visitor center and park. Even from here, the iconic Mitten landmark was visible. They paid the entrance fee, picked up a visitor's guide, and declined to take a guided tour.

"Aw, those open trucks look like fun." Matthew laughed as they looked at the guided tour vehicles, basically small buses with no windows.

"Looks like a lot of dust," Kim said.

"We're in luck," Melissa said as they headed back to their cars. "The dirt road is fine for trucks, but tour buses can't make the trip. We'll have a fairly solitary journey. It should take about two hours to see the sights along the seventeen-mile loop. At least that's what I've planned for. It gives us about a half hour leeway before we're setting up camp in the dark." Melissa passed out lunch items to snack on.

They climbed back in and made the trek down the dirt road, the fifteen-mile-an-hour speed limit helping to keep their dust off Matthew's truck, though he stayed back a ways.

Melissa read from the guide. "There are eleven viewpoints. The first right up here are the Mittens."

They continued to drop down to the valley floor. The slow speed gave them plenty of time to take pictures out the window and enjoy the view such as the Elephant Butte and the Three Sisters, which were rock spires that looked a bit like a nun teaching her pupils. The road turned sandy just before John Ford Point, named after the man who made these iconic views famous with his western movies. They stopped to look out across the valley dotted with red spires and mesas carved by the elements and time.

Kim shot a number of pictures. "At sunset or sunrise, this would be amazing."

There was a large parking lot where locals sold their jewelry and other wares. A man offered to pose on his horse out on a bluff for a few dollars. Kim took him up on it.

The intensity of the scenery made it impossible for Allie to think about work, much less worry about it. Her problems seemed awfully small in light of the towering rock formations and God's magnificent creation.

At Camel Butte, the road narrowed and became a one-way track as it would loop around and rejoin this trail later. Rain God Mesa was the geographical center of the park, according to Melissa, their own personal tour guide. There was a lot of sand but not much in the way of springs at Sandy Springs Aquifer. The Totem Pole was another iconic point, set apart from another grouping of spires. To get closer, they would have to hire a guide with a four-wheel drive. But the photos they got from the road were pretty amazing too. Allie couldn't think of any other people she'd rather share this experience with.

The road began its return loop, and they passed the Balanced Rock, a large rock seemingly teetering on a much smaller one. At Artists Point, they stopped and got out, taking in the panoramic view that had captured the imagination of so many people around the world, defining what the American West looked like.

Two people were actually painting the view. Kim and Matthew stopped to chat with them. When Kim rejoined the group, she told them that the artists were staying in the area and came out every day at different times to capture the light and shadows playing across the scene. She nudged Matthew. "Sounds like fun, right?"

"I'm up for it."

Allie glanced at Melissa. Matthew coming back to the same scene day after day? Didn't sound like him. He liked new and exciting. Maybe Kim was a good influence on him.

At the Window, they got out and walked along a short trail to get a view of the Mitten between two buttes. Like at the Grand Canyon, Allie felt oversaturated with awe and beauty. It was almost too much to take in. She let it wash over her soul and fill up the tender places.

The final view was the Thumb, and they headed back on the main route. Even though they'd been on this road before, coming in the opposite direction made everything look totally different.

When they returned to the visitor center, Matthew joked, "We could stay here. It's only about two hundred dollars a night for a room. Then we could come back, and Kim could sketch in the good light."

Kim beamed up at him.

What had happened to Allie's little brother? Maybe the same scenery that was getting her mind off work was working its magic on him.

Chapter Fifteen

____

Collins was ready to get back on the pavement. His shoulder hurt from the jostling of the dirt road, though it was decently graded.

Matthew brought his phone over to Melissa. "When Kim and I talked to those painters, they told us about these great side roads with amazing views. And all of them are on the way to Moab. It'd just be a side detour."

Melissa shook her head. "I don't know, Matthew. We don't have that much leeway before the sun sets."

"Come on, Lis. It won't take that much time. We'll be fine." He gave her a grin that must melt female hearts everywhere.

Melissa looked at Collins. "What do you think?"

He glanced around at the group. He wasn't thrilled with more jostling. But that was his problem. They were out here and probably wouldn't be again for a long time. He shrugged his good shoulder. "Might as well see what there is to see. I'm in if you all are."

"Awesome!" Matthew brought his phone over and showed Collins what he was talking about.

But in case they lost GPS because the cell service wasn't great, Melissa brought over the map she had of the area, and they traced the route, though some of it wasn't on her map. It wasn't detailed enough.

"Don't forget, we have to stop at Forrest Gump Hill," Matthew said as they climbed back into the trucks.

Collins shook his head and laughed. But sure enough, as they left the visitor center and headed northeast on Highway 163, they came across a marker and pulled over. The sign read, THIS IS WHERE FORREST GUMP FINISHED HIS CROSS COUNTRY RUN. Looking behind them, they had another iconic view of the highway leading to Monument Valley.

Matthew hopped out and ran up the road, turned around, and came back as Kim took pictures of him. She also grabbed a few of the mesa-filled skyline.

They continued on to the little town of Mexican Hat on the San Juan River. They turned off onto a dirt side road that after a short jaunt led them to the rock formation the town was named after. On a red mesa, a balancing rock that looked a lot like a sombrero hovered over a stack of smaller rocks.

Matthew and Kim tried to get a picture that made it look like he was wearing the rock sombrero.

Allie took some deep breaths when they were outside the truck. She looked a little green.

Collins slid his arm around her shoulders. "Are you okay?"

She nodded. "I think I'm just a little stressed about the Data-Corp thing. Trying not to be." She smiled at him, but it wasn't very convincing. "I'm going to grab a water. I think it'll help. Lunch isn't sitting well on my stomach."

Once they got back in the truck, his eyes drifted to the rearview mirror more often. She didn't say anything, but he didn't think she looked well. He hoped she wasn't coming down with something. There was nothing worse than being sick on vacation, unless it was being sick on a road trip.

Back on the main highway, they continued to Highway 261, where they turned east to Highway 316 and Goosenecks State Park. Which was aptly named. The San Juan River made three ox-bow bends tight together, making the river look as crooked as a goose's neck. They enjoyed the spectacular view perched on a dirt overlook a thousand feet above the river's edge.

"Man, if you camped here, you wouldn't want to wander around at night. You'd find yourself over the edge." Matthew peered down.

"It would be a good rafting trip, though. I saw a sign back in Mexican Hat." Scott slipped his arm around Melissa. "We should come back. This looks like a cute little place off the beaten path."

Kim shot photos from various angles, trying to capture the play of light and dark across the river-carved layers.

Collins popped Matthew on the shoulder. "You were right. This was a worthy detour."

Matthew grinned. "See? Told you, Lis."

Collins hoped he wasn't contributing to sibling rivalry. And the roads hadn't been too bad. Still… "Allie, do you have any more ibuprofen?"

Her brow furrowed. "Sure. How's the pain?" She dug in her backpack.

"Not too bad, but I'm hoping to head it off."

She spilled two pills into his hand. He downed them with half his water bottle. "Thanks. How are you feeling?"

"Better. I think the water helped."

"Next stop," Matthew hollered as they got back in the trucks. "Valley of the Gods. With a name like that, it has to be good."

They made their way back to Highway 163 until they reached Valley of the Gods Road. It was a less-iconic and less-traveled version of Monument Valley. They oohed and ahhed at the mesas, spires, and balancing rocks. It was a peaceful trip and exactly the kind of off-the-beaten-path place that Collins loved to find on vacations. Matthew had chosen well. And he'd probably hold that over Melissa's head for a while.

When it dead ended at Highway 261, they turned north on

the Moki Dugway. Collins pulled over and studied the map on his navigation system. Looked like a lot of switchbacks. He pulled up more information on the road and studied Melissa's map of the area. "Why is it called a dugway?"

"Because the miners used it to haul ore down for processing." Of course Melissa would know the answer.

Matthew appeared at Collins's window. "What's up?"

"Just seeing what kind of trouble you're getting us into. This road looks pretty tight in a few places. Are you sure it'll work pulling the trailer?" Something he didn't think Matthew had thought to mention to the folks who had told him about this side road.

Melissa flipped through her guidebook of the area. "Hmm."

"What?"

"Vehicles over twenty-eight feet aren't recommended." She leaned into the center console between Collins and Scott.

Matthew frowned for a minute then brightened. "Well, that makes sense for a long RV, but you can bend in the middle with the hitch. The trailer's only twenty-seven feet. We should be fine." Matthew tapped the window frame.

He glanced over at Scott and Melissa. "What do you think?"

Melissa sat back. "It's your call, Collins. You're driving. If you don't feel comfortable, that's fine. Matthew will get over it."

Scott glanced at the map and at the road. "I think we can do it. I'll drive if you want."

If they ruined Daniel's trailer, maybe it'd be better for Daniel to be mad at the guy who would likely be his brother-in-law soon.

Nah, if something happened, he'd rather be at the wheel. He looked at the map again. Well, why not? It was a road trip. Time for adventure. He just hoped he didn't regret it. Glancing back at Allie through the rearview mirror, he didn't think she looked any better, but she gave him a brave smile. Maybe the sights would keep her mind off things.

He put the truck in gear, and they headed out. The road

ascended on the side of a mesa, clinging to the cliff face, and eventually became dirt. But the views of the Valley of the Gods were spectacular. Collins concentrated on driving and not looking, since there were no guardrails, and he was pulling the trailer. If they survived, it'd be worth it.

On a couple of the switchbacks, the turns were tight enough that he was sure he was scraping the trailer against the rocks, pulling to the far side of the road so the trailer wheels wouldn't slip off the edge as they turned. He was glad there were no oncoming cars. His shoulder ached, since he needed both hands on the wheel. But he'd be more nervous if Scott were driving.

As far as the eye could see, there was no evidence of humans other than the road they were on. At the very top, 1,100 feet up from where they began, they started across the top of the mesa along Muley Point Road.

"I need to get out." Allie's voice was frantic, and he pulled quickly to the side of the road. She bolted out the door and to the nearest bush, losing whatever she'd had for lunch.

He hadn't been watching her, needing to keep his eyes on the road. He was just glad she was able to wait until there was a place to pull over.

Melissa followed her, bringing napkins and a bottle of water.

After a few minutes, the women came back to the car. Scott climbed in back. "Allie, sit up front. It will help."

She started to refuse, but Scott had already climbed in the back. "Thanks. I guess I must have gotten car sick. It's been so long since I rode in the back. I was fine on the highways, but I think the jostling on the dirt roads and the switchbacks got to me."

"You okay now?"

She nodded. "I feel a lot better."

"I'm just glad you made it out of the car," Melissa said from the back. "The last time you got car sick, you waited too long. We spent the rest of the day in a puke-filled car."

Allie's face reddened, but she didn't say anything. Just fiddled with the bottle cap on her water.

He studied her a minute longer then, satisfied she really was doing better, he pulled back onto the road. It was nice having her up here next to him. And he was glad he didn't have a sibling to tell stories about him.

They visited both east and west Muley Points. Here they really did feel like they were on top of the world. The view stretched far and wide, the mesas and canyons below them. It was a great contrast in perspective from the valley floor where everything soared above them. From here, it all looked like carvings into the crust of the earth.

When they got out, he slipped his arm around Allie, and she curled hers around his waist. What was even more spectacular was that they had all these amazing views to themselves. Vast, wonderfully lonely. It felt like they were the only ones in the whole area. That was a feeling you never had in Southern California. It was hard to believe there were still places as desolate as this.

His chest tightened at the thought of something going wrong—a blown tire, a medical emergency, or worse—that would make all this isolation a negative instead of a plus.

Reversing their path, they headed back up Highway 261 to State Route 95 headed east. They'd be making a big loop and generally heading toward Moab. He caught Melissa looking at her phone. She must be calculating how much time they had before it'd be dark.

For their final detour stop—which Matthew promised was unlike anything they'd seen to this point—they pulled into a small parking lot.

Collins's shoulder ached. He wanted to put ice on it, and the last thing he wanted was to hike up a rock-strewn trail. He could have stayed at the truck, but then Allie would have felt obligated to stay with him. And even if she hadn't, he didn't want to see pity in anyone's eyes. Scott had been through far worse than a stupid shoulder injury. He'd suck it up. It would be worth it. Melissa always planned well, and even though she hadn't planned this side trip, Matthew hadn't been wrong yet.

He joined the rest of the group on a two-mile hike along the Mule Canyon Trailhead to cliff dwelling ruins.

Once again, Matthew had called it. The rock had weathered away the roof on the cliff dwellings, and the shape and color of the remaining stone looked like tongues of flame licking at the roof. It was unlike anything he'd ever seen.

"It's so desolate out here. And with these abandoned ruins, it almost seems like we're the only people left on earth." Allie shivered.

"I was thinking the same thing. It's been weird to see so few cars." Collins squeezed her shoulder. If they had to survive some difficulty, could they do it? He figured the odds were in their favor.

Melissa nodded. "That's why this was such a good time to come. Not hot and not many people. Plus, this is more off the beaten path. Good call, Matthew." She looked at her Apple Watch. "But we've got to hustle if we don't want to set up camp in the dark."

He was not looking forward to that. He was going to let Scott drive the rest of the way and put ice on his shoulder.

***

MATTHEW FELT PRETTY PROUD OF HIMSELF AS HE followed behind the trailer on the highway toward Moab. Even this smaller state route was pretty, with steep rock walls lining both sides of the road at some points.

He turned to Kim. "See? It pays to talk to people and ask questions, to be willing to try something new and go off plan now and again."

"True, but I'm actually finding the plan freeing. I don't have to think about what's the best thing to do next because Melissa has already done that work. And we always know what we're going to eat." She laughed.

For once, Melissa had taken his suggestions seriously, and everyone had had a good time. They saw some spectacular things they wouldn't have seen otherwise.

Kim had been a great partner in this adventure. Instead of resenting being stuck with her, he loved it. She was as up for adventure as he was. "How did it go today? I bet you got some amazing shots."

"I hope so. It's so hard to take it all in. The vastness of Muley Points and the Goosenecks. I kept flipping between wide-angle and zoom lenses, trying to capture the wide-openness and the details that tell the story. The House on Fire ruins were unbelievable. Anyway, I can't wait to see what all I got on something bigger than the LCD screen on the back of my camera. I brought my iPad, so I can load the photos onto that and see what's up. I was part of a photo shoot last month with this famous fashion photographer, Zander Jakes. I wish I'd thought to ask him some questions."

She touched his arm, and white-hot electricity shot through him settling in his chest. "Thanks for thinking of this. I know it's got to be hard to go against Melissa's ideas sometimes. I know something about older siblings. But this was absolutely fabulous. I love going places other people don't know about."

He glanced at her briefly before turning his eyes to the road again. "Me too. I think we're going to have a lot of adventures together." He looked at her again. "Are you up for that?"

A smile brighter than the desert sun lit her face. "Oh yeah."

Now they just had to set up camp before dark and Melissa's wrath was unleashed. He grinned. He liked living dangerously.

THEY TURNED NORTH ON HIGHWAY 191 AND WERE BACK on their original course. Scott was driving, and Collins had insisted that Allie sit up front. She protested, because it meant Collins had to sit in the back. But given that the road still had some curves and hills, and her stomach wasn't quite itself, she was grateful for his insistence.

And she was glad that Collins had ice on his shoulder. She bit her lip. Should they find an urgent care and get it checked out?

Melissa's phone rang. "Matthew, what's up?" She rolled her eyes and lowered the phone, putting it on speaker. "You guys want to stop up here at Wilson's Arch? He says you can see it from the highway." She glanced at her phone. "We can make it quick. A few minutes won't matter at this point."

At everyone's nods, she told Matthew yes.

"I see the signs." Scott glanced back at Melissa in the rearview mirror. "Matthew's giving you a run for the money as activity director."

She scoffed. "He's just showing off for Kim."

The rest of the truck laughed. They weren't wrong. It'd been a long time since Allie had seen Matthew be so attentive to another person. He was growing up. On the other hand, she hadn't spent much time with him since he'd graduated from college and started his career. This trip was one way of making up for that. And she was glad Melissa had taken his suggestions in stride. Perhaps Scott had something to do with that.

But she also felt Melissa's anxiousness to get to the camp. Allie understood that. One way or another, she needed some good Wi-Fi. She'd given up on Rachel at this point, but she needed to get to her cloud server and get the information to DataCorp.

She debated explaining the delay. On one hand, she didn't want Edward to think she wasn't responsive or good with follow through. On the other hand, anything she'd say could make her look like she couldn't handle things. Her assistant was a flake, and Allie didn't have a good backup plan for when she was out of the office. Neither of those made Allie look good. So maybe she'd just let Edward draw his own conclusions. There was nothing she could do about it. And maybe it wouldn't even be a big deal to him.

Scott pulled over at the turnout. It was good to climb out of the truck and stretch her legs. The sandstone rose above them, and an arch broke through the middle of it. The late afternoon sun hit the rock nearly square on, lighting it with a warm glow. Kim was already out, Matthew helping her, getting her shots set up.

They didn't have time to climb up to the arch, but they did scramble a ways up the dirt mound that led away from the highway to get a better view.

Collins took her hand. "How's your stomach?"

"It's fine. Better, now that I can see the whole road." She smiled up at him. "Thanks for giving up your seat."

"Of course. No question." He turned and met her gaze. "I'd do anything for you, Allie."

Her heart did a funny flip in her chest, but she didn't quite know what to make of his words. She was used to doing the helping, not being helped. She squeezed his hand. "How's your shoulder?"

"It's fine."

She laughed. "That's my line."

After a few quick pictures, they got back to the trucks. "You want to ride up front now?" Allie paused with her hand on the door.

Collins studied her a minute. "Nope, you stay up there. We're almost there, anyway."

Back on the road, they passed Hole in the Rock, an unabashedly tourist stop with a giant lizard on the sandstone wall looking out over the highway. "No, Matthew, we're not stopping," Melissa said, even though he hadn't called. They all laughed.

Allie had to admit Melissa had been a good sport about Matthew's hijacking of her plans. But his ideas had been good ones. If they hadn't been... well, Matthew wouldn't have the opportunity to offer any other ideas the rest of the trip.

The sun hovered over the horizon as they drove through quaint Moab and pulled into the RV park. The red sandstone cliffs hid the sun as it made its final descent, washing the park in shadows as Melissa checked them in and directed them to their site. Luckily, it was a deluxe one without neighbors, allowing room for the tent and Matthew's truck. Since they had done this before and the lots had easy access, it wasn't difficult to get the trailer in position and unhooked.

Allie looked at her phone. "Melissa, did they tell you what the Wi-Fi was?"

Melissa pointed to the map sitting on the trailer table. "It's supposed to be on that."

Allie picked it up and found the name and password. "Hmm. It's not coming up. I'm going to check at the front desk. Can you handle the rest of this?"

"Sure. All the ingredients for the Texas Skillet Hash are precooked. I just need to mix everything together and warm it up."

"Thanks. I'll get the paper goods out when I get back."

Allie headed to the office in the darkening shadows. They had pulled in and gotten set up just in time, though they did have to use flashlights for the last part. They were all pretty wiped out, so she didn't think there would be a campfire tonight. It'd be close to eight thirty by the time they ate.

The office was dark. There was a sign in the window with an emergency number. She didn't think they'd consider the lack of Wi-Fi an emergency, even though it was for her. A smaller sign said, SORRY, THE WI-FI ISN'T WORKING. HOPE TO HAVE IT FIXED TOMORROW.

Great. That didn't help her tonight. Now what? She scanned the area as if the answer would magically appear. Perhaps Collins wouldn't mind taking her into town to find some Wi-Fi at a coffee shop. She hated to bother him with his shoulder being sore, but she knew he'd say yes. If it weren't so important, she wouldn't ask.

She hurried back to the trailer.

"Any luck?" Melissa looked up from stirring the skillet.

Allie pulled out the paper goods. "Nope. The office is closed. The Wi-Fi is down. I'm going to have to go into town." She surveyed the trailer. There was nothing else she could do. They were just waiting for the food to heat through. Restless, she stepped outside the trailer with the lantern and set it on the picnic table. The guys had finished setting up the tent.

Collins met her gaze. "What's up?"

"No Wi-Fi. Can you take me into town after dinner to find some?"

"Sure." He grinned and leaned close. "It'll be nice to have some alone time with you."

She gave him a soft smile. "Once I get those documents off to DataCorp, I'll be able to relax and enjoy it."

He squeezed her hand.

Melissa came to the trailer door. "Dinner's ready."

Everyone filed in and filled their plates then filed out to the picnic table lit by a lantern. Matthew asked the blessing and they dug in. The spiced meat with peppers, onions, tomatoes, and rice filled her mouth with flavor. Her appetite had returned as soon as they'd gotten to camp. Plus, everything tasted better camping.

It was Matthew and Kim's turn to clean up after dinner, so Allie grabbed her phone and her fleece and climbed into Collins's truck. They headed back down the highway until they came upon a little coffee shop. They turned in, and soon she was seated with a steaming London Fog tea latte and a cookie next to her phone. Collins had a cappuccino and a cookie.

"That caffeine won't keep you up?" Allie nodded at his drink.

"Nope. Never does."

"Sorry to work in front of you. I just hope this works" She logged onto the shop's Wi-Fi.

"Don't be. I'm happy to watch."

She gave him a wry grin. "Great. I don't feel self-conscious now or anything."

He gave her a devilish grin back. "Reminds me of our study sessions in high school. I spent a lot of time studying you."

She rolled her eyes at him, secretly pleased, then dropped her gaze to her screen and worked on accessing her cloud backup. She got to the site but couldn't find the files. It was designed for a computer, not a phone, so she had to keep enlarging the screen and moving it around to see everything.

She clicked on the help button and entered *downloading files.* A series of help articles showed up, including one on using mobile devices. She clicked on it, discovered she needed to download an app. She did. Then finally, she was able to find the files. Whew. She wasn't sure this was going to work.

Digging through the hierarchy of files, she found the one she was looking for. She opened the Davis file and sorted through it, clicking to download the files she needed. She sipped on her London Fog while they downloaded. She could even send them directly from the app.

"Despite my getting car sick and your sore shoulder, today was a pretty good day."

Collins nodded. "It was. Some spectacular scenery. And considering how many people there are where we live, I'm amazed that we found someplace as desolate as it was today."

"Tomorrow should also be amazing, but with more people."

"True."

Her files had finished downloading. She opened them, making sure they were what she thought they were. Okay, so far so good. Yes, Edward should like this.

"What's wrong?"

"There's a key file missing. It must not have gotten backed up to the cloud. So I still need someone to get to my laptop." She picked up her phone and tried Rachel again. Voicemail. She left another message and sent another text.

Why did she think this trip was a good idea? This DataCorp project could make or break her company. Rachel was nowhere to be found, which wasn't a shock. The only reason Allie came was to make sure Melissa had the trip she wanted. Well, and to spend time with Collins, if she was honest.

But was all of that worth the cost of her company? This could cost her everything she'd worked so hard for. She was always looking out for everyone else's interests, but no one seem interested in what she needed. Irritation built inside her and she sighed, staring at her phone.

"What?"

She met Collins's gaze. "This was part of what I was heading back to the office for that night I got rear ended. It's on my laptop. Maybe I should just figure out a way to go home. I don't know why I thought I could pull this trip off with the big proposal out there. Rachel's nowhere to be found, big surprise, and my company is hanging in the balance. I don't know." She opened another app on her phone. And it wasn't like she was anywhere near an airport to catch a flight back home. Though maybe she could find a rental car…

Collins reached across the table for her hand. "Allie, look at me."

She glanced up.

"Let's think this through. The missing document is just extra, right? Not something Edward asked for or even knows exists."

"Right. But it shows how perfectly I could do this job since I've done it before. It could make me stand out from the rest of the competition. And I need to do that."

He nodded. "Is it worth trying to reach your former client? Only you know the pros versus the cons."

She thought for a moment. His warm hand enfolding hers was reassuring. And it was nice to have someone working through a solution with her. Usually she was on her own. And even though Collins didn't know her business like Glenn did, he was still good at helping her talk through options and the decision-making process. He actually cared. Tears pricked her eyes. And she was forgetting the most important thing: God was in control. He knew what she needed, and He would provide.

She squeezed Collins's hand. "I'll send off what I have to Edward. If it looks like I should send him more info, I'll get in touch with Jim Davis if Rachel hasn't returned my call. In fact, I'll shoot him an email and let him know that DataCorp will likely be reaching out to him." She shook her head. "My neighbor has a key to my house, but she's not computer literate. I wonder if I could walk her through the process of how to access the files and send them to me." She drummed her fingers on the tabletop, thinking.

Collins drained his drink. "We could get a copy of your key made and FedEx it to someone. Maybe Glenn? He'd get it Wednesday."

She stared at him, then leaned over the table and gave him a quick kiss before she knew what she was doing. "You're brilliant!"

Then what she did soaked in. Her face heated. She hadn't just kissed him, had she? Oh she had. And it was their first kiss. Way to go. So romantic.

He just grinned at her.

Chapter Sixteen

The next morning, Kim was up early. She got ready quickly and began getting her gear together inside the trailer, while staying out of Melissa's way. Allie was in the tiny bathroom getting ready, and Kim was careful not to block the door. Kim wanted to get to Arches early to get some shots of the sunlight hitting a few of the key features. Melissa had suggested last night they see part of the park today and then explore some of the surrounding scenic areas and see the rest of it tomorrow.

When Allie and Collins had returned last night, they'd mentioned that they'd need to go to town again to take care of something, so they were also motivated to get to Arches early too. Maybe they could all get a group photo by the Greetings from Moab mural in town that looked like a retro postcard.

"Can I help with anything?" she asked Melissa, who was pulling items out of the cupboards.

"You can start the coffee, if you'd like."

"Sure."

Melissa started breaking eggs into a bowl. "What did you and Matthew do last night while everyone else was gone?"

While Allie and Collins had been gone, Scott and Melissa

had taken a walk around the RV park. "We sat in here and went over the photos I'd taken. I was able to put them on my iPad and play around in Photoshop. I put a few into black and white. The monochrome really emphasizes the geometry and land features. I thought they turned out well."

Melissa nodded, a smile playing around her lips. Did she suspect something more between Kim and Matthew?

Kim's face heated, and she focused on getting coffee cups out.

Allie began helping Melissa, and they discussed the day's schedule.

Other than focusing on a few key shots she wanted to get, Kim didn't care much about the itinerary. Her mind swirled with possibilities. Which also frustrated her because the little sketching she'd done in the car yesterday was far short of her imagination.

But she was enjoying the time with Matthew. Too much. His excitement was contagious, he had great ideas, and he was interested in her work. They were almost halfway through the trip, and it had become second nature to be paired with him in everything.

Which was a problem. She was falling hard for him. More than she should, but her heart didn't want to listen. And guys like Matthew were great until they moved on to the next shiny object. She and Matthew didn't even live in the same state.

She needed to rein in her heart. Maybe she wouldn't spend so much time alone with him. She'd seek out the other women. Except they were always tied up with their own men. Sigh. Well, she'd do what she could to stay part of the group.

Since there wasn't anything left for her to do, she double checked all her gear and battery levels. Coming home with a broken heart was not on her agenda.

Allie helped Melissa and Kim with breakfast, stirring the scrambled eggs in the pan, but her mind was on last night. The lack of sun definitely let them know it was early. Kim was up early, too, so they were all eager to see what Arches had to offer.

Allie still couldn't believe she'd kissed Collins last night. If she hadn't been so exhausted by the trip yesterday, it probably would have kept her up. She'd wanted him to kiss her. She'd never expected their first kiss to be instigated by her or in a coffee shop. She'd hoped for some romantic under-the-stars kiss. But she'd been impulsive and blown it.

Collins didn't seem to mind, though. Still, maybe they'd have a more romantic opportunity tonight. Plus, they needed to get back into town today in time to make any cutoff times. There was a hardware store in town and a copy center that did next-day shipping. She'd call Glenn and tell him to expect the key tomorrow.

"Did you put salt and pepper in the eggs yet?" Melissa held up the shakers.

"I can't remember." Her thoughts had definitely been elsewhere. Allie suppressed a sigh.

"I guess everyone can add it to their own." Melissa took them out to the picnic table.

As they were cleaning up breakfast, she wondered if she was making too big a deal out of the key. Going to all the trouble to FedEx her house key to Glenn in order that he could get a document off her laptop just so she could send it as an addendum to a proposal. In the light of day, it seemed a bit much. *Lord, I could really use some direction. Is it that important to rearrange everyone's schedules just to send off something that might not even be needed?* Could she let it go? Should she?

They repacked the ice chest with drinks and snacks. Scott had grabbed more ice from the resort store. And soon they were ready to hit the road. After looking at the map, Collins suggested Allie sit up front. Scott concurred, and Allie reluctantly took the front seat. But once they hit the road, Collins reached over the center console and took her hand. That was more than nice.

Once again, they crossed over the Colorado River, and in ten minutes, they were entering Arches National Park. The rocks seemed to greet and embrace them as they hugged the road on the way in.

After stopping at the visitor center, where Kim got shots of the Moab Fault glowing in the early morning light, they followed the road up the Moab Fault to the plateau that most of the park was situated on.

"Given the curviness of this road, it's a good thing you're sitting up front," Melissa said.

Allie nodded. Yes, she didn't need Melissa telling more embarrassing stories about her.

The fault made a 2,600-foot difference between the two sides of the valley. Four- to five-hundred-foot red sandstone mono-liths lined the road. Once again, her mind struggled to find perspective when everything was so huge.

The first pullout was Park Avenue, the eroded sandstone looking like New York skyscrapers, giving it its name. As they continued around the road, the next stop was the La Sal moun-tain vista. The still-snow-topped peaks in the distance contrasted with sandstone in the foreground. Back on the road they passed more sandstone formations with names. The Three Gossips looked a lot like the Three Sisters back in Monument Valley. In addition to the monoliths and sandstone formations, water, ice, and wind had eroded the sandstone into the stone fins that dotted the park.

They passed another balanced rock, this one 128 feet high. "It seems like every place has its own balanced rock," Allie said.

Melissa looked up from her guidebook. "Another one nearby fell over in the seventies. This one will too, someday."

Scott looked back. "Don't stand under it!"

Melissa rolled her eyes and laughed.

They kept going to the end of the park and the Devils Garden.

Melissa read from her park guide. "It's an easy hike on a sandy trail to the largest natural rock span in the world, Landscape Arch. It's 306 feet from base to base. But you can't walk on it. I can just see Matthew trying it so Kim would have a great shot."

At the trailhead parking lot, Collins came around and took Allie's hand. "Guys will do a lot of things to impress a woman they like." He winked at her.

Her face went hot. They weren't going to have any time alone today unless they went back into town together before taking the scenic route to Dead Horse Point. She didn't want to inconvenience everyone, so she'd reserved making her final decision until she saw how much time they had. But she really wanted to know what Collins thought about last night's kiss. Yet, she didn't want to ask him. So she'd spend most of today torturing herself, trying to read his mind and determine his thoughts.

She shook her head at herself. She was so ridiculous sometimes.

Matthew and Kim joined them, and they headed down the trail, walls of rock climbing up both sides. Signs everywhere warned them to stay on the trail and DON'T BUST THE CRUST, the fragile soil made up of microbes that were part of the delicate ecosystem of the park.

"Hey, there!"

They all turned around. The man they'd met at the Watchtower at the Grand Canyon was waving to them. Willie.

Allie pasted on a smile, but Collins stiffened next to her.

"Hey, I see you found us." Matthew grinned. "How long have you been at Arches?"

"Got here last night." Willie pointed back toward the road. "I'm staying in the Devils Garden campground. What about you all?"

"We're in an RV park in Moab." Matthew stepped closer to Kim.

Collins cut a sharp glance at him.

Willie gestured down the trail. "Looks like we're going the same place."

Collins nodded and tugged Allie down the trail, leaving the others to entertain Willie. What did he have against the man, anyway? Was he just being protective of her? If so, he was assuming a lot, considering there was much they hadn't talked about.

Determined to enjoy her surroundings, she pushed it all out of her head. Collins was a cop. It had to be hard to turn that off. She'd give him the benefit of the doubt.

Besides, Willie couldn't be a threat. It wasn't on Melissa's schedule.

The walls of rock hid the morning sun from view, casting them in the cold shadows. She hurried her steps to keep warm. The land opened up as they reached Pine Tree Arch.

Kim set up and took her shots of the warmly glowing red stone. "Okay, group shot."

Everyone assembled under the arch where Kim directed.

"Just show me what button to push, and I'll take the photo so you can get in there too," Willie offered.

Kim made a few more adjustments. "Sure. Thanks. Just push this button here. You'll hear the shutter click." She ran and jumped in next to Matthew.

"Say cheese!" Willie hit the button a few times.

Kim jumped out of the shot. "Thanks. Want me to take one of you in front of the arch?"

He waved her off. "No thanks."

They continued down the trail, more open and in the sun now. Allie studied Collins's profile. He was staring straight ahead, but his mind was clearly a million miles away.

She lowered her voice, though the others were behind them. "What don't you like about Willie?"

His gaze shifted to her for a moment, then he lifted his good shoulder. "Just don't. Can't really explain it other than when you've seen what I've seen over the years, you get a sense for people. It's not perfect. And maybe he's just got a lot of speeding tickets or whatever. But promise me something." He paused, glanced back, then looked at her steadily. "Don't go anywhere alone with him."

Allie's stomach twisted. Collins was serious. And she trusted him. Plus, why would she go anywhere alone with Willie? "I promise."

THE TRAIL TURNED SANDY, AND ANOTHER HIGH WALL OF stone blocked the sun. Allie shivered. Was it from what he'd told her about Willie? He'd debated bringing it up. He wanted her to have a good time, and she had enough to worry about with DataCorp. He didn't want her to worry about Willie too. That was his job.

What he really wanted to do was find a place where he could finish that kiss she started last night. For half a second, he'd been surprised. Then he'd only wished he'd done it first. But he'd been waiting for the perfect time, the perfect memory. Still, he had some ideas about tonight.

Matthew's voice floated up to him. "That one looks like Jabba the Hut."

He glanced at Allie and grinned. Matthew was irrepressible, but maybe Collins needed to have a talk with him. He was a little too free with their information. Normally, it wouldn't be a big deal. But given Collins's bad feelings about Willie, he wished Matthew would be a little less friendly and a little more circumspect.

"That one looks like Obi-Wan Kenobi," Scott said. "See the hood?"

"Yeah but we're looking at him from behind. It could be any Jedi. Darth Sidious even."

Allie laughed. "You'd think those two were brothers."

Landscape Arch came into view, delicately rising above the tumble of boulders beneath it. The morning sun shone on it, and Kim took her time getting all her shots.

Collins pulled Allie in front of him and wrapped his arms around her. "Better?"

"Yes, thanks. It's chilly."

"It's still early."

There were a number of arches and formations in the sandstone. Collins resolved to put Willie out of his mind. Short of the guy pulling out a weapon, there wasn't anything he could do to hurt any of them out here with plenty of people around. The trail looped back, and Collins let some of the tension drop from his shoulders. Even the one that still ached a bit.

The red sandstone contrasted with the dusty green of the pinyon pines and junipers. Kim would probably appreciate the design aspect of the color scheme, but it occurred to him that nothing ever clashed in nature.

At Navajo Arch, it was big and deep enough that they walked under it. Kim got a photo of them, but he noticed Willie slipped out of view. In fact, he hadn't been in any pictures or taken any selfies. Collins had seen him with his phone out but never saw him taking any actual photos. No crime in that, just unusual. Maybe Willie was just a weird dude who lacked social skills.

Partition Arch acted like a window with a view out onto the expanse of the Utah desert. As Kim and Matthew discussed the best angles and moved her gear around, Collins kept an eye on Willie. He never seemed to let Collins slip behind him. That awareness itself put him on alert. But as Collins watched him, nothing telling showed up, other than maybe a gaze that strayed toward Melissa a bit more often than anyone else.

The trail led up and on top of one of the fins that dotted the park. The rock looked slippery but felt more like sandpaper. Still, it was another excuse to keep Allie within arm's reach.

They finished the loop and returned back the way they came to the original trailhead.

"Have you folks been to Windows yet?" Willie asked.

"Nope. We're hoping to do that tomorrow night and catch the stars," Kim volunteered.

"We're actually leaving now and heading to Dead Horse Point and the Shafer Trail after lunch," Matthew said. "Ever driven that or any other scenic routes up here? Some artists at Monument Point told us about some great ones on our way here yesterday."

Collins glanced back to see Willie shake his head. "I haven't. This is the first time I've been in this area. But that sounds like a can't-miss spot."

"That's what I've heard." Matthew loaded Kim's gear into his truck.

Collins waited to see which vehicle Willie got into, but he just waved and headed toward the campground. Maybe that was the end of him. Collins considered following Willie to his campsite to get information on his vehicle. Though if the scenic routes today were as deserted as the ones yesterday, it'd be obvious if Willie got within twenty miles of them.

He stepped over to Matthew. "Let's keep our plans to ourselves. We don't know anything about this guy, and something about him rubs me the wrong way."

Matthew shrugged. "It's a public road."

"And given how desolate the roads were that we were on yesterday, it wouldn't take much for us to get into trouble fast." He clapped Matthew on the shoulder. "Look, it's an occupational hazard with me. I'm sure it's fine. But I'd rather be safe than sorry."

He walked over to Allie. "Do you want to run into town before we head out? Have the key with you?"

She tilted her head. "I don't know. I've been thinking about it. One, it'll take at least an hour to get the key made and send it off. And it seems like a bit of overkill." She bit her lip.

Melissa eyed them and walked over. "Honestly, I think you're fine. If they reach out to Jim Davis, he can send it on to them."

"True. Maybe I'll just check my email in town and see if Edward has replied."

It was unusual to see her uncertain. He pulled her into a hug. "Whatever you need. We should get gas anyway. I don't want to risk running out on those deserted roads."

"Good plan."

Matthew said he didn't need more gas, so he and Kim would meet them at the Greetings from Moab mural in town. They stopped at the visitor center to pick up their passes for the Fiery Furnace hike tomorrow.

As they passed the Colorado River and Lions Park, Collins had an idea, if they had enough time. He'd take Allie out on a real date tonight and then a walk in the park under the stars. And he didn't care if it messed with Melissa's plans. He grinned as they pulled into town.

ALLIE WAS THRILLED TO SEE BARS ON HER PHONE AS Collins pulled into the gas station. Melissa and Scott went inside to get more snacks and drinks to add to the ice chest, and she pulled up her email. Edward had sent back a short email that he had gotten her additional information and he'd be in touch with any more questions. Whew! That was good. And it made her lean toward not FedExing her office key.

And yet, last night it had seemed like such a perfect solution she'd kissed Collins. Her face heated. Well, maybe that was more about his support and a long-held dream than keys. Plus, she'd been about ready to throw in the towel last night and figure out a way to get home.

That decision was reinforced when she got Glenn's email. He

would love to help her, as usual, but he was heading out of town for the rest of the week. And still no word from Rachel. She blew out a breath. Okay.

Collins opened the door. "What's the verdict?"

She gave him the rundown. "I'm going to enjoy the rest of the day and not worry about it unless Edward reaches out and needs something else. And if so, Jim Davis can send it to him."

"Good plan."

Melissa and Scott came back, and a minute later they were parked on the street in front of the Greetings from Moab mural. Matthew and Kim were already set up there taking pictures. They joined in for another group picture.

Melissa, Collins, and Matthew studied the map of the area on the hood of Collins's truck and made a plan.

"Let's head to Dead Horse Point first. It's got a nice overlook where we can eat lunch. Then we can stop at Island in the Sky visitor center to make sure Shafer Trail is still passable." Melissa traced the route with her finger.

Matthew tapped a spot near the Colorado on the way back to camp. "Cool. Kim wants to stop by the Corona Arch. It's right on the way."

"And up to that point, the road doesn't look too bad, but I think once we leave Dead Horse Point, Allie needs to ride up front." Melissa folded up the map.

Irritation flared in Allie. She didn't like being treated like the weak little sister. Even if Melissa was probably right.

They took Highway 191 north of town, past Arches National Park until Highway 313, the road cutting through the red rock on both sides. A giant dinosaur greeted them as they turned, heralding the entrance to the Giant Dinosaur Park.

"Those aren't quite as big as the ones near Cabazon." Allie looked at Melissa. Off I-10 between San Bernardino and Palm Springs sat giant replicas of dinosaurs that were some inventive person's idea of a tourist trap in the middle of what used to be nowhere and now was surrounded by casinos and outlet malls. "Remember whenever we would drive by those when Matthew was little, he would insist that they were proof that dinosaurs weren't extinct?"

Melissa laughed. "That's when he was in his dinosaur phase. I couldn't even pronounce most of those names, and he had them memorized as a four-year-old."

"He hasn't lost his exuberance over his interests, has he?"

"Um, no."

The road was uneventful until they hit a few tight switchbacks between the sandstone rocks as the road climbed a mesa. Allie kept her eyes straight out the front window.

Collins's gaze glanced back at her in the rearview mirror. "You okay? That's the last of it."

She nodded and took a swig of water. She wasn't going to think about it. She was tired of being coddled over her finicky stomach, something she'd thought she'd outgrown. Instead, she'd concentrate on the scenery.

Did the people around here ever get used to the stunning beauty surrounding them? The top of the mesa flattened out to an endless horizon. There were several viewpoint stops, but they had agreed to stick to the plan today. Because there were so many beautiful vistas, they'd never get to their destination otherwise.

They passed several campgrounds, and Allie let the peaceful scenery speak to her soul. They followed the signs and the road until it dead ended in a parking lot. Scott and Collins grabbed the ice chest between them, and they took a concrete path to a covered area and found a spot along the low rock wall.

Before unpacking the lunch items, Allie took a moment to be in awe of the view. They were on a butte that jutted out into and above Canyonlands National Park. A sign near the overlook read A LAYER CAKE OF TIME. That was exactly what it looked like two thousand feet above the Colorado River goosenecking its way below them once again. It had been fascinating to see this river in its various forms and environments.

Everyone made their own lunch from the meat, cheese, fruit, and cracker selections. She could get used to eating her meals outside, especially with views like this to enjoy. The La Sal mountains stood sentinel in the distance, their white caps looking salt-covered like their Spanish name.

"I bet we can see for a hundred miles in any direction." Scott peeled an orange then handed it to Melissa.

"According to my guide, this was one of the last places in the continental US to be explored and mapped because it's so isolated and desolate." Melissa popped an orange section into her mouth.

Kim threw her trash away and began setting up her shots. "What are those cobalt-blue ponds over there?"

"Potash ponds from a mining operation. We'll drive by them on the way back to camp." Melissa packed up the rest of the lunch items.

"The light isn't as dramatic now as it would be at dawn. I can see why you need several days here if you wanted to shoot certain places in their best light. But it's still amazing." Kim took a series of shots.

Matthew pointed. "There's the Shafer Trail down below. Hard to believe that we can get from here to there. Kim, there's some rocks down below that we can get to if you want to get some different shots."

The two of them went off, scrambling over boulders below the lookout point. Melissa glanced at her watch.

Scott slipped his arm around her and pulled her close. He was good for her. Allie wished Melissa could just relax and enjoy the trip. Though given Allie's own meltdown last night at the coffeeshop, she wasn't really one to make judgments.

Collins touched her shoulder. "You up for the next leg of the journey?"

The Shafer Trail switched back and forth across the face of the mesa, carving its way down to the valley floor. From here it looked fit only for animals. "The rangers at Island in the Sky will tell us if it's not safe, right?"

He nodded. "Don't worry. I won't let anything happen to you." He pulled her close.

She didn't realize twisty roads bothered her until the other day. But then again, before this trip it had been a long time since she'd ridden in the back seat. She just hoped she didn't lose her lunch again today. She hated to put Scott in the back seat with his long legs. But she supposed everyone would prefer that to her being sick. And Melissa would never let her forget it.

They made their way back to the trucks. Allie climbed up front and took a deep breath.

Collins winked at her. "It's going to be okay."

Famous last words.

Chapter Seventeen

Willard grinned, watching from his truck while the other two trucks passed in front of him leaving Dead Horse Point. Go for the weak link, and the whole chain falls apart. Worked every time. And Matthew was the weak link. He'd given Willard valuable information.

He didn't like the other two men at all. But Scott and Steve were definitely wary. They would be his biggest obstacles. He couldn't take them directly, of course. He wasn't stupid. But he was certain he could outwit them. It would make the chase that much sweeter.

He glanced in the rearview mirror at the two gas cans secure in the back of his truck. He didn't think he'd left Matthew with too much gas. They'd been gone a long time having their lunch, and not many people were around. It'd been easy to siphon off most of his tank.

Terrible thing to get stranded in this desolate area. The folks in the other truck would have to leave to get gas and that would take awhile, leaving Matthew and Kim all alone. They wouldn't all fit in one truck.

Willard chuckled and put his truck in gear, following at a

safe distance where he wouldn't be spotted. It didn't matter if he lost them. There was only one road, and he knew where they were going.

He'd follow them and wait for an opening. And one would happen. He'd make sure of it.

ALLIE SETTLED INTO THE FRONT SEAT AS THEY backtracked on Highway 313 to Island in the Sky Road. From the top of the mesa that stretched in all directions, it was hard to believe that a deep canyon wasn't far away.

Collins ran into the visitor center and came back out a minute later. "We're good to go. Road has been graded not too long ago. He said it was better than it looked, that there was even room to pass."

"Awesome," Melissa chimed in from the back seat.

Allie wasn't sure it was awesome, but she didn't want to disappoint anyone. They retraced their steps a bit and took Highway 142, better known as Shafer Trail. She gulped as they stopped at the Shafer Trail lookout. The last point of smooth riding before the red-dirt road became as twisty as a plate of pasta.

The road began its descent clinging to the side of the mesa. The mesa was close to her side window. She couldn't imagine driving, since the view out Collins's window was of a sheer drop-off. Yet, the rangers were right; the road was about two cars wide. Which came in handy when they had to pass a group of mountain bikers. As Collins moved closer to the cliff edge to pass them, she tried to ease her grip off the seat.

"So, Melissa, what's the story on this road?" Melissa would know, and it would take Allie's mind off things, knowing why someone would choose to build this particular road here.

"It's named after the Shafer brothers. They used this trail to drive their cattle into this closed canyon below."

"I wonder how many cattle they lost over the side. Or are they smart enough to stay on the trail and follow the road down to the river? I heard cattle can smell water a long ways away. That was the cause of stampedes during old cattle drives of yore." Yore? Who talked like that? She did, when she was trying not to freak out. The view was amazing. She tried to appreciate that.

"Uranium prospectors in the forties made the roads wider," Melissa continued.

The road began to flatten out after about ten minutes, and Allie cautiously let her breath out. That wasn't so bad. The views here were spectacular, magnificent mesas on either side. They were on a wide, flat plain with several intersecting dirt roads. They came to a T.

Collins stopped. "This is a good place to get out and stretch our legs. We can wait for Matthew to catch up with us, and then figure out which way to go. We wouldn't want anyone to get lost."

Allie climbed out. She had survived. Her stomach was fine once they were on flat ground and it felt good to get out and walk around. There was no one else in sight, not even Matthew. A shiver coursed through her. The quietness was almost a presence itself.

Collins and Melissa consulted over the map. "We actually don't want to go straight. We want to turn here. Then we can descend to the lower part of the canyon. This road goes to the White Rim. It'd be cool to take that sometime."

Allie wandered off a bit, mostly stretching her legs, but also taking in the magnificent scenery. Worry had just started to snake through her stomach when a plume of dust announced Matthew's presence.

He and Kim pulled up and hopped out. "Cool trail, huh? That road is something else. We stopped a few places to take pictures."

Allie couldn't blame him, but she'd feel better if he stuck

closer to them. Still, he was a grown man, something she seemed to forget. Too many years of looking after him and the others.

Kim shot some pictures looking back where they had come from. Melissa showed Matthew which road they needed to take.

"Where does this one go?" He pointed to the road straight ahead.

"That's the White Rim trail. A much longer way to get back to camp."

He nodded. "Kim and I will probably stop more places than you to take pictures, so don't wait for us. We'll see you back at camp. Plus, we want to stop by the Corona Arch."

Allie shot Melissa a look.

Melissa bit her lip. "Look, we're better off sticking together. If something happens, there's no way to reach anyone."

A high whine of an engine floated to them and soon a couple of motorcycles appeared over the hill of the White Rim Trail. They slowed as they came to the crossroads and pulled to a stop next to the trucks. "How's it going?"

"Good. How about you? What's it like down that way?" Matthew asked.

"Some amazing canyon views, but watch out for the mountain bikers. There's a group of them."

"We're heading down the rest of the Shafer Trail." Collins pointed.

"How is it on the top part?"

"A lot better than you'd think. You'll do fine."

"Thanks, have a good one." The riders eased off slowly, careful not to drown them in dust.

Matthew grinned. "See? Someone will always come by and help out if you need it."

Melissa shook her head. "Do you have enough food and water?"

"I can always take more snacks." Matthew reached into the bed of Collins's truck and pulled out a few things, transferring them to his own.

"Ready to head out?" Collins opened his door.

Everyone piled back in, and they headed down the correct road. Allie studied the rearview mirror until they rounded a bend, but Matthew's truck didn't move.

MATTHEW CLIMBED BACK IN THE TRUCK WITH KIM. "DID you get the shots you wanted?"

"I think so. There's just so much. It's overwhelming. I wish I'd studied photography more. I just don't use it enough to remember. And now I wish I did."

He loved watching her work. She got so focused, she hardly noticed he was there. Until she did. Then her smile could light up a room and made him a little weak in the knees. He liked that they were on their own today.

"Let's go down the White Rim Trail a bit. I want to see where it goes."

Kim nodded. "I'm up for it."

They crested the hill and saw that it wasn't much different than the area they were currently in. "I was hoping maybe it'd go close to the rim of a canyon. If I had Melissa's map, I could see how much farther until it did that."

They passed a group of mountain bikers, and the road got sandy. He had four-wheel drive, but he wasn't stupid, even if Melissa seemed to think he was at times. Plus, he had Kim to think of. He didn't want to put her in an unsafe situation. "Let's turn back. It doesn't seem like there's anything interesting nearby that I can see."

"I agree. Plus, I don't want to get too far behind the others. And I know there will be more places I want to stop and see. Like the Corona Arch."

Matthew swung the truck into a three-point turn, gunning it a bit to get through the sand. It sputtered before catching again. What was that? It had never done that before. They crested the top of the hill just as it sputtered again. Now they were heading downhill, and the engine caught. What on earth? He checked the gauges. It wasn't overheating, the battery charge was fine. But the gas gauge rested below E. What? He had half a tank when they left Moab. That should have been plenty. And they'd been going downhill most of the day. What was wrong with his truck?

Worse, what would Melissa say? He didn't have to guess. He knew.

"What's going on?" Kim's brow wrinkled.

"Not sure, but it looks like we're out of gas."

"But you had plenty."

"I know. I don't know what's going on." He pulled over at the T with the Shafer Trail, where they'd been not long before. He hopped out. "I'm going to take a look." Maybe they'd cut something scraping on a rock. But he hadn't felt anything, and the road had been graded pretty decently. He popped the hood. Everything looked good under here. Nothing loose or leaking. He dropped down and looked under the truck. No leaks or scrapes that he could see. It didn't make sense at all.

Kim got out with him. "What are we going to do?"

He glanced at his phone, but the lack of bars wasn't a surprise. He tossed it on the truck seat. Now he had put Kim in a potentially unsafe situation. He should have known better and stayed with the group. "We've seen mountain bikers and motor-cyclists today. There's bound to be a truck or something come by. Someone can take us into town, and we'll bring back some gas."

"It won't be quick, though."

"Nope. It won't." He grinned at her. "Let's make the best of it."

She tilted her head to the side. "Do you always see the bright side of everything?"

He shrugged. "Yeah, I guess I do. Wouldn't you rather focus on the good instead of the bad?"

"Sometimes the bad is just overwhelming though."

"I can still usually find some good in it. Yeah, the bad is there. It's inevitable, so why dwell on it if you don't have to?"

She fiddled with her camera strap. "I think the light and dark of emotions fills out the tapestry of life. Sometimes bad things make us appreciate the good that much more. Like sunlight breaking through clouds after a storm. It's more powerful than if it was just sunny all the time."

He studied her profile while she wasn't looking at him. "I like how you see the world. I know I tend to gloss over the dark parts in search of the next exciting thing. But I'm learning to see things a bit differently after spending this time with you. You have a unique perspective."

Her mouth tilted up, teasing him, before she met his gaze. What would she think if he kissed her? He leaned a little closer.

She brought up her camera and took a step back, snapping a picture of him. "Guess we'd better chronicle this part of the adventure as well, huh?"

COLLINS GLANCED AT ALLIE AS THEY LEFT THE FLAT clearing and descended to the lower portion of the canyon. But he couldn't look at her long since the road turned rough and rocky, and he had to concentrate on dodging the larger ones. "Reminds me of some of the roads around Holcomb Springs after a rain or a freeze-thaw cycle. Rocks get dislodged and tumble down the mountain sides into the road."

He was glad for his high-clearance truck. And the ranger had been right. The top section was the easy part. They came to a flat clearing with nice views before descending to the lower portion of the canyon. The road narrowed, and they crossed a wash that he wouldn't want to chance after a rain. Thus, the stop at the ranger station for road conditions.

Allie kept glancing in the side mirror, even though the road twisted enough that there was no way she'd know if Matthew was behind them. As an only child, it wasn't a feeling he was familiar with, having to take care and look after a younger sibling. Yet Kim was his partner's little sister, and he had promised to keep her safe. That thought niggled at him.

He glanced back at Melissa, who was doing the same thing. As carefree as Matthew was, he wasn't stupid. He and Kim would be fine. And if the women got too worried, he could always turn around and go back until they met up with them.

The trail became a broad shelf above the Colorado River with cliffs 1,200 to 1,500 feet above them. But now his side was close to the mesa, and Allie's side was close to the cliffs. She kept her gaze straight out the windshield. Dead Horse Point was far above them, and it was hard to believe they'd been up there less than an hour earlier.

An oxbow bend in the Colorado River carved out a mesa in the middle from the cliffs on either side. At the pull out, they stopped and got out. Greenish-brown water played against the red rocks. A rim of greenery skirted the river.

"Such a spectacular view, and we're the only ones to enjoy it." He reached for Allie's hand.

"Matthew and Kim should catch up with us in a few minutes," she said.

Melissa gave a short laugh. "Unless they got caught up in a photoshoot or got sidetracked."

Was there a bit of romance igniting between Matthew and Kim? He'd seen some glances that made him think he might need to have a conversation with Matthew. On the other hand, if Collins had time alone with Allie, he wouldn't be in too much of a hurry to rejoin the group either. Maybe that's what Matthew and Kim were doing. Still, he should probably have a talk with Matthew since he'd promised Kyle he'd look after Kim.

Scott pointed to the river. "Next trip we'll explore these water routes. There's some cool ones we've come across. Can you imagine floating down that, looking up at us?"

Allie laughed. "I think my stomach would like it better."

They took a few pictures, and when it was clear Matthew and Kim wouldn't catch up with them, they climbed back in the truck. But he didn't miss the looks that both Melissa and Allie gave back down the road. Should he mention his suspicions about romance between Matthew and Kim? Had they noticed anything?

"We can go back for them if it'd make you feel better." He looked at Allie and then in the rearview mirror.

Scott touched Melissa's knee. She bit her lip then shook her head. "No, he's a big boy. I'm sure they are just stopping every few minutes for pictures. If they're not back at camp by the time we're making dinner, then we can come back for them."

He put the truck in gear and pulled onto the road. He didn't think they had anything to worry about, but he wanted to be sensitive to their concerns.

Down the road, they came across the cobalt-blue potash evaporation pools they had seen from Dead Horse Point. It made a striking contrast to the red, tan, and green landscape.

The road continued to drop down to river level and get rough. There were dirt roads going off in various directions, and he was more concerned that Matthew would take one of them accidentally. Collins had Melissa to keep him on the straight and narrow.

"Hey, there's another balanced rock," Scott said from the back seat. "We've hit one at every scenic spot, I think."

"Are you keeping track?" Melissa elbowed him.

"No, but maybe I should. We could call this the Balanced Rock Tour."

"Just as long as Matthew doesn't try to climb them or unbalance them," Melissa added.

They passed a boat dock along the Colorado, and the road became paved again. Greenery sprouted alongside the road as it followed the Colorado River on the right and great sandstone cliffs on the left.

Several feet above the road there was a sign for Indian writing, petroglyphs and pictures carved into the dark varnish of the rocks.

Then they passed the rock-climbing section, the easy area. "Scott, I might be up for river rafting, but I'm not going rock climbing. Not a fan of heights." Melissa said.

Collins rubbed his shoulder and agreed.

"Aw, come on. This is a world-renowned climbing area." Scott laughed.

"I can enjoy it from down here," Melissa insisted.

"I'm just happy to be on pavement and a road that's not twisting back on itself." Allie's gaze kept cutting back to the road.

"Some of this looks like it's either from the Flintstones or Cars Land at Disneyland. It almost doesn't seem real," Scott said.

"That's just what I was thinking," Collins agreed. But truth be told, he just wanted to get back to camp, put his feet up, pop some ibuprofen, and put ice on his shoulder until the pain calmed down enough that he could persuade Allie to go to dinner with him in town. And if Matthew didn't get back in time, that'd put a real crimp in his plans.

***

KIM HELD HER CAMERA IN FRONT OF HER LIKE A SECURITY blanket. Was Matthew going to kiss her?

She stepped away from his truck and shot more photos of the area around them. But her mind wasn't on the pictures. She had plenty to inspire her clothing line and ideas, even when she returned home. And she loved the concept of being the chronicler of their trip. Putting a movie together was going to be fun. Breaking down was part of the experience, so she made sure to get a shot of Matthew lounging against his truck.

But his gaze on her almost made her drop her camera. Was he really into her? Or was she just the distraction of the moment? They'd spent enough time together that she was beginning to feel like she was getting to know the man behind the good-time exterior.

He lowered the tailgate and hopped up on it.

She put her camera in the truck and, bringing a couple of bottles of water and a bag of trail mix, joined him.

"Thanks." He laughed. "I think I'm getting sick of trail mix, and I never thought I'd say that. Especially this kind that has M&Ms in it."

"It's eating it every day that gets old. But it's hard to have a lot of variety when you have to bring everything with you."

The silence surrounded them, broken by an occasional bird call or rustle in the brush. Not hearing any human-generated sound was cool… and eerie. Especially since they were stuck here. They'd been on the move so much from place to place, and she'd been so eager to capture everything, that just simply being still was refreshing. As long as she didn't dwell on the reason for it. She shivered.

Matthew patted her knee. "Don't worry. This is the great thing about having Melissa as a big sister. If we don't show up at camp when she thinks we should, she'll send out the posse." A shadow flicked across his gaze.

She smiled at him, acutely aware of his warm hand on her knee. "I'm not worried." It came out breathier than she expected.

His usually sparkling eyes darkened. "This has been a great trip, Kim. I'm glad I got to spend it with you."

"Me too."

Matthew slid his hand up her arm and around the back of her neck. "I don't want to go back home to my ordinary life that doesn't have you in it. There's that job opening in OC. If I took it, I could see you a lot easier than if I lived in Phoenix."

"Not even a week ago you didn't know who I was. I don't want you to change your life for me and then regret it."

"I don't think I could ever regret doing anything for you."

He leaned in, his gaze dipping to her lips and back up, seeking permission.

She leaned closer, letting her lips meet his, her fears swept away by his confidence. The assurance in his kiss took her beyond the moment, and her hands clung to his shoulders, bringing him closer.

He deepened the kiss, and she surrendered to being here and now with Matthew, not thinking about the future, not thinking about anything other than feeling cherished in his arms.

Some sound niggled for attention at the back of her brain, and it took a moment before she realized what it was. An engine.

She pulled back.

Matthew's gaze was dark on her, his thumb caressing her jaw. "I've wanted to do that since the first time I saw you in Daniel's yard."

She wanted to say *really?* But what came out was "I think I hear something."

He gave her another quick kiss before looking around. "Yeah, can't see anything yet. But sound bounces around these rocks." He gave her that heart-stopping grin as he hopped off the tailgate and wrapped his hands around her waist, lifting her down. "But whoever it is, we're in luck!"

She didn't step back when her feet hit the ground, instead relished the feel of his hands on her. But the unmistakable sound of rocks popping under tires greeted them as well as a now-visible dust plume. A truck was heading toward them from the Shafer Trail. It wasn't Collins's—which would be coming from the other direction anyway—but an older model green one.

It was almost on them before she could make out the single driver. Willie, the guy they'd run into a few times. Relief surged through her. It was even someone they vaguely knew.

Matthew let her go and stepped toward the truck.

Willie pulled even with them and rolled down his window. "Hey there. Car trouble?"

"Yeah, I think we're out of gas. Not sure what happened. If you don't mind giving us a ride into town, I can have Collins meet us once we get a phone signal and come back with some gas cans."

Willie grinned and opened his door. "I can do you one better. I've got gas cans in the back. Always carry some for emergencies like this."

"Wow. Even Melissa doesn't do that."

Willie went to the back and opened the low-profile shell over the bed and pulled out two cans.

Matthew opened the fuel door and gas cap on his truck, and Willie poured the gas in. After the first can, Matthew turned the key enough to see the gas gauge rise to above a quarter tank. "That should get us to a gas station. Thanks."

Willie started with the other can. "Let's put this one in too. Just to be on the safe side."

"I don't want to take all of your gas and leave you without any."

"Nah, it's no problem. I'm just glad we had talked earlier about this scenic road and I decided to take your advice. Looks like it worked out well for both of us."

"The least I can do is offer you dinner. Why don't you follow us back to our camp and have dinner with us tonight? I know we're grateful and everyone would love to have you, especially since you rescued us and Melissa didn't have to come bail me out." He laughed. "I'm grateful for that."

Willie capped the final gas can. "That's really nice of you. Thanks. I'd be happy to spend the evening with you folks. It gets a bit lonely traveling by myself after a while."

Kim climbed back in the truck, relieved. It was amazing how everything had fallen into place. She hadn't quite been worried, but she wasn't looking forward to spending hours alone out in the desert waiting for help to come.

Even if Matthew's kiss had rocked her world.

He climbed into the cab and leaned over, giving her a quick kiss. "And we are on our way! See? Things usually work themselves out." He started the truck and pulled onto the road.

Now if she only knew how she and Matthew were going to work things out.

Chapter Eighteen

Collins couldn't miss Melissa's and Allie's anxious looks that flitted between their Apple Watches and the RV campground road. It was Matthew and Kim's turn to cook, but it was brat-and-potato packets, which didn't take much work since they were already put together. But because they needed to be cooked in the fire, a good bed of coals would be helpful.

He and Scott set about getting firewood from the camp store and got the fire going. He wished there was something Allie and Melissa could do to get their minds off things.

Melissa brought out the map and itinerary and sat at the picnic table. "Scott, want to go over this with me? I want to talk out the plans for tomorrow since we're going in different directions."

Collins walked over to Allie and took her hand. "Let's walk around the campground."

With a glance over her shoulder, she nodded.

Once they were a few sites down from theirs, Collins squeezed her hand. "Scott and I will go look for them in a bit if they're not back. Okay? Matthew's a grown man and out of your sight most of the time. Why are you so worried today?"

She shook her head. "I know. It's silly. There's just something about this trip that is making us all fall into our usual roles. When we camped as kids, Matthew was always wandering off or getting into some sort of trouble. Melissa and I were afraid the police would pick him up and figure out what was going on in our house. It's only been lately that I realized how much worry we carried on our young shoulders. I haven't spent as much time around him as an adult, so I guess it's hard for me to have confidence in him.

"But even this past Thanksgiving, he said he was going to take care of the turkey, so we didn't need to worry about it. The problem was, he didn't know turkeys were frozen and needed to be thawed, so when he went to cook it Thanksgiving morning… well, we didn't have turkey for Thanksgiving. It's that inability to plan ahead that really gets to Melissa. I don't like that it puts everyone else out." She glanced at him. "I guess we sound just like big sisters."

He shrugged. "I don't have a lot of experience in that department. But I'm beginning to see how much you and Melissa had to deal with back when we were in high school. I just never knew."

"No. No one did. We never told anyone what we went through. Melissa was afraid we would get sent to foster care and split up. One time in high school, the teacher embarrassed Melissa in front of the class for not getting her project done. But she wasn't able to say why she hadn't. It was because we'd all been sick and she'd been taking care of us." She looked off into the distance. "Our whole goal was to make it until Melissa was eighteen. We thought that was the magic number."

She gave a harsh laugh. "That night I made Melissa work on her school assignments while I made dinner and took care of the other kids. We had a little tuna, a little cheese, some saltines, peanut butter, and the last of the lettuce. Melissa didn't have time to go to the store because of her schoolwork, and I didn't want to leave the younger kids to bother her. So I made do, tried to make it a fun smorgasbord, and the five of us sat down to eat."

"Where was your mom? Was she just never around or just in her own world?"

"Most of the time she was in her own world. In her manic stage, she'd start a painting or a pottery project, and we wouldn't see her for days. And if she was depressed, she'd stay in bed with the lights off. But that night she wandered out in paint-splattered clothes and noticed that I'd made dinner. Except that I hadn't counted on Mom showing up. There wasn't enough food. So I gave mine to Matthew." Her voice caught on the last word. "I wasn't that hungry anyway. It was more important for the other kids to eat."

She let out a breath. "The kids had tests and homework they needed to work on, but Mom decided to be a mom that night and play board games. But what got me the most was that there were two crackers left with peanut butter on them, and she just dumped them in the trash. I hadn't even eaten." Her hand gripped his more tightly. "I wanted so badly to pull them out of the trash, especially when my stomach growled all night. But at the same time, I didn't want Mom to be upset. I wanted her to stay and play board games and ask about our days. It was such a rare thing."

She met his gaze. "We didn't know until we were adults that she was bipolar. I think she's stayed on her meds for a few years now, but I don't think she was even diagnosed back then. I guess that's why Melissa and I are so protective of our siblings. It just brings back a lot of memories."

He stopped and pulled her into a hug. "I'm so sorry you had to go through that. I had no idea. I knew you had a lot of responsibility, but I never knew how much. I wish I would have known."

Her head lay against his chest, her words muffled. "We never told anyone."

Standing on the pavement in a campground in Moab, Utah,

with the sun hovering over the horizon, one moment Collins had thought of Matthew as an irrepressible, fun-loving guy whose antics might irritate his overprotective sisters. Now he realized what Matthew represented: the fear of losing the family they so desperately tried to hold together with wisdom beyond their years. The complexities of moving their childhood relationships into adults with jobs and responsibilities… he could see the seams of the fabric between the past and present straining under the changes. But would they? Could they keep relationships forged in survival intact through thriving as adults? Maybe that's what this road trip was supposed to represent.

He kissed the top of her head. "Scott and I will go look for him."

"Really?" She lifted her head and pulled back. "I'm sure he's fine. But…"

"I'm sure he is too. It's you I'm worried about. If it puts your mind at ease, it's not a big deal." Not considering all she had overcome. He never realized quite how resilient she was. They finished the loop back to their site.

Scott and Melissa sat at the picnic table, heads together in deep discussion. They looked up when Collins and Allie walked into camp.

"Scott, want to go with me to look for Matthew and Kim?"

"Sure. Melissa and I were just discussing that. Let me grab a jacket."

Collins squeezed Allie's hand. "How about when we get back you and I head into town for dinner tonight? It's about time we had a real date night."

Hesitancy flashed through her eyes. Until Matthew returned, she wouldn't be able to relax. But once Matthew and Kim were okay, they needed some time alone. He needed some time with her.

She nodded. "Sounds like a good idea. I'll tell Melissa."

Collins pulled his keys out and was standing next to his truck when another truck pulled in and headed toward their site.

Matthew. Whew. A load of tension dropped from his shoulders. He turned to Allie and smiled. "He's back!"

Melissa scowled.

Matthew pulled into the site and hopped out. "Hey, guys. Sorry we're late. We ran into a bit of trouble." His gaze dropped for a moment, and he stuck his hands in his pockets. "The truck ran out of gas."

Melissa stalked over, fire in her eyes. "Matthew! Why didn't you get gas when we filled up in town? That was so irresponsible of you. You always think everything is going to work out just fine."

He put up a hand, his tone more strident than Collins had ever heard. "First, Lis, everything did work out just fine. Willie stopped and had extra gas in his truck for us. And second, I had plenty of gas. Something went wrong with the truck. I don't know what. That could happen to anybody. But I handled it."

"Hey, there."

Collins stomach clenched at the voice as he turned.

Willie.

"I invited him to have dinner with us since he bailed Kim and me out. I figured it was the least we could do."

Melissa walked over to Willie, her expression transforming into one of hospitality. "Absolutely. Thanks so much, Willie, for helping out Matthew. Scott and Collins were just going to look for him."

Willie's head twitched at Collins's name.

He'd introduced himself before as Steve, and Willie had noticed the difference. Interesting.

"Glad I could save you guys the trip."

"Allie and I are headed into town. I can take your gas cans in and refill them." Collins gave a fake smile he often used in inter-rogations. "That way you'll be ready to help the next poor soul."

Willie gave him a steady look. "Okay, I'll go grab them."

"I'll go with you."

"No need." Willie started walking toward the visitor parking area.

"Not a problem." Collins wasn't going to let him off the hook. When they approached an older model green truck, Collins began taking mental notes. The truck didn't fit with the upscale, REI way Willie dressed. He expected a top-of-the-line rig.

Willie went around back, and Collins snapped a quick photo of the license plate. California. Good. He'd send it to Kyle and see what turned up. He hustled around to the rear as Willie was pulling the cans out and took them from him.

"So you're from California too. What part?" They headed back to the campsite.

"Northern. Near the Bay Area."

Collins nodded. "Nice area up there." He put the cans in the bed of his truck. "Thanks for rescuing them." He nodded toward Matthew and Kim. "Good timing."

"Yep." Willie walked off toward the campfire and chose a chair next to Melissa.

Collins slipped his phone out and snapped a photo of Willie just as he turned, catching Collins in the act. He swiped a few more things on his phone, acting like he was using it. "Hey, Allie, you ready to go?"

"Yeah, just let me change into jeans and grab a jacket." She disappeared into the trailer.

Willie met his gaze and smirked.

Collins held his gaze steady. His instincts were right. Willie was up to something. Worse, he knew Collins was on to him and didn't care. That sent a chill through him.

Allie came out of the trailer, and Collins moved to his truck, opening the door for her, but keeping his gaze on Willie.

Willie tossed him a salute and then began talking to Melissa.

Collins clenched his fist, then made sure that Allie was tucked safely inside before closing the door on her. He hopped in his side, and they left the campground. His mind was whirling, and he forced himself to pay attention to where they were going.

"What's wrong?" Allie's brows were drawn together over her clouded eyes.

He shook his head and let out a breath. "This was supposed to be a date. Something else Willie ruined," he muttered. Probably just what Willie hoped for.

"How does Willie play into this? I know you don't like him, but he did rescue Matthew and Kim."

Another thing that seemed a bit too convenient. It rubbed him raw that this guy was back at camp with his friends. It went against all his protective instincts to let them sit there unaware while he was out on a date.

"It's his attitude. He knows I don't trust him, and instead of trying to prove he's a good guy, he just smirks at me. I know it sounds ridiculous, but this is what I do for a living. I've seen guys like this that think they are too smooth to get caught. What he's up to, I don't know. That's what scares me."

Allie put her hand on his arm. "If you want to go back, we can."

He thought about it. "I have an idea." He pulled into a parking lot. "You okay with pizza tonight?"

"Sure."

"Do you have enough bars to find a pizza place and make an order with enough for everyone?"

"I do."

"Good." He texted Scott.

I'm going to grab a pizza and bring it back. Humor me. Don't let Willie near the trailer, tent, or vehicles or let him out of your sight. I'm texting Kyle his license plate.

Scott's reply came back a second later. Good, the text went through. He wasn't sure it would.

Will do. Pizza's a popular choice.

He texted Kyle Willie's license plate and the photo he took with a brief note about the guy. He hoped Kyle got back to him soon because once they headed back to camp, his signal was intermittent at best, likely blocked by the sandstone cliffs behind them.

He looked at Allie. "Where's the pizza place?"

"Just down the road." She pointed.

Collins pulled back out onto the street. He filled the gas cans, and a few minutes later they were in front of Zax's. "How much longer until the order's ready?"

"About ten more minutes."

"At least we'll get some time alone." He grinned and slid his arm along the back of the truck seat. Then he sobered. "Look, maybe we should cut the trip short. We don't know what's wrong with Matthew's truck. Melissa's upset. You're stressed out over DataCorp. And I have a bad feeling about Willie. Unless we can figure out a way to ditch him, I don't know why he's obsessed with hanging around with us, and I don't know what he's up to. I'd hate for something bad to happen just because we were afraid to be rude. It's what predators count on."

She bit her lip. "I trust you and your instincts. If you think Willie's dangerous, then we need to do whatever you recommend. But is there a way to do it without cutting the trip short? We've been having a good time for the most part, and I'd hate to disappoint everyone if there was any way to salvage it." She sighed. "Or maybe this trip has been doomed from the beginning. Maybe we shouldn't have tried to go without Daniel and Brittany."

He rubbed his hand over his face. Could it cost him his relationship with the others or even Allie if he insisted they needed to go home? Maybe. Willie hadn't done anything yet. And Collins wanted to keep it that way. All he needed to do was keep Willie away from everyone else. Something he should be able to do.

Willie had the attitude of a predator, a cocky one who thought he couldn't get caught. Which meant the women were the ones he was likely targeting, waiting for a moment to make his move. If they were never alone, he couldn't get to them and would move on to easier prey.

Unless he already had a rap sheet and a warrant. In which case, he could be arrested and put away. Something Kyle could find out. But Willie's cocky salute led Collins to think Willie thought he was untouchable.

His phone buzzed. Kyle was calling. He picked up.

"Ran that plate like you asked. Comes back to a Robert Warren of Irvine. No warrants. He's clean. No known associates. But his driver's license picture doesn't match the guy you sent me. I'll text it to you."

"He goes by the name Willie, but I don't have a last name. Might even be made up." Collins looked at the text that came in. Nope, wasn't Willie. "The truck's not been reported stolen?"

"Nope. He could have loaned it to this Willie guy. Might be a friend or relative. But we don't have any reason to ask him about it. I'll dig a little further, see if I come up with anything."

"Thanks, Kyle." He wanted to ask about the assault cases and the guy who'd hit Allie's car, but didn't want to do that in front of Allie. Plus he knew Kyle would tell him to remember he was on vacation. Collins dropped his phone. "Pizza ready yet?"

Allie studied the app. "It is now."

"I'll go in and get it. Lock the doors after me." He went inside and grabbed their order. The sun was setting, making a fiery show above the red rocks. It would have been a beautiful night for a date. Once they separated themselves from Willie, Collins was going to have that date with Allie, one way or another.

WILLARD CARRIED BOTH GAS CANS AS HE WALKED BACK TO the truck. Once the cop showed up with pizza, he knew he'd been outplayed. Tonight anyway. He ate a couple of slices and then took off, noticing neither Scott nor Collins let him near anything, instead bringing him a plate with pizza and a drink. He pulled the bottle of ipecac out of his pocket and tossed it on the seat as he climbed in. How did they know he'd planned to spike the guys' drinks to make them sick?

At least he'd gotten free gas out of it.

He pulled out of the RV campground and headed for his own. It didn't matter. Collins had gotten a picture of his license plate and when it came back registered to his half-brother Robert, it wouldn't be too much longer before they found out who he was, no matter how well he covered his tracks. In the meantime, everyone other than the cop thought he was a nice guy.

The stakes had gotten high. One wrong move and he'd be back in prison. He was searching for that adrenaline rush that came from playing close to the edge. But it hadn't happened tonight. There were easier targets. He knew where Allie worked and lived. He could bide his time and get her when her guard was down. Maybe he should give up and head back home. This was getting dangerous. The cop was smart enough to know what was going on. Given enough time, he'd put the pieces together.

But was he as smart as Willard? Tomorrow they'd find out.

He tapped his phone and the tracking app it contained.

He'd show the cop who was the smart one. It was his last chance.

EMOTIONS SWIRLED THROUGH ALLIE, LEAVING NO ROOM for s'mores even after Willie left. Everyone's mood was subdued, and Matthew didn't pull out his guitar. Melissa was still irritated at him, believing he hadn't kept a close eye on the gas gauge. Kim had defended him, saying the tank had been half full in Moab; she'd seen it.

Collins had updated them on what he knew about Willie and what he suspected.

Scott was the only one who didn't seem upset. He and Willie had swapped stories about the Bay Area and favorite camping and fishing trips. Willie had seemed like a genuinely nice guy who was embarrassed that he had stumbled into some awkward family tension. Which was probably why he'd cut out right after the pizza.

The whole point of this trip was for them to have fun together. And the fun had gone out like a deflated balloon. Maybe Collins was right. Maybe they should just head home.

"Here's the deal." Collins's face glowed in the waning campfire. "Willie knows where we're staying now. He knows our cars. He knows my full name. I'm not comfortable with any of that. If it wasn't already full dark, I'd suggest we pack up and leave. I want you girls to lock the trailer up tonight in case he tries to come back."

"We lock you guys out every night." Melissa gave a halfhearted grin. "So are you saying we should leave tomorrow morning and go where? To Bryce?" Melissa leaned forward to see around Scott.

"Yeah, that would be the best idea. I know that messes with your plans, but I'd rather be safe than sorry. If we move on early, he won't know where we are. He doesn't know that's our next stop, right?" He looked at Matthew.

Matthew looked over at the now-dark picnic table. Their maps lay open with notes and times written on it from when Scott and Melissa had been discussing tomorrow's plans. "I don't think we had to say anything."

Allie studied Collins as the tension radiated off him. She hadn't seen him this upset since high school when Amber Tinney lied about copying off his paper, saying he had copied off hers. And the teacher believed her and gave him an F. He stalked over to the picnic table and brought the paper back, tilting it toward the firelight. "This has our whole itinerary on it. The times we're planning for the Fiery Furnace Hike, the trip up Highway 128, and Bryce and Zion." He sank into his camp chair. He wore the responsibility for keeping all of them safe like a heavy sack. He'd always been responsible, but this was an entirely new level.

Everyone was silent for a moment. Scott spoke up. "Here's how I see it. If he's a predator, he's after the women, right? Or maybe fixated on just one of them?"

"Yeah. He can't seem to keep his eyes off Melissa."

Scott's mouth formed a tight line. "I noticed that too. Okay, so that means he has to get one of the women alone. That doesn't happen anyway. So we'll just be extra vigilant until we hear something more concrete from Kyle."

Collins gave a stiff nod. "I looked inside his truck and the shell when we got back. Everything was locked up tight, and I didn't see anything but some camping equipment in the back. Doesn't necessarily mean anything either way." He rubbed his face. "Because of the bad reception, I won't hear anything from Kyle till tomorrow. While you, Matthew, and Kim are at the Fiery Furnace hike, I'll hang out with Allie and Melissa. Then we'll meet up here for lunch and take the scenic Highway 128. At least it's paved, and we'll stick together. Matthew, let's get a good look at your truck in the morning before you guys take off. Just, everyone, please be alert and don't go anywhere alone. Not even to the bathroom."

A somber assent went around the group. The guys put the fire out and took care of the pizza boxes.

Allie shivered, and Collins came over and wrapped her in a hug. "I'm sorry we didn't get our date. I'll make it up to you." His voice was low in her ear, comforting and reassuring.

"I know. I just don't know what to think. He seemed like a nice guy. If it weren't for your warning, I'd invite him along with us because he looked lonely. But if you're right, then it means he's still out there waiting for a chance to get us. Especially now that he knows our whole trip."

"I won't let anything happen to you." He kissed her forehead.

But later that night as she lay in her bunk, she couldn't turn her brain off. When did you draw the line against helping people? And Willie had been helpful, even if Collins suspected it was just to get an in with the group. Wasn't everyone's motivation for helping others always a little bit selfish at the root? Even she, who liked to help people, could admit in her frankly honest times that she liked the good feelings she got from helping, she liked how others viewed her. At the root, was that any different than Willie? Her head hurt with all the deep thoughts.

She rolled over and tried to sleep but couldn't help but wonder about every sound she heard outside. She knew Collins and Scott would be vigilant and protect them.

But did Willie know that too?

Chapter Nineteen

Matthew was determined to get Melissa back on his good side this morning. He was up early and knocked on the trailer door. "You ladies up? I'm at your service to help with breakfast."

Melissa pushed open the door, her face unreadable. For a moment, he felt like a scolded little boy. He hated how she'd come after him yesterday in front of Kim. And Kim had come to his defense. Last night had been weird, and he was ready to get past it.

Kim's face appeared next to Melissa's shoulder, her face bright with a smile. "Morning, Matthew."

"Hey, Kim."

Melissa pushed the door open the rest of the way and smiled. "Come on in. We'll put you to work."

While Melissa got the coffee going, he pulled out a dishtowel and tried to tie it around his waist like an apron. It didn't reach, so he tucked it into his jeans. He flipped the spatula like a Japanese hibachi chef and started to work on the pancakes. The mix just needed water added then it was shaken. He had fun with that, too, getting the women doubled over in laughter as he pretended it was a maraca.

He was looking forward to the Fiery Furnace hike this morning. He knew this would be a hit-the-highlights trip, but he liked a little more adventure than his sisters. "Kim, looking forward to our hike this morning?"

She bit her lip. "I'm a little nervous. What if I don't like squeezing through those slot canyons or climbing under that arch? I don't want to freak out."

He reached out and grabbed her hand. "I'll be with you. Nothing will happen. We'll have fun. Haven't we always had fun?"

"Yeah. We have." The soft smile on her face about melted him like chocolate over a blackened marshmallow.

He winked at her. "Good." He turned to Melissa. "That leaves you, Collins, and Allie Cat to explore Arches or find something else to do in Moab."

Melissa turned to Allie. "Anything in particular you want to do?" She grinned. "Perhaps I should leave you and Collins alone."

"Hey, hey, hey." Matthew tossed a hot pad at her. "No one's to be left alone. Collins's orders. So you're stuck being the third wheel. Unless you want to come on the Fiery Furnace hike with us. I'm sure we can find you a pass."

"No thank you. Don't like tight spaces."

"Not even with Scott?"

"Only if a fire is chasing us." She shuddered.

Yeah, that had happened last year to her. He should give her a bit more of a break than he usually did. She'd been through a lot last year, and he knew a schedule was how she coped with things. And while she didn't embrace spontaneity as much as he did, there was much to be said for knowing that they would have a place to sleep every night and food to eat. But he couldn't help wish she'd see him as a grown man instead of a little boy.

He slipped his arm around his sister's shoulder and gave her a squeeze. "You can have the first pancakes then."

After breakfast, Collins and Scott looked over Matthew's truck. None of them could find any obvious problems or leaks to explain the missing gas.

"You said you still had half a tank in Moab?" Collins asked. Matthew nodded.

"The only place where we were away from the trucks for any length of time was at Dead Horse Point. Someone could have siphoned it off then. It's the only explanation that makes sense."

Matthew stroked his chin. "And we went downhill for quite awhile after that. It was after we went up a small incline that it began to sputter."

Collins thought it was pretty convenient that Willie just happened to come upon them with two gas cans. But he didn't say anything. He said his piece last night. He just hoped he heard from Kyle soon.

"I think it's fine for you to take it into Arches today. It's populated all the way, and it's not a far trip. If you don't have any further problems, then we'll still plan on the scenic road trip when you get back. At least this one's paved."

"Sounds good." Matthew nodded, and swung his backpack and Kim's into the bed of the truck. Kim slid in, followed by Scott. It'd be a bit of a squeeze, but it wasn't a long trip.

"Have fun." Allie waved as they pulled out of the campsite. She turned to Collins. "What do you want to do this morning?"

"Get another cup of coffee." He hadn't slept well last night. Mostly just dozed, his ears straining for sounds of Willie returning. Probably just what the guy wanted.

They headed inside the trailer. "Melissa, you have any idea what you want to do this morning?" Collins poured himself another cup of coffee and slid into the dinette.

"I thought we'd straighten up the trailer, organize the food better, see what we need to replace, and then poke around Moab. What do you think?"

"Sounds good to me." Allie started cleaning up the breakfast dishes. For the next bit, it was comfortable as the women puttered around the trailer putting things to rights. He sipped his coffee. Everyone thought he was overreacting. He hoped he was. But he didn't like the feeling he got around Willie. He spent some time trying to predict what Willie would do next. Was he into the mind games, keeping Collins on his toes and jumping at shadows? Or was he planning his next move, now that he knew their agenda?

Kim would be safe on the Fiery Furnace hike with Scott, Matthew, the ranger, and other hikers. And Allie and Melissa would be with him today. His guess was that Willie would be somewhere down the road, waiting for their guard to fall, and try to grab one of the women when they were alone.

Collins would make sure that didn't happen.

He sat back and watched Allie and Melissa work together like they'd done it a thousand times before. Probably because they had. He thought about her life growing up. If he'd known more back then… Well, he was a kid. What could he have done? Maybe something to make her load lighter. But instead, she studied with him on a regular basis. One more thing on her plate.

When they were satisfied that the place was in order, they headed out to downtown Moab. For once they weren't trying to solve a problem in town, just enjoying it. They wandered through the shopping district, noting the local-made, one-of-a-kind offerings, a clothing shop, a bookstore. He grabbed another couple of postcards while Allie wasn't paying attention.

He checked his phone often, but no word from Kyle.

They got back to the campsite just before Matthew, Scott, and Kim pulled in. Allie and Melissa laid out lunch.

"So how was it?" Melissa wrapped her arms around Scott's waist and kissed him on the cheek.

"It was fun. The ranger information was interesting, and I'm sure we would have gotten lost if we'd been back there on our own. It was a complete maze."

"I'm glad you got back safely. Hungry?"

"You bet."

They ate lunch, and soon after hit the road for scenic Highway 128 along their good friend, the Colorado River. Collins couldn't help but feel relieved that there had been no Willie sightings and the group was all together again.

They took Highway 191 toward Arches but turned off onto Highway 128 before they crossed the river. The road was a paved two-lane that ran with the red cliffs rising up on the right and the Colorado just off the road to their left. It was a different experience viewing the Colorado from this perspective, deep in the gorge, since most of their viewing had been done from much higher vantage points.

He glanced back to make sure Matthew was right behind him. He was. And Allie was beside him, since the road was twisty.

The greenery that grew along the banks of the Colorado striped color between the red sandstone cliffs on either side. With a bright blue sky above, it looked like someone was playing with the basic pack of crayons.

The walls parted at Grandstaff Canyon Trail.

"Someday we'll have to take that trail." Melissa read from her guide book. "It was named after William Grandstaff, an African-American prospector and rancher who grazed his cattle here in the late 1800s. There's a spring a ways down the trail. Makes me wonder how he found it. It's the perfect way to feed, water, and protect your stock."

"There are a lot of things to do around here," Scott said from the back seat. "We definitely need to come back and explore. I picked up one of the brochures from the outfitters. We could do full or half-day rock climbing or canyoneering. Or part of the day on the river. And they have levels geared for beginners, so everyone can enjoy it. Maybe that should be the next sibling trip, huh?"

Melissa laughed. "So you're making yourself one of the siblings, then?"

He shrugged. "Of a sort."

Collins glanced at Allie and grinned.

They passed several campgrounds right on the river. "That would be convenient if you were floating down the river." Collins glanced back at Scott. "Add that to your list for next time."

"Might be a bit more primitive than I want," Melissa said. "I don't see any RVs or trailers. But you guys will be fine. You're used to sleeping in a tent." She patted Collins's shoulder over the seat.

"I see how it is. We're left roughing it."

"Yep."

A pullout had a few cars in it. The Big Bend bouldering area was littered with pieces of the mesas and spires that had broken off and tumbled down, creating boulders perfect to practice climbing on. Collins wished they could stop and have some fun clambering over things. On the other hand, his shoulder still hurt, so maybe it was another thing better left for "next time."

Melissa glanced back and then spoke up. "So you didn't find anything wrong with Matthew's truck?"

Collins glanced back at Scott and shook his head. "We couldn't find anything."

"He did forget to put gas in his truck."

Scott shifted closer to Melissa. "I don't think that's what happened. Even Kim said she saw they had enough gas in Moab."

Melissa rolled her eyes. "She's half in love with him. She'd say anything."

Scott laughed. "In this case, I think they're both telling the truth. I asked them more about it on the hike. It was awfully convenient Willie was there to rescue them. I don't think this one is on Matthew."

Collins was glad Scott was the one to tell Melissa. She sat back in the seat and stared at Scott.

The gorge opened up, and some of the flat land was used for agriculture, including a winery. A network of dirt roads left the main highway, some leading to where iconic western films had been shot. Which was probably why, once again, Collins felt like he was driving through a movie set. He probably was. The highway disappeared to a point on the horizon between two red mesas. Now he felt like he was in a Road Runner and Wile E. Coyote cartoon.

After passing that point, the gorge narrowed in on them again as the Colorado took another wide bend. The road was back hugging the cliffs and the river. It would be a bad place to break down or have an accident since shoulders or pullouts were few and far between. He glanced back to make sure Matthew was still with them.

Which made him think about yesterday. If Willie had any kind of weapon, he could have taken Kim yesterday when she and Matthew had broken down. Of the three men, Matthew was the youngest and least imposing. So if kidnapping one of the women was his goal, why didn't he take Kim then? Had another vehicle come along? Did Matthew seem to present too much of an obstacle? Or was Kim not who Willie wanted? Playing the hero certainly would win him credibility with the rest of the group and cause them to let their guard down.

Collins didn't know, but there was some bigger game here Willie was playing. He hoped he heard something from Kyle today. But as Kyle had reminded him on the phone yesterday, he was on vacation. This wasn't his jurisdiction. He didn't have access to his normal resources, and the local LEOs wouldn't want his help. The best thing he could do was relax and have a good time with Allie.

And keep his eyes open.

Melissa piped up as they passed a road. "That's called Top of the World Safari Route. Weird name. Let me see where it goes on the map." Paper rustled. "It ends up at a place called Top of the World Moab. That's definitely got to go on our 'next time' list. It looks like it ends up at the edge of the mesa. Maybe like Dead Horse Point."

They crossed the Colorado and pulled into a gravel lot on the other side of it. They climbed out of the trucks and headed down the paved path. The remains of the Dewey Suspension Bridge were in view, steel towers rising on either side of the river with steel cables connecting them and nothing else.

Melissa read from her guidebook: "This was the longest suspension bridge in Utah from 1916 until April 2008 when it was destroyed by a boy playing with matches who started a grass fire. It originally carried this highway across the river. It was an all-wood deck about ten feet wide and over five hundred feet long, designed to support six horses, three wagons, and nine thousand pounds of freight. It was the second-longest suspension bridge west of the Mississippi. Can you guess the longest one?" She grinned.

Matthew waved his hand. "I know! Pick me!"

"Matthew," she said in a game-show announcer voice.

"Tanner's Crossing bridge we saw in Cameron, Arizona."

"Give the boy a prize. Both bridges were built by the Midland Bridge Company with the same basic plans. See, it pays to pay attention." She tossed him a bag of trail mix.

"Gee thanks, Lis. Though I find it interesting that the best constructed bridges of their time were defeated by sheep and a boy."

It felt good to get out and stretch their legs.

Collins edged over to Matthew. "Any trouble with the truck?"

"Nope, it's running fine."

"Good. Flash your lights if you need to pull over. I don't think we have much cell reception here."

He nodded.

When they headed back on the road, the rocks here were more tan in color, and the land flattened out horizon to horizon. That meant a different geological era, but he couldn't keep them straight. The colors were easier.

The road dead ended at a T, and Collins swung left to hop on I-70, a less scenic route but a faster one that made a big loop back to Moab. At the intersection with Highway 191, they headed south, approaching Arches from the north instead of from the south as usual.

He looked at the rearview mirror and addressed Melissa. "Head back to the camp site first?"

"Yep. We can pack up things for dinner, grab some warmer clothes and the camp chairs, and then head into the park."

They did exactly that. Collins was tired from the drive and the lack of sleep the night before, but they wanted to take in the most iconic arch in the park, Delicate Arch.

Kim grabbed her tripod and had a few red-light flashlights. Hopefully other people would be as considerate and not ruin their night vision.

They would start at the Windows section, head to Delicate Arch to catch the sunset, then make their way to the lookout at Panorama Point. Knowing Melissa, she'd timed everything just right. It should be pretty spectacular, which was saying something given what they'd seen on this trip. He just hoped he stayed awake long enough to see the stars after the sunset.

Back inside Arches, they turned off the main Scenic Drive onto The Windows Road. They took the side loop through the Garden of Eden and continued on to loop around to the Windows trailhead. They parked, and Collins took Allie's hand as they started out across the dirt trail. The stone steps made the incline easier and reminded hikers to stay on the trail. And the windows in the rocks in the distance peeked at them, reminded them of their goal, beckoning them on. It was amazing to see something so fragile and elegant carved by nature into stone.

The contrast was striking. Because this area was elevated, they had a panoramic view of the park.

They hiked the Windows loop trail up and around and then hiked between the parking areas to Double Arch. Kim had fun playing with angles in her images in the waning afternoon light as one arch branched off of another.

The sun was making a descent toward the western horizon when they drove to where the Delicate Arch hike began at Wolfe Ranch. A cabin by the trailhead was all that remained of the family who eked out a living here for over twenty years in the late 1800s. Their daughter had taken one of the first photographs of Delicate Arch. Collins couldn't imagine what the early residents endured to live here with the scarcity of water and the heat in the summer.

The trail climbed up a dirt-and-rock trail that gradually became a steep slickrock slope. Just like before, the slickrock wasn't so much slick as it was like sandpaper. There was no shade, so this would be brutal in the summer afternoon heat, but this time of year and day it was perfect.

After hiking up for almost a mile and a half, the trail narrowed to a sloping rock ledge for about two hundred yards. He squeezed Allie's hand. "I'll go first. Just keep your eyes on my feet and don't look downslope. It'll be worth it."

She swallowed and nodded. "Okay. Let's do it."

He looked back at the rest of the group trailing behind them before heading out.

"After the Fiery Furnace today, this will be easy," said Kim.

When they reached the other side, a giant sandstone bowl hollowed out by wind and rain greeted them. On the far side, perched on the edge of the bowl before dropping off the cliff behind it, was the iconic Delicate Arch, a symbol so representative of Utah that it was on their license plates. The rock glowed red under the setting sun, with the La Sal mountains as a backdrop. A number of people had gathered with the same idea.

Kim studied the area then picked a spot. The rest of the group followed.

The air was growing cooler as the sun lowered. Collins sat close to Allie and put his arm around her. "Having a good time?"

"I am. The beauty is incredible."

He turned to Matthew. "How was the Fiery Furnace?"

"It was awesome. We started out at the visitor center to watch a movie about it, then we drove to the trailhead. Even though the hike was only about two miles, it twisted like a maze. There was a place where we had to crab between the walls with our hands and feet on the rocks where they made a vee because it was too narrow to touch the ground. A couple places had some tight squeezes, including an arch you had to crawl under. But it would be easy to get lost there for sure."

Allie touched Matthew's arm. "I'm glad you went. Why is it called the Fiery Furnace?"

Kim stepped back from adjusting her camera on its tripod. "It's kind of like the House on Fire ruins we saw. I guess the already-red rocks almost glow at sunset, which would be awesome to watch. And with all the fins and twists and turns, I could see why you'd call it a Fiery Furnace. The rocks almost look like they were roiling and then froze in that position. It was remarkable. Even though a few places made my stomach drop, with all the people around and the rangers, it felt perfectly safe. It was unforgettable. I'm glad we did it." She smiled at Matthew and touched his arm. "He's had some great ideas on this trip."

Allie glanced at Collins and smiled.

Kim turned her attention back to her camera and took a number of shots as the sun slowly sunk.

Collins sat with Allie snuggled up next to him. The whole area became silent as everyone witnessed the ritual of nature celebrating the end of the day in a most spectacular way. He was thrilled to have Allie next to him to share it with. It was one of those perfect memories from this trip that he wanted to tuck away in his mind and pull out in the future.

As the sun faded behind the horizon, they scrambled to get back down the trail while it was still light. Collins led the way through the narrow slope with Scott bringing up the rear. But as the trail flattened out and became downhill, he took Allie's hand until they reached the trailhead.

As they approached the trucks, he noticed something stuck under his windshield wiper. He unlocked the vehicle for the others and grabbed the note. Is THIS YOURS? IT'S IN THE MEN'S BATHROOM. He frowned. That didn't make any sense. He felt his pockets. He had his cell phone and keys. What could he have dropped? Suspicion rose, but he wanted to look at all the angles.

"Anyone lose anything?"

Everyone shook their heads.

He showed the note to Scott. "I'll go check this out. I'm sure it's a ploy, but if Willie is behind it, this is a chance to see what his story is."

Scott studied the note. "Let's think this through. If this is some trick to get one of us alone, what's his plan? To isolate one of us? Or to come back and grab one of the girls?"

They both scanned the area. The parking lot was wide open and in full view. It'd be hard to approach the vehicles without being seen. "There's only one way to find out, and that's to grab him. Besides, if we don't, what if some unsuspecting person comes up on him and gets hurt?" Collins was tired of living with the tension of this guy hanging over him. He was tired of not having access to his usual resources or even being in his own jurisdiction where he had any kind of authority. He wanted this to end and now.

"Then I'll go with you. If it is him, you'll want backup."

"Agreed. Matthew, keep an eye out. It's better if everyone is in the trucks with the doors locked." He and Scott strode over to the bathrooms at the trailhead, the night quickly darkening with a few of the early stars poking out.

He lowered his voice. "You go around this way; I'll go around the other way. See if we can surprise him wherever he's hiding."

Scott nodded and went around the far corner of the building.

Collins took the closer one.

ALLIE SAT IN COLLINS'S TRUCK, IN THE BACK SEAT WITH Melissa, fiddling with her fleece zipper. What was taking them so long? Were they talking to someone? "They've been gone longer that I expected."

"I was just thinking that." Melissa peered out the windows.

The moments stretched into long minutes.

She looked at Melissa. "What's going on? Should we go after them?"

Melissa opened her mouth to answer but then pointed. "Here they come."

Allie turned. Scott had his arm under Collins, who was holding his head. What on earth? She hopped out of the truck and ran over to them. "What happened?"

"He was just staggering to his feet when I got around the building to where he was," Scott said. "He's got a gash on his head."

"Collins, what happened?" Allie spotted blood seeping between his fingers.

"Not sure. I turned the corner of the building. I think I got whacked on the back of the head. I woke up on the ground."

She lowered the tailgate. "Sit up here and let me look at that."

Scott eased him onto the tailgate and kept his hand on him.

Allie climbed up and turned her phone flashlight on. "Let me look."

He moved his hand out of the way. There was a gash, but it looked pretty superficial. It wasn't gushing blood. "Melissa, grab me some of those paper towels." She took the wad handed to her and pressed them on his cut, not missing the hiss of pain he gave. "Sorry."

Scott waved Matthew over. "Go find a ranger. Tell them we have someone who was attacked."

Matthew nodded and climbed in his truck.

Scott looked at Collins. "I didn't see who it was. There were a few people off in the distance on the trail, but in the growing dark, I couldn't make out anything identifying them."

Allie's thoughts went to Willie. Collins had been right. Though there was no way to prove it unless Willie's prints were on the note, and they probably didn't even know his real name.

She lifted the paper towels. "The bleeding has slowed. It's mostly seeping, but we should go get it cleaned out and stapled."

"Plus, you should be checked for a concussion with that loss of consciousness." Scott grimaced. "I know a few things about head injuries, unfortunately."

Matthew pulled back into the lot with the ranger's truck behind him. The ranger came over. "What happened here?"

Collins told her about the note and their scouting out the situation. Scott brought the note over and told her what he'd seen. Collins also mentioned that he was a detective with LVPD and what he'd learned about Willie, which he admitted wasn't much.

"Are you able to get yourself to a hospital to get that head checked out, or do you need me to call an ambulance?"

"We can get him there," Scott said.

She nodded. "Okay, I'll check the campground for the truck you described and see if anything comes up. But you know as well as I do that in cases like these, there's not much I can do unless you can identify him or there was a witness."

Collins started to nod then winced. "Yeah. Thanks for your help."

"Sure." She handed him her card. "I'll be in touch if I discover anything. Let me know if you learn anything else."

"Will do."

She got into her truck and drove off.

Collins eased off the tailgate. "No need for everyone to miss the stars tonight. Plus, I'm sure you're hungry. Matthew, can Allie drive me in your truck and you all can fit in mine?"

Matthew nodded, frowning. "Of course, but are you sure that's what you want?" He handed his keys to Allie.

"Yeah."

Scott helped Collins over to the passenger side of Matthew's truck while everyone shifted gear around. "Sorry you were the one he beaned. It could have as easily been me."

"I'm glad it wasn't. You've already had one head injury. You don't need another."

Allie snagged a couple of pieces of fruit, cheese sticks, and trail mix from the ice chests and stuck them in her backpack before climbing in the driver's side of Matthew's truck. She opened her maps app and typed in *hospital,* figuring it would pop up once she got into town and got a signal. Given the nature of the activities in and around Moab, they had to be used to all sorts of injured people coming in. And given that Collins wanted her to drive, he must really be injured.

They pulled up to the emergency entrance, but Collins didn't get out. "No, go ahead and park. I don't want you alone."

She studied him, not convinced.

"Come on, Allie. I don't want you walking through the parking lot alone."

She sighed and found a parking spot, luckily close by.

Collins seemed steady enough on his feet, but she gripped his hand tightly anyway. He checked in at the desk in the emergency department. There were only a few other people in the waiting room.

The triage nurse called him back after a short wait. Then she reappeared and motioned to Allie. "You can join him right through there." She pointed to a curtained off area.

Allie slipped through. Collins lay on a hospital bed with an ice pack on his head. She took the chair next to him.

"You're bearing the brunt of injuries on this trip. First the shoulder, now the head." She smiled.

He reached for her hand. "It's all a misguided attempt to get your attention. Is it working?"

She laughed. "You had my attention."

"Oh, well I wished I'd known that before I went to all this trouble."

She shook her head, and her stomach growled. "Are you hungry for anything? Will they let you eat?"

"They didn't say, but I'm not hungry. You go ahead, though. You missed dinner."

She pulled an apple out and took a bite. It did taste good. "So do you think it was Willie who hit you?"

"That's my best guess. No other answer makes sense. But proving it will be difficult." He eased back against the pillow.

"What would he hope to gain by it?"

"Not sure. But if I'm out of commission, that's one less obstacle between him and his goal. Plus, it throws everything into confusion, and maybe he's hoping to take advantage of that."

"Do you think the others are safe?"

"They're in a public place out in the open. No good way for Willie to get to Kim or Melissa. Plus Scott and Matthew are there, and they all are on alert. But—" he pulled out his phone — "I'm going to text Kyle the latest and see if he's found anything out."

He was still texting when the doc came in.

"I see you had a run-in with a hard object." He performed an exam on Collins and asked him questions. "Where are you guys staying?"

"At the RV resort campground up the road."

He looked at Allie. "You'll want to check on him throughout the night, make sure you can still wake him every couple of hours."

She nodded.

"I'll get a nurse in here to clean this wound, then I'll be back to staple it shut."

Collins finished texting Kyle, snapping a picture of the ranger's card as well. "Now we wait. I said I wanted to see the stars tonight. I just meant the kind in the sky, not the kind that fly around your head."

Allie laughed. "Yeah. I'd be happy just sitting around a campfire with you instead of in the emergency department. Speaking of which, I never told you how much I enjoyed your guitar playing with Matthew. I wasn't sure you still played."

He gave a small smile. "I hadn't for a long time before that night. Couldn't you tell?"

She shook her head. "No. I mean, I'm sure you don't play as much as you used to, but the guitar seemed as natural in your hands as it always was. I imagined you'd go on to be a music major in college or continue to play with a group."

He let out a sigh. "I almost did. Remember Mr. Paul, our music teacher?"

"Yes. I had choir with him."

"He was really encouraging to me. He'd gotten me in with a community ensemble, and I had worked on this complicated piece we were playing. I think I was the youngest person there. I came home excited and told my parents I wanted to major in music."

His face lit up then dimmed, the emotions playing across his face as he went back in time to something he hadn't even shared with her.

"I remember my dad saying that I couldn't make a living as a musician, that it was only good as a hobby. He was the one that encouraged me to major in business. I didn't want to believe him. I saved all my money working one summer to buy that Martin. Didn't go to the movies or hang out with friends. Didn't save for a car like the rest of them did."

"I remember that summer. You just disappeared."

He nodded. "I thought I could convince my dad I was good enough, that the Martin showed I was serious." He shrugged. "In the end, I didn't have the courage to go against him. But I didn't get a business degree either. When I switched to criminal justice, I found I did well and I enjoyed it. Working with a partner, being part of a team, it was kind of like being in a band. I told myself I'd never stop playing, that I'd find groups to play with. But life gets in the way and until this trip, I had hardly picked up my guitar in years."

She squeezed his hand. "I'm glad you brought it. I hope you play it more."

He nodded. "Life's too short not to do those things you enjoy."

"Have you been in touch with Mr. Paul at all?"

"Nope. I'm not on social media, remember?"

She laughed. "Yeah, you Luddite. Actually, it probably saves you a lot of angst. But we do have a school page and every once in a while, one of the teachers will pop up. I think he's on there and still living in the area, if I remember correctly."

"Who was an influential teacher in your life?"

Allie took a deep breath and traveled back in time. It was easy. "Mrs. Carmean. She picked up on my love of books in intermediate school and let me help in the school library. But she actually listened to me and asked my opinion on books and why I liked them. I liked staying after to help because it was better than going home. I got noticed and appreciated for what I did.

"One day, she found me crying in the library. I don't even know why now. But she didn't try to fix anything. I felt like I could trust her, even though I still didn't tell her anything about my home life, just that as one of the oldest of five kids, I had a lot to do. Looking back, I think she read between the lines. But it's one of the few times I felt seen and known. At the end of the school year, she gave me a complete set of Laura Ingalls Wilder books. I still have them."

Collins squeezed her hand. "You had so much on your shoulders when you were young. You and Melissa. I wish I would have known and been able to help."

Allie blinked back tears.

But before she could reply, the nurse came in with a tray. "Let's get that head washed out." She put absorbent pads around his neck and shoulders and began squirting saline into his wound.

He held Allie's gaze and made a few faces that made her laugh.

"Okay. All done." The nurse put her supplies back on the tray. "The doctor will be in here in a moment to staple that shut."

He raised his eyebrows at Allie. "Fun times."

"Bet you never thought this sibling road trip would be so exciting."

"It's definitely been unexpected." He ran his thumb over the back of her hand. "I wouldn't change a thing, since it meant I could be with you. I'm so glad we've reconnected, Allie."

"Me too." She glanced down and then back up. "This may sound petty, but I need to ask. Lauren seems glad you've reconnected as well. Is she still texting you?"

He slid out his phone, unlocked it, opened the texts, and handed it to her. "See for yourself. I don't have anything to hide from you, Allie. I'm not interested in Lauren."

She scrolled through. Lauren initiated all of them. Collins's responses were bland, and he worked Allie into the conversation whenever possible. Oh. He was being honest with her.

She handed his phone back. "Thank you. It's just Lauren and I... I always felt like I was competing with her. Her mom would tell my mom something Lauren had accomplished, and it seemed like I was supposed to do the same thing. And then when you were dating her, well… I guess she's always been a little like competition."

He opened his mouth to say more when the doc walked in.

"Okay, let's get this wound closed up and get you out of here. You'll feel a pinch with the Novocain shot, but after that you shouldn't feel anything." And in a little bit, with a few *thunks*, Collins's wound was stapled shut and they were getting discharge papers and heading back to camp.

He wouldn't let her bring the truck around, insisting that he could walk and was tired of sitting.

They got to the truck, and Collins stopped her with a hand on the door. He glanced up. "It's you I want, Allie. It's always been you. We're under the stars, not that we can see many of them from here, but I've always wanted to do this." He leaned in and slid his arm around the back of her neck, tugging her close as his lips met hers.

Feathery light at first, then stronger and deeper. Allie lost herself in his arms as the dreams of a thousand nights came true in that moment. Collins cherishing her, returning her feelings, holding her close. She never wanted it to end.

Chapter Twenty

Collins woke with a headache. He hadn't slept much. It was hard to find a place on the pillow that didn't set his gash to pounding. And Scott woke him up about every two hours, or just when he'd drifted off to sleep. Allie had offered to give up her bunk and share with Melissa so he could have a soft bed, but he wouldn't hear of it.

He picked up his phone. It was early, but they had to pack and get on the road today, so there was no point in trying to go back to sleep. No new text from Kyle either. Not that he expected one. They had texted a bit last night. Kyle was concerned about Collins's injury but hadn't had time to check into Willie since they'd been working on the Realtor assault case. Collins had reassured him that it wasn't urgent, especially since they were leaving Arches and hopefully Willie.

His stomach growled. Time to get up and get some coffee. He and Allie had stopped for a burger last night after leaving the hospital. Plus, there was that amazing kiss they had shared. It wasn't ideal, but he was tired of waiting for ideal, since every one of his plans for some romantic time with her had been trashed.

He popped another ibuprofen and washed it down with bottled water then proceeded to pack up his sleeping bag and pad. He grabbed his duffle and headed for the bathrooms. He'd bet money Melissa would be up and making coffee by the time he got back.

And he was right. He knocked on the trailer door, and it opened immediately.

"How's the head?" Melissa waved him in.

"Sore, but coffee will help." He grinned and slid into the dinette.

Allie handed him a cup and slid in next to him. "Sleep okay?"

"Eh, but I'm not driving today, Scott is, so I can nap."

Her fingers feathered through his hair as she studied his gash. "It doesn't look too bad."

And it felt fine as long as she kept doing that.

But she stopped and asked, "What kind of muffin do you want?"

"Blueberry, please."

She handed it to him then brought over a plate of microwave bacon. Soon everyone else was up, and they ate quickly then packed the trailer to move out. The earlier they got to Bryce, the more chance they'd have of getting to see some sights today.

Scott expertly pulled the truck and trailer out of the campsite with Matthew and Kim following behind. They were leaving the farthest point on their road trip and heading back west for their last two stops. He only had three more days with Allie, and he was determined to enjoy them, headache or not.

They drove north past Arches and took the I-70 headed west. The land here was flat from horizon to horizon.

"How did the star watching go last night? I forgot to ask," Collins said from the front seat.

Scott's gaze darted to Melissa in the back seat via the rearview mirror. "Good. We were able to get our chairs set up and food out before it was full dark. We were there about an hour or so. Kim was trying some night photography, but I don't know how well it went. I heard Bryce will be even better because of its higher elevation."

At Green River, they pulled off the interstate and into town to fill up the gas tanks, including the extra one Collins had picked up in town yesterday, and use the restrooms.

They turned south on Highway 24. The two-lane was a bit prettier than the interstate.

Lighter-colored mesas and rock formations dotted the landscape. They passed a sign for Goblin Valley state park.

Melissa spoke up from the back seat. "I know we don't have time, but this would be a fun place to visit someday. The rock formations look like weird mushrooms and aliens. You just wander around wherever you'd like. It was so hard planning what places to stop at for this trip. There's just so much to choose from and not enough time."

After a while, the scenery grew greener, with more trees and some farms. Some red rock formations began to pop up, and the road ran alongside the Fremont River.

They passed the sign for Capitol Reef National Park. "That's another place I wish we could have visited," Melissa pointed out.

"Why is it called a reef? Was this area under water at some point?" Collins asked.

"Here's what the guidebook says. It's actually at the top of a fold in a mostly flat valley. The rocks are white, which reminded earlier settlers of the US Capitol building. And a reef was what they called any obstacle. Apparently it was difficult to get over the fold. There's also some old uranium mines back there. This highway wasn't even paved until the 1940s."

"Once again, I wonder if the people who live around here appreciate the odd beauty around them," Allie said.

"I suppose we take the Pacific Ocean for granted," Melissa pointed out.

"Probably true," Allie agreed.

Collins dozed, lulled to sleep by the soothing scenery, Journey's *Greatest Hits* album coming through the speakers, and the rhythm of the tires on the road. Something rough jolted the truck, and he sat up and glanced at Scott, who was gripping the wheel tightly. He checked the rearview mirror. Black tire tread streamed out beside them. "One of the trailer tires blew."

Scott nodded and eased the truck over to the edge of the road. Luckily, there was a shoulder.

Both men got out and examined the tire. Looked like the sidewall had blown out.

Matthew pulled in behind them and got out. "Flat tire?"

"Shredded. There's a spare in the back, but we'll need a tow truck to replace it." Collins squatted down. "There's a lock nut on here. Do you remember seeing the key anywhere?"

Scott blew out a breath. "No. Let me ask Melissa. Do you have any cell service?"

His phone was in the truck. "Let me check." He walked back to the cab and grabbed his phone. No bars. "Nope, do you?"

Scott shook his head. "Melissa, do you remember seeing anything in the trailer that looked like a lug nut? Did Daniel mention it?"

She chewed her lip. "I don't think so, but let me get in the trailer and look." She climbed out and headed back to the trailer.

"I'm going to pick up the pieces of tire we left on the road so no one hits them." Scott jogged off.

Collins leaned over to the back seat. "You feeling okay?" he asked Allie.

"I'm fine. The road hasn't been bad. So we lost a tire?"

He nodded. "It's not uncommon on trailers. But Daniel had gone over them with us before we left and said they were fairly new. So I'm surprised." Or was he? "Need anything?"

"No, but I am going to help Melissa look for that lug nut thing."

He opened the cab door for her and stood back, giving her hand a squeeze as she climbed out. Then he headed back to Matthew. "Since we don't have cell service, you'll have to drive to where you either have service or a town where you can call for a tow for us. Keep track of your mileage to tell them where we are, or find a mile marker or something for reference. We can't even give them GPS coordinates." He handed Matthew his roadside assistance card. "I added RV coverage before we left, so we should be good, if there's a truck anywhere close that can help. Also, call Daniel and see if he knows where the locking lug nut is."

"Will do." He climbed back in his truck and drove off back the way they had come from.

Collins bent down to look at the tire. It was hard to see because it had shredded, but it sure looked like one of the breaks was a straight line, like it had been cut, and not jagged like if it had been a blowout. He nodded to Scott. "What do you think about this? Seems like a cut, doesn't it?"

"We didn't run over anything. I would have known." He met Collins's gaze. "Thinking Willie's behind this somehow?"

Collins shrugged. "Possibly. We were gone from the campsite a lot. He knew where it was. But if he'd slit the tire at the site, it would have been flat and we would have noticed."

Scott picked up a couple of the pieces he'd retrieved. "Unless he just weakened the tire with a slice, figuring it'd blow out at some time."

"But he wouldn't know when that would happen, if he was planning on ambushing us."

"Maybe he just wants to mess with your head, make your life difficult."

Collins nodded. "Could be. By the time the truck gets here, changes the tire, and gets us back on the road, we'll be lucky to pull into the campground by dark. Did you check the spare?"

"Not yet. Let's do that." Scott stuck his head inside the trailer. "Lis, do you have the keys to the storage compartments?"

Melissa handed him the lanyard with the trailer keys on it. "No luck yet. I've looked every logical place. Now we're looking in all the illogical ones."

"Maybe it's with the spare. We'll look." Scott headed toward the back storage area where the spare was kept.

"We kept this locked, right?"

"Yeah, all the time. If you don't, they tend to stay ajar and then critters can get in." Scott unlocked the compartment, and they both lifted the door. The spare was covered by some camp chairs, so they moved those out of the way, and Scott lifted the tire off its mount. They looked it over.

"Looks fine. Might need a bit more air." Collins patted the tread. "Let's dig around in here and see if we can find that lock nut."

They spent the next fifteen minutes pulling everything out and looking in every crevice, but the key to the locking lug nut could not be found. After they loaded everything back in other than the spare, Scott locked the compartment back up. "I'm sure the tow truck driver runs into this all the time. He probably has an assortment of them."

Allie leaned out of the trailer. "You guys want lunch? It's a little early, but we might as well eat while we're waiting." She handed out a plastic basin with a bottle of water, soap, and roll of paper towels.

"Sure." Collins took it from her.

"Okay, you can use that to wash up with."

When he and Scott were done, they entered the trailer where the women had laid out lunchmeat, cheese, fruit, chips, crackers. Their typical lunch fare. They filled up paper plates and took them outside.

"If we have to picnic by the side of the road, it's nice to have such a great view." Collins patted the bumper next to him for Allie to join him. "Well, this wasn't exactly according to plan."

Allie laughed. "No, it wasn't. But something always happens on a trip. I thought we'd used up our quota already with your injuries and Matthew's running out of gas."

"Apparently not. But once the tow truck gets here, he'll have us back on the road. The worst that will happen is that we'll have to set up in the dark. But we've got the process down, so we'll be fine."

She nodded. "How's your head?"

"Now that I've eaten, I could use more ibuprofen." She started to rise, but he put his hand on her arm. "It can wait. Just sit here with me a bit more."

She smiled at him. "Okay."

Yes, this would be nice if it weren't for the circumstances. They hadn't even seen another car pass since they'd been here. Scrubby chaparral spread out along their side of the road and rolling hills sat in the distance on the other side. They really were in a remote area.

The sound of an engine reached their ears, and Matthew's truck grew larger as it neared until it reached them. He hopped out, and Kim followed.

"I see you didn't wait on us for lunch."

Allie smiled. "Food's in the trailer. Help yourself. There's a wash basin on the steps."

Kim headed that way.

Matthew handed the roadside assistance card back to Collins. "It's gonna be awhile. They have to send in someone from one of the bigger towns. I also got ahold of Daniel, but he didn't remember anything about any locking lug nut. So it's possible the people he bought it from didn't give it to him."

"Okay, thanks." Collins turned to Allie. "Wanna go for a walk?"

She looked around. "Sure. Let's get you that ibuprofen first." She gathered up their plates and took them in the trailer, then headed to the truck. Scott and Melissa were sitting with the front seats partially reclined, doors open. "Just going to grab some pills for Collins then we're going to take a stroll. I'm sure you'll be able to see us for miles."

"Just don't get hurt," Scott said.

"We'll try not to."

She dropped the tablets into Collins's hand, and after he

washed them down with the rest of his bottled water, he took her hand and they headed across the rocky land. The silence became a living thing, heavy over them like a blanket, broken only by the sounds of birds and insects. They were busy watching their steps over and around brush and rocks since there was no trail. Still, it was nice to get out and walk. The throbbing in his head would subside soon, once the meds kicked in.

Most of all, he liked being with Allie, the feel of her hand in his.

She looked up at him. "I almost forgot. Your home inspection is happening tomorrow. Jay is my first-choice inspector, and he'll do a good job. He's going to text me what he finds and then email the report. He knows I won't have much Wi-Fi or cell phone service, so I'll have to make sure I check in at the visitor center to get connected around that time."

"I'm curious to see what he'll find. I'd almost forgotten about the house on this trip."

"Hopefully nothing major. I think Melissa had some hikes planned for us tomorrow. I'm sure we'll discuss rearranging things since we won't make it to Bryce until tonight most likely."

"She won't be too upset, will she?"

"Nah. She's more flexible than she lets on. Her plans have contingency plans because she knows things happen. I think she just wants everyone to have a good trip and make the most of the time."

"She has done a fantastic job of planning out where to stay and what to do. That takes a lot of time." He squeezed her hand. "So what do you do for fun?"

She squinted up at him. "Fun? What's that?" She laughed then gestured to the land around her. "This. The last time I left the office for any length of time was Thanksgiving when Melissa and I went to Phoenix to be with our family. And that was fun. We did some hiking. But I've been so consumed with my business, which doesn't always stick to regular business hours, that I haven't made time for much else other than church and Bible study." She shrugged. "Until you came back into my life, I didn't have a real reason to make any room."

Warmth that wasn't from the sun flooded him. He liked being back in her life. "Just good mental health and all that. But I'm guilty of the same thing. So can we hold each other accountable to keep reasonable boundaries on work and find fun stuff to do?"

She grinned and swung his hand back and forth. "I like that idea a lot, accountability partner."

"Me too." He stopped and pulled her around to face him. "I like you a lot." His voice dropped, and he lowered his head touching his lips to hers, gently and then more insistently as he pulled her closer, his hands skimming across her back. Hers found the back of his neck. The world collapsed to just the two of them, just this moment. Desire flashed through him, and he pulled back, leaning his forehead on hers, catching his breath, feeling a bit like a man who couldn't quite slake his thirst. He had a feeling when it came to Allie, he might never feel like he had enough of her.

A hazy look filled her gaze as she met his, her lips rosy. He ran a thumb across them then gave her a quick kiss. "Maybe we should head back."

Her hand found his, and they headed back across the broken landscape.

After some silence, Collins spoke. "You're going to help me decorate my house, right? I mean, I've got no idea where to start with any of it."

"I could be persuaded." She gave him that smile that was only for him, that made the heat gather low in his belly.

"Oh really? What kind of persuasion?"

"I'll let you know."

He laughed. This was going to be fun.

WHEN THEY ARRIVED BACK TO THE VEHICLES, SCOTT AND Melissa appeared to be napping in the front seat of Collins's truck. Matthew and Kim were tossing rocks into the brush. Allie shook her head. Matthew always found a way to make a game out of things. He and Kim probably had a contest going.

She was thinking of going over tomorrow's plans with Melissa so she could be available for Jay's text.

"Did you hear that?" Collins turned and scanned the highway.

"What? Wait. Sounds like a truck." The unmistakable sound of a heavy engine reached Allie's ears just as a truck came into view. It quickly became apparent it might actually be their rescue.

"I hope that's it. I haven't seen hardly any traffic on this road since we've been sitting here." Collins rapped on the door frame. "Hey, Scott, I think the tow truck is here."

Sure enough, it slowed as it neared and pulled in behind them. Scott and Collins walked over to meet the guy. Allie climbed into the driver's seat vacated by Scott.

"Did you get a nap?" she asked Melissa.

"A little." A sly grinned crossed her face. "Did you have a good walk with Collins? Though from here, it looked a lot more like kissing than walking."

Allie's face heated. She just wiggled her eyebrows then sighed. "We talked about how we both work too much. I'm going to have to figure out how to make time for a relationship while trying to keep my business afloat."

"Have you heard from Rachel?"

"Not a peep. But then DataCorp hasn't asked for anything else either. Tomorrow I need to be near Wi-Fi around eleven to get the inspection report on Collins's house. I think the only place that has it is the visitor center."

Melissa nodded. "Yeah, we'll have to adjust our plans tomorrow. Tonight's our only night in Bryce, and Zion is two hours away. But because of the trailer, we have to have an escort through the tunnel on the highway, and that closes at six. So we'll have to plan the time carefully."

Collins appeared at the driver's window. "The tow truck guy didn't have a lock nut key that fit. He's going to have to go back to his shop and MacGyver something up."

Dread sunk deep into Allie's stomach. Sitting alongside of the road wasn't the best way to spend a vacation. Her thoughts spun to Willie. Would he come along and try something? Surely not with everyone, especially Collins and Scott, here. But this was a deserted place. On the other hand, how would he know this was the route they were going to take? Oh, it was on Melissa's itinerary that he had gotten a look at. She sent up a quick prayer for protection and for peace. She didn't want to worry about something that was a bunch of conjecture.

"Well, we have plenty of food. We have board games, cards. I have some magazines and a book. We can entertain ourselves for a while. I'm sure Matthew will come up with something fun."

Collins smiled and touched her arm. "We're definitely getting away from it all."

Melissa raised her seat upright. "I'm going to pull out the camp chairs. I've been in this seat too long."

"Good idea." Allie reached for her backpack then opened her door and climbed out. "Let's find a sunny spot." She gave Collins a kiss on the cheek as she passed him. "If you're bored, I can loan you one of my magazines. I have *Real Simple* and *Magnolia Journal* and *Better Homes and Gardens.* You can get ideas for your house."

He gave her a slow grin. "Save me a spot next to you."

Her senses were even more heightened than usual around him after that toe-curling kiss. As he pulled out the camp chairs with Melissa, she couldn't help but notice how his muscles flexed under his dark T-shirt. The whole camping trip had been a good opportunity to watch him in action. He set up four chairs. Matthew and Kim were off walking the landscape and…

Allie nudged Melissa. "Look."

Matthew was kissing Kim. Huh. When had that happened?

Melissa smiled. "I knew putting those two together was a good idea."

"You did? You planned that?"

Melissa shrugged. "I hoped."

She turned her gaze to Collins, who winked at her. Maybe there was something magical about that landscape after all.

ALLIE TUCKED HER MAGAZINES INTO HER BACKPACK, AND helped Melissa put the camp chairs away. It was mid-afternoon, and they were finally ready to get back on the road. The tow truck driver had a few choice words, but he managed to get the old tire off and the new one on. Collins had slipped him a hefty tip.

Melissa wanted to find a camping supply or tire store as soon as possible to see about getting that lug nut key in case one of the other tires blew. Collins and Scott had inspected all the other tires and their pressure. Everything looked okay. But no one wanted to spend another day like today.

"We won't be able to take the scenic route the rest of the way." Melissa looked over her map with Scott. "I don't think it's worth the risk, and we can't spare the time." She glanced at Allie. "It's not too twisty. Other than one spot, I think we're through the worst of it. You'd have to sit up front for the scenic route, though. So that's one good thing about going this way. Anyhow, we've probably got another three hours, so that will give us about an hour to get set up before dark."

"Great." Allie climbed in the back seat with Melissa.

Melissa kept her itinerary and guidebook open, rearranging tomorrow's plans.

The landscape turned into more farmland and red rock formations popped up along the road. For the non-scenic road, it was still pretty scenic. She was thankful the tire had blown when it did. For long stretches of the road, there wasn't much shoulder.

When they eventually turned onto Johns Valley Road, the road got a bit twisty. Collins turned and looked at Allie. "You doing okay? Do you want to sit up front?"

"I'm okay. As long as I keep my eyes out the front windshield, I'm okay." After a while, the road straightened out, and she was able to relax a bit. As they neared Bryce, pinyon pine and juniper gave way to ponderosa pine and manzanita along the road as they climbed to the higher elevation.

When they pulled into the visitor center, the air was much cooler, and not only because it was evening. Allie would need to pull her fleece out when they set up camp. Melissa got their campsite assignment, and after stopping to fill their water tanks, they headed over there. The ponderosa pine forested site was a welcome one from the wide-open dirt sites they'd been at.

As soon as the guys got the trailer situated on the site, Allie hopped in and grabbed her fleece. Then she and Melissa got to work setting things to right. They were at a campground with no hookups, but they could run the generators from six to eight p.m. and eight to ten in the morning. That would give them enough time to charge their phones and not overly deplete the trailer's battery backup.

The guys were cooking tonight, and lunch had been a long time ago. They were making brat packets that hadn't been eaten on pizza night, so they needed wood to create coals and for tonight's campfire.

Melissa stepped out of the trailer. "Hey, we've got some time, even though I know we're all starving. We can walk the rim from Sunrise Point to Sunset Point. It's about a mile there and back, but at least we could see some of the amphitheater. Then we can hit the camp store on the way back and get firewood. But if we start the fire now, someone has to stay here and watch it."

"Good plan." Scott snaked his arm around her waist. "But I'm grabbing some of those cowboy cookies to take with me."

"The light should be great this late in the afternoon," Kim said.

"I'll grab your gear." Matthew headed for his truck.

Allie exchanged a glance with Melissa and raised her eyebrows.

Collins came over and took her hand, and they headed out. The Rim Trail was a dirt path close to their campsite. The evergreens parted to reveal part of the amphitheater, which—as Melissa had informed them—was the correct term as it wasn't really a canyon, even though it was called that. It was the top step of a grand staircase that sat around 8,000 to 9,000 feet.

In the distance peeking between the trees they could see the colorful hoodoos created by erosion and the multi-colored layers of rock. In places, it looked like the rock had just melted away between segments. It was a beautiful walk and felt great after sitting for most of the day. The trail became paved as they neared Sunrise Point. They ascended the ramp to the raised viewing area. The horizon stretched on forever in the clear, high-elevation air.

She leaned back into Collins's chest. His arms came around her waist. It had grown chilly, and she was grateful for his warmth. She watched Matthew help Kim set up her shots with new eyes, kind of surprised she hadn't seen the attachment there before. "I can see why this would be a beautiful place to watch the sunrise. The vista really opens up to the east."

"If you're up early enough tomorrow, we can come out here and do that." His breath tickled her ear and sent goosebumps over her arms.

"Let's."

After another group shot, they continued down the trail. It was literally along the rim, and the same sense of falling over with a wrong move that had stunned Allie at the Grand Canyon returned here. She thought about the girl Collins had saved and her brother. What would they be like here where nothing would stop you from a long, thousand-foot fall to the bottom? She shivered.

The rocks here were more sculptural and less massive than in Arches. It was amazing to see the variety of ways nature carved itself through the land with water and wind. In places, the land scooped down below them, the rocks looking like a giant had raked them, creating grooves and furrows. This trip had certainly put her life and problems into perspective.

They arrived at sunset point and admired how the changing light and clouds shifted the colors and shadows across the rocks in the amphitheater. But Allie was starving and was glad to head back to camp.

She touched Matthew's arm. "The guys are cooking tonight, so why don't you and Kim stay here until sunset? You've got over an hour."

"That's a great idea."

She grinned. At the general store, she and Melissa looked around while the guys loaded up with firewood. "Better them than us," she told Melissa, who agreed.

Back at the campsite, the guys got the fire started. As soon as it was going, Allie stood next to it. It felt good in the cool evening, even though the sun was still up. The trees cast long shadows, and even the sun had lost most of its warmth. "It's going to be cold tonight. Will you guys be warm enough in your tent?" She held her hands to the fire.

Collins jabbed Scott. "We'll just huddle up. We'll be fine."

Scott gave him a playful shove to the side.

Once some good coals had formed, the guys placed the foil-wrapped packets in the fire to cook. They steamed and hissed. Packet meals were some of Allie's favorites. They seemed to represent camping. And cleanup was easy, which was a plus on her night.

Matthew and Kim came back just as it was nearly dark to join them.

After dinner, Melissa gathered the foil and the paper plates. "Keep some of those coals. We've got a special campfire banana split dessert."

Collins raised his eyebrow at Allie. "How does that work?"

"You'll see." She brought out more foil-wrapped pouches. "These don't need as long. Just about five minutes or so." She handed him one.

Collins used long-handled tongs to place the packet in the coals. When it was almost done, Allie handed him a clean paper plate and a spoon. He pulled the packet out, placed it on the plate, and carefully opened it. Inside was a peeled banana covered in now-melted mini marshmallows and chocolate chips. He took a bite. "Wow. That's good."

She smiled and handed him more packets.

"I'm going to start hot water for cocoa." Melissa stood on the step to the trailer. "Any takers?"

Every hand went up.

Allie leaned her head back and looked up at the purple sky, stars dotting it between the treetops. Contentment settled over her. Collins reached over the chair arms and took her hand. "This is about perfect." She turned her head to look at him. "The food, the sky, the fire. You." She smiled.

His gaze on her darkened, and she remembered their earlier kiss. Her face heated, and it wasn't from the fire.

His thumb stroked the back of her hand. "It is. Does my backyard have a fire pit? I can't remember."

"Hmm. I don't think so, but we can always put one in. There's space for it."

"Okay, first project in our accountability plan. Let's build a fire pit and enjoy it on a regular basis. That'll get us away from work."

"I like how you think."

"I like you." He leaned across the chair and kissed her gently.

Matthew ducked into the tent, coming back with both guitars. "Campfire sing-along time."

Collins slid a look at Allie and let go of her hand, taking his guitar from Matthew. "How did I let you talk me into this?"

"Chicks dig musicians." Matthew winked at Allie.

Firelight flickered over Collins's face and fingers as he picked and strummed through a song. She sang along out of rote but was more fascinated by watching him. He caught her at it and tossed her a wink. One thing she could do would be to encourage him to play the guitar more. Even though she could see his frustration born of his lack of practice, she could also see the joy that spilled through. He wanted to build a fire pit? Fine, but he'd have to serenade her. She smiled at the thought.

Chapter Twenty-One

The sky was just beginning to lighten when Collins stepped out of his tent and headed to the bathroom to clean up. He and Allie were going to watch the sun come up over Sunrise Point, ostensibly to see if it lived up to its name but really just to get some alone time with her. It was hard to believe they only had two more days left before returning to the real world and their busy schedules. They'd become close on this trip, but would their relationship survive their schedules? He'd like to think so, but they'd both have to make some changes.

He was about to knock on the trailer door when it opened. Allie stepped out. "Morning," she whispered. "Ooh, it's chilly out here. I made some coffee to take with us." She handed him a travel mug then stepped out and closed the trailer door behind her.

He reached for her hand. "I'll keep your hand warm."

She smiled at him. "How's the head?"

"Getting better." The coffee would help, but he was looking forward to being in a real bed again. But then he wouldn't have these earlier morning times alone with Allie.

They walked in silence along the trail, retracing their steps from last night. The forest around them was waking up, with sounds of birds and small animals rustling the brush and branches. They reached Sunrise Point, and a few other people had joined them, but everyone spoke in low murmurs, nature somehow commanding the same respect as a great cathedral.

He wrapped one arm around Allie—the other held his coffee —and pulled her against his chest as they watched the eastern sky lighten. They sipped their coffee and just looked, embraced by the silence that surrounded them while nature put on her daily show, painting the sky in rosier hues by the moment. Neither of them took any pictures. They simply enjoyed the moment.

He wanted more of these moments with her.

Once the sun had crested over the amphitheater, casting the rock formation in golden light, he kissed her cheek. "Great way to start the morning."

"Mmm." She nodded then sighed. "I kinda hate to leave here, but we do get to find out about your house inspection later this morning."

He didn't anticipate any surprises. In fact, he'd had enough surprises between his shoulder, his head, and the tire blowing. But there had been no sign of Willie yesterday, other than his apparent handiwork on the trailer tires. Maybe that was the extent of it. He hoped so. But he couldn't help but think if his head didn't hurt so much he'd be able to see what he was missing. Something seemed just out of his reach about Willie. He hoped Kyle would be in touch today.

His stomach growled. "Guess we should head back. I'm ready for breakfast."

"Me too." She curled her fingers through his, but their return to camp wasn't hurried.

After a quick breakfast, they packed up and were ready to go other than hooking up the trailer. They had several hours before they had to check out, and one place Melissa had put on their list was Mossy Cave. It was outside the park and would be easier to drive to if they weren't pulling the trailer. So that was their first stop. Then they'd come back, hook up the trailer, check out, and park near the visitor center so they could spend the afternoon exploring the rest of the park before they had to get on the road to Zion.

Outside the park entrance, they stopped at the Bryce Canyon National Park sign to get a group picture, then headed on to Mossy Cave. His phone dinged with a text from Kyle. He must have coverage now.

Have info. Call me ASAP.

Collins tried dialing but couldn't get a connection. Must have been just enough for the text to go through. He'd have service at the visitor center. Should they go back? Kyle said ASAP. On the other hand, they weren't going to be gone long, and he didn't want the others to wait for him. He couldn't think of anything that wouldn't wait until they got back.

They continued on the highway out of the park and turned on Highway 12 until they got to the trailhead pullout. The dirt-and-gravel path was an easy walk lined with ponderosa pines and other evergreens and canyon walls rising up both sides. The trail followed along a creek with water rushing through it, likely snowmelt given that it was still March. They crossed over the creek via a wood-and-steel bridge. The sight and sound of the water so close by was as refreshing as the trees, considering they had been in a desert environment before this, viewing water from a distance.

Collins tried to relax and enjoy the hike, but Kyle's message ate at him. The sooner he got the info, the better.

They turned left when the trail made a T, heading toward the towering rocks. The vegetation grew denser, and he could see the dark shadow of a grotto. The trail climbed, and a railing and then a fence appeared between the trail and the drop off. The grotto dripped water from its moss-covered stones, creating a lush contrast to the rocks around it.

"In the winter, this would be cool to see with the drips turning into icicles," Melissa added.

After taking in the view, they headed back to the trucks at the trailhead and then to the campsite to hook up the trailer. He tried Kyle's phone again as they drove back into the park and got through to his voicemail. He left a message that he'd try to call back in an hour or so when he got coverage.

They were nearly done hooking up the trailer when he noticed Allie frowning at her phone.

"What is it?"

"It's nearly eleven. Would you mind if I walked to the visitor center so I can get Jay's call about your house? I don't want him to have to wait on me."

He started to say it was fine. They didn't need her help to finish up here. But Kyle's text flashed through his mind. What if it was something about Willie? They'd already agreed not to go anywhere alone. "Take someone with you. And go inside the visitor center. Don't hang around outside."

She nodded. "I will. I'll meet you inside by where they play the movie about the park."

Relief washed through him. He was afraid she might think he was being a bit overbearing. He grabbed her hand and pulled her in for a quick kiss. "Be safe. And let me know what Jay says. I'll see you in a few minutes."

"I will." She moved off and asked Kim to go with her, and the two of them headed toward the visitor center. He watched until they disappeared among the trees. Had he done the right thing? Unease swirled in his gut. Best thing was to get finished, checked out, and headed to the visitor center.

***

ALLIE AND KIM HEADED THROUGH THE CAMPGROUND, THE trees' shadows making for a cool walk. She'd be glad to get inside the warm visitor center.

She turned to Kim. "How have you liked this trip so far? Getting everything you need?"

Kim's cheeks turned faintly pink. "It's been better than I expected. I've got a larger following on Instagram, including a couple of creepers, and I'll have more ideas than I know what to do with for my clothing line. Plus… Matthew." She gave a shy grin.

Allie returned it. "Yeah, I noticed that. I'm happy for both of you."

"We'll see how it works out. Long distance and all."

"Only six hours if you drive, one hour by plane."

"You and Collins made it work for a few months, didn't you?"

Allie shrugged. "We reconnected last November, but we weren't dating until he came back."

"Anyone can see he's awfully attached to you."

Now it was Allie's turn to flush. "It's mutual."

They entered the visitor center. Allie stationed herself outside the room where they showed the film, *Shadows of Time* that talked about the park. She checked her phone; she had coverage. The visitor center served as an information center, gift shop, and museum. The exhibits wove back and forth, creating their own aisles. Allie leaned against the wall at a corner so she could see in two directions.

Her phone rang. Jay.

Kim motioned to the gift shop area. "I'm going to look around. I won't go far."

Allie nodded and answered. Jay gave her the rundown of the inspection. Everything looked good, except for a small leak in the water supply behind the refrigerator. The travertine tile was stained by it, but it hadn't created any structural damage. He said he'd email her the pictures. Maybe she could go over them with Collins when he arrived. She thanked Jay and hung up. She sent a quick text to the listing agent asking for the leak to be fixed then pocketed her phone.

She looked for Kim but couldn't spot her. Perhaps she was behind one of the racks. She walked over to the gift area, worry pricking the back of her neck. She couldn't find Kim anywhere in the gift area. She tried texting her as she moved over to the exhibits. There were a few people around, but it wasn't crowded. She glanced at the ranger manning the info desk. Kim wasn't a child, so it seemed weird to ask for help finding her. Walking behind the display of the rock formations over time, she spotted a thin man disappearing around the end.

Fear washed over her like a tidal wave, and she couldn't catch her breath. That couldn't have been Willie. Her mind was playing tricks on her. No, she should talk to the ranger. And say what? She thought she saw a guy who creeped her out, and her grown adult friend had wandered out of sight? It sounded ridiculous even to her.

She needed to find Kim. That's all there was to it.

KIM WORKED ON GETTING A SHOT OF THE GREAT MURAL they had on the back of the visitor center wall, behind the exhibits. She'd spotted it when she was wandering around and ducked back to take a quick picture before Allie knew she was gone.

"Hey, Kim. Run out of gas lately?"

Kim turned at the voice. "Hi, Willie. I didn't know you were planning on coming to Bryce." The guy was a bit odd, showing up wherever they were. But he had rescued her and Matthew, so she at least owed him some courtesy. He was one of those clueless, gregarious people who thought everyone wanted his company.

"Seems like we all had the same idea of doing the big loop. Where's everyone else?"

"Allie's here with me. She's on the phone." She gestured in Allie's general direction. "The others are packing up the trailer."

"You guys are leaving today?"

"We'll spend some time in the park first. I'd better get back to Allie before she wonders where I'm at." She turned, but Willie grabbed her arm.

"Let's go find her together. And if you do anything I don't like, you'll never see Allie again."

Kim's knees couldn't hold her, and she stumbled against a display. She couldn't quite believe what she was hearing. "What does Allie have to do with it?"

"Quite a lot. Now stop talking and start walking." He gave her a little shove and flashed a knife at her which he pointed at her ribs.

She took a few steps, scanning the area for help. But it being the off season, there weren't many people in the visitor center, and she and Willie were behind some displays. She rounded the corner where Allie should have been. "She's gone." Relief and fear battled through her. Had he already gotten to Allie? No, he wouldn't have had Kim bring him to her.

But if he couldn't find Allie, what would he do to Kim?

COLLINS PULLED THE TRUCK AND TRAILER INTO A PARKING spot. "Do you mind checking us out, Melissa? I've got to call Kyle. We can meet back here."

Melissa climbed out. "No problem. Scott and I are going to walk down to the rim for a bit. When we meet up, we can decide if we want to eat lunch and take the Queen's and Navajo loop hike or take a driving tour instead."

"Sounds good." He had his phone out and was swiping Kyle's name. He didn't much care what they decided.

Kyle picked up. "Glad I got ahold of you. Have you seen that Willie guy around?"

"No, not in Bryce. But we had some trouble yesterday we thought might have been caused by him. Why?"

"His name is Willard Dumas. He's currently our best suspect for those attacks on the Realtors. Heather finished the composite sketch. It matched the owner of a Porsche that showed up on one of the neighbor's doorbell cams. We showed his driver's license photo in a six pack to Amanda Park, and she picked him out as her attacker. So did Elaina Gonzales. And it matched the photo you sent me, except now he's clean shaven."

Collins hopped out of his truck and nearly sprinted toward the visitor center. He had to get to Allie. Odds were that Willie wasn't here, but he wasn't taking any chances.

"That truck registered to a Robert Warren? Turns out that's his stepbrother. We're heading out to talk with him to see if he knows where Dumas is. Be careful. Dumas has served time for assault. He was originally charged with rape, but they pled it down. We'll put out a BOLO to the Park Service, the sheriffs in the surrounding counties, and Utah Highway Patrol. I'll text you the info so you can show it to a ranger if you spot him."

A cold sweat broke out over Collins as he said a few words to Kyle and pocketed his phone, yanking open the visitor center door.

***

ALLIE WASN'T SURE WHAT TO DO. SHE'D LOOKED ALL OVER the visitor center for Kim, even in the bathroom. She wasn't there.

She wanted to look outside, but she remembered Collins's warning. Had she told Kim? She couldn't remember. She headed for the closest door, wanting a peek outside to see if she could spot Kim. There were several doors, so she'd check all of them. She stepped outside, just to see Kim's blonde head disappear around the corner.

Darting out after her, she let the door slam shut behind her. "Kim!"

She turned. And so did Willie. Grinning at her. With a knife pointed at Kim's ribs.

"Run!" Kim screamed. "He wants you!"

Allie froze, trying to comprehend what Kim was saying. She needed help to save Kim, but she couldn't let her be carried off by Willie if she went to get help. How could she stop him?

Willie took a step toward Allie, dragging Kim with him. "Come here, Allie. Let's all go on a road trip together." He grinned.

She grabbed the door and darted back inside, tears clogging her throat, hating every minute of what she was doing. She ran to the info desk, not caring that the ranger was helping someone else. "Help! This man took my friend. He's out there with a knife." She pointed to the door she'd just come through.

"Calm down and tell me what's going on." The ranger studied her.

Being calm was the last thing she wanted. "Please, he's getting away. He's going to hurt her! Send someone out there."

The ranger picked up a radio, spoke into it, and asked Allie for descriptions then ran outside. Another ranger came over, and she followed him into an office. It was all she could do to keep the tears at bay so she could speak clearly and do everything she could to help the rangers rescue Kim.

It just felt like so little. She'd failed to help Kim when she needed her most. One moment Kim was in the visitor center with her, and Allie was on the phone. The next moment Kim was gone, like the nightmare Allie'd had often as a child, that one of her siblings would go missing. And Allie once again had been helpless. Surrounded by images of fantastic natural beauty, of fun-loving families, and adventure seekers, her emotions felt sharply out of place. Alone, except for the company of a park ranger and the chatter over her radio.

KIM USED THE DISTRACTION OF ALLIE'S APPEARANCE TO kick Willie in the knee and spin out of his grip. She expected the pinch of the knife, but it didn't come. She darted for the door behind Allie, but Willie grabbed her arm.

The door to the visitor center was just out of reach. Maybe Allie would look back and see her. She tried to scream but couldn't get more than a squeak out. Kyle's words rushed through her brain. *Never let anyone take you somewhere else.* If Willie was going to kill her, he could do it right here in front of the visitor center.

She reached back, grabbed his thumb off her arm, and twisted.

He yelped and loosened his grip.

She dashed for the door, grabbing at, missing, and finally grasping the handle and yanking it open. She ran inside, not looking back until she was at the info desk. "That man tried to grab me. He's got a knife. My friend got away." She could barely get the words out.

The ranger spoke into a radio then came around. "Is your friend named Allie?"

"Yes." Relief poured over her and tears flowed. "Is she okay?"

The ranger opened a door. "She's in here."

Allie rose from the chair in front of a desk. "Kim? Are you okay?" She pulled Kim into her arms and held her.

COLLINS NEARLY TORE THROUGH THE WHOLE VISITOR center. He didn't see Kim or Allie anywhere. Why hadn't they stayed put? Maybe they were forced to leave. He couldn't think of any other explanation for Allie not being where she said she would be.

He spotted a ranger, but she was on her radio, something about a missing girl. If they were looking for a lost child, that would take priority over looking for two grown women who weren't where he thought they should be. He ran back outside, colliding with Matthew coming in.

"I need your truck. Allie and Kim are missing. I want to alert the rangers at the entrance, and then I'm going to go look for Willie's truck."

Matthew's face paled, but he tossed Collins the keys as they sprinted across the way to the park entrance. Collins showed the rangers his badge, the BOLO from Kyle. "I think he's taken two women." He gave a quick description of Kim and Allie and of Willie's truck.

"We already got this information just a few minutes ago. We're not letting anyone leave, and there's only one way out." The ranger said.

Collins scanned the area, barely processing how they'd gotten the info about the missing women so quickly. But just past the visitor center, pulling out of a far parking lot was Willie's truck. "There he is. That green truck."

He didn't wait for the rangers but dashed across the parking lot to Matthew's truck and jumped in. He barely registered that Matthew had joined him before he gunned it, squealing out of the lot and down the park road following Willie deeper into the park.

"Why's he going this way? Ultimately it dead ends." He pressed the gas, narrowing the gap between him and Willie.

"Maybe he's not thinking." Matthew pulled out his phone. "Nothing from Kim."

"Look at this map of the area." Collins tossed him the park map off the dash. "Maybe there's a spur or dirt road that leads out of the park."

Matthew tapped the paper. "Yeah. The service road leads to a dirt road that heads out of the park. I bet that's where he's headed."

"Got enough signal to call the rangers and tell them?"

"Think so." He grabbed the permit off the dash and dialed the emergency number. Just as he was explaining, Willie swung off the road, as Matthew had predicted. He pulled the phone away. "Lost the signal. But they're right behind us. They gotta know where this road goes. He won't get away."

Collins ran through all the options as they tore through the park employee housing. Luckily they weren't in the main park area where other people could get hurt. With the shell on the back of Willie's truck, it was hard to see if the women were with him. But they had to go on that assumption. Which meant that many maneuvers he could use to stop Willie could hurt them.

They bounced along the road, the trees thick along the side. Collins did his best to keep Willie within his sights. What was Willie's end game? Everything about this guy pointed to his having a plan. That didn't sound like a guy who'd panic and head down a dead-end road. Unless he was so narcissistic he thought he'd get away with it.

Matthew studied the map. "The road splits off up here. The right goes right to the main highway. The other goes somewhere off the map. I don't think he'd take that one."

"He'd want to hit the highway so he could get away fast and hide. He'll have to change vehicles if he doesn't want to get caught. This isn't a metropolitan area, so that's going to be hard." What was his plan? Could he have another vehicle stashed in the woods out here somewhere?

Collins lost sight of Willie as the road veed in two different directions and trees limited his line of sight. Which one to take? He didn't know where the left one went. He slowed and swung to the right, toward the highway. The ranger behind him took the other road.

After a while, when Willie's truck didn't come into view, he knew he'd made the wrong choice.

He had to pray that they could succeed where he had failed.

Chapter Twenty-Two

Kim shivered in Allie's embrace. "I'm okay. You distracted him enough that I was able to get away from him. But I think he took off." She held on to Allie, not sure her own legs could hold her up.

Allie led Kim back to the chairs, and they sat. It was then Kim realized there was another ranger in the room, seated at the desk.

Kim told him what happened, holding on to Allie's hand for strength. They had pulled up the surveillance camera footage that backed up her story.

Allie stared at her phone. "I haven't been able to get ahold of Collins. He's got to be frantic with worry."

The ranger gave a soft chuckle. "Is he a cop?"

"Yeah." She frowned.

"He was already at the front gate looking for you. He saw the suspect's truck and took off after him. We've got our officers on it too."

Kim met Allie's worried gaze. "Do you think he knows we're safe?"

"I don't think so." Allie shook her head. She turned to the ranger. "Is there any way to let him know we're both safe? I don't want him putting himself in danger chasing Willie because he thinks Willie has us."

He picked up his radio and spoke into it. Kim didn't really understand what all they were saying on the radio, but the ranger smiled.

"He'll be one happy man to see the two of you."

COLLINS WASN'T SURE HIS LEGS HAD EVER FELT SO WOBBLY as he strode into the visitor center, Matthew right behind him. The rangers manning the roadblock to the highway had informed him that the women were unharmed. At that point, as much as he wanted Willie to pay for his crimes, he was more interested in seeing Allie for himself, wrapping her in his arms.

The ranger at the info desk smiled and pointed to the door that said Authorized Personnel Only. Collins yanked open the door to see Allie and Kim sitting in front of a desk opposite the ranger. He'd never seen such a wonderful sight. Somehow, Allie was in his arms, and he was holding her like he never wanted to let her go.

He barely noticed that Matthew was doing the same to Kim. He probably felt the same way.

Allie's phone buzzed, and she pulled away to answer her text. "It's Melissa. She and Scott are back at the trailer wondering where we are and where Matthew's truck is." She glanced at the ranger. "Can I tell them to come here?"

He nodded.

Soon Melissa and Scott joined them. The room was too small, and the ranger needed to take their statements. He started with Kim and the rest of the group waited outside. Allie, clinging to Collins's hand, told her part of the story.

So she *had* listened to him. He squeezed her hand as she continued. "I just wish I'd told the rangers when I first spotted him. Even if I didn't know all about his criminal past, I could have had him detained or something."

"But you didn't know." Melissa laid a hand on her shoulder. "And it all turned out okay. You girls were brave and amazing, rescuing yourselves. It's true how those self-defense moves that feel so silly when you're practicing them come in handy when you really need them."

"I didn't feel very brave."

Kim came out and straight into Matthew's arms. If they were hiding their relationship before, they weren't now.

The ranger called Allie back. Collins's hand felt empty when she removed hers from it. He heard Kim's side of the story as she told it to the group. Then he and Matthew gave their versions.

When they were finally free to go, Melissa looked at her watch. "We're going to miss the cutoff time to get an escort through the tunnel at Zion. Plus, we haven't eaten. Why don't we go into town and get food? We can make a decision then."

He was grateful for Melissa and her clear thinking. He handed Scott the keys to the truck and took hold of Allie's hand. He wasn't going to let her out of his sight unless absolutely necessary.

—

As the adrenaline drained from Allie, she was glad they had chosen to eat in a restaurant attached to the Best Western. The table was mainly quiet while they placed their orders. And since it was late for lunch and early for dinner, they had the place nearly to themselves.

Melissa pulled out her itinerary. "We've got some options tonight, depending on what you all want to do. We can still go to Zion, but we'll have to take the long way around. It'll take an extra hour, meaning we've got a three-hour drive ahead of us. We'll likely have to set up in the dark."

No one said anything. Allie couldn't imagine trying to set up the trailer tonight. She wasn't sure she had enough energy to even eat.

"Or we could stay here at the motel tonight and make a decision tomorrow. If we decide to head to Zion still, we could get there by ten or eleven and find a place to park the trailer until we can check in. Or we could head toward home and I could start looking for places for us to stay between here and there."

The idea of a hot shower and a real bed almost made Allie want to cry. Heads nodded around the table.

Scott leaned back. "Honestly, I think staying here tonight is the best plan. No one wants to drive three hours and still have to set up on the other side. Let's get some good sleep and see what tomorrow looks like."

Allie noticed Melissa hadn't mentioned going back to Bryce as an option. She shuddered at the thought. Willie was still on the loose, but staying in a motel with doors that locked felt a lot safer than the trailer. Maybe she'd feel different later.

"I'll go call and cancel our reservation for tonight." Melissa stood and moved toward the waiting area of the dining room.

"We should see what kind of rooms they have for us tonight," Scott said. "We'll need to figure out a third bed in the guys' room."

"I can sleep in the trailer again," Matthew volunteered, but Kim's hand tightened around his.

Collins shook his head. "No. We're all going to stay inside together. I'm not taking any chances. Even if it means we have to pile sleeping bags on the floor."

Melissa returned just as their server brought their food. "It's taken care of. If we decide to go on to Zion, we'll be able to check in early."

They ate in relative silence, and when the meal was over, they headed to the motel next door and got two rooms close together. All the doors opened to interior hallways, and they were able to get a rollaway for the guys' room.

They headed back out to the trailer to grab their bags and then returned to their rooms. "Kim, you want the shower first?" She'd been through the most trauma, so Allie thought she might want to shower and head to bed.

"Sure. Thanks." She dug through her bag, grabbed a few things, then headed to the shower.

Allie flopped on the bed next to Melissa.

"Are you okay?" Melissa's brow furrowed.

Allie shrugged. "I guess. I mean, nothing really happened to me other than being afraid for Kim."

"Don't underestimate what you went through."

"Here's what bothers me the most. The moment I couldn't find Kim, my instinct was that she was in trouble. But I didn't want to make a scene." Allie shook her head. "It's just this whole trip I've been focused on everything else: the DataCorp account, Rachel, Collins's home inspection. If I hadn't been on the phone with Jay or waiting for him to send the email with the pictures, Kim and I would have been together. She would have been safe. My job and my desire to make nice for everyone else isn't a positive thing; it's become a negative. I'm so distracted by what I have to do for other people that I don't notice the people I'm with and what they need." She rubbed her hand over her face. "I don't know what to do." She stared at the textured ceiling as if it might have some answers.

Melissa pushed a strand of hair off Allie's face. "Look, Allie, you and I had to put our siblings first as a matter of necessity. I think when we have to do that from such a young age that it becomes ingrained in us. Everyone around us feels like our responsibility. Not to mention the desire for security. I see what's happening with you and DataCorp. I went through that last year with Broadstone. I couldn't imagine a life without that company. It took some pretty serious things happening for God to get my attention, to help me see that he had a better life waiting for me."

Melissa glanced at the bathroom door, but the shower still

ran. "You're not responsible for what happened to Kim. She could have stayed right by you. Yes, you should listen to your instincts. God gives them to you for a reason. And you should reconsider if DataCorp is giving you the life you want. Especially if you want a future with Collins. Things will have to change. I know this from personal experience." She gave a soft smile.

Allie reached for Melissa's hand and squeezed it. "Thanks, big sis. You always know what to say."

"I've learned the hard way, and I'd like to spare you some of my pain, if at all possible."

The water shut off. "I'd better get my stuff together if I want to hop in next." She gathered up her toiletries and a fresh change of clothes.

Kim exited the bathroom in a cloud of vapor.

Allie hopped in and soon steaming water was pouring down on her. The token showers at the campgrounds only gave you about five minutes to wash and rinse, so there was no luxuriating in the warm water like this. She let the spray pound her neck and shoulders, washing away the tension. Now if it would only wash away the memories so she could sleep tonight.

Matthew knocked on the women's room door.

Melissa opened it. "Hey, Matthew." She pulled the door open wider.

Kim sat on a bed, her head wrapped in a towel, studying her phone. She looked up, a smile not reaching her eyes.

"Thought you might want to go down to the lobby and find some hot chocolate." He took a step in the room, his foot bracing the door so Melissa didn't have to keep holding it. He shoved his hands in his front jeans pockets. Maybe this wasn't a good idea, but he needed some time with her, to make sure she was okay. The shower was running; that must be where Allie was.

Kim looked at Melissa then back at him. "Sure. Just let me comb out my hair." She pulled the towel off her head as she bent over her bag, then she dragged a comb through her damp-darkened blonde hair, the comb leaving tracks. She grabbed a clip out of the bag and twisted her hair up.

Turning and spotting him watching her, she gave another tight smile. "I need some shoes." She grabbed some flip-flops and slipped them on.

He looked over to see Melissa watching him watching Kim, something like concern in her eyes. "Don't forget to grab a room key." Melissa pointed to the dresser with the TV.

"Right." Kim swiped it up. "Ready." She turned back to Melissa. "We won't be late."

Melissa nodded, and Matthew followed Kim out of the room, letting the door *thunk* closed behind them. He reached for Kim's hand, and she let him take it, but something didn't feel right. It was like she'd retreated inside herself. He didn't know what to do with that.

Downstairs, they found the station that had tea, coffee, and hot chocolate. He made them cups and then headed toward the deep, leather couches that faced the stone fireplace. The whole area had a western lodge vibe. They sank into the cushions. He handed her a cup and slipped his arm around her shoulder, pulling her close. She didn't resist, but she didn't lean into him the way she usually did. And he couldn't help but feel it was his fault. He should have gone with Allie and Kim to the visitor center. But he'd liked the idea of the woman he was interested in spending time with his sister. He'd never suspected what would happen.

"Talk to me, Kim."

She lifted a shoulder. "I was an idiot. I wandered off like a little kid, even though I told Allie I'd stay put. Willie grabbed me. Until I saw the knife, I thought he was a good guy, that

Collins was overreacting because he was a cop, like my brother. How could I be so wrong about someone?" Now she looked at him, tears pooled in her eyes.

He trailed his fingers along her shoulder. "I thought he was a good guy too. Especially when he rescued us when we ran out of gas. Collins thinks Willie siphoned the gas from my tank so he could play the hero. We both saw what he wanted us to see. I don't want to be the kind of guy who goes around thinking the worst of people."

Kim was silent for a long time. Matthew wasn't sure what to do or say. He'd never been in a situation like this before, and all he wanted to do—desperately—was to make Kim happy, to see her smile light up her eyes like it usually did. He'd never felt so helpless.

"When I saw the knife, I knew immediately that I'd made the wrong choice, and I just wanted to take it all back, return to standing next to Allie."

"You couldn't know." He swallowed, the knot in his throat feeling like a cue ball, making it hard to get the words around it.

She shook her head. "He was awfully brazen, coming into the visitor center. He knew how to play on my fear for Allie's safety. And then when I saw her, it was like she was my hope and my nightmare all at once. Yes, she had seen that Willie was taking me, but she was the one he wanted. And I'd just been the bait to get her. And I felt terrible about it. When she ran back inside, it was like the feelings reversed. I was glad she was safe and terrified for myself.

"I'll never tease Kyle again about being overprotective. If he hadn't made me practice those self-defense moves over and over, I wouldn't have been able to react." She started shaking. "Who knows where I'd be now, where he would have taken me." Her shoulders shook with sobs.

Matthew pulled her close, letting her soak his T-shirt as he wrapped both arms around her. He held her, but he had no idea what he was doing. He rarely saw his sisters cry. Brittany cried more than any of them, and he was usually able to make a joke or tease her to make her feel better. But nothing came to him, and he couldn't find anything about the situation to joke about.

Not to mention he wasn't sure what to do about his own feelings. Short of wanting to flatten Willie for scaring his girlfriend, he didn't quite know how to handle the residue of the fear he'd had when Collins had told him what was happening, and they'd taken off in his truck. He'd been riddled with disbelief for the first part of it, thinking at first that either Collins was joking—until he looked at his face—or that the girls were. And a lot of guilt came with that.

Once he wrapped his brain around Collins's words, it had been such a roller coaster of trying to figure out what was really going on, thinking Willie had gotten away with the girls, then finding out they were safe, then seeing Kim for himself at the visitor center, not quite believing she was safe until he felt her in his arms. He didn't want to think about those feelings, never wanted to feel them again.

Normally he just thought about something he could look forward to or some silver lining. But he was having a hard time doing that right now. He couldn't find any good thing about what happened today other than how it ended. And he was having a hard time getting his brain to think about something good in the future. Like tomorrow. Zion should be fun, shouldn't it? But he couldn't get his brain to go there.

So maybe, just for now, he'd let Kim cry in his arms. He didn't know what else to do. But he knew he'd never let her be in danger again.

<hr>

THE GOOD THING ABOUT THE MOTEL ROOMS WAS THAT Collins would get a real bed tonight. The bad thing was he felt isolated from Allie, when all he wanted to do was hold her. The shower had stung his stitches when the spray hit his head, but it still felt good. The first time he'd really felt clean on this trip, not that you expect to feel real clean when you're camping. But after today, he needed it.

Scott was laying on one of the beds channel surfing.

"Where's Matthew?"

"He was going to see if Kim wanted to go to the lobby and get hot chocolate. I think he needed some time to make sure she was really safe. I remember that feeling all too well from last year when Melissa and I crawled out of that burning building."

Collins ground his jaw. He didn't like the idea of any of them being out of his sight, but he figured the lobby was safe enough. And he understood Matthew's need to get Kim alone after today.

In fact, it wasn't a bad idea at all. "How about I go next door and send Melissa over here for a few minutes?"

Scott gave him a wry grin. "Need to check on Allie?"

"Something like that."

He opened the door but flipped the swing bar privacy lock so it kept the door from closing all the way. He knocked on the women's door.

Melissa swung it open. "It's like Grand Central Station here."

Collins tilted his head. "You can head over and visit with Scott for a while, if you'd like."

"If I'd like?" She gave a half smile and glanced back over her shoulder. "Sure." But she flipped the lock like he had so the door didn't shut all the way.

Collins moved over to where Allie sat on the bed and sat next to her. "Hey."

She had showered and changed into a T-shirt and yoga pants, wet hair pulled into a pony tail. A soft smile lit her face. "Hey yourself. How'd your head handle the shower?" She reached up to feather his hair away from his staples.

"It was a little tender, but it felt so good taking a shower longer than five minutes that I didn't mind." And he certainly didn't mind her touch, which was sending lightning up and down his body.

"Yeah, the shower was definitely the best part of today."

He slid his hand up her neck and pulled her close, planting a kiss on her temple. "How are you doing? Really."

She let out a long sigh. "I'm okay. I'll be fine. I just hate how today went. Especially since if I'd been paying closer attention to what was going on instead of being obsessed with work, it never would have happened."

He ran his hand down her arm to her hand and took it in both of his. "You don't know that. If he hadn't gotten you there, who knows what he would have done. Who knows but we'd foiled other plans of his? You did interrupt his attack on Amanda Park."

"Not on purpose."

"Still. She's grateful to you."

Allie nodded but didn't say anything. Finally, she looked up. "I'm just glad it turned out okay. Thanks for coming to my rescue." She lifted her hand to his jaw.

He covered her hand with his own, not ready to lose her touch. "I'll always come for you, Allie. Whenever you need me." His voice was low and rough. If he thought for a second about what could have happened, he'd lose it. He pulled her hand to his chest and kissed her, soft and tender. "You going to be able to sleep tonight?"

"I think so." She gestured to her backpack. "I have a book in there to help. What about you?"

"I'll be all right." He planted a kiss on her forehead as he levered himself from the bed, knowing each second he stayed, the harder it would be to leave.

But later in his room—with Matthew on the rollaway and Scott in the other bed, the lights out—he couldn't sleep. His brain was in after-action report mode, analyzing everything that happened, what he could have done differently. He should have made Allie stay with him. Who cared about the dumb house inspection? It was no big deal.

He was the cop here. He was supposed to keep them all safe. So how was it his girlfriend and his partner's sister both were taken right from under his nose? He'd talked to Kyle after dinner and before his shower, giving him the update on Willie and what had happened.

Kyle's silence had spoken volumes. He'd expected Collins to keep his sister safe. Yeah, Collins was disappointed in himself. Willie had shown his true colors with the gas incident and the rock to the back of Collins's head—not that he could prove either one. Sure, it might not have been enough evidence to convict him in court, but it should have been enough to cancel the rest of the trip and head back home, to make better decisions. How much more did he need?

Unless Willie knew where they lived. He couldn't. Could he? Before today, he'd figured Willie to be an opportunist. But when he realized that Willie had been Amanda Park's attacker, there was no way it was a coincidence that Willie happened to now be two states away from home. Right where they were. So how had Willie found out where they were going? Yes, he'd looked at Melissa's itinerary, but before that? How did he know where to find them?

And until he figured that out, he didn't know if home was the safest place for them to go.

Chapter Twenty-Three

Collins's phone rang just as they were heading down to breakfast. One of the park rangers from yesterday let him know they'd apprehended Willie last night. Collins had offered to come in to help and provide information, but he was politely and clearly told to stay out of the way. As much as he wanted to be a part of catching Willie, the locals weren't interested in his help. Still, it was good news, and should put everyone's mind at ease. He texted Kyle the news, even though the ranger had said they'd be in touch with LVPD.

After they'd gotten their food, Collins put the question to the table that had kept him up all night. "After everything that happened yesterday, and knowing that Willie's been caught, do you all want to head home or continue on to Zion? If we head home, we'll still need to find a place to stay overnight, so we'll only end up home a day early."

There were a few shrugs, but everyone's gaze turned to Kim.

She wrapped her arms around herself and didn't say anything.

Matthew draped his arm over her shoulders and looked at her. "We can do whatever you want."

"I hate to put a damper on everyone's trip." Kim spun her

coffee mug. "Willie's not a threat any more. So let's try to finish up this trip on a good note."

Matthew gave her a squeeze. "That's my girl. We'll still have fun."

She didn't look convinced, but she didn't say anything.

Collins looked at Allie. "What do you think?"

"I like being with you." Her voice was soft, but it made his heart want to break out of his chest.

They packed up their motel rooms, checked out, and were on the road early. They hadn't lost a whole day since the original plan was only to reach Zion in the afternoon yesterday and they'd be there by lunch today. They could still have a good time.

Collins let Scott drive again, and as the landscape swooped by the window on Highway 12, he turned over how Willie might have known where they were. Kim had been posting on social media, but Willie would have had to know where to look. Which meant he needed to know Allie's name. His mind went back to the guy who'd rear ended her, but he didn't look like Willie at all and wasn't a known associate. That was most likely just bad luck.

Still, until he could figure out how Willie knew Allie's name before the trip, he wouldn't rest easy. When LVPD got custody of Willie, it'd be a question he'd have one of the detectives ask. He and Kyle wouldn't be allowed on the case because they were too close to it.

The scenery was stunning as it had been for the whole trip. He glanced back at Allie. She had looked at the map and insisted that she'd be fine. They passed the area—and a tourist stop— that highlighted where Butch Cassidy was known to hang out.

They headed south on Highway 89, roughly following the Sevier River, the landscape flattening out and becoming low hills of chaparral. He tried to put it all out of his mind. They'd have a good trip. If the RV park would let them in early—and they should—then after a quick lunch they could hit the park. As they got closer, the scenery became dotted with more pines and other evergreens, and the hills became more mountainous. The east fork of the Virgin River began accompanying them, and resorts and river tour companies dotted the highway. Highway 89 turned into Highway 9 past Mount Carmel. They were getting close.

The rest of this trip was going to be a good one. He was determined of that.

THE RIDE TO ZION WAS QUIET, BUT KIM DIDN'T MISS THE glances Matthew shot her way. She wanted to put in her earbuds and listen to music, tune everything out, but considering how close they'd become on this trip, that just seemed rude. So she'd asked him to sync his phone to play music through the car speakers. The silence was too much.

But the music didn't drown out the soundtrack in her head that she'd been the victim of an attempted abduction. And that it could have gone very, very bad. She wanted to get back to the easy relationship she'd had with Matthew, but she couldn't. All she really wanted to do was curl up in her bed at home and watch Netflix while downing Ben and Jerry's Chunky Monkey.

She could have spoken up this morning, and the group would have headed for home. But they'd still have a long drive ahead of them, and they wouldn't be home today. Besides, she didn't want to be the party pooper.

She'd be home soon enough.

She pulled her knees up on the seat, wrapping her arms around them, and closed her eyes. Maybe if she could actually sleep, it'd make time go faster.

At the east entrance to Zion, they paid the oversized-vehicle fee for the Zion-Mount Carmel tunnel. The road looked to get quite a bit twistier as they went on. Allie studied the map and tried to decide if she should gut it out or not.

Collins made the decision for her. "Allie, you should sit up front the rest of the way." They pulled over at a scenic lookout. The soaring cliffs rose in the distance. It was a good break to stretch their legs, and she got a long hug from Collins before he climbed into the back seat with Melissa.

She glanced over at Kim who studied the scenery with an uninterested stare and didn't take one picture.

Allie sighed. It would just take time, she supposed, but she wanted to help Kim. She just didn't know how.

They were now following Pine Creek, and the road seemed to twist as much as the creek did, cutting through the rock and almost folding back on itself.

They passed through two tunnels in quick succession carved into the golden rock. But they were nothing compared to the big tunnel that was to come. The Canyon Overlook Trail parking came up just before the tunnel.

Melissa spoke up from the back seat. "I think this might be the place to come back to once we get settled. It's a great overview of the canyon from the top, whereas most of the trails are at the bottom and go up. There's just no place here to park with the trailer."

As they moved along, a tunnel ranger directed them to where to go to be measured and wait to be allowed through the tunnel.

When it was their turn, Allie's heart rate ticked up. She didn't like tunnels, especially when you couldn't see through to the other side. The truck's lights turned on immediately. Unlike most tunnels, this one didn't have any overhead lights. The over-a-mile-long tunnel felt much longer driving in the dark. Occasionally there would be "windows" or galleries on the passenger side with amazing views. There were six of them total. But her eyes barely adjusted to the bright light before plunging back into the dark.

She was glad when they safely reached the other side, and she could breathe freely. And they'd have to do it again coming the other way to get to the trailhead, but then they wouldn't be pulling the trailer and have to wait for the one-way traffic control.

But the road moved through a series of switchbacks, making her glad Collins had insisted she sit up front. The scenery was striking, and she focused on that, not the swirling in her stomach or the fact that the road was clinging to the side of the mountain. Luckily breakfast was a long time ago. They crossed the Virgin River over a bridge that spanned the gorge. And the road finally straightened out as they reached the valley floor. They exited the other side of the park and headed for the RV campground in Springdale, just a half mile outside the park.

The RV campground let them in early, and they had another shady site. She and Melissa got lunch items out while Collins, Scott, and Matthew got the trailer and tent set up and ready. Kim sat at the dinette, pulling out paper goods. She looked at her phone, made a disgusted noise, then swiped a few times before putting it away.

Allie raised her eyebrows. "What was that?"

Kim let out a long sigh. "Some creeper. The disadvantage of having a lot of people follow you."

Allie hugged her around her shoulders. "I'm sorry. That's the last thing you need."

They ate lunch and packed up snacks and water for the trip, and drove back through the park and the tunnel, coming out the other side. It wasn't as bad this time, since Allie knew what was coming with the twists, turns, and tunnel.

They parked at the trailhead and piled out. Kim didn't bring her camera or tripod. Allie worried for her. How was she handling what happened yesterday? She'd been quiet, which was understandable. But her not bringing her camera gear… well, it just showed how drained she must feel at every level. Allie wished there was something she could do to help Kim. But it would just take time. And frankly, she was a bit wrung out herself. Still, she'd keep an eye out for her. She caught Matthew's worried looks too.

They crossed to the stone steps that ascended the ridge. A large cave greeted them with its coolness. The trail hugged the cliffs, the drop-off steep. The railings helped, as did Collins's firm grip, but her stomach swirled, and she stayed away from the edge. "Whoever was the person who came out here and thought it would be a good public hiking trail must have been a bit crazy." Her voice shook a bit, but she tried to keep it light. She couldn't imagine trying to install the railings. They would have had to hang off the cliff. Still, she was very grateful for them.

Then they came to the place where there were no railings. The trail didn't get much wider and an overhang of rock kept hikers from scrunching too close to the cliff face. She squeezed Collins's hand, suddenly having visions of herself plummeting over the edge, taking Collins with her. It almost looked like a grotto or sea cave with its bits of green fern and lichen. She took some deep breaths and focused on that.

"Maybe I could just wait here for you guys to go and come back."

Collins shook his head. "You can do this. I'm not going to let you fall."

Her legs shook, and she wasn't sure they'd carry her across. But other people were doing it successfully. *You can do this.* She scanned the area for something to focus on. Bushes and small trees clung to the edge of the path. Worse came to worse, she could grab one of those if she started to fall.

"Okay, let's go."

Collins squeezed her hand and let her stay close to the wall, hunched over. Soon they were on the other side of the opening, a large boulder keeping them from the abyss's edge, and the railing started up again. But it was attached to a planked boardwalk that cantilevered out over the edge. Once they were across and the trail widened, her heart rate began its descent into somewhat normal. She was able to appreciate the soaring mountainous forms around her, the trees clinging to the sharp ridges. Kinda how she felt.

When they reached the cliff overlook, the views were amazing. The whole expanse of Zion canyon spread out before them. They could also see the road they had traveled winding like a slithering snake back and forth through the mountain descent.

She found a boulder to perch on, Collins behind her, arms wrapped around her, holding her safe. The views were stunning, reminding her of Ooh Aah Point at the Grand Canyon with the views of the canyon in front of them and the canyon walls rising above them. For a moment, everything was perfect. The stress and trials and worry of the past days fell away. God's presence surrounded her, holding her, reminding her that nothing was out of his control. Not what happened yesterday or what would happen tomorrow.

She leaned her head back against Collins. "It just seems like God is closer here. No distractions, just us stunned by his amazing creation. Maybe it literally has to be in front of my face to take time to notice it and appreciate it."

She felt more than heard his rumbled assent. "I like to think I'm in control until it's painfully obvious that I'm not. This reminds me how little I am in the scheme of One who can create something as majestic as this."

They sat in quiet for a moment, letting the peace wash over them.

She snuck a peek at Kim, who sat with her legs pulled up, arms wrapped around them. Matthew sat nearby but not touching her. He was pointing things out in the rocks and cliffs. Kim nodded absently. But she didn't take one picture.

THEY MADE THEIR WAY BACK ALONG THE TRAIL TO THE trucks, through the tunnel, the twists, and finally back into the visitor center parking lot. Allie wanted to congratulate herself for all she'd accomplished today. Like with many hard things, there was usually a reward at the end. She was thinking tonight it would involve chocolate.

Melissa had asked everyone what they wanted to do next. She suggested the Emerald Pools trail, and everyone agreed. They drove to the Zion Lodge and parked near the trailhead. It was an easy, paved trail with trees and greenery lining it.

Allie lagged a minute, tugging on Collins's hand, so she could come even with Melissa. Kim and Matthew moved ahead of the group.

"Thanks for doing all this, Melissa. I know it was a ton of work figuring out all the options and what we could do with limited time."

Melissa waved her off. "It was my pleasure. I mean that. I love to plan things." Her face darkened. "I just wished we hadn't had to factor in Willie. If there'd been some planning technique to keep him away, I would have been all over it."

"I know." She gave her sister a soft smile, then moved ahead of her with Collins.

The trail ran alongside the Virgin River before turning deeper into the canyon. The trail etched into the side of the mountain. She let go of Collins's hand as he moved in front of her, pointing out tricky spots and holding back the occasional brush or branch. If there were any snakes, she hoped he saw them first. From here, there was no sign of civilization. It was amazing how quickly they could get away from it all. That feeling of desolation came over her again, one she'd experienced a few times on this trip.

Matthew and Kim were ahead of Collins, but no one did much talking. The canyon rose up in front of them and soon they joined a few other hikers at the emerald pools. Water cascaded off the rocks above them and the path wound behind the waterfall, which dropped into the rocks below. After gazing at it for a few minutes, they continued hiking up and around to the top of the falls. Here the rocks were scooped out and worn smooth by the rushing water. A chain guarded the waterfall. But more people and several kids splashed in the water that was accessible.

A woman turned in circles. "Macy, where are you? Have you seen your sister?"

The boy shrugged and went back to tossing rocks in the water.

Allie recognized the boy's Marvel heroes backpack. Was his sister the girl with the unicorn backpack that Collins had saved? The mom looked familiar.

Collins scanned the area then stepped up to the woman. "Is your daughter missing?"

"Yes, she was right here."

"What's she wearing? We'll help you look for her. Her name is Macy?"

She nodded. "Yes, she had on a pink sweatshirt and purple leggings."

"Okay. Was there any part of this trail she was fascinated by? Some place she might have lingered or gone back to see?"

The mom bit her lip, but the boy looked up. "We've been playing hide and seek, jumping out and scaring each other. She's probably hiding."

Collins squatted down to eye level with the boy. "That's very helpful. Thanks. Any place you think she might have tried to hide?"

He shrugged again. "Maybe a big rock. That's what I would do."

"Good thinking." Collins stood. "How about Scott and I head up the trail farther? Allie, you and Melissa want to go back down the trail and see if she's hiding somewhere? Matthew and Kim, can you stay here, look around, and keep Mom company? If anyone sees a ranger, let them know. And ask people along the way to look for her. Meet back here in thirty minutes if we haven't found her."

Even though they were phrased as questions, they were assignments. Collins was in his element. Allie was proud of him. He knew just what to do, and she was confident he'd rescue this little girl yet again. She reached for his hand and squeezed it before following Melissa back down the trail.

"You want to focus on the left, and I'll take the right?" Melissa said.

"Sure. Hopefully purple and pink will show up against the trees and brush." Allie strained her eyes on the brush off the trail, looking for anything that might make a good hiding place or a flash of color.

"I hope so. Some of this is pretty thick. She wouldn't have gone in too deep, I don't think."

"I hope not. It drops off not too far from here." And the fall wouldn't be survivable.

They continued their search in silence. The mom must be worried to death. She tried to think like the little girl. She'd want to stay close to the trail if she was trying to jump out at her brother. Maybe behind a tree or a rock?

She glanced down the trail. Melissa's side of the trail went straight up. Not many hiding places. So she was moving faster than Allie. When Allie looked again, she wasn't in sight. She'd gone around a bend.

Just as Allie was going to hustle to catch up with her, something caught the corner of her eye. A flash of pink behind a fallen tree.

"Macy?" Allie stepped off the trail and eased herself over the log. The girl huddled behind it. "Are you playing hide and seek?" Allie smiled.

The girl nodded.

"Well, your mom is looking for you. How about I go take you to find her? I'd say you found a good hiding spot."

"The man told me to stay here. He said I'd win the game." But Macy got to her feet.

The man? Allie's blood ran cold. Why was this girl away from her mother? "Yeah, I'd say you won. Let's go find Mom." She held out her hand to help the girl up.

They stepped back on the trail. She needed to let Melissa know. "My sister is helping me look for you. I need to let her know I found you. She's just down here." Allie took a couple quick steps down the trail and around the corner. Rustling in the brush caught her attention. Some animal?

No, Melissa. Being pulled back into the trees by Willie with his arm around her neck.

Chapter Twenty-Four

Collins searched the trail. It had gotten a lot steeper up here. He turned to Scott. "I find it hard to believe she'd come up this far."

"I was thinking that too. On the other hand, kids do the craziest things."

"Yeah." He turned and scanned back down the trail. What had they missed? Below him the trail switchbacked up the mountain. He caught a glimpse of Allie and Melissa far below. Allie stepped off the trail. His vision laser-focused on to the scene below him. A man stepped out from a tree behind Melissa. Willie!

He yanked Melissa off the trail, and they both disappeared.

"Scott!" Collins shouted over his shoulder as he took off down the trail. "Willie's back, and he's got Melissa."

Scott's feet pounded the trail behind him. He was torn between getting to the women as fast as he could and being careful on this potentially slippery trail. Closer to the pools there were more people as well.

They dashed past Mom, who shouted, "Did you find her?"

He gave a quick shake of his head, "Not yet." He hoped she

stayed out of their way. They didn't need more people to be Willie's potential victims.

The women were out of sight and would be until he and Scott could get there. He only hoped they arrived in time. Because he was certain Willie was using Melissa to get to Allie.

How had it come down to this? Willie was supposed to have been captured, and yet, here he was again, knowing exactly where the women were. And Collins conveniently out of reach. How had all the luck broken the bad guy's way?

If all his training as a cop didn't come down to this moment, to protecting the people he loved, then what was it good for? What was the point in saving the whole world if he lost the woman he had loved for more years than he could remember? She was such a part of his past, and he wanted her to be part of his future. He was not going to let anything take her out of his life again, no matter what it cost him.

He prayed for answers. And fast.

***

ALLIE WAS TORN BETWEEN HELPING MELISSA AND GETTING this girl back to her mom. She definitely didn't want this girl around whatever might happen. And she wasn't going to leave Melissa.

She bent down. "Macy, you're a big, brave girl, so I need you to do something for me, okay?"

Macy nodded.

"Good. Follow this trail straight back up to the pools, okay? Your mom is there. And tell my friends that are with your mom that I need them to come down here quickly. Can you do that?"

Macy nodded.

"Good girl. Go straight there but don't run. You might fall and get hurt." And they didn't need that.

Macy spun and power walked up the trail, unicorn backpack bobbing behind her.

Okay. One problem solved. Next one, find Melissa.

She eased down the trail, hugging the mountain side, listening. As she came around the corner, she heard Melissa's voice, calm, reasoning, even though Allie couldn't make out the words.

There. He was on the downslope side of the trail, where it wasn't as steep, but it was thick with brush. He had his arm around Melissa's throat, the knife raised into her line of vision. To intimidate her by reminding her of its presence.

Melissa had her hands on his forearms. She was attempting to tuck her chin, but he was blocking her.

Allie slipped behind a tree. She had an idea.

COLLINS CAME DOWN THE TRAIL JUST IN TIME TO SEE THE little girl in pink and purple marching determinedly uphill. Macy. He let out a breath. The women must have found her.

He slowed a bit. "Hey, Macy. Your mom's just up here. Keep on going until you find her."

"Okay, are you friends with the lady who found me?"

"Yeah, I am."

"She said to tell you to come quick."

He exchanged a quick glance with Scott. "Good, I'll do that. Don't stop until you get to your mom."

He and Scott picked up the pace and came around the corner in the trail just to see Allie slip off the trail into the woods just out of sight. He couldn't call to her or he'd risk drawing Willie's attention to her. What did she think she was doing? Her propensity to help could cost her her neck. And Collins didn't think he could survive losing her. The urge to run in there, grab Allie, and snatch her away to safety was almost overwhelming.

He slowed at the corner, and Scott panted up behind him. He pointed and lowered his voice. "Allie went in there, probably after Melissa and Willie. No cell service here. We're on our own."

Scott nodded. "So we'd better make sure Willie knows we're here and keeps his attention off Allie."

"Yeah, when Allie interrupted his attack on Amanda Park, he ran. Maybe we'll get lucky and he'll do that again."

The look on Scott's face said he didn't want to gamble these women's lives on the propensity of a deranged man. Yeah, Collins didn't either.

And it looked like Allie was trying to sneak up behind Willie. What was she thinking?

They needed to get closer without putting either woman in more danger.

ALLIE MADE HER WAY DOWN THE FLATTENED SLOPE, grabbing onto trees to steady her in the loose debris and rocks. Willie was on a flatter section, but to stay out of his sight, she had to take a steeper route. Maybe this was a bad idea. One wrong step, and she'd tumble off the cliff. Her heart pounded.

No, she had to help her sister, give her some sort of opening. She had an idea, a crazy one, but it was the only thing she could think of. She couldn't sit on the trail and not help.

Besides, it was her fault. Willie was after her. So maybe if her plan didn't work, Willie would take her instead of Melissa. The thought made her want to throw up. She hoped it wouldn't come to that. That her plan would provide a distraction for Collins to find them and move in or for Melissa to use her self-defense skills. They just needed an opening.

Allie swallowed and let go of the tree branch, planning her next step. She slid slightly, clamping her mouth shut against a squeal. But she didn't slide any more. She took two more angled steps, dirt spilling in over her hiking boots, and reached another tree. She saw a limb perfect for her purpose. She snagged it and used it as a walking stick on the downhill side to help her make her way along the slope parallel to where Willie had pulled

Melissa. She'd slid down far enough that she couldn't see them. She only hoped her sense of direction continued to work, that she'd come up at the right point.

When her shins and calves were screaming from the awkward angle of traversing the slope, she thought she'd gone far enough. Willie was talking. Good. She moved past his voice then began her slow crawl up the slope, dirt under her fingernails, tree branch clasped in her hands. Knees and feet dug into the loose soil.

Slowly raising her head, she spotted them. She was a few feet behind Willie and Melissa.

Now her timing had to be perfect, and she had to be perfectly quiet. Moving inch by inch, she levered the tree branch onto the ground in front of her.

Willie was ranting about his perfect plans, still moving back.

Because of how Willie had Melissa's neck craned, she couldn't see Allie.

Allie slid the branch behind Willie's heel.

And hoped she hadn't just killed her sister.

"Willie, what is it you want?" Collins stepped into the brush to cover the rustling in the trees. He didn't give away what he suspected by glancing in Allie's direction. He shot a look at Scott, who had followed him off the trail.

Willie jerked his head up and tightened his grip on Melissa. He took a step back. "I'm taking what's mine. I deserve it. That little Allie Cat ruined my plans." He gave a wicked grin. "But I'm adaptable. That's why I always win. So, new plan. This one here will do just fine." He ran the knife along one of Melissa's dark curls.

But it was back at her throat before Collins could even move. They were too far away, and there was too much undergrowth between them.

Willie laughed. He'd done it on purpose to tease Collins.

Anger at being played washed through him, and he shoved it back. It wouldn't help and would only cloud his thinking. "It's gonna be hard to get her away from here, down the trail. And what are you going to do when someone else comes up the trail?"

"None of that is your concern."

Melissa maintained a rigid posture, but fear shadowed her eyes.

"Yeah, I guess you're smarter than us, Willie. But I'm not sure what you want us to do at this point. Give up? Just let you walk away?"

"Yeah, that's exactly what I expect you to do if you want Melissa to remain unharmed. I'll return her when I'm done with her." He grinned again.

Scott's knuckles turned white, and Collins hoped he didn't do anything stupid.

How to let Melissa know she was going to have to act, that she was going to have an opening? He made eye contact with her and nodded.

"Hey, Willie. Watch your step."

"Pickle!" Allie yelled from her hiding spot behind them.

Willie's foot came down on the tree branch, which rolled under his weight and knocked him off balance.

Melissa pushed his arms away and ducked while Scott and Collins leaped toward Willie.

Recognition lit Willie's eyes. He turned and sprinted between the trees. Scott and Collins chased him. But Willie jumped off the cliff and to the Virgin River hundreds of feet below. He hit the rocks and didn't move.

Collins and Scott looked at each other, breathing hard.

"Let's check on the women." Collins gave Willie a final look then headed back into the woods.

Allie had joined Melissa, and the two sat on a log, arms wrapped around each other.

Every bit of worry and anger poured out in his voice, and he didn't have the willpower to check it. "What were you thinking!? You could have gotten yourself killed or your sister. You're not a police officer, Allie. Even Scott here was waiting for me to move first."

Allie paled and seemed to shrink even as she held her sister tighter.

No one said anything.

ALLIE HUDDLED WITH MELISSA IN A ROOM AT THE RANGER station remarkably like the one they'd been in yesterday. Only today Melissa was the one needing comforting. But unlike yesterday, today they knew after they all gave their statements that Willie was unable to harm them. He'd never actually been captured. They'd apprehended the wrong guy, but that message had never gotten to Collins.

Matthew and Kim had gotten Macy's message, saw the commotion from the trail, and had run down in record time to get help. A team was in the process of retrieving Willie's body.

Macy had told her mom that Willie was the nice man who showed her a good place to hide. No doubt knowing that the group would split up to find her.

When they were finally able to go, they were hungry and exhausted. No one wanted to cook, so they headed to a Mexican cantina near their RV campground. Chips and salsa seemed like the perfect comfort food.

Dinner was quiet. Allie dipped a warm chip in salsa and broke the silence. "It's weird that we're going home tomorrow. Then Monday we'll be back at work, and I won't be spending every waking minute with you all."

Melissa nodded. "I wish we'd been able to see more of Bryce and Zion. But aside from that, it really was an amazing trip, even given how it had ended." She looked at Allie with a grin. "I can't believe you remembered our old code word."

She scanned the table, meeting everyone's gaze, her eyes welling. "I couldn't have asked for a better group of people to be on this trip with. It was supposed to be a sibling trip, but I think you all are my family now."

Scott squeezed her hand. "We'll come back and see more. We've got some river rafting to do."

Melissa nodded and gave him a watery smile. "I hate that you fly back on Monday."

"Me too." He picked up a chip. "Allie, did you hear any more from DataCorp on your proposal?"

She'd hardly thought about it. "No. I guess they had what they needed, one way or another. It's in God's hands." And she truly believed that. After everything they'd been through, a work contract seemed insignificant. She tilted her head at Collins. "And the leak in his new house is going to be fixed, so everything is proceeding just fine in that area."

Her smile felt a bit forced. Things were definitely different between the two of them. Something had shifted and neither of them could find their footing. And she didn't know if they would. Maybe the magic of the road trip could only last so long. Then real life intruded and brought them back to the fact that they were two very different people.

His gaze on her was troubled, searching. But she wasn't sure she could ever get out of her head the tone of disgust and disbelief he'd used on her after she'd saved her sister's life. He was a cop and saw the world from that perspective. But she didn't. And perhaps that was a canyon they couldn't bridge.

Kim helped Allie and Melissa pack up the trailer after dinner. She emptied the cupboards and handed the food items to Allie.

Melissa shook her head. "All this food we didn't eat. At least three meals worth. Though I see the cowboy cookies are gone."

"Better too much than too little." Allie stacked items in the collapsible crate.

"True." Melissa closed the ice chest lid. "Tomorrow's going to be a long day. Thirteen hours in the truck. Doing in one day more than we did in two on the first two days."

"Can't be helped. We all have to get back to work." Allie took the last item from Kim. "Let's just grab coffee and breakfast burritos at that coffee place across the highway. That way we don't have to deal with any food or cleanup tomorrow. We could hit the road at six a.m."

"Great idea." Melissa picked up her phone. "I wonder if they have an app. We could probably place the order tonight and have it ready in the morning."

Kim couldn't believe how well Melissa was handling everything. She'd been in more danger than Kim but wasn't as shaken. Maybe it was because she was older. Or maybe it was because of everything she'd been through last winter when her life had been threatened then too. Kim didn't know. But she wanted to.

A knock came at the trailer door. "Everyone decent?" Matthew's voice. Kim's heart jumped before sinking back down again.

"Yes." Humor laced Melissa's voice. "Come on in."

The door opened, and Matthew's head appeared, his classic grin lighting up his face. "Kim, if you're not busy, I thought we could take a walk. The stars are amazing."

She tugged her hoodie over her hands. Her heart pulled in two directions. "Um, I don't want to leave Melissa and Allie with all the work."

Melissa waved her off. "Go. We're almost done anyway. Just give me your breakfast order."

Kim told her what she wanted, then followed Matthew out the trailer door.

He reached for her hand, and she let him take it as they

walked away from the site and down the road through the campground.

He swung their hands a little and gave hers a squeeze. "Hey, it's over now. And since it's our last night here, I thought we should spend some time together. We could go into town or…" He turned his gaze to her.

She knew what he wanted. Heck, she wanted to put all the bad behind her and just focus on the good. But she couldn't. Today, when she saw Melissa in Willie's grasp, her mind immediately put her own face there. It was exactly what Willie had intended to do to her. She couldn't wait to get home and give her big brother a hug for making her practice her self-defense moves with him.

What she really wanted was for Matthew to hold her and let her talk and cry. So maybe… "I wish there was a place we could sit and talk privately."

"We could go to a coffee shop."

She shook her head. "Too many people."

"Maybe we could find some live music in town, take your mind off things."

She sighed. He was trying, but he just didn't get it. The Virgin River ran along the backside of the campground, and she pointed to the access trail. "Let's go sit by the river." It was darker over here, but they found a downed log to sit on. She tried not to think about Willie's demise upstream.

Matthew draped his arm around her shoulders and pulled her close. "I'm going to miss seeing the night sky like this." He turned to her. "I'm going to miss seeing you. But I decided I'm applying for that job in Orange County with DataCorp. And if Allie gets the job with them and I do too, then we'll be working together for a while. For a long time, I felt like Melissa and Allie were just my bossy older sisters. And I didn't need more of that in my life. But this trip has shown me a different side of them. They're people I actually like hanging out with. And their guys are pretty cool too. So I won't mind being closer to them." He paused. "I don't want to stop seeing you."

Kim didn't want to hurt Matthew's feelings. She did want to keep him in her life, but right now, it was too much pressure. She'd been through a lot and needed time to process that. Time he didn't want to seem to give her.

She gave him a soft smile that she didn't know if he could see in the moonlight. "I don't want to stop seeing you either."

He leaned in for a kiss, but she put a hand to his chest, stopping him.

She didn't miss the hurt in his eyes as he pulled back. "What's wrong?"

She shook her head. "I don't even know. I just feel so mixed up after everything that's happened."

"But you're safe. Willie's…no longer a threat. You don't have anything to be afraid of."

She shot to her feet. "You just don't get it. I need time, Matthew. It doesn't just disappear overnight."

"It would if you'd stop dwelling on it." His retort was fast, but so, apparently, was his regret. "I'm sorry, Kim. You take all the time you need."

But did he really mean that? "I'm going to head back now. We're leaving early in the morning." She spun and returned to their site, but Matthew didn't follow her.

Chapter Twenty-Five

Collins felt every bit of their trip weighing on him as he rolled up his sleeping bag and pad in the dark. His staples throbbed in his head, and he hadn't slept much. Based on the rustling in the other sleeping bags, he didn't think Matthew or Scott had either. In one respect, he'd be glad to get home to his own bed and shower. On the other hand, he'd miss spending so much time with Allie.

He shouldn't have yelled at her yesterday. But he'd been so worried, so angry that she'd put herself in harm's way. Her desire to help people once again had the potential to hurt her. He let out a breath. It was something they would have to work through. But she had retreated. Was it from their relationship or was she just worn out from everything that had happened and the normal melancholy that came at the end of a trip? Time would tell.

Scott and Matthew got their bags rolled and packed, the tent emptied and put away before they saw any stirring in the trailer. But when he returned from the bathroom, the trailer door was open and the women were standing outside.

With practiced moves, he, Scott, and Matthew got the trailer hooked up, and they pulled out of the campground. Scott pulled in front of the coffee shop while Melissa and Allie went in to retrieve their orders. Before the sun had done much more than lighten up the sky, they were on their way to Phoenix.

The striking scenery was muted by the pre-dawn. Normally it would save them about thirty minutes to exit the east entrance with the tunnel, but since they would have had to wait until eight a.m. to get a tunnel ranger, it ended up being better to continue out through Springdale on Highway 9 following the Virgin River until they turned south and left it behind. By the time they hit Highway 59, the scenery had become flat and vast. Which fit his mood. He was glad Scott was driving. He tried to doze before the sun was full bright, but his thoughts wouldn't let him completely rest.

They crossed the border into Arizona and the highway became 389. Because Arizona didn't do Daylight Saving Time, they had gained an hour, putting them on the same time zone effectively as California. Didn't make the drive any shorter, though. The sun was over the horizon by the time they turned on to Highway 89A. The truck cab remained quiet. No one needed to stop anywhere, and the sounds of Boston's *Greatest Hits* played through the speakers.

By the time they reached the Vermillion Cliffs, they had been traveling through Arizona's mountains for a while. Collins checked back to see if Allie looked like she might want to sit up front. The turns had been more wide and sweeping than many they had been on previously, but he didn't want her to get sick. They passed the Cliff Dwellers Stone House, but no one wanted to stop, and Melissa didn't read any fact from her guidebook. He couldn't help but think how different this journey was than the one they had started on ten days ago.

They crossed their old friend, the Colorado River in Marble Canyon, the blue-green river far below in the gorge in the once-again desert landscape. And finally, they crossed the Little Colorado back through Cameron, where they first stopped at the historic Tanner's Crossing Bridge. They'd come full circle. Collins remembered their first stop here, where Matthew had been silly, Kim had taken his picture, and he had comforted Allie about Rachel and DataCorp. Who would have guessed back then everything they would have been through?

Highway 89 took them to Flagstaff by eleven a.m. They needed to stop for food and gas and to stretch their legs. After a quick stop, they picked up the I-17 into Phoenix and arrived at Daniel's house by 1:30. As the guys unhitched the trailer, the women unloaded everything into Collins's truck. Nikki came out to help them.

As he and Scott were telling Daniel about the tire blowout, out of the corner of his eye, he saw Matthew tug on Kim's wrist as she grabbed her things from his truck. A pleading, "Kim…" came from him, but she pulled away and climbed in Collins's truck.

With a glance at Kim, Collins headed to Matthew, whose head was down. Collins reached out his hand. "Hey, thanks, man, for driving and calling in the cavalry yesterday. I know your sisters are glad you came along. I'm glad I got to know you."

Matthew nodded, his eyes clouded. "Sure. It was a good trip. Thanks for making it happen by bringing your truck."

Allie and Melissa came over and gave him hugs, and Collins stepped back.

According to Allie, Lauren had been commenting on the social media posts. She had sent them both a text asking to meet up for dinner again. He was glad they weren't. He let Allie handle the reply.

They thanked Daniel for the use of his trailer and headed out to grab something to eat and hit the road again.

Allie looked back at Melissa. "Did you see Nikki's ring?"

She nodded. "I asked her about it, and she said he proposed Saturday at a fancy restaurant."

"Guess they both preferred that to camping with us."

Collins barely noticed that Nikki was at Daniel's house, let alone that she was wearing an engagement ring.

Without the trailer and having a straight shot down the I-10 until the Inland Empire, Collins felt up to doing the driving. They headed west, following the sun, until it disappeared about an hour before they got to Melissa's townhome. They unloaded the supplies and Melissa's and Scott's bags.

He shook Scott's hand. "Thanks, man. I couldn't have done this without you. Have a safe trip home."

"I will." He nodded to the women. "Keep an eye on them for me, will you?"

"You got it."

Next stop was Kim's condo. They hauled her stuff up to her door. She gave Allie a hug and disappeared inside.

Then he and Allie were alone. She sat up front on the trip to her house. He didn't know where to begin, but it was late. Probably not the best time to have a conversation when he didn't even know what to say.

He unloaded her bags and brought them inside her house.

"Just leave them in the entry. Everything has to be washed anyway. No point in hauling it upstairs and back down again."

He pulled her in a hug and kissed her cheek. "I'll call you tomorrow, okay?"

She nodded.

As the door closed behind him and he waited to hear the lock click home, he hoped this was more of a beginning than the ending it felt like.

Chapter Twenty-Six

Allie slapped her alarm off, regretting she'd planned on coming into work the day after getting back from a long trip. Rajah wouldn't leave her alone, sleeping curled up next to her. She'd be upset that Allie was going into the office today. But she'd been away from the office too long as it was. And she was curious to see if Rachel would show up. She hadn't heard a word from her.

As she made coffee and got ready, Rajah twined through her legs, happy to see her. She was grateful for her own bed and hot shower, but she'd need more than a good night's sleep to feel normal again. If that was even possible. Home didn't even feel the same, though she knew she was the one who had changed.

Her mind reeled through everything they'd been through. She was still stung by Collins's words. He had apologized, but she knew he meant what he said. And she couldn't really blame him. He was thinking like a cop, and he always would.

And she was always going to want to take care of the people in her life. It almost seemed mutually exclusive. Maybe this trip proved something. Maybe their high school crush couldn't survive the real world.

That didn't seem right either. But she couldn't see the way

forward. Her brain was too clouded, and she was too close to the situation and too tired after the trip and the drama. They really needed to talk, but Collins was going to be swamped getting back to work, and she was too.

She took an Uber to the office and let herself in. Besides, right now she had to get her car fixed and deal with Rachel. She started coffee brewing while she took her laptop that she had retrieved from her dining room table into her office and opened it. It seemed empty and quiet after spending days in close quarters with others.

Here she had perfect access to all the information, now when she didn't need it. It was in God's hands, she reminded herself. Cup of coffee in hand, she emailed her agent that she was back and would like to get a rental car today. She answered the emails that had piled up while she was gone, listening for the front door.

After all she'd been through, firing Rachel should be the easiest thing. Like ripping off a bandage, she was just going to do it.

She worked through her bookkeeping program and printed out a final check, with a generous bonus. She grabbed it off the printer when the front door opened. She headed to the front.

"Hey, how was your trip?" Rachel slid behind the receptionist desk.

"Fine. Why didn't you respond to my texts, calls, or voicemails? I needed you to come into the office to get something important." Allie was tired. Tired of always trying to think of other people, of putting their needs first to her own detriment. And she'd had it. Done. Finished. Tapped out. She was putting her business first. And Leroy would just have to understand.

Rachel flipped on the computer. "I was having a few days at the spa with my friends. You said I didn't have to be in the office."

"I also said you'd need to respond when I needed you. I warned you before I left." Allie was proud of how firm her voice sounded. She handed Rachel the check. "This is your final check with a bit of severance pay. You'll see I paid you for not being here. You're fired, Rachel. I need someone I can depend on."

Rachel stared at her and then the check. Then a smirk curled across her lips. She huffed. "Fine. Uncle Leroy will hear about this. And see if I'm here to give people info when they walk in looking for you." She opened her designer bag and began opening desk drawers, tossing stuff in. Including some office supplies, Allie noted but didn't care.

Allie tilted her head. "When does that ever happen?"

"The day before you left on your trip. This thin guy with brown hair, kinda preppy looking, said his company was looking to hire you."

Allie frowned. Had Edward stopped by? She didn't think he was even in the area. But then why would he have called? It didn't make any sense. She pulled up a photo of Edward from his company's page. "Was it this man?"

Rachel made a face. "Ew, no. That guy's ancient. This one was younger. Brown hair."

Allie's stomach dropped. With shaky fingers, she pulled up a photo of Willie. "Was this the guy?"

Rachel gave a quick nod. "Yep. I see he found you. I told him you were headed out of town on a road trip around the Southwest, so you wouldn't be able to help him until you got back. See, who are you going to get to help you with your clients?" She shoved a drawer shut and stood.

"You told him where we were going?" Cold sweat broke out over her.

"Not everywhere, just the Grand Canyon, those biblical places."

"Leave the key, please."

Rachel wrenched it off her keychain and slapped it on the desk. "It's been real. But it hasn't been fun." She flounced out and let the door slam shut.

Allie locked the door behind her. She returned to her office and texted Collins what Rachel had told her. Then she sent two emails. One to Leroy, telling him what she'd done and apologizing for not being a better mentor. And one to an employment agency looking to hire a receptionist.

Collins's heart jumped when he saw Allie's name come up on his text. He was glad to hear from her. He'd been wanting to text her all day, but he'd been swamped with work, including wrapping up the Willard Dumas case. His heart stopped when he read her words.

Just fired Rachel. She ID'd Willie and said he came by my office before we went out of town and she gave him the list of the places we were going. That's how he knew to find us.

Collins supposed that answered that question. The other question was how Willie had known where in the park they were. Though Willie had seen the Emerald Pools on Melissa's itinerary, there were other hikes listed there as well.

But that had been answered by the rangers who had searched Willie's body. They'd given Kyle the update that they had found a tracking app on Willie's cell phone linked to Kim's phone. Kyle had immediately had Kim bring in her phone so their techs could go through it.

She remembered Willie offering to take a picture of her and Matthew that night he had joined them for dinner and then had kept her distracted. He must have added it before he gave her phone back. Even though the cell service wasn't great, it helped him narrow down the options of where they might be.

As a cop, he was relieved to find the answer to something that had been puzzling him. As a boyfriend, he was terrified and incensed. And glad she'd fired Rachel.

His own thoughts stopped him in his tracks. Would Allie consider him her boyfriend? She'd been cool to him, understandably, given all that had happened. He'd apologized for yelling at her. Mostly he was mad at himself for not protecting them all better from Willie. Which made him even wonder if he should get into a relationship. He knew this job was hard on them. He'd seen that firsthand. And he knew Kyle had had similar concerns with his fiancée, Heather.

The last thing he wanted to do was hurt Allie again or put her in danger. But the thought of life without her, now that he had her back in his life hollowed him out.

Kyle rapped his knuckles on Collins's desk. "Earth to Collins."

Collins glanced up. "Yeah?"

Kyle gave him a wry grin. "Let's make a dent in this pile then see if Joe is available to shoot some hoops when we get done. You look like you need to blow off some steam."

And that's what happened when you'd worked with someone for five years. They knew you better than you knew yourself sometimes.

"You got it."

* * *

COLLINS WASN'T SURE HOW GREAT HE'D BE AT SHOOTING hoops with his still-sore rotator cuff. He had an appointment with his doctor Friday to get his stitches out and check on his shoulder. But he did need to blow off some steam. They met Joe at the park near his house, and they tossed the ball around, taking turns making baskets.

"So how was your trip?" Joe went in for a layup then tossed the ball to Collins.

"Other than the serial rapist stalking us, me ripping up my shoulder trying to keep some kid from taking a header into the Grand Canyon—said kid being used by said serial rapist to lure us into a trap, and getting my skull split open by said serial rapist, it was great." Collins tried for a jump shot and the ball bounced off the backboard.

Kyle caught it. "Hey, but you solved a case for us, so there's that."

"Allie should probably get the credit." He gave them the highlights of the trip.

"So how come you're here shooting baskets with us instead of hanging out with Allie?" Joe took a pass from Kyle.

Collins swiped the ball. "I could ask you two why you aren't with your women."

"Stop trying to change the subject." Kyle blocked his shot. "What's up with you and Allie?"

Collins shook his head. "I yelled at her when she put that branch behind Willie's foot. All I could see was him turning on her. I said I was sorry, but we haven't had a chance to talk. I think this trip might have just proved to her that she doesn't want to date a cop." He stopped and wiped the sweat off his face with his shirt. "She's one of those people who sees the good in others. She wants to help everyone." He shrugged. "My job gives me a different view. I didn't like Willie from the beginning. And in the end, I didn't protect them from him. Not good enough, anyway."

Kyle put the ball under his arm. "None of us is Superman. Not even Scott. He'd be the first to tell you that now. I talked to him this morning while he was waiting for his plane. He likes you and respects you. He wishes they'd listened to you better about Willie. You kept them safer than they would have been on their own. You know guys like Willie. They have a plan, and they are determined to carry it out. All we can do is hope to intercept them somewhere along the line before they do too much damage. Sometimes you just have to trust that God is in control."

Joe nodded. "None of us have safe desk jobs. But we're trying to make the world a better place. Allie's perspective can help balance you out, keep you from being jaded. Sarah and Heather both had to work that out for themselves. I don't know Allie that well, but I think she'll come around."

Kyle tossed Collins the ball. "Why don't you talk to Melissa? See if she has some insight."

Collins shot the ball at the hoop and heard the satisfying *swish* of it passing through the chain net. His friends actually had some good ideas. And they were killing him at basketball.

Kyle grabbed the ball from underneath and shot it to Joe. "And when are you going to pop the question to Sarah?"

Instead of shooting, Joe tucked the ball under his arm. "Actually, I was going to ask you guys for some help with that."

Chapter Twenty-Seven

<hr>

Allie opened the door to a smiling Melissa. She wasn't sure how Melissa could be smiling this early on a Saturday morning.

"You ready to go?"

"Yeah, just let me grab my bag." Allie picked up her tote and followed her sister out the door. When she'd called two days ago telling her they were taking a spa day, her first response had been to decline. But Melissa wasn't taking no for an answer.

It had been a long week, so a spa day wasn't the worst idea. Soon they were wrapped in towels sitting in the steam room cleansing their pores. The heat seeped into her bones and made her feel like melting. This actually was a great idea. They also had a massage, a facial, and a mani-pedi planned.

Melissa propped her feet up on the wooden bench. "So how've you been since we got back?"

Allie shrugged. "My car's being fixed, which is good. I fired Rachel. The agency has already sent over a few people for interviews. I heard from DataCorp yesterday that I'm in the top three for the job, so I have interviews with them and their top execs next week. I feel good about whatever happens."

"I knew you could do it. Talked to Collins much?"

"We've texted back and forth. He's swamped at work." She sighed. "It feels like we're back to where we were when he was in Holcomb Springs. Friends keeping in touch."

"Allie. You guys are more than friends. I've seen it with my own eyes."

"I don't know, Melissa. We agreed that the trip would be a good way to see what we had together as adults. Maybe it can never be more than a vacation romance. Our real worlds are too different. I'm always going to want to help my friends and family, sacrifice myself for them even."

Melissa reached out for Allie's hand. "You did a great job making sure we had a great trip."

"It wasn't quite what we'd dreamed of as kids, was it?"

"Those golden dreams of childhood vanish in the harsh reality of adulthood. This trip as adults was different, but then so are we. It was a good trip. And it's not your job to make sure we are happy. We can be trusted to find our own happiness."

Allie gave a short laugh. "Maybe not Matthew."

Melissa grimaced. "What's up with him and Kim? Did he tell you?"

"No, but he's convinced she'll get over it."

"Did you talk to Kim?"

Allie nodded. "Yeah, I wanted to make sure she was okay. She is. She had a good talk with Kyle, which helped. I think she just needs some time. And she doesn't think Matthew is taking what she went through seriously enough."

"He's not. Serious stuff is not his forte. But he's going to need to learn to deal with it. It would be a shame if he lost Kim over his immaturity."

"I told Daniel to talk to him. I think Nikki's helped mature him."

Melissa lowered her gaze at Allie. "This is exactly what I'm talking about. You want everyone to be happy, but honestly, it's not your job. It's between all of us and God." She smiled. "Hon, you're not Mom bailing on us. I know you and I are so used to

making things work for the family in her absence that we don't
quite know when it's time to let go. You have great value just by
being you. And I bet Collins sees that. Let him help you sometimes." She grinned. "Let him pamper you. He wants to do it."

Allie rolled her eyes. "How do you know?"

"Because this whole day was his idea and his treat."

COLLINS WIPED HIS HANDS ON HIS DRESS PANTS. ALLIE
should be here any minute. Melissa had texted him that she'd
given Allie his note and she was on her way. He hoped his plan
worked.

He looked around the dining room of what would soon be
his new house. He'd contacted the seller's Realtor, told her what
he had in mind. She was immediately on board. Everyone loved
romance, he guessed.

It wasn't as fancy as he'd like, but he thought she'd at least
appreciate the gesture. A folding table covered with a tablecloth,
folding chairs pulled up to it. Candles and flowers graced the
table. Food was keeping warm in the kitchen, take-out from
California Grill, ready to be plated on china borrowed from
his mom.

And his guitar sat in the corner. He hoped he wasn't too
nervous to play it.

The front door opened. "Collins?" Allie's voice floated to
him. She'd seen the sign on the front door to come in. Her footsteps echoed across the tile.

He lit the candles and headed toward her. "Hi. You look
beautiful. Thanks for coming."

Her eyes were wide. "What is this?" A little laugh graced her
words.

He held out his hand. "Dinner."

She took it, and he led her into the dining room, pulling out
her chair. She sat. "Why here?"

He sat across from her and took her hand. "We've never been on a proper date. And since this will soon be my house, I thought it was a great place for new beginnings."

Her cheeks flushed.

"How was your day?" He gave her a grin.

She laughed. "Wonderful. Melissa said I have you to thank for it."

"I just want you to know how much I want to take care of you. You look after everyone else, but occasionally, I'd like you to let me take care of you." He met her gaze. "I love you, Allie. I have since I was fifteen. I learned on our trip that what I dreamed about in high school isn't something that we can ever go back to. But we have something richer, better now. I want to see what kind of life we can create together."

Her eyes sparkled in the candlelight with unshed tears. "I love you too, Collins. I always have."

He came around the table and pulled her to her feet and into his arms. Who cared if dinner got cold? His hand cupped her cheek, and he lowered his lips to hers, promising all the hope for the future he could. He pulled back and leaned his forehead against hers. "We're better together, Allie. We can work through any obstacles as long as we do it together. I need you. I'm a better person with you in my life."

She nodded. "Me too."

He pulled back. "I do have dinner." He prepared their plates and they ate, enjoying the easy conversation they always had. He told her about getting his staples out and that the doctor had said his arm was healing fine.

He handed her a thick, square envelope. "Something for you."

Her eyes held questions, but she took it and opened it. Inside were the postcards he'd collected at each of their stops, with a short note written to her about a memory of that day. She was a part of every one of them.

She laughed. "So this is what you were doing with all those

postcards. Collins, this is so sweet." Her eyes misted. "I love it. Thank you for thinking of this." She reached for his hand.

He kissed her fingers. "I have another surprise for you." He opened his guitar case, hoping all his practice paid off. He strummed the first few chords, glancing between his fingers and Allie's face. He saw when she recognized the song.

"It's 'You and Me' by Lifehouse." She smiled, and he could see her remembering their first dance at Cait and Grayson's wedding.

He made it through the song and put the guitar away then reached for her hand. "One more thing." He led her out to the back yard, to the patio that reminded him so much of his own growing up. He pulled her into his arms. "I know the stars aren't as bright here as they were on our trip, but I always want to dance under the stars with you, Allie."

And they swayed to the music only they could hear.

Epilogue

Allie grinned as she handed Collins the key to his new home. "Here you go, new homeowner."

He gestured to the front door. "You do the honors. I couldn't have done this without you."

She slid the key in and pushed the door open, the memories of the special night they'd had here a couple of weeks ago rushing through her. Collins was right. This house was a good place for new beginnings.

He swept his arms underneath her knees and lifted her up as her arms flew around his neck.

"Collins!"

"What? You don't carry your Realtor across the threshold?" He stepped inside and kicked the door shut, dropping a kiss on her lips.

She rolled her eyes at him. "We've got work to do, mister."

"Yes, ma'am." He lowered her feet to the floor. "I'll grab the TV out of the car."

"Priorities, I see."

"If we're going to see this movie Kim made of our trip, yes it is."

It was a BYO lawn chair, since he had no furniture here yet.

But all their friends were coming over to see what Kim had created. Plus another surprise or two.

They had an ice chest with drinks plus a box containing movie-theater type candy and popcorn.

Kim was the first to arrive as Collins was hooking up the TV. She looked much more like her sparkly self. She and Collins figured out how to get her movie to show up on the screen.

Kyle and Heather were next, Joe and Sarah on their heels. Joe looked a little pale. Allie gave the girls the tour of the house while they oohed and aahed.

As they came back downstairs, Melissa walked in the door with Scott. That was surprise number one. He'd flown in just for the weekend and was staying with Joe. For moral support.

The group had gotten their chairs arranged in the family room in front of the built-ins that held the TV. Allie was passing out snacks and drinks and keeping an eye on the door.

"Heather, how are the wedding plans coming? You've got what, less than three months?"

Heather grimaced. "It's nearly a full-time job. I'm hoping our sisters will help. Hint, hint, Kim."

Kim grinned. "I have some great ideas for a bachelorette get away weekend. When's your sister Kellie coming down so we can plan it?"

"We need to get something on the calendar."

The doorbell rang. Allie hurried to answer it. Matthew stood there grinning, Uber driver pulling away from the curb. Surprise number two. She gave him a hug. "Come on in. How was the flight?"

"Fine. Short." He shoved his hands in his pockets, looking like he did when he brought home a report card he wasn't sure about.

Allie tilted her head toward the family room. "She's in there."

He nodded and started walking. Allie trailed behind, watching for Kim's reaction.

Matthew rounded the corner, and a cheer erupted.

Kim was sitting in her chair, laptop open, waiting to begin. She looked up. The corners of her mouth tipped up before dropping back in place.

Matthew circled the room shaking hands and giving hugs. He got to Kim. "Hey, Kim. Surprise." He held his hands out to the side.

She gave him a wry grin. "Sit down so we can start the show."

Allie laughed. Kim could handle Matthew, whether she knew it yet or not.

Allie settled in next to Collins, who reached for her hand. The movie started. Kim had done a great job of interweaving the stills and videos of their trip to the same 80s classic rock soundtrack they had listened to on the trip. Her titles gave the location and a few funny comments along the way. Seeing their trip from this perspective made the good memories flood back. And watching the trip through Kim's eyes, it was obvious she had great talent. She was able to tell the stories of the relationships through their body language. Allie had no doubt of Collins's feelings for her after seeing pictures of them together.

And whether Kim knew it or not, it was obvious to everyone in the room, Matthew had eyes only for her.

Bryce and Zion had fewer pictures, but Kim still captured the grandeur of both places without the bad memories. Allie didn't even remember her taking any pictures at Zion, but the others had and sent them to her. The difference was kind of obvious.

The soundtrack faded out and became The Fray's "She Is" romantic ballad. Pictures of Joe and Sarah filled the screen. Bonfires, friend gatherings, and the video of when his fellow firefighters had surprised Sarah with an unusual tour of Joe's fire station.

Allie watched Sarah out of the corner of her eye and kept her own expression neutral.

Sarah furrowed her brow and looked from Kim to Joe, but no one seemed to be surprised by the change in movie at all.

Joe just shrugged and smiled, but his fingers tapped on the arm of the chair.

Finally, Joe himself was speaking directly to the camera. "Sarah, it's been an amazing journey with you. I wouldn't trade a moment of it. Will you build a future with me?"

Sarah turned to the real Joe next to her, who dropped to one knee, pulling a ring out of his pocket. "Sarah, will you make me the happiest man and marry me?"

Her hands went to her face as she nodded. Then she threw her arms around his neck. "Yes!"

The room burst into applause.

Surprise number three.

Joe kissed her, then slipped the ring on her finger.

Sarah wiped her eyes. "Were you all in on this?"

Everyone laughed. Yes, they'd all been in on it. It was why Scott had wanted to be here this weekend.

Allie leaned her head on Collins's shoulder and looked around the room. These friends had become her family. Maybe you make your own family out of the friends you go through life with. Her circle was getting bigger, not smaller. And that was something to celebrate.

Are you curious about Kim and Matthew? Will they be able to resolve their differences?

When will Scott and Melissa get engaged?

And what did Collins do while he was on assignment in Holcomb Springs?

Find out by signing up for my latest news and updates at www. jlcrosswhite.com. You'll get a short story about Collins's time in Holcomb Spring and the prequel novella to the Hometown Heroes series, *Promise Me*— Grayson and Cait's story.

My bimonthly updates include upcoming books written by me and other authors you will enjoy, information on all my latest releases, sneak peeks of yet-to-be-released chapters, and exclusive giveaways. Your email address will never be shared, and you can unsubscribe at any time.

If you enjoyed this book, please leave a review. Reviews can be as simple as "I couldn't put it down. I can't wait for the next one" and help raise the author's visibility and lets other readers find her.

Keep reading for a sneak peek of *Out of Range: In the Shadow book 2.*

Acknowledgments

The expertise on all things police related come from Deputy J. Roy Crosswhite.

Many thanks to marketing colleague and friend, Glenn Hunter, who allowed me to use his real name and likeness in this book. I couldn't think of anyone better to give Allie marketing advice.

This book would not be possible without the patience and willingness to read early drafts by Diana Brandmeyer and Jenny Cary. Jenny gets an extra dose of thanks for helping me brainstorm when I got stuck. Special thanks to Sara Benner for her expert proofreading! Many thanks to my beta readers Anita Stafford, Lisa Canton, and Malia Spencer and my early reviewers!

Much thanks and love to my children, Caitlyn Elizabeth and Joshua Alexander, for supporting my dream for many years and giving me time to write.

And most of all to my Lord Jesus, who makes all things possible and directs my paths.

Author's Note

I love road trips. My kids and I have driven across the United States four times, with various numbers of animals in tow! But each time, I've been struck by the variety of scenery and how much I didn't have time to see.

I hope someday to recreate the trip this group took. With Google Maps and its street view feature—which allows you to look at many part of national parks, including trails—I felt like I was on the trip with them.

There's also a great YouTube series of videos that covers this area called The West Is Big. I highly recommend it. And of course the national parks have great websites and fantastic social media. I love following them on Instagram so I can see the beautiful pictures.

I've created a Pinterest board for this book, which you can check out at http://pinterest.com/jtiszai.

The idea for this book has been with me a long time. I wanted to explore how a first love from a long time ago—possibly romanticized—might stand up under the pressures of adulthood. I know a number of people who are happily married to their high school sweethearts, and I wondered how that might look if they weren't able to get together in high school, but found each other later in life. And what could be more fraught with potential tension and conflict than a road trip with people you don't know well?

I also wanted to explore how challenging it can be to trust God, even when that is literally all you can do. I hope you come away from reading *Off the Map* with a little clearer sense of how God is working things out behind the scenes, no matter what our circumstances look like.

About the Author

My favorite thing is discovering how much there is to love about America the Beautiful and the great outdoors. I'm an Amazon bestselling author, a mom to two navigating the young adult years while battling my daughter's juvenile arthritis, exploring the delights of my son's autism, and keeping gluten free.

A California native who's spent significant time in the Midwest, I'm thrilled to be back in the Golden State. Follow me on social media to see all my adventures and how I get inspired for my books!

www.JLCrosswhite.com
Twitter: @jenlcross
Facebook: Author Jennifer Crosswhite

Instagram: jencrosswhite
Pinterest: Author Jennifer Crosswhite

facebook.com/authorjennifercrosswhite
twitter.com/jenlcross
instagram.com/jencrosswhite
pinterest.com/jtiszai

Sneak Peek of Out of Range: In the
Shadow Book 2

Kim Taylor searched for inspiration at the end of a precisely sharpened drawing pencil. She tapped it on the paper in front of her in their open workspace at House of Elan. It was old school, but she needed inspiration. Plus, her hands ached from being at the computer so much. Design Review was coming up, and it was her chance to get her work in front of the big names at the studio. Junior designers presented a portfolio of their top styles to the head designers at Design Review. Top designers would choose the winner to work with them for the next year. It would be a huge jump for her career.

She had sewn up several of her designs into actual outfits, one of which she was wearing. A few others had become computer designs, and she was creating her portfolio to present. But which were the best ones to choose? She'd gone over the trend reports until her eyes were bleary. Her trip through the Southwest had given her a ton of ideas. But it had also left her with nightmares, thanks to being grabbed by Willie Dumas. Thankfully, he couldn't ever hurt her again.

Her mentor, Lynnae MacKenzie, owned a boutique in Newport that Kim had worked at in high school and college. She learned much of what she knew about the business from

Lynnae, who'd always encouraged her to pursue design. She would showcase Kim's clothing and often sent clients to her for custom work, especially if they were hard to fit. Kim was bringing her designs to her tonight for her summer wear fashion show next month.

"Searching for brilliance?"

Henry's voice behind her made her jump then flip over her sketchbook. A quick glance at her computer showed that it was on screensaver.

Henry Smythe was her biggest competition. With his spiky black hair and retro New Wave fashion sense, his designs had a lot of flair, but were more appropriate for clubbing than women looking for something to wear to work or out with friends. Still, he'd managed to get some face time with the senior designers. He had connections in the industry. And he never failed to let her know it.

She gave him a sweet smile. "Just letting my creativity wander, now that I've got my presentation all locked up." It wasn't a complete lie. She'd picked her portfolio items; she just hadn't decided if they were final. She hoped Lynnae would give her some input tonight when they met.

His gaze scanned her head to toe. It wasn't a come on; he was evaluating her outfit. He swirled his finger in front of her. "Is that one of yours?"

He knew it was. This outfit, and ones she was bringing to Lynnae she'd sewn up at home. It wasn't like she didn't trust leaving them at work. But she wanted to try them on herself. She specialized in clothes for every woman, but with those unique touches that made the outfit look one-of-a-kind.

And she *didn't* trust leaving them at work. Design Review was too important. Not that she thought anything would happen. She didn't. But better to be safe than sorry. Besides, seeing her clothes on the dress form at home or even wearing them had often given her an idea for a change or alteration.

She didn't bother to answer him. "Did you need something?"

"Just wondering how your portfolio was coming along. Only two weeks left, so if you need to get a design made up, you'd better get it to the seamstresses today."

"Got it covered. Thanks."

He gave her another appraising look then turned on his heel.

She'd learned early on not to give Henry any fuel for his rumors. Or even his innuendo. She turned back to her drawing. She seriously doubted he came by to give her a friendly reminder. More like he wanted to see what she was working on. This business could be cutthroat, but she'd been fortunate enough to work with really great people. Henry was the exception rather than the rule.

Her phone buzzed, and she snatched it up.

But it was Matthew.

I'm in town. Want to catch dinner?

She dropped the phone on her desk and rubbed her hands over her face. Matthew. She hadn't seen him in nearly two months. They'd gotten close on the Great American Road Trip—he'd even kissed her, twice—but after she'd been grabbed by Willie Dumas, she'd been shaken. And she realized that Matthew couldn't handle her breadth of emotions. He was a fun guy to hang out with, but expecting anything more from him was a recipe for heartache. And she had too much on her plate as it was.

But she knew this day was coming. They'd texted, and he'd told her he got the job with DataCorp and was relocating to Orange County, but she'd pushed it out of her mind, not wanting to think about what it'd be like to be in the same geographical region, with the same friends, as he was. But it looked like that was coming to an end. She did have a reprieve for tonight: an appointment with Lynnae.

But she couldn't put off meeting him forever. What was she going to do about him?

She texted his sister Allie. And after a moment's thought, added in Jessica.

Matthew Ellis tried to keep his attention on what the HR person was saying. He hated all these forms and video training on how not to be an offensive coworker as well as learning about company values. His flight this morning had been early, and he was struggling. Until DataCorp finalized the lease on their own building, they were meeting in the conference rooms at the hotel where they were all staying. His sister Allie was the relocation specialist coordinating all the details for the company.

He had an appointment with the Chief Operating Officer, Edward Jacobsen, and the Chief Marketing Officer, Anne Radcliff—the woman who'd hired him—about the timeline for opening the Orange County, California, branch of DataCorp. He knew it was necessary; he just wanted to get on with it and get to the good part.

Which he hoped would include dinner with Kim. But she hadn't answered his text yet. He knew she was busy preparing for Design Review. And her brother was getting married next month. She had texted with him a bit over the past two months since their Great American Road Trip. They'd gotten close on the adventure, but he'd screwed it up. Now it was his chance to prove to her that he could do better.

But it was hard to do that if she wouldn't see him.

He signed the papers the HR person pushed across to him and smiled and thanked her. Then he headed over to the next room. He'd just grabbed the coffee carafe to pour himself a cup —he'd need the caffeine to stay awake—when his phone buzzed. He set the cup down and looked at his message.

Sorry, I can't.

From Kim. His mood soured. This was going to be harder than he thought. Just being in the same town as her wasn't going to be enough. He picked up his coffee and took a sip. He knew someone who would have dinner with him.

And he still had another plan up his sleeve.

It had been two months, but she had never left his mind. Or heart, if he was honest. So all he wanted to do was to get through these meetings and have dinner with her. Maybe tomorrow. He let his mind wander about where they could go, what they would talk about, how she would look—

"Matthew?" The director of sales, Chris Chang, called his name. He and the chief marketing officer, Anne Radcliff, had been discussing something about the Seattle headquarters. Nothing that had to do with him. Or so he thought.

"Sorry, could you repeat that?" Matthew scrambled to figure out what he'd missed.

"I think you should join us, get the pulse of the team." Chris frowned. Even though Anne had hired Matthew, Chris would be his boss. It wouldn't be good to get on his bad side. "About a third will be relocating down here. You can give us some input on what holes we'll have in our team, and who we should be looking to add."

"Sure, I can do that." Getting to know new people would be a lot better than hanging around in these boring meetings.

"Great." Anne looked at her phone. "Our flight leaves in two hours. Why do you go grab what you need from your room and meet us in the lobby in twenty minutes? I'll have our admin send you your boarding pass via email."

He nodded. "Sounds great." But inside he was a little panicked. What had he just agreed to? He didn't want to admit he had spaced out. Usually if he played along, it would become clear. Apparently he'd agreed to get on a flight somewhere.

They stood and headed out of the room toward the elevators together. Chris turned to him. "I like your perspective on things. You have your feet on the ground and are closer to knowing what our clients what and need, what will make them say yes and close the deal. We need a few more like you. Maybe you can help us find them."

"Sure, I'd like that."

The elevator doors opened, and Anne stepped inside first. As the doors closed, she said, "Edward's not completely convinced that the OC branch needs its own sales department. He thinks they can travel down from Seattle just as easily, since so much work is remote these days."

Chris scoffed. Matthew didn't say anything, but inside he was screaming *no, no, no, no, no!* He had relocated his whole life to Southern California. For this job and to be with Kim. Long distance wasn't going to cut it for either of those things. He needed to help convince Edward that an OC sales department was in the company's best interest.

He didn't know how he was going to do that. He wasn't even sure where they were flying to. Seattle, maybe?

Only one thing was clear. Kim wasn't on the agenda for today, but maybe the job he had barely started was.

Order here. www.Amazon.com/dp/B08WWMCR66

Books by JL Crosswhite

Sign up for my latest updates at www.JLCrosswhite.com and be the first to know when my next series is releasing.

Romantic Suspense

The Hometown Heroes Series

Promise Me

Cait can't catch a break. What she witnessed could cost her job and her beloved farmhouse. Will Greyson help her or only make things worse?

Protective Custody

She's a key witness in a crime shaking the roots of the town's power brokers. He's protecting a woman he'll risk everything for. Doing the right thing may cost her everything. Including her life.

Flash Point

She's a directionally-challenged architect who stumbled on a crime that could destroy her life's work. He's a firefighter protecting his hometown… and the woman he loves.

Special Assignment

A brain-injured Navy pilot must work with the woman in charge of the program he blames for his injury. As they both grasp to save their careers, will their growing attraction hinder them as they attempt solve the mystery of who's really at fault before someone else dies?

In the Shadow Series

Off the Map

For her, it's a road trip adventure. For him, it's his best shot to win her back. But for the stalker after her, it's revenge.

Out of Range (Spring 2021)

It's her chance to prove she's good enough. It's his chance to prove he's more than just a fun guy. Is it their time to find love, or is her secret admirer his deadly competition?

Over Her Head (Summer 2021)

On a church singles' camping trip that no one wants to be on, a weekend away to renew and refresh becomes anything but. A group of friends trying to find their footing do a good deed and get much more than they bargained for.

Writing as Jennifer Crosswhite

Contemporary Romance

The Inn at Cherry Blossom Lane

Can the summer magic of Lake Michigan bring first loves back together? Or will the secret they discover threaten everything they love?

Historical Romance

The Route Home Series

Be Mine

A woman searching for independence. A man searching for education. Can a simple thank you note turn into something more?

Coming Home

He was why she left. Now she's falling for him. Can a woman who turned her back on her hometown come home to find justice for her brother without falling in love with his best friend?

The Road Home

He is a stagecoach driver just trying to do his job. She is returning to her suitor only to find he has died. When a stack of stolen money shows up in her bag, she thinks the past she has desperately tried to hide has come back to haunt her.

Finally Home

The son of a wealthy banker poses as a lumberjack to carve out his own identity. But in a stagecoach robbery gone wrong, he meets the soon-to-be schoolteacher with a vivid imagination, a gift for making things grow, and an obsession with dime novels. As the town is threatened by a past enemy, can he help without revealing who he is? And will she love him when she learns the truth?